GIDEON SMITH
AND THE
MECHANICAL GIRL

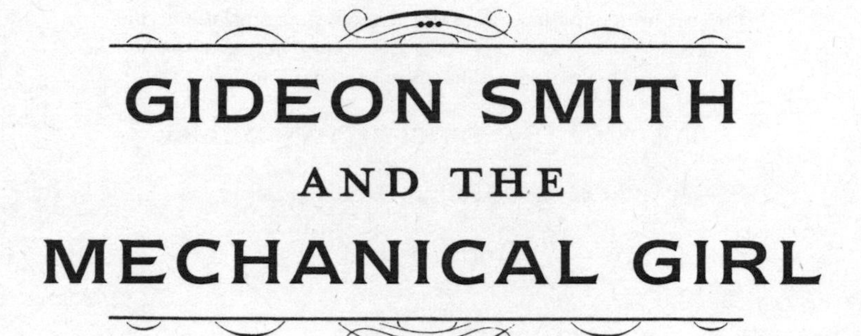

GIDEON SMITH AND THE MECHANICAL GIRL

David Barnett

A TOM DOHERTY ASSOCIATES BOOK
New York

This is a work of fiction. All of the characters, organizations, and events portrayed in this novel are either products of the author's imagination or are used fictitiously.

GIDEON SMITH AND THE MECHANICAL GIRL

A Tor Book
Published by Tom Doherty Associates, LLC
175 Fifth Avenue
New York, NY 10010

www.tor-forge.com

Library of Congress Cataloging-in-Publication Data

Barnett, David.
Gideon Smith and the mechanical girl / David Barnett. — First edition.
p. cm.
"A Tom Doherty Associates Book."
ISBN 978-0-7653-3424-4 (trade paperback)
ISBN 978-1-4668-0908-6 (e-book)
1. Fishermen—England—Fiction. 2. Ship captains—England—Fiction. 3. Robots—Fiction. 4. Great Britain—History—Victoria, 1837–1901—Fiction. I. Title.
PR6102.A7689G53 2013
823'.92—dc23

2012043365

First Edition: September 2013

Printed in the United States of America

0 9 8 7 6 5 4 3 2 1

To my wife, Claire,
the hero of our empire

ACKNOWLEDGMENTS

The journey to publication for Gideon Smith has been one that feels as fraught with trials as the adventure that follows, and just as Gideon would be nothing without the cast of characters around him, so this novel has relied upon the hard work, encouragement, and support of many people.

I would like to thank all at Tor for their unswerving support of Gideon Smith, principally my editor, Claire Eddy, Patrick Nielsen Hayden, and Kristin Sevick, but not forgetting all those who have worked to turn a manuscript into a book, illustrate it, produce it, and sell it.

John Jarrold, my agent, deserves special mention for his constant belief in me since taking me on as a client in 2005. He did warn me we were in for the long haul, and seven manuscripts later he was proved right.

Kudos, also, to Eric Brown for his long-term championing of my work, Darren Nash, Jon Courtenay Grimwood (who said, when I got the Tor deal, "It's about bloody time"), and Nick Harkaway, among many others.

Thanks to Mum and Dad for instilling in me a love of books and never telling me I was reading too much science fiction, and to my mates who I've bored to tears over many a pint with my plans for literary world domination.

This book is dedicated to my wife, Claire, for always being there and for her words of encouragement, which can be summed up thus: Just get on with it.

And extra-special thanks to our children, Charlie and Alice, who listened spellbound around a fire on a wet Welsh camping holiday to episodic (and slightly sanitized) adventures of Gideon Smith, and always asked for more.

I hope there are a lot more people out there like you.

—David Barnett

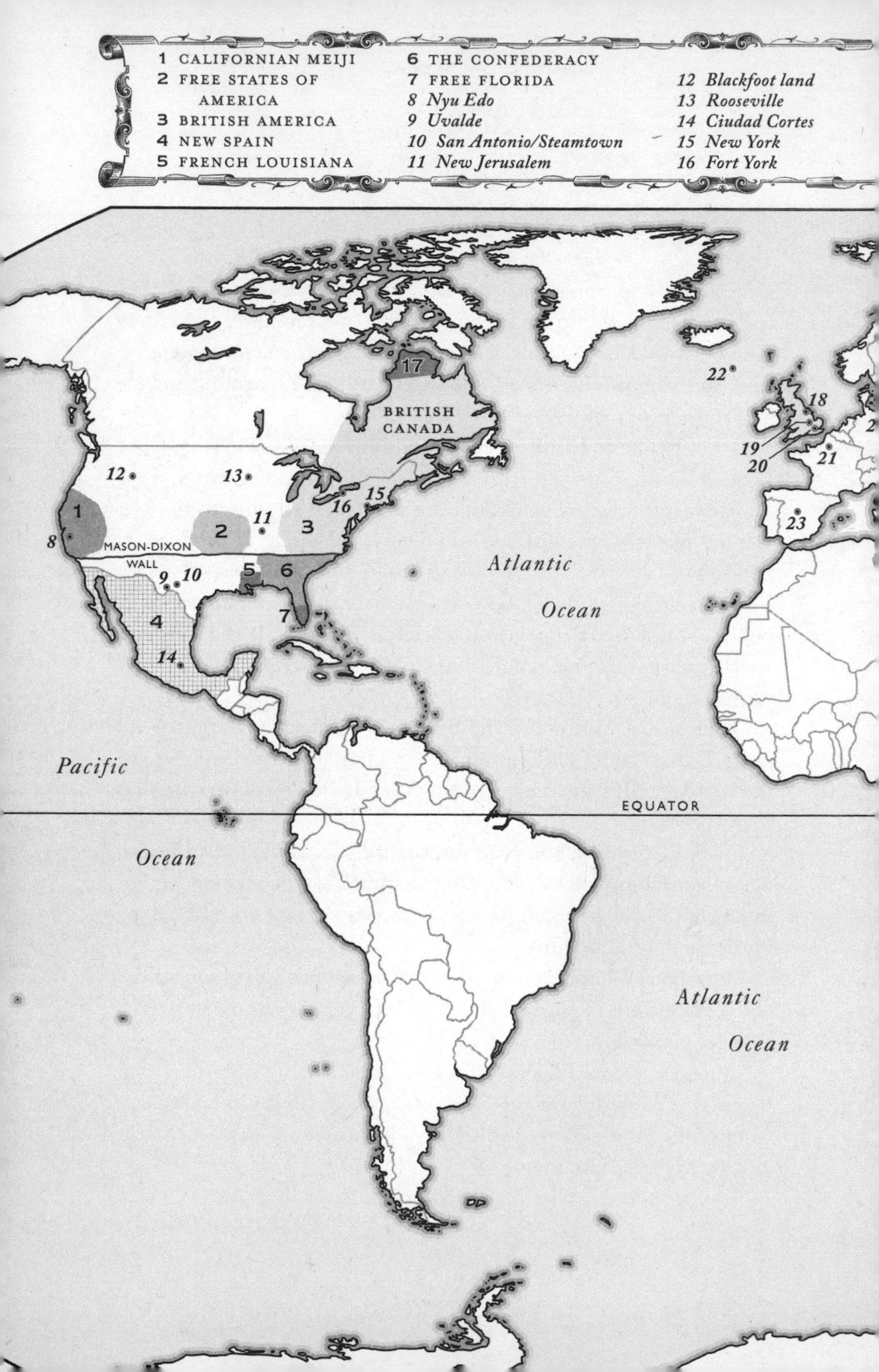
1 CALIFORNIAN MEIJI
2 FREE STATES OF AMERICA
3 BRITISH AMERICA
4 NEW SPAIN
5 FRENCH LOUISIANA
6 THE CONFEDERACY
7 FREE FLORIDA
8 Nyu Edo
9 Uvalde
10 San Antonio/Steamtown
11 New Jerusalem
12 Blackfoot land
13 Rooseville
14 Ciudad Cortes
15 New York
16 Fort York
17
BRITISH CANADA
MASON-DIXON WALL
Atlantic Ocean
Pacific Ocean
EQUATOR
Atlantic Ocean
18
19
20
21
22
23

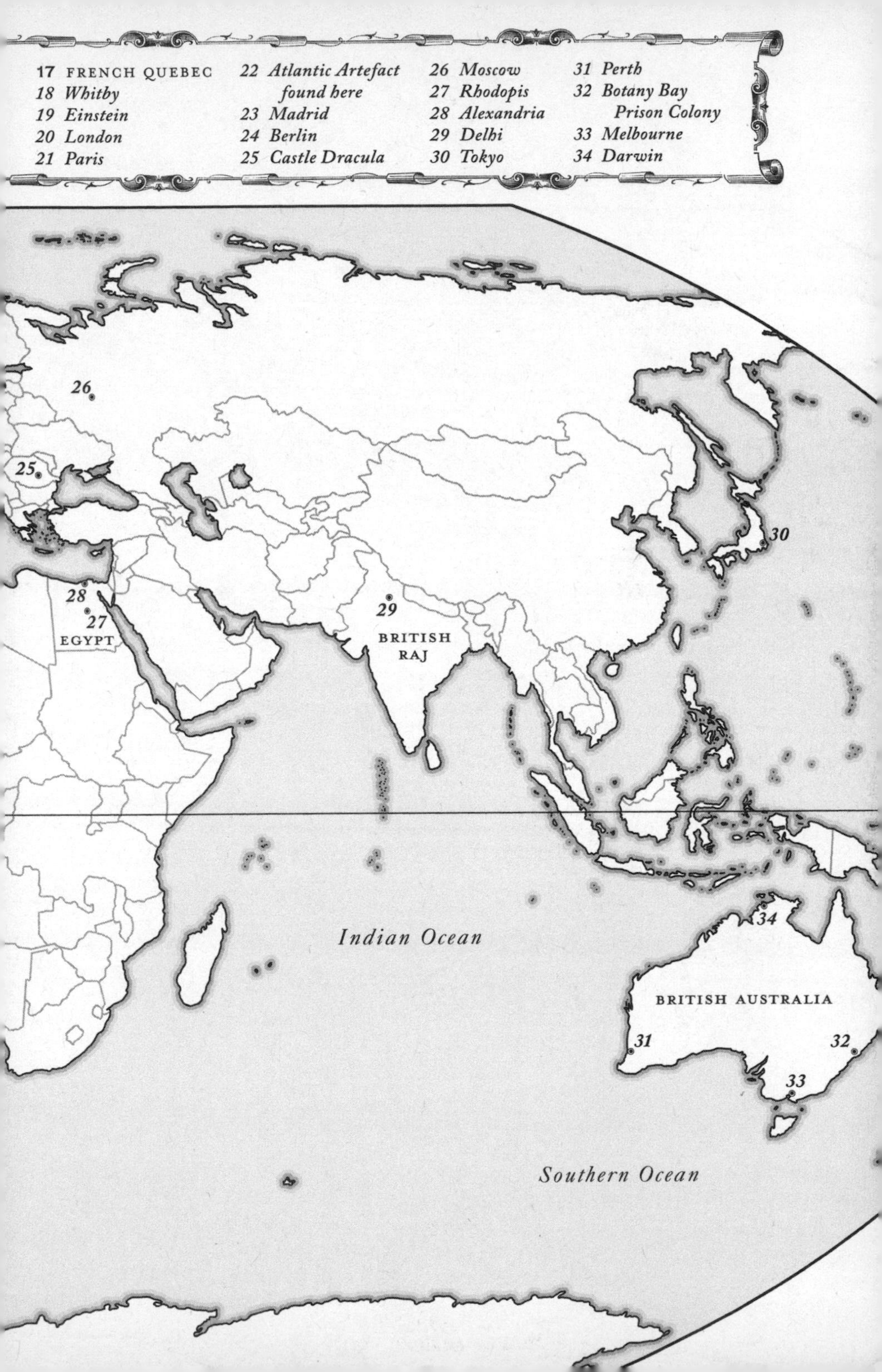

17 FRENCH QUEBEC
18 Whitby
19 Einstein
20 London
21 Paris
22 Atlantic Artefact found here
23 Madrid
24 Berlin
25 Castle Dracula
26 Moscow
27 Rhodopis
28 Alexandria
29 Delhi
30 Tokyo
31 Perth
32 Botany Bay Prison Colony
33 Melbourne
34 Darwin
26
25
30
28
27
EGYPT
29
BRITISH RAJ
Indian Ocean
34
BRITISH AUSTRALIA
31
32
33
Southern Ocean

Poets and heroes are of the same race, the latter do what the former conceive.

—ALPHONSE DE LAMARTINE
(1790–1869)

GIDEON SMITH
AND THE
MECHANICAL GIRL

Two Years Earlier

Annie Crook never read newspapers. If she had, she might have known what was coming.

But she never read newspapers. She passed soot-grimed boys on the streets, shrill voices jostling to present the wares of the *Argus*, *London News*, *Gazette*, and a dozen others. France and Spain at each others' throats. Skirmishes along the Mason-Dixon Wall. A dirigible crash in Birmingham. All a fog of hollered headlines to her. Annie Crook never read newspapers, because she was in love.

Not that it mattered whether she read the papers or not, because there were plenty of customers who came into the shop where she worked, eager to offer their opinions on the day's events. Queen Victoria should take hold of the European problem and impose her will on France and Spain, they said, perhaps utilizing the German armies under her command. The Texan rebels in the southern regions of America should be thoroughly bombed out of existence by airships from the British enclaves in Boston and New York, they decided, as punishment for seceding from the Crown. The dirigible crash in Birmingham . . . well, that wasn't anyone's fault. At least it hadn't been London.

Annie paused on Cleveland Street, where she had rooms. It was mid-June and quite a scorcher, though the sun had dipped over black-slate roofs. The flare of gaslight at Sickert's window meant he was working. But it would not be Annie who posed for him tonight, glad as she was of the extra shillings. Tonight was for Annie and her man.

Cleveland Street was not far from the towering gothic spires and massive ziggurats of central London, from the Lady of

Liberty flood barrier on the Thames, and Highgate Aerodrome. It was just off the Tottenham Court Road, where costermongers plied their trade and where Annie worked in a small tobacconist shop. The street was the haunt of the streetwalkers and cutpurses who lurked between its tall tenements. Every other window held an impecunious artist raging against the ever-present smog or a grizzled writer churning out some romance for Grub Street. But it was Annie's home, and she was blind to its faults, because she was in love.

In her tiny bedroom, she considered herself in the cracked mirror. Her Irish brogue and mass of jet-black curls suggested a more pastoral life for Annie, but she had always lived in London. She would like a bath before he came, but a quick wash would do, and she would change into the scandalously close-fitting Chinese silk dress he had gifted her at Christmas. He would have to take her as he found her. He always did. She wasn't, she had to admit, what you might call a *good* Irish Catholic.

Annie had barely fastened the last hook on the dress and arranged her hair into a bun with black wisps trailing to frame her angular, pale face, when there was a rap at the door. A flush rose on her cheeks, and she could barely contain a girlish squeal as she threw open the door.

He smiled broadly beneath the black bowler and silk scarf he always wore around his face when he visited, whatever the weather.

"Darling Annie!" He took her in his arms and kissed her. Annie wanted to shout it from the rooftops. She had a sweetheart, and he was a toff to boot.

❧

To be young and in love in London in spring was very heaven. Not quite the words he'd read to her as they lounged in Hyde Park that sweltering July day the previous year, taking refuge from the merciless sun in the shadow of the platform of the stilt-train that criss-crossed Westminster, but close enough. They'd watched the first pinkish stones of the Taj Mahal that had been shipped over from India being relaid in honor of Queen Victoria's golden jubilee. He told her it had first been built as a declaration of love.

"Is there nothing Victoria can't do?" Annie had sighed.

A rare cloud had passed his brow. "No," he'd said thoughtfully. "Nothing."

Annie had met Eddy in that spring of 1887, while modeling for old Walter Sickert. Any given day could find Sickert drinking in the gin houses with bright-eyed villains or lunching in gentlemen's clubs. Some of his acquaintances looked hungrily at the girls who posed. Eddy was different. The first time Annie met him, she was sitting astride a felt ottoman, aping the act of riding horseback. Eddy, curled into an easy chair, smoking cheroots and drinking brandy, never took his eyes off her.

"Is it true, Sickert," he'd drawled nonchalantly, "that there's what they used to call a molly house on Cleveland Street where the *earnest* young men go for solace?"

"I wouldn't know," rumbled the painter. Annie snorted to herself; Sickert knew full well of the brothel down the road. "Perhaps you should ask Annie; she is of the common classes."

Eddy smiled mischievously. "I doubt it, miss, looking at your angelic beauty."

"I could take you to the molly house," she'd said, surprising herself. "If that's your thing."

Eddy had chuckled. "A raven-tressed colleen, and saucy with it. What say we go for a more intimate soiree, dark-eyed Annie Crook?"

"Don't be a fool," Sickert had hissed, his teeth clamped around the shaft of a paintbrush. "She works in a tobacconist, and she's no stranger to coining it on street corners, if rumor be true."

Annie pursed her lips. "I *am* here, Mr. Sickert," she said. "I'd thank you not to talk as though I were some stray dog off the street."

Sickert shrugged; evidently that was as high as his opinion

of Annie rose. But Eddy continued to stare, and when the session was done he insisted on taking her for a drink.

"I'll have a drink off you," she conceded. "But nothing else. Despite what Mr. Sickert thinks, I'm not that sort of girl. What did you say your name was?"

"Eddy," he'd said. "Just Eddy."

❦

Over the next year he courted her properly and chivalrously, and if Annie had, in the past, lain with someone for a few shillings as rent day approached, she foreswore such behavior for Eddy. She was his and his alone. They lay in a tangle of bedsheets in the darkness, listening to each other's gradually slowing breathing. Night had fallen, and Annie stepped naked from the bed to light the gas lamp on the wall.

Eddy whistled. "You're a fine figure of a woman, dark-eyed Annie Crook."

She smiled thinly as she got back into bed. "That's what you called me the first night we met."

"A lot has changed since then," he said, rooting in his trousers for his cheroots.

"Yet so much remains the same," she said thoughtfully. Annie always fell into a funk after they made love. "I know nothing about you, not even your full name. You could have a wife and children, for all I know."

She thought he'd laugh, but he said softly, "I've not treated you well, have I, Annie?"

She took his thin face in her hands and kissed his lips. "You have your reasons, I'm sure. You're my sweetheart, Eddy, but you're a toff. It wouldn't be right, me hanging on your arm in polite society."

He enclosed her hands in his. "But that's what I want!" he whispered fiercely. "They've finished the Taj Mahal. We should go and see it. Tomorrow."

"And will you be wrapped in your scarf, like last time?" she asked. "Even though it was July?"

Eddy looked broodingly at his cheroot. "No," he said with finality. "That's over. I've decided. We should be together."

Annie's heart skipped, but she kept her voice steady. "And we should also take a dirigible to New York and walk in the Albert Gardens on Manhattan Island. There are many things we should do, Eddy."

"The Albert Gardens aren't all that," he muttered.

She stared. "You've seen them?"

"Many times." He took her hands in his. "It's a big world out there, and my . . . and Queen Victoria has most of it in the palm of her hand." His eyes shone. "We could go to New York, you know, see the vast gothic towers. We could take a dirigible ride over the vast, untamed land that stretches right over to the Pacific, and the Japanese territories, or see the Mason-Dixon Wall they built to keep the Texans out. We can do all this together, if . . ."

She raised an eyebrow. "If?"

He dug into his pocket again and withdrew a small, dark box. "Annie," he said seriously. "Look at me."

She did. Something in his eyes made her heart take flight and stampede in her chest. He said, "I love you, Annie Crook. I want you to be my wife."

She opened her mouth, but he quieted her with a finger on her lips and pressed the box into her hands. Fingers trembling, she opened it, and gasped. It was a gold ring, set with a huge, intricately cut stone glowing redly in the dim lighting. "Eddy," she whispered. "It's beautiful."

"A mere gewgaw from my family's coffers. We have thousands like it. Not one of them holds a candle to you for beauty, Annie."

She placed the ring on her finger. "Thousands?" she said as she admired it. She looked at him. "Who exactly is your family, Eddy?"

He took a long drag of his cheroot, and the door to Annie's rooms crashed inward with a shriek of splintering wood.

There were six of them. Four were tall, stocky, with bowlers pulled over their eyes, wearing black leather gloves that screamed danger at Annie. Of the other two, one was a short, fat man carrying a leather doctor's bag, and the last was tall and thin, dressed in dapper tails and carrying a cane. He had a topper on his greased gray hair, and a thick mustache dangled beneath his hawkish nose.

Annie screamed and pulled the sheet around her nakedness, while Eddy gawped at the intruders.

"Do quiet the woman down, sir," said the tall man mildly. It took Annie a moment to realize he was talking to Eddy.

"Walsingham! What is the meaning of this?" demanded Eddy, shuffling into his trousers. "What are you doing here with those . . . those gorillas? And Gull! You bloody bone saw!"

"I'm afraid this has gone quite far enough," said the man whom Eddy had called Walsingham. "It would be best if you came with us now, sir."

"I won't!" said Eddy stoutly. "You have no right!"

At last, Annie found her voice. "Eddy, who are they? Do you owe them money?"

Walsingham laughed. "My dear . . ." He paused, frowning. "Do you not know?"

Annie felt her cheeks burn. "It's Eddy," she said quietly. "We are to be married."

The short man, Gull, barked a laugh, then stared at her. He said, "I don't think she does."

"It's true!" said Eddy, standing. "Annie Crook is to be my wife."

Walsingham shook his head sadly. "I think not, sir. Gentlemen."

Two of the bull-necked men shouldered their way into the room, and in a swift movement clambered over Annie's screaming form and took each of Eddy's arms. The one called Gull laid down his bag and took from it a dark bottle and a handkerchief.

"This is an outrage!" cried Eddy. "When Grandmama finds out . . ."

Gull tipped liquid from the bottle into the handkerchief and clamped it over Eddy's surprised face. In seconds, he slumped, and the men began to drag him to the parlor.

Walsingham lit a cigarette and looked pityingly at Annie, cowering in the bed.

"I am truly sorry for the trouble you have been put to," he said almost tenderly. "Things should not have gotten this far."

"Where are you taking Eddy?" she wailed.

He exhaled a plume of blue smoke. "Do you not know who he is, really? Do you not read the newspapers?"

Annie shook her head.

Walsingham told her.

Annie's eyes widened and her jaw dropped. She was about to tell him she was not falling for his sick joke, when she noticed Gull withdrawing a brace of cruel-looking metal instruments from his bag.

"What are those?" she asked in horror. "What are you going to do to him?"

Walsingham looked down at Gull, who waited by the bed. "He will spend some time in a private sanatorium, perhaps in Switzerland. He will recover. He will get over you. We have a match planned for him with a German girl." He stepped forward and took a lock of Annie's hair in his thin fingers. "Not a patch on you in the beauty stakes, but more his social equal."

"Then . . . ," said Annie, unable to tear her eyes away from the devices in Gull's hands.

"Those are for you," said Walsingham, as the other two men entered the room and roughly took hold of Annie's shoulders. "We can't have you running around London talking about this. It shouldn't hurt. . . ."

"Much," said Gull, grinning.

Walsingham waved his cigarette. "Much," he agreed. Then he took his leave as Annie began to scream, "Eddy! Eddy! Save me!"

1

The Smiths of Sandsend

The night before, Gideon Smith had dreamed a dragon ate the sun. But there was no dragon in the blue sky, only a gull hovering on the hot air rising from the dry sand, seemingly screaming, *save me, save me.* And the sun had risen as usual, just ahead of Gideon, emerging from the iron-gray sea and traversing the cloudless blue until it began its descent toward the Yorkshire moors far from where he now stood. *Save me, save me,* cried the gull, its black face to the sea.

"And me," whispered Gideon as he leaned on the tarnished railings, watching the men drag the day's meager catch from their trawlers moored alongside the ancient wooden jetty to the tarpaulins laid out on the fine golden sand. Gideon's day had been as unremarkable as the sun's, and as he observed the men standing and shaking their heads at the small piles of haddock and cod glittering in the dying day, he idly prayed a dragon really would come and devour them all, if only to give them some respite from the unending boredom that was life in Sandsend. But the only things that came were the hovering gulls, their minds on eating only fish.

As the fishermen shooed the gulls away, one of the men detached himself from the muttering trawlermen and walked wearily up the beach to the stone jetty, as though the heavy oilskins and thick leather boots made each step a chore. He paused to light his pipe, then climbed the stone steps and rested his thick arms, clad in a cable-weave woolen sweater despite the summer heat, on the railing.

"How's the leg?" he grunted, not turning his weathered face away from the knot of fishermen.

Gideon rubbed the thigh of his serge trousers. "Shooting

pains when I woke this morning," he said, the lie stabbing him sharper than his imaginary ailment. "It isn't so bad now."

Arthur Smith nodded and puffed on his pipe. "That's why I didn't wake you when we went out. Thought we'd give it another day. You'll be fit for tomorrow?"

A week before, a hook had gashed Gideon's leg while he'd been out on the trawler. There'd been a lot of blood from the fleshy part of his thigh, but it had looked worse than it felt. He looked at the paltry pile of fish, which the trawlermen were now loading up into barrows ready for delivery to Whitby to the south and the villages to the north and inland. He couldn't with an honest heart delay any longer.

"Aye, Dad. I'll be fit for tomorrow."

Arthur Smith put out a hand as big as a spade to ruffle the black hair hanging over Gideon's frayed collar in loose curls. "Good lad."

Like a protective arm, the rocky promontory of Lythe Bank at the top of the village reached out to sea, as though pointing with silent accusation at the long, dark shapes of the factory farms on the distant horizon. The farms belched columns of black smoke into a deep blue sky broken only by the high, stately passage of a dirigible. Gideon had read in the *Whitby Gazette* there was talk in London of making a special dirigible with some kind of unheard-of engine, so they could plant the Union Flag on the very moon. He wished he could be on it when they built it.

"We should complain," said Gideon, shaking the collar of his white cotton shirt to allow some of the sea breeze to circulate around his chest. "Write to our Member of Parliament."

His father sighed heavily. "What's the point?"

Gideon suddenly felt angry. "Look at that haul! It's a tenth of what we were doing five years ago. The Newcastle & Gateshead shouldn't be so far south, not at this time of year!"

His father shook his head sadly. "Remember the *Wheeler*?"

Everyone remembered the *Wheeler*. Three days before it sank with the loss of its fourteen crewmembers, its skipper had gotten an order from the assizes preventing the Newcastle & Gateshead factory fisheries from entering within a ten-mile boundary of Sandsend. Nobody could prove anything, but tough old trawlers like the *Wheeler* didn't just sink without a little help.

"How old are you next birthday, Gideon? Twenty-four?" asked his father, spitting on the stone promenade.

Gideon nodded. His father said, "We've been trawlermen for four generations. When I was a lad, I thought we'd do four generations more. Five or six, even. I thought fishing was a job for life. . . . But now, I wonder, Gideon. When I'm gone . . ."

"Dad," protested Gideon.

His father laid a hand on his arm. "When I'm gone . . . it's no life for a young man, Gideon. Not anymore. I thought you'd be settled down by now, maybe have young'uns yourself, ready to take charge of the *Cold Drake* and let me retire. But the world's changing quicker than I can keep up with it." His eyes stared into the middle distance. "I'm just glad your mother's not here to see the state we're in."

She had died fourteen years ago, in childbirth with his brother, who had lasted only a day. In another world, Gideon would have been the middle boy of a family of fishermen. But six years ago, his older brother Josiah had fallen victim to the influenza. Now there was just Gideon and his dad.

"What did you get up to today?" asked his father.

"I walked along the sand to Whitby," said Gideon, glad to speak of other things. "Picked up some bread and vegetables from the market."

His father gave a crooked smile. "And did you buy anything else?"

Gideon flushed, then nodded. "The latest issue of *World Marvels & Wonders* had just come in on the steam pantechnicon. . . . I had a penny spare. . . ."

His father laughed and ruffled Gideon's hair again. "Why don't you put us something on for supper, and maybe you can read me a couple of chapters before we turn in? The carriages are here for the catch."

Three horse-drawn carts and one steam-truck, the latter in the black-and-white livery of the Magpie Café. How long before these faithful few finally succumbed to the cheaper supplies from the Newcastle & Gateshead was anyone's guess, but for now there was work to be done. Gideon watched his father stride back down the beach, and he was just turning to go when he caught sight of a smaller figure, a little way along the shoreline, struggling to push a rowing boat three times longer than himself into the shallows. Gideon shielded his eyes against the sun. It looked like little Tommy, the son of Peek, who skippered the *Blackbird*. What was he up to?

Gideon walked along the sand and stood to watch the boy—only seven or so—loading a leather bag into the rowing boat. Gideon hailed him and waved.

"Where are you off to, Tommy?"

"America," said the boy stoutly.

"Ah," said Gideon, squatting down beside him. "Does your daddy know?"

"I'll send him a letter when I get there," said Tommy, heaving against the stern of the rowing boat. "Can you give me a hand with this?"

Gideon nodded, then scratched his chin. "Have you got enough for the journey, though? It's an awfully long way to America."

Tommy dug enthusiastically into his leather bag. "I have a loaf and a jar of pickle. Two apples." He looked at Gideon. "Will that be enough?"

"I don't know, Tommy. I've never been to America. Which part are you heading for?"

Tommy reached into the bag again and pulled out a magazine, then bit his lip. "Oh. This is yours." It was an old edition of *World Marvels & Wonders* that Gideon had lent Tommy. The boy had a skill for drawing and liked to copy the illustrations of Captain Trigger's adventures.

"That's all right. It's the one with the Bowie Steamcrawlers, isn't it?"

Tommy nodded enthusiastically. "Captain Trigger teams up with Louis Cockayne, the American adventurer, and they defeat the Texan rebel Jim Bowie and his steam-powered armored desert-wagons. I thought I'd go there, see the Mason-Dixon Wall they built to keep the Texans from attacking the pioneering families."

Tommy separated another sheet from the magazine, a map he'd clipped from an old book. "Do you know where that would be? It isn't on this map."

Gideon took it from him. "Let me see . . . here on the East Coast is British territory, Boston and New York. Over here on the West Coast, that's ruled by the Japanese, or the son of the old emperor, at any rate. Nyu Edo."

"That's New Spain," said Tommy, pointing to the south. "And Ciudad Cortes. I learned that at school."

Gideon jabbed his finger in the middle of the map. "Then this must be where the adventure took place, north of the Texan strongholds, where they keep slaves and make them dig for coal."

Tommy frowned. "Would they make me dig for coal?"

"Possibly. If they caught you. Might be best to go somewhere else first, maybe New York? They have tall buildings there called skyscrapers."

"Taller than the ones in London?"

"So they say," said Gideon.

Tommy put the map and magazine back into his bag. "I'll go to New York, then."

Gideon stood up, then put a hand on Tommy's shoulder. "One more thing," he said, pointing out to sea. "That's east. America is west. You need to be on the other side of the country if you're going to sail there."

Tommy's shoulder slumped under his hand. "Really?"

Gideon nodded. "Sorry."

Tommy looked out to sea, then shrugged. "I don't really like pickle, anyway. Maybe I should go home."

Gideon nodded. "Me, too."

❧

"Is it cold for July, or is it these old bones?" asked Gideon's father. Gideon grunted noncommittally as he cleared away the dishes from their supper and lit half a dozen candles and small oil burners.

Gideon retrieved the July 1890 issue of *World Marvels & Wonders,* its cover depicting a fearsome ape-beast menacing a lithe, heroic figure with brilliantined hair and an impeccable mustache, framed within a Union Flag border. He kept his penny dreadfuls stacked in piles in his bedroom, where he could, in summer, get the rays of the sinking sun to light his bedtime reading. *World Marvels & Wonders* was always his first choice, if only for the adventures of Captain Lucian Trigger.

This adventure was called *The Man-Monsters of the Forty-Ninth Parallel,* sandwiched between a lurid account of the latest victims of Jack the Ripper, who was slicing up streetwalkers in the capital, and a slew of advertisements for labor-saving kitchen devices and telescopes that could see the craters on the moon. Gideon read breathlessly aloud to his father in the flickering flames how Trigger had been dispatched by Queen Victoria herself to investigate reports of Frenchie bandits running amok on the border between Britain's interests in the New World and Canada. His father's eyelids began to droop after half an hour, so Gideon retired to bed to complete the story, reading with wide-eyed amazement how Captain Trigger had uncovered a conspiracy going back to Paris, but had been betrayed and abandoned in the frozen wastes. Near death, he had been discovered by a pack of grotesque, hair-covered demihumans, known to the local Red Indian aboriginals as *sasquatch.* Despite their horrific appearance they had proved benign, and with their help Trigger foiled the French plot to assassinate the British Governor of Michigan.

It was a chilly tale for a summer edition but a thrilling one. And like all the Trigger stories, it was prefaced with: *This adventure, as always, is utterly true, and faithfully retold by my good friend, Doctor John Reed,* followed by the flourish of the good Captain's signature.

One day he would leave Sandsend, Gideon promised himself for the hundred-thousandth time. One day he would seek adventure, just like Captain Trigger. Gideon Smith would be the Hero of the Empire, and he would meet his one true love, and he would truly live in a world of wonders and marvels. One day, but not today. Maybe tomorrow, thought Gideon, as he drifted into sleep.

❧

Arthur Smith awoke before dawn from the disturbed sleep that sometimes troubles those who live their lives in tune with the sea. While not given over to whimsy as much as his son Gideon, Arthur had learned over the years not to ignore the insistent little voices speaking at the back of his mind. When he drew back the drapes in his bedroom and saw the thick sea mist rolling up the cliffs and making black islands of the ramshackle roofs of the fishermen's cottages, he felt a slight shiver. He would have given anything to close the curtains and return to his bed, but there was a living to be made.

In the darkness, he creaked open the door to Gideon's bedroom and for a long moment observed his son, snoring gently with the bedsheets wrapped around him, the pale square of a penny dreadful on the rug by his bed. Arthur felt a sudden wave of love for his only remaining flesh and blood. He'd told Gideon to be fit for work this morning, but his troubled sleep still bothered him, and he didn't like that sea mist rolling in off the bay. Arthur fingered the polished piece of jet hanging around his neck on a leather thong. Gideon had found it on the beach fifteen or sixteen years ago and fashioned it into a good luck charm for his daddy. Arthur Smith never put out to sea without it, and he had a feeling he'd need it on this early morning more than any other. Let the boy sleep, he decided. Another day of dreaming wouldn't kill anyone.

❧

The *Cold Drake*, like all the Sandsend trawlers, was a gearship, built seventy-odd years previously on the Clyde. Arthur remembered the first time he had skippered her, taking her out beyond the bay just three hours after they had buried his father in St. Oswald's churchyard on the top of windblown Lythe Bank. As his boots slapped along the wet stones, he could hear Milton's heavy breathing as the old first mate cranked the paddle-gear, but couldn't see him for the fog.

"Ho," called Arthur.

"Skipper," grunted Milton, his lined face framed by his oilskin hat emerging from the mist. "She's cranked up and ready to go, the old girl." He paused and chewed his ever-present tobacco. "We're the only ones out, you know."

Arthur grunted. "More for us, then, and more fool them. We got a full crew?"

"Aye." Milton nodded, then squinted over Arthur's shoulder. "Except . . . no Gideon?"

Arthur said nothing. Milton, like him, would have had that feeling in his bones that today was not going to be a good day. He muttered, "Shall we get moving? Those fish won't catch themselves."

❦

The pace of a gearship was slow, and it was two hours before they reached the deep waters where they could drop the nets for cod. The sun was rising somewhere ahead of them, but the fog stubbornly refused to lift, so they were little better off. Arthur applied the shaft-brake, and the *Cold Drake* drifted in a silence that unnerved him. There weren't even any gulls crying overhead.

The nets down, Arthur settled into the wooden chair he kept on deck and lit his pipe. The sea was millpond calm, and all there was to do was wait for the cod to flock into their nets. He puffed on his pipe and wondered what Gideon was doing.

At first, he thought the knocking was a gear slipping, or one of the springs wearing. He sat up in the chair, suddenly alert, and peered around. "Anybody else hear that?"

Arthur frowned. There it went again. He stood and walked to the port side. Probably a piece of driftwood or rubbish hauled over the side from one of the factory farms. He leaned over and looked at the black, oily water.

The first one came at him so quickly he didn't have time to yell. He stepped backward in surprise, slipping on the damp deck. His first thought was that it was a seal, such as could be seen sporting out at sea on balmy days. Seals, though, rarely clambered up the side of a trawler, as far as he recalled. As the shape sat itself, hunched over, on the steel balustrade around the deck, he heard the other men find their voices, and he looked madly around to see panic on the deck. His hand went instinctively to the jet charm at his throat, and with his other he fumbled at his belt for his gutting knife, but it was too late. The *Cold Drake* was overwhelmed.

2

THE FATE OF THE *COLD DRAKE*

The sun burned off the sea mist a little after dawn, revealing the night's dark bounty: the *Cold Drake*, drifting a hundred yards offshore, her gear-driven paddles wound down and still, her torn, empty nets spread out on the still sea behind. Arthur Smith and the rest of the crew were gone; the *Cold Drake* was abandoned.

By ten o'clock a crowd had gathered on the beach, the wailing wives of the *Cold Drake*'s crew side by side with Sandsend's other fishermen, who ruminated and spat tobacco on the sand, wondering at the rare but not unknown feeling deep in their collective guts that had caused them to roll over in the small hours of the morning and decide not to take their trawlers out. The parishioners of St. Oswald's Church, high up on Lythe Bank, had assembled around the dour, white-haired figure of the Reverend Bastable, and were joining him in a ragged rendition of "Eternal Father, Strong to Save." Gideon Smith stood to one side by the wooden spurs of the breakwater, blinking back tears as their voices rose to sing, "Oh, hear us when we cry to Thee, for those in peril on the sea!"

One of the fishermen, Peek, broke away from the huddle of his crew and walked up the wet sand toward him. He stared at the toe caps of his boots and muttered, "Sorry for your loss, Gideon."

Gideon nodded miserably. Peek turned to look at the *Cold Drake*, where she had been anchored by his crew. "I suppose she's yours now. Will you put together a new crew? I could lend you Peter from the *Blackbird* for a couple of months, if you like, 'til you get on your feet."

Gideon stared at him as the song of the parishioners swelled into a climax and then tailed off. Skipper the *Cold Drake*? Of course. It was expected.

"That would be good of you," said Gideon flatly. Peek made way for a thin stream of mourners, the last in line being Reverend Bastable, his eyes shining pinpricks beneath his bushy white eyebrows. "The sea is a bountiful provider," he rasped, "but a capricious mistress."

Gideon felt an unaccountable anger at the thin, hook-nosed man rise in his gut. "Why did your God take my dad? What has He done with him?"

"You may think God has abandoned you, but He has not. Do not abandon Him. You need His succor now more than ever. His reasons for taking Arthur Smith are His own; your father is in a better place."

Gideon thought back to the night before, his father half-dozing in his armchair as Gideon read the Lucian Trigger story to him, his belly full of the day's catch, his blood warmed by a tot of brandy.

"No, he isn't," said Gideon. "God is wrong. He should have let my dad be."

Bastable pursed his thin lips and seemed about to speak harshly, then thought better of it. Eventually he said, "You are grieving, Gideon Smith. Come and see me at St. Oswald's. I will remind you of what Scripture teaches us of God's love."

Gideon watched him go, then spat on the footprints he left in the moist sand.

❧

Gideon was not given to drinking, but at the cottage he dug out his father's bottle of brandy, then found a quarter of a bottle of whiskey and, wincing, forced it down. His head swimming, he turned his father's chair toward the window, staring down the hill to the sea, the distant dots of the trawlers bobbing in the sunshine.

Where was the adventure tantalizingly presented to him in the stories of the penny dreadfuls? He spied the *World Marvels & Wonders* he'd brought downstairs with him that morning, wondering why his father hadn't woken him for the day's work, and suddenly he hated it. Its stupid stories and wild claims, its tales of far-off lands and improbable escapades. He regarded it with loathing for a moment before angrily tearing it up and letting the pieces fall from his fingers like snow before he slumped into the chair and an empty, black sleep.

❧

That afternoon brought a visit from old Peek, who had young Peter with him. Gideon, bleary eyed and sick to his stomach, let them in, and Peek raised an eyebrow at the empty liquor bottles rolling on the hearth.

"I've brought Peter," said Peek unnecessarily. Gideon nodded at him. "He's happy to come aboard the *Cold Drake* for a spell."

"Two of us can't handle her," said Gideon.

Peek nodded and said, "There's Walter's lad, Eric, and young Clifford Griffiths."

"Am I to crew the *Cold Drake* with children, then? Do no men want to sail her?"

Peek shifted uncomfortably. "You know what fishermen are like."

Gideon looked into the middle distance. "He should have woken me," he said softly. "I should have died out there with the rest of them."

Peek laid an awkward hand on his shoulder. "Don't be saying that, lad. What happened, happened. Best not to dwell on it. Say you'll think it over, at least."

"I will," said Gideon.

❧

After Peek and Peter had gone, Gideon packed some bread and cheese, took his father's old spyglass and a handful of *World Marvels & Wonders,* and headed out. He didn't know where he was going, but his feet took him up the winding road toward the imposing shape of Lythe Bank.

When he'd eaten and washed down the food with water from his canteen, Gideon trained the spyglass on the horizon, bringing the factory farm into sharp focus. Could it be nefarious deeds by the Newcastle & Gateshead that had done in his father? It seemed doubtful, as the *Cold Drake* had been undamaged. Gideon swept his spyglass left and right, some small kernel of hope inside him insisting that he might pick out a tiny figure swimming to shore. But, aside from the factory farm and the three trawlers fishing closer to shore, there was nothing.

Gideon turned the spyglass on the *Cold Drake*, and duty wrestled with desire, his calling to continue the family business at odds with a longing to see the world that ached more fiercely than ever. Gideon sighed and stared out to sea as the sun began to descend behind him.

He heard a sound from over the lip of the promontory, from the beach far below. The coastline was full of crags and pebbles, and Gideon crept to the edge of the grass-tufted cliff and crouched down. The tide had already advanced to cut off the beach, and he could make out no boat moored by the breakwater. But there came the sound again, something wet slapping the large pebbles below. Gideon thought then of the caves and tunnels marbling the interior of Lythe Bank, which everyone said had once been used by smugglers and even pirates. He felt a sudden thrill. Adventure, of a sort, beckoned, and . . . his breath caught in his throat. Something to do with the disappearance of the *Cold Drake* crew? Gideon edged forward, training the spyglass on the beach below. He could see nothing. He wondered whether he should try to scale the cliff and get a closer look, but if there were indeed villains, then they would have the upper hand, and he'd be trapped by the rising tide. Quickly shuffling backward and packing up his knapsack, he decided to go back to the village and alert the village constable.

To get to Clive Clarke's cottage he had to pass Peek's, where the fisherman's youngest, Tommy, was sitting cross-legged in the small front garden, drawing with a worn pencil on a scrap of paper. Peek was a prodigious sire of children and Tommy was his tenth or eleventh—and final, after Mrs. Peek had called a halt. Tommy was a sharp child, and keen on drawing, and from the copies of *World Marvels & Wonders* Gideon sometimes allowed him to borrow he taught himself his letters and copied the illustrations with uncanny skill. The boy waved and gave a gap-toothed grin, all thoughts of adventuring to America apparently forgotten, and his father appeared at the door.

"Get help," called Gideon. "There's trouble at Lythe Bank! Smugglers, perhaps!"

Peek shook his head sadly. "Go home, lad. And stay off the liquor."

Gideon growled with frustration and left the cottage, making for Constable Clarke's. The officer worked from his own dwelling overlooking the East Beck. Oil lamps already illuminated the window, and Gideon pounded on the door. Clarke, in his shirt and braces, opened at once, his jowls wobbling.

"Gideon Smith," he said. "I was sorry to hear about your dad. A fine fellow. What's to do?"

"I want you to get a party of men up," said Gideon. "Investigate at Lythe Bank. Smugglers, or worse!"

"Not tonight," said Clarke kindly. "Go home, Gideon."

Gideon looked back at the shape of Lythe Bank, black against the indigo dusk. "Then I'll just have to investigate myself."

Investigations, however, were not quite so straightforward. Gideon brooded in his father's chair, staring out the window until the black sky and the black sea were indistinguishable. And even then, no answers offered themselves; no course of action seemed the best. He could investigate Lythe Bank himself, of course, but he was no fool. If there were villains, what good could he do alone? Like every other Sandsend boy, he knew better than to venture inside the caves and tunnels that crisscrossed the interior of the promontory. Every generation of Sandsend boys had a cautionary tale of one of their number who had ignored the warnings drummed into them since before they could walk. For Gideon's, it was Oliver Thwaite, who'd gone in there looking for pirate gold one spring day in 1875 and never come out, his ghost joining the grim roll call of those forever lost.

Over a breakfast of coffee and stale bread, Gideon flicked through his collection of *World Marvels & Wonders,* hoping some guidance from Captain Trigger would present itself. Lucian Trigger was an agent of the Crown, charged by Queen Victoria herself with tackling the more unusual threats to her globe-spanning empire. Trigger rarely worked entirely alone; he had a coterie of friends who shared his exploits, from the distinguished Yankee Louis Cockayne to the Tibetan mystic Jamyang, to the beautiful dirigible pilot Rowena Fanshawe, the Belle of the Airways. Wherever Trigger roamed, be it the lawless, untamed lands squabbled over by the British, Japanese, and Spanish at the heart of America, or the vast penal colony that was Australia, or even the wolf-haunted forests of Middle Europe and the bejeweled clockwork mysteries of the Tsarist lands beyond, he always had help. And ever waiting for him at home was his faithful friend and companion Doctor John Reed. Who did Gideon have? No friends, as such, because he'd always been a lonesome, bookish child, happy with his own company and that of his family. No family, not now. He had tried Peek, and Peek had thought him a drunkard. He had been to the Law, but Constable Clarke had not seemed of any mind to investigate. He sighed and turned the pages of the magazine, the drawing of the Hero of the Empire proudly standing tall. If only Trigger could guide him.

His eyes fell on the box giving the address and telephone number for the offices of *World Marvels & Wonders.* Who, indeed, was to say Captain Trigger couldn't offer assistance?

Gulls as big as cats wheeled around the lighthouse at the end of the stone jetty that pointed out to sea, hoping for scraps of battered fish from the tourists who flocked to Whitby. Waiting in line out of the door of the Post Office was a line of holidaymakers wishing to send telegraph messages or buy stamps for picture postcards. He shuffled along, glancing repeatedly and anxiously at the page where he had folded open *World Marvels & Wonders*, as though the telephone number might shift or change or disappear altogether. As he neared the kiosks he realized he hadn't used the public telephones ever before, and was not really sure what the protocol was. He glanced around and met the gaze of a benignly smiling tall man with a tidy, reddish beard and dark suit, waiting in line behind him.

"You need a chitty," said the man in a pleasant Irish brogue, pointing to a prim woman sitting at a desk beside the kiosks. "You take a number from that lady, and when you have made your call she calculates the cost and takes your money."

The man saved his place in line, and when Gideon had procured his chitty his new friend held out a shovel of a hand. "My name's Stoker. Abraham Stoker. Most friends call me Bram. I am in Whitby holidaying." He adopted a conspiratorial tone. "I am supposed to be writing, but the weather and location are simply too beautiful for work."

Gideon blinked. "You're a writer?"

"I try." Stoker smiled. "Success eludes me thus far, though I'll have my first novel published later this year, so perhaps we shall see."

Gideon brandished the magazine at him. "Do you know *World Marvels & Wonders*?"

Stoker peered at the penny blood. "Ah. I am familiar with it, of course. And the adventures of stouthearted Captain Trigger. Although I have worked for some of the story-papers, I have never been published in *World Marvels & Wonders*."

"Oh," said Gideon. "I must get in touch with Captain Lucian Trigger quite urgently. When you said you were a writer, I thought perhaps you might be acquainted with him. There is . . . there is something of an emergency in Sandsend."

There was a thin, sharp cough that echoed around the marble floors. "I believe it's your turn," said Stoker gently, and Gideon turned to see the woman glaring at him and the door to the middle kiosk hanging open.

"Good luck with Captain Trigger," said Stoker. "I hope your emergency is quickly and sufficiently resolved."

❧

"What number do you require?"

Into the flowerlike transmitter mounted on the top of the central column Gideon enunciated loudly and slowly the string of numbers printed in the magazine. The voice said, "Very good, please hold."

After a few seconds another voice said, "You are through to the London Newspaper and Magazine Publishing Company. To whom would you like me to direct your call?"

Gideon's dry mouth worked wordlessly for a second, then he blurted, "Captain Lucian Trigger! It is a most urgent matter!"

"I am afraid I cannot furnish you with a private number for Captain Lucian Trigger," said the woman. Gideon's eyes narrowed; was there a hint of mockery in the voice? She continued, "There is a coupon in the latest edition, which, if you mail it to us with two shillings, enrolls you for membership in Captain Lucian Trigger's Global Adventurers. You will receive two newsletters each calendar year, a membership card, and a pin brooch."

"I do not wish to join the Global Adventurers," said Gideon through gritted teeth. "This is an emergency!"

There was open laughter in the voice now. "I am afraid Captain Lucian Trigger is adventuring and cannot be contacted. Good day to you, sir."

❧

Bram Stoker closed his eyes and held the earpiece so close it hurt to encourage the illusion that his dear Florence was indeed whispering into his ear in the confines of that beeswaxed telephone kiosk, rather than hundreds of miles away in London.

"I miss you, too, dear," said Florence. "But Noel is just too sickly to travel, I am afraid. The doctor suggested another ten days, perhaps a fortnight."

"Then I shall return to London at once," decided Stoker.

"You will not," said Florence distantly. "You have worked hard, Bram, and Noel will not improve any more quickly with you pacing up and down the house. Stay in Whitby, relax, and work on your new novel. Noel and I shall join you as soon as he is well enough."

"Well, if you're sure . . . ," Stoker said, sighing. "I shall ring again tomorrow."

Florence was right, of course; he acted as manager for the actor Henry Irving, and it had been an exhausting season. Stoker didn't know where Irving got the energy. He swore the man would breathe his last on some stage somewhere. Bram emerged into the sunshine and breathed deeply of the briny air. Noel had but a fever, he told himself. But as he himself had been an invalid until he was seven years old, Stoker did sometimes worry that Noel, now eleven, had inherited some weakness. Still, Stoker had made up for lost time, and he had excelled in athletic and scholarly pursuits at school and college. Noel was of the same makeup as Stoker, and he would be as tall and strong.

Bram had the publication of his first novel, *The Snake's Pass*, to look forward to later that year, but he was already bored with it. His mind buzzed with ideas, notions, and fancies. He had spent his weeks in Whitby listening to the fascinating tales of the salty old fishermen, or walking along the West Cliff and climbing the wild, craggy East Cliff, home to the ruins of the old abbey. They were like two opposing forces, those cliffs encompassing the fishing town, the ancient and modern, the civilized and primeval halves of the same place. If he could unlock his big idea anywhere, it would be here, in Whitby. All he needed was the key.

Gideon was circling the red mailbox like one of the gulls spiraling above the lighthouse on the harbor, desperately trying to think of his next move. Captain Trigger would not be so indecisive, so without an idea what to do next. How could he hope to even try to emulate his hero, when he could not even get in touch with him for advice?

He saw the tall Irish writer—Stoker?—striding out of the Post Office. Hadn't he said he worked for the magazines? Yes, this was what Trigger would do. Avail himself of help. Perhaps Gideon wasn't so useless. He put up his hand and shouted, "Mr. Stoker! Over here!"

Gideon was not short, but the Irishman towered over him. He looked down at Gideon and smiled with recognition. "Ah, Mr. Smith, isn't it? Was your emergency dealt with?"

"No," said Gideon. "They would not put me in touch with Captain Trigger."

"Unfortunate," said Stoker, looking contemplatively down the cobbled street and toward the harbor. "I wonder . . . might I share your burden? My own scribbling is not in the league of the illustrious Captain Trigger's adventures, but I might be able to offer assistance in some small way."

Gideon nodded enthusiastically.

"Excellent," said Stoker. "There is a most agreeable little teashop I have been frequenting. Allow me to buy you some refreshment."

⁂

Over tea and buns Gideon told Stoker what had happened since the *Cold Drake* had been found abandoned. In the bustle of the busy seaside resort, the sun blazing down, Gideon found his concerns about the noises beneath Lythe Bank seemed somewhat foolish, and he could tell Stoker thought the same from the shrewd gaze the writer cast upon him.

"A sad tale," said Stoker. "I am sorry for your loss."

"You agree an investigation is in order?"

"I am not a maritime man, I am afraid," said Stoker carefully. "I would not know just how unusual an abandoned ship is."

Gideon sighed, but the writer's attention had been diverted to a commotion outside.

"Curious," said Stoker. "Allow me to settle the bill and let us take a look."

Gideon saw a body of people moving down the street toward the harbor. Being tall, Stoker could peer above the heads of most men, and he reported a crowd gathering near the little beach between the pier and the East Cliff. Stoker said, "There appears to be a ship perilously close to land, observing a most erratic course."

"A Russian, they say," said a passing man breathlessly. "Schooner, about to run aground on Tate Hill Beach. They reckon it's deserted."

Stoker let the man go and Gideon met his eyes. He said, "Two abandoned ships in the space of a few days is not a usual occurrence around here, Mr. Stoker."

The writer stroked his beard. "Then, Mr. Smith, I suggest we investigate."

Son of the Dragon

From the Journal of Abraham Stoker

A most diverting day. After breakfast, I met an interesting young man with a strange tale. He had lost his father to a mystery of the sea—the family trawler had turned up utterly abandoned. I confess I was about to gently suggest that such occurrences, while tragic, were not utterly unknown. Then there was commotion at the harbor, and we saw a rather curious sight: a schooner, sails set, drifting haphazardly toward port and ignoring bullhorn calls from the harbormaster and the coast guard to identify itself and arrest its course.

The crowd drew back with a gasp as the schooner, with no sign of crew on deck, ran aground on the stretch of sand beneath the East Cliff, Tate Hill Beach. The harbormaster, Randolph, led a small contingent of the local constabulary to the beached vessel. They had been on for mere moments when the police officers, their faces pale and grimly set, returned to the beach and began to move the crowd back to the promenade. There were mutterings of it being some kind of plague ship, and one old maritime type, chewing tobacco and fixing nets with his gnarled fingers, commented, "A ship like that has to fetch up somewhere, even if it is hell."

As he spoke, one of the men opened up the hold and from the depths leaped the most vicious-looking black hound. It had a shaggy, lustrous pelt as dark as midnight, and it bounded from the deck to the sand, baring its white, glistening teeth at the crowd, before making for the East Cliff and disappearing. The parallels between this and young

Mr. Smith's own tale were, of course, difficult to ignore. Two abandoned ships in the space of a few days? A mystery was unfolding for certain.

I had struck up a relationship with the harbormaster, and we had swapped many tales over the preceding weeks. He remembered I had a smattering of Russian, and he asked me if I would cast my eye over the log of the schooner.

The *Dmitri* was registered in the port of Varna, on the Bulgarian Black Sea coast. According to the log, the captain had accepted a fortnight prior a commission to deliver a cargo to Whitby, with instructions that the crew was to await delivery at the stroke of midnight precisely a week ago.

The cargo—three long wooden boxes—arrived in horse-drawn coaches, each one driven by two of, according to the captain's log, the most beautiful young women he had ever seen in all his travels. Due to the late hour, some of the crew had imbibed liquor, and one seaman announced he had quite taken a shine to one of the women. I had expected to read that the captain immediately put a stop to such dishonorable talk, but it seems he merely encouraged the man, who went off in pursuit of the coaches.

He was not seen again . . . and his was not the last disappearance on the *Dmitri*'s ill-fated voyage. After becoming becalmed near an archipelago of Greek islands, another crewman vanished in the night. The *Dmitri* stopped for supplies at Gibraltar, and a crewmember absconded. The journey continued, but relations between the captain and the mate, who were Russian, and the remaining jack tar, a Romanian, were strained. The Romanian talked of creatures that inhabit the night and drink the blood of men, but the captain dismissed him as a mere uneducated yokel.

As they passed the south coast of England, a sea mist drove the Romanian mad, and he leaped over the side. The first mate did not last until dawn before he, too, was taken by whatever plagued the *Dmitri*. Driven half mad, the captain vowed in his final log entry he would never abandon ship. He charted a course for Whitby and lashed himself to the wheel.

It was this sight that greeted the harbormaster and the police when they boarded the beached schooner. The *Dmitri* had completed its journey with its captain utterly drained of blood!

The ship's log noted that delivery of the boxes was to be taken by an F. Billington, Attorney, of Royal Crescent, Whitby—mere doors from my own lodgings. A swift inquiry turned up the fact that Billington had been subcontracted by a firm of London attorneys, who were in turn acting for a practice in Roumania. Several telephone calls were made at my behest until the name of the procurer was at last obtained.

The *Dmitri* had been commissioned from the Transylvania region of Roumania by a party of the name Dracula.

While the log and manifest made no mention of any dog, the beast was witnessed leaping from the ship by half the town. It has not been seen since.

Mrs. Veasey rapped smartly at Stoker's door, and she was so flustered she forgot her hitherto impeccable manners and blustered in, waving the *Whitby Gazette* at him.

"Oh, Mr. Stoker! Russians! Dogs! Whatever will become of us? And the papers say you are helping in the inquiries!" She halted in her rapid-fire speech. "Forgive me, sir, I'm all of a flutter this morning. Your young man, Mr. Smith. He is here to see you."

While Stoker had earlier pored over the ship's log, Gideon had grown more anxious in the enclosed quarters, stalking up and down and staring out the window toward the sea, where *something* had happened to both the *Dmitri* and his father's vessel, the *Cold Drake*. To save the boy's fraying nerves—and Mrs. Veasey's threadbare carpet—he dispatched Gideon to the library to see what he could turn up on the name Dracula.

"Mr. Smith!" said Stoker. "How did your investigations at the library go?"

"Fruitfully," said Gideon, waving a sheaf of notes at him. "Though I admit I'm not sure where this is leading."

"Let us take a walk on the promenade," said Stoker. "Mrs. Veasey keeps an impeccable house, but it gets damnable hot in here."

He led Gideon out of the guest house and toward one of the wrought-iron benches on the stone jetty. The sun was low, and a refreshing breeze was blowing off the sea. Stoker nodded at the papers in Gideon's hands. "So. What did you learn?"

Gideon began to leaf through the pages. "Vlad Dracula the Third was a Prince of Wallachia," he said, as though reciting for a schoolmaster. "He was a voivode, which I think is a type of nobleman. He was an enemy of the Turks and was known as Tepes, which means The Impaler. Wallachia is in Roumania, or was." Gideon shrugged. "He died in 1476, or thereabouts. I've got sheets and sheets of this. How much do you want, and how relevant is it to anything?"

Stoker smoothed his beard. "You seem a little frustrated, Mr. Smith."

Gideon handed the pages to Stoker. "I am seeking answers to my father's death, Mr. Stoker. You seem to have had me on an errand for the past afternoon which seems nothing more than . . . well."

"Perhaps you are too polite to say *a waste of time*, Mr. Smith?"

Gideon met his eyes and held his gaze. "Is it? Some wild goose chase? What can a long-dead nobleman from . . ." Gideon glanced at the papers in Stoker's hands. "Wallachia. Transylvania. Wherever. What can he have to do with my father? Your Dracula has been dead for four centuries."

Stoker looked out to sea. The boy had fire in his belly. One saw so little real passion in London, where everything was *old* and *boring* and *unexciting* to the young men who moved in the theatrical circles. Perhaps Gideon Smith could give some of his peers in the capital lessons on how to be alive.

"Dracula," said Stoker thoughtfully. "It means *Son of the Dragon*."

He felt Gideon glance at him, then look out to sea. "The night before my father died, I dreamed a dragon ate the sun," Gideon said quietly. "But I still fail to see—"

"If you will allow me," said Stoker, raising a hand. In it was a small, leather-bound notebook. He had brought many books with him to Whitby, which he had arranged on the bookshelves in the living room. This one was a journal filled with closely written words in a tight, crabbed hand. Not his hand, however. He flicked it open to show Gideon the title page, on which was scrawled *Being an Account of JS Le Fanu's War Against the Darkness, by Himself.* Inside the cover was a folded piece of vellum, on which, in the same handwriting, was a short note, which he again presented to Gideon. It read:

> *Dearest Bram, Please forgive me for the abrupt nature of this missive, but I fear time is short. I am about to embark upon an adventure from which I fully expect I may not return. If that is the case, it shall be an untimely death, because my work is far from done. Just as the baton was passed to me many years ago, I in turn intend to ensure the flame of my work remains lit, and hand the torch to you. There are others to whom I am posting copies of the enclosed work, but for your own safety and sanity I intend to keep you ignorant of each other for now. There may well come a time when your paths cross, but for now I entrust you with a task that is necessarily lonely. May God go with you. Joseph.*

Stoker had received the package a year ago, and within a month Le Fanu had indeed turned up dead, near Macroom in County Cork, Ireland. Stoker had thought the book a literary joke for Le Fanu's friends, and had given it a brief read. After Le Fanu's body—horribly maimed and almost bloodless, by all accounts—had been discovered in the ruins of Carrickaphouka Castle, Stoker gave the book more careful study. It purported to be a journal of Le Fanu's war on vampires, following his being entrusted with the role of hunter and slayer by a mysterious old European, and the final chapters detailed Le Fanu's final assault on his bête noire, a revenant High Sheriff called Cormac Tadhg McCarthy who had died in the seventeenth century yet who returned as a *derrick-dally*, in the local parlance, to feast upon the living and continue the evil deeds that had marked his life.

Even after the troubling death of his friend, Stoker still largely regarded the work as merely another of Le Fanu's excellent supernatural fictions. But sometimes, in the dark, he wondered if the writer really had lost his life battling the undead Cormac Tadhg McCarthy, and whether he had managed to dispatch the vampire with his final breath. That was his problem, Stoker thought ruefully, a problem often pointed out gently by Florence. He had lived his life so long among theater folk, had spent so much time in stories and fictions, had immersed himself so deeply in artifice and pretense, that he had trouble separating truth from fancy. The facts as he knew them wrestled with what he hopelessly believed to be true. On the one hand, as his feverish imagination married the tales of the undead bequeathed him by Le Fanu with the reports of the slavering hound that had leaped from the ship, the *Dmitri* had brought with it a supernatural entity from the wilds of Transylvania, now abroad in England. On the other hand—the one that cautioned sense and logic—the *Dmitri* was merely an unfortunate ship that had run aground, a starving dog of a very prosaic nature fleeing as soon as the vessel landed.

In the end, fancy won out. Why else had Stoker ordered all those items from the hardware store, doubtless being delivered at that moment to Royal Crescent? Why else, after allowing Gideon to peruse Le Fanu's notebook, did he now find himself murmuring, surprising even himself, the words "Mr. Smith, it is my profound belief that Count Vlad Dracula still thrives in a most unholy state, four hundred years after his death. It is not inconceivable he could be responsible for your father's disappearance. Tell me, what do you know of vampires?"

❧

The sky was already black on the horizon, and to the west the sun had dipped behind the hills and moors, painting the underside of the straggling clouds bloodred. The imagery was not lost on Gideon, who quickened his pace on the coast road. He didn't know what to make of Stoker's theory. If Peek thought Gideon's fears about the *Cold Drake* outlandish, what would the fishermen make of the tall Irish writer? They'd think him mad, and Gideon wasn't wholly sure he didn't agree. But Captain Trigger himself had faced the undead. Gideon searched his memory and recalled *The Endless Night of the North*, in which Trigger and the Yankee adventurer Louis Cockayne had battled an undead creature that preyed on young girls in the Swedish city of Gothenburg. He hurried to his cottage and let himself in, checking that all the doors were locked before taking an oil lamp upstairs where he sought out the issue of *World Marvels & Wonders*. He read the story until drowsiness overtook him. Gideon made to blow out the lamp, then paused as the shadows danced. Just this once, he would leave the light on while he slept.

❧

The beaching of the *Dmitri* had brought excitement to Whitby, but in summer excitement was by no means rationed in the port town. It had been the destination of holidaymakers for half a century, and one such tourist was Robert, a good-looking, tall young man from mill-owning stock in Bradford, who had paid Ella Rainford a good deal of compliments as he bought cod and chips from the shop where she worked. She had seen his like often enough, but she had allowed herself to be flattered by his attentions and had primly agreed to meet him after her shift. They had looked at the wreck of the *Dmitri*, then taken a small beer from the street vendors. Ella informed Robert that she must be home by ten, and he was welcome to walk her. The alley they now found themselves in was just two narrow streets away from Ella's family cottage. She had found him agreeable enough company, and she was ready to consent to meeting him the next evening if he suggested it. Robert, however, was not planning to wait.

"Robert?" she queried, as he shoved her hard against a shadowy alcove. "Robert! What is the meaning—"

"You know full well," he said, then planted hot, wet kisses on Ella's bare neck, and took a rough, stolen handful of her skirts. "I've heard you Whitby girls like to entertain the tourists."

Robert placed his body scandalously close to Ella's. "Like that, do you?" he breathed heavily, just before realizing Ella had not gone slack in submission, but in reaction to a presence he now felt at his back, making the hairs on his neck stand on end and his skin crawl. "Who's there?" he asked, turning and peering into the darkness. The shadows in the alley deepened and fell upon him before he even had time to scream.

Stoker gasped, convulsed, and shocked himself awake with a throbbing head. He reached from the tangled bedsheets for his pocket watch on the bedside table and peered at its face in the moonlight shafting through the open windows. A little after three. Burning shame colored his cheeks as he realized he had ejaculated. How odd. He hadn't done that since he was little more than a boy. Half-glimpsed dreams clouded his mind and disappeared like dandelion clocks as he tried to grasp them. One thing was certain: His dreams had not been of Florence. He considered changing his sheets, but he felt tiredness weigh down upon him and lay back in the bed. As he did so he heard a distinct tapping sound, and he blinked away the sleep enveloping him. Stoker looked up and let loose a small cry.

There was a pale face at the window, shadowed within the confines of a voluminous hooded cloak, a pair of blazing eyes regarding him balefully as a long, thin finger tapped insistently on the glass. Was it Dracula, come to claim him?

Then the eyes became two moths, banging in unison against the pane before parting and fluttering off. The face was nothing more than the moon, within not a hood, but the branches of the plane tree outside his room. The components of the hooded face had disassembled, and Stoker forced a smile. He lay back again, laughing at his own foolishness. But his departed dreams still left a strange taste of something incredibly old and forbidden on his dry lips, and it was a long time before sleep embraced him again.

❧

There was excitement in town that distracted Stoker from his intention to telephone Florence, and from his brooding of the incidents of the night before: a crowd at the entrance to one of the cobbled side streets stretching in a haphazard warren up from the harbor. Stoker spied the chief of police, Superintendent Jackson, glowering grimly as a uniformed officer murmured in his ear, and he hailed him.

"A bad business, Mr. Stoker," said Jackson, his mustache waggling. "A bad business all around." He leaned in close and whispered, "Murder most foul." He pointed at a shapeless lump in the shadows of the alley, covered by a sheet. "Holidaymaker," said Jackson. "Son of a Bradford wool family."

"A thief?" asked Stoker. "He was murdered for his money?"

"It doesn't appear so. He had a full-to-bursting wallet in his jacket pocket. We've got witness reports saying he left the harbor area at quarter to ten, with a local girl."

"Aha," said Stoker. "A suspect."

"A doubtful one," said Jackson. "She was at the scene, in a dead faint. Still in the infirmary, not properly conscious. And I doubt a fish-and-chip shopgirl could do that to a man."

"Do . . . what?"

"Rip his throat out," said Jackson grimly. "And leave a corpse drained of blood, with barely a drop spilled on the cobbles."

❧

Stoker met Gideon at their appointed time and led him to the harbormaster's office to return the ship's log of the *Dmitri*. More mysteries worried the harassed Randolph; he had discovered that the three wooden boxes were filled with nothing but earth, and overnight someone had stolen one of them.

"Now, who'd do a thing like that? A six-foot-long box of soil? Take three men to carry it." He shook his head. "What's the world coming to?"

Or one man, thought Stoker. One man with the unnatural strength of the vampire. They left Randolph poring over the translated notes, shaking his head and puffing again, and stepped out into the afternoon sunshine.

"Well," said Stoker. "Most exciting. Did you know, Mr. Smith, that vampires like to hide away from daylight in coffins? According to Le Fanu, they favor a layer of soil from their homeland." He paused and stroked his beard, regarding Gideon. "You are not yourself today, Mr. Smith, if I might say so."

Gideon sighed. "All this talk of vampires, Mr. Stoker. I'm not sure . . ."

"We need to get back into the chase," said Stoker. "Perhaps some lunch at the Magpie Café . . . ?"

"Mr. Stoker," said Gideon, "if this Count Dracula really is in Whitby, and if he is responsible for the deaths of this tourist and my father's crew, perhaps we need help. You have worked for the magazines . . . maybe they'll listen to you at *World Marvels & Wonders*, put you in touch with Captain Trigger."

Stoker laughed, then regretted it as Gideon's face fell. "I didn't mean—" he began, then stopped. "Look, Mr. Smith, this is my story, and while I'm grateful for your assistance . . ."

"Story?" asked Gideon sharply. "You mean this is all some kind of . . . of research project for a novel? I thought you were helping me investigate my father's disappearance."

Stoker bit his lip and directed Gideon to a wooden bench. He sat down and said kindly, "Look, lad, I went through the ship's log again . . . when did your father go missing?"

"Three nights ago." Gideon frowned. "Why?"

Stoker took a breath. "The log quite clearly charts the course of the *Dmitri*. The night your father was lost it was hundreds of miles away. I don't think that Dracula could have been responsible for the fate of the *Cold Drake*."

"Oh," said Gideon. "Then . . ."

"Perhaps an unfortunate accident?" said Stoker softly. "I am no expert, but I suppose these things do happen. . . ."

There was silence as Gideon stared morosely at his boots. "Still," said Stoker, "nothing to stop you continuing to help me. Take your mind off things, eh? We've still got Dracula out there somewhere." He dropped his voice to a murmur. "I need your help, Gideon."

Gideon looked at him. "I must go, Mr. Stoker. Home. I must go home and think about things."

Stoker nodded, and Gideon walked like a sleepwalker toward the West Cliff, and the coast road to Sandsend.

4

The Shadow Over Faxmouth

Peek let Gideon in to a house that seemed to be full of children, though they didn't sit still long enough for him to count them. Except Tommy, drawing with his tongue poking out of his mouth in concentration.

The cottage was filled with the smells of cooking, and Gideon's stomach rumbled. "Sorry to interrupt you at teatime."

Peek shrugged. "It isn't ready yet. You're not interrupting."

Gideon looked over Tommy's shoulder at the pencil drawing of a gull on a breakwater. Very lifelike, and evidently drawn from memory. The boy was astonishingly good. Gideon felt a momentary pang of sadness. Tommy's talent would not be nurtured; that didn't happen in Sandsend. Not through malice, but because its inhabitants didn't know anything else. He would fish, like his brothers, like his daddy, like everyone.

"I won't keep you long," said Gideon at last. "I've come to tell you I'll be taking the *Cold Drake* out as soon as possible. Day after tomorrow, perhaps. I need to look over her, and get some supplies."

Peek screwed up his eyes. "What's changed your mind?"

Is this what Trigger would do? It didn't matter. Gideon Smith was not Lucian Trigger, nor would he ever be. Despite the salutation at the start of each story—*This adventure, as always, is utterly true, and faithfully retold by my good friend, Doctor John Reed*—real life was never as neat as the stories. Trigger never failed; he was never turned away from his adventures by anything as *ordinary* as a death in the family. Trigger was impervious to personal tragedy, or if he wasn't, then he gamely adventured on regardless. Gideon didn't have that luxury. He needed to put food on the table and pay the bills, and neither searching for whatever truth lay out there about his father's death nor hunting for Bram Stoker's vampiric nobleman would do that. He said, "It's the right thing to do."

"Peter's ready when you are, and I've spoke to the others and their dads."

Mrs. Peek, who had thinning hair and a look of perpetual, ingrained exhaustion, appeared at the kitchen door, wiping her hands on a tea towel. She nodded at Gideon. "Sorry about Arthur. He was a good man."

Gideon nodded. Peek said, "So you've given it up? All this talk of investigations? And your . . . noises? At Lythe Bank?"

Gideon shrugged. "I told Constable Clarke. It's his business if he cares to look into it."

The look that passed between the Peeks was not so brief that Gideon didn't catch it. His eyes narrowed. "What?"

Peek said, "Clive Clarke's . . . missing. He started his rounds, called in on Mrs. Higginbotham, as is customary, then . . . well, no one saw him after that."

"Maybe he's out of the village," said Gideon. "Called to Whitby, or Staithes."

But Peek glanced out the window, at the darkening sky, and Gideon saw in his furrowed brow that same look he'd had the day after the *Cold Drake* was lost. He said quietly, "Old Mrs. Higginbotham said he'd been planning to go to Lythe Bank. Check out a *report* he'd had."

There was a moment of awkward silence, then Mrs. Peek said, too brightly, "You'll stay for tea, Gideon?"

"No. I've taken up enough of your time."

"He'll turn up," he said. "Clive Clarke."

"Yes." Gideon nodded.

They both looked at their feet, then Gideon said his goodbyes and left, heading down the hill toward the beach. On the horizon a thin, pale line was advancing, indicating another sea mist was going to crawl inland. The last time it had come, the sea mist had claimed his dad. Gideon wondered what fresh terror this new incursion would herald. In truth, he was famished and would have gladly sat at Peek's table, but he had suddenly felt so very sick to his stomach. He had sent Clive Clarke off to investigate those noises from Lythe Bank . . . had he sent the police officer to his death? Had whatever overwhelmed the *Cold Drake* insinuated itself into the tunnels beneath the cliffs, awaiting more victims? Bram Stoker said it couldn't be his fanciful vampire crawling in under cover of the sea fret, so it must be something more solid . . . and much, much worse.

"Why'd you say that to him?" asked Mrs. Peek as she dished up the stew. "About Clive? You said yourself he's apt to be a little away with the fairies. Who knows what he'll make of that?"

Peek dipped a hunk of bread into the brown soup. "He'd have found out anyway. Better he can put this sort of thing into . . . oh, what's the word, Harold? When something seems one way or another depending on what sort of place you're at when you looks at it?"

Peek's son, Harold, who was a whiz with his spelling, shrugged. "Perspective?"

Peek considered. "Sounds right. Better he can put this sort of thing into *perspective* while he's in a sensible frame of mind. Even if Clive is missing in Lythe Bank, and God knows no one wants that, at least Gideon'll be able to see it's just one of those things and not one of his mysteries." He winked at Harold. "Perspective. Bloody good word, that."

"Well, he looked half starved to me on top of it all," said Mrs. Peek. "I bet he hasn't had a square meal since his daddy died. After tea you can take a bowl of stew over to Gideon."

Peek sighed and Tommy perked up. "I'll take it."

Mrs. Peek was about to protest, but her husband held up his hand. "Aye, let the lad. It's only five minutes." He turned to his son and waggled his spoon. "No letting him fill your head with nonsense, mind. I know you're almost as much of a bugger for those penny dreadfuls as he is."

❧

Before Gideon returned to the cottage, there was a ghost to lay to rest, a more looming presence than Stoker's Transylvanian phantoms or the disappearance of Clive Clarke.

He hadn't set foot on the *Cold Drake* since the crew was lost, had barely had the stomach to look at it. He wanted to run from it, in fact. But Trigger wouldn't do that. Trigger would face the beast in its lair. He walked with measured footfalls along the rickety pier until he was alongside the ship. The other trawlers were moored farther along the beach, black shapes in the dying day. Why didn't they look as foreboding as his father's ship? Why didn't they fill Gideon's gut with butterflies? They just looked like gearships wound down for the night, awaiting preparation for tomorrow's fishing, once the sea mist had lifted. The *Cold Drake* looked like something else. Something *other*. Gideon could see, now, why none of the more seasoned fishermen of Sandsend would take to the sea with her, why trawlermen were so superstitious. A pall hung over the *Cold Drake* like a cloud of flies. She was cursed, plain and simple. There were no rules about these things, nothing written down, no guidebooks. But Gideon knew the Sandsend fishing community would not put up with the abandoned ship moored on the beach for long. It was bad for business, bad for morale. Bad for Sandsend. There was only one way the curse of the *Cold Drake* could be lifted, and that was by Gideon taking her out as though nothing had happened. Only he could break the hold the black shape of the Smiths' trawler was exerting on Sandsend.

Steeling himself, Gideon placed a shaking hand on the strut of the wooden pier and jumped.

No earthquake split the land when his feet hit the deck of the *Cold Drake*. No tidal wave consumed Sandsend. The sky did not fall; fire did not rain from the heavens.

No dragon appeared to eat the sinking sun.

There was no clue as to what had happened. Gideon's fingers trailed along a series of shallow gouges in the decking.

Were they fresh, or had they always been there? It was difficult to say. A belt buckle rusted by the bow. Had it been lost by one of the crew that fateful night, or had it sat there for months? Gideon completed another circuit, walking clockwise as though he might ward off any bad luck clinging to the trawler. He had not ventured belowdecks, and did not intend to as the sun dipped redly over the rooftops. That was enough for one day. As he made to leave, though, the last of the sun's rays bounced off a reflective sliver by his feet, hidden by the long shaft-brake. Arthur Smith's gutting knife, the blade sunk a half-inch into the plank. Gideon pulled the knife from the deck and inspected the point of the blade. The knife had pierced and fixed to the decking what appeared to be a small square of dirty white cloth. Gideon plucked it from the end of the blade. It *was* cloth, though as dry as paper. It crumbled to dust in his fingers and was whipped away on a sudden and unexpectedly cold breeze playing over the *Cold Drake,* chilling Gideon into a hurried exit from the trawler and a rapid return up the hill to his cottage. He did not dare to cast a single look over his shoulder.

❦

Gideon closed the windows against the advancing fog and sat in his father's chair, leafing through his copies of *World Marvels & Wonders* by candlelight. He was just thinking how hungry he was and how good Mrs. Peek's stew had smelled when he heard a startled cry, followed by the crash of something breaking. The fog was thick and he could see nothing from the window, but then the air was rent by a scream that could have been dragged from within Gideon himself. A small boy, calling for his dad.

In seconds Gideon was out of the front door, and his scalp crawled as he saw Tommy Peek half lying on the path outside Gideon's cottage, a pot in pieces around him, the brown gravy from his mother's stew soaking into the dry earth. But the boy was moving, wide-eyed and drawing breath for another cry. Gideon squatted at his side.

"It was a monster!" Tommy hissed. "It came out of the fog. Its teeth . . ."

Monster? Teeth? Was it Stoker's Count Dracula after all? "Inside," Gideon said. "We'll get you cleaned up, then get your daddy."

A shape loomed out of the curling white fog, and Gideon's heart raced, but it was only his nearest neighbor, a crippled old fisherman who had not been out on the sea for a decade.

"Go get Peek," said Gideon, his mouth dry. "Tell him Tommy's had a bit of a fright, but he's all right."

Inside the house Gideon gave Tommy a cup of water and sat him in the chair. He remembered the portrait of Count Dracula he'd seen in one of the books in the library. "Did the man have a long nose? A jutting lower jaw? A thick black mustache?"

Tommy shook his head. "It wasn't a man. It was a monster." He put his hands to his face and burst into tears again.

Gideon hushed him. "Can you describe him? *It*, then?"

Tommy looked at his hands and sniffed. Gideon thought for a moment and said, "Can you draw it?"

He fetched a notepad and a pencil and went to make some coffee while the boy haltingly began to sketch. The water was about to boil on the stove when there was a hammering on the door and Peek let himself in.

"Tommy!" he said, glaring at Gideon. "What happened?"

"It was a monster," said Tommy.

Peek shook his head. "You're as bad as Gideon for your tales. You dropped the pot and now you're trying to cover it up with some daft story. Your mother was right. I shouldn't have let you out in this fog." He turned to Gideon. "Thank you for looking after him. I'll take care of it now." He ruffled the boy's hair. "We'll think of something to tell your mammy, don't worry."

Tommy nodded and Gideon marveled at the resilience of the young. Either he really was lying, or he was more scared of his mother than he was of Count Dracula. Gideon saw them out and returned to the chair, where Tommy had left the sketch.

At first he took it for the product of an overactive imagination—*It takes one to know one.* It was technically very good, as were all Tommy's pictures. But the subject matter . . . it really was a monster, thin and wiry of body, ragged strips of cloth wound around its chest and festooning its arms, gnarled but viciously clawed hands. The thing had a bulbous, bald head into which were set bulging round eyes without pupils, giving them the appearance of milky orbs. Tommy had managed to make its skin look dry and thin and seemingly stretched over its ball-like skull. But the true terror lay in its mouth: thin lips, curiously elongated and froglike, and rows of pointed, black fangs slavering with clear, viscous fluid.

Something about it was awfully, terribly familiar. Gideon stalked up and down the small living room, his fist to his mouth. Think, think, think. Then his eyes fell on the pile of *World Marvels & Wonders* by the chair. He *had* seen the thing before.

❧

It was one of Gideon's favorite stories, *The Shadow Over Faxmouth.* While a guest of Professor Reginald Halifax in British-American Massachusetts, Captain Trigger is taken to witch-haunted Arkhamville by the enthusiastic professor to see a rather grotesque mummy the academic has found near the Nile. Gideon's finger found Trigger's description of the thing: "The grayish skin looked parchment dry, stretched over a hairless skull surely more globular than any normal human's. The eyes were unnaturally round, and pupilless, staring from the face like gray, smooth stones. The nose was almost rudimentary—merely two nostrils etched in the dry skin—and below it hung a most horrible mouth, froglike in its width and aspect, but with rows of black, cruel-looking teeth as sharp as razors."

He put down the story-paper and picked up young Tommy's drawing. Trigger could have been describing the boy's vision.

Gideon finished the story, reading how Trigger was awoken in the early morning by a message from the university where Halifax worked in the Egyptology department. The Professor was near death, having been attacked, his offices ransacked. The mummy, and a valuable ruby locket, had been stolen. But it was no burglar, whispered the gravely injured Halifax. It was the mummy itself, roused from its centuries-long slumber, that had attacked him, grabbed the amulet, and made off for the coast.

Trigger tracked the creature to Faxmouth, a bleak place populated by dour backwoodsmen. He was unable to stop the thing escaping into the cold Atlantic, but stole back the purloined amulet. Halifax died of his injuries, taking the mystery with him to the grave, and Trigger kept the ancient stone, inlaid with enigmatic hieroglyphics, for his trophy room.

The candle on the mantelpiece burned down as Gideon stared at the story-paper on his lap long after completing the tale. Common sense told him there were a million reasons why he should ignore this. Tommy Peek was only a child with an overactive imagination. Tommy had often shared the stories in *World Marvels & Wonders* with Gideon, and it was likely his young, impressionable brain had absorbed *The Shadow Over Faxmouth*. And wasn't it patently ridiculous anyway, the idea a mummy from ancient Egypt was lurking in the fog-bound coastal village of Sandsend, Yorkshire, England?

Perhaps it was the eerie quality the sea mist had lent to the night, perhaps the look of terror on young Tommy's face. Perhaps it was Gideon's own predilection for the fantastic. But as he read the story he had felt a shivering *something* grip his spine, and it refused to let go. While the artist's rendition of the Faxmouth horror wasn't quite identical to Tommy's sketch, they were so near alike for the differences to be negligible. Coupled with Gideon's own feelings of unnameable dread at hearing those strange sounds at the foot of Lythe Bank, the disappearance of Clive Clarke, and the scrap of cloth he'd found pinned under the knife on the *Cold Drake*, Gideon was convinced the thing that had haunted Faxmouth was now just outside his very door.

His first instinct was to seek out Stoker, but he paused. Stoker had already made it clear the whole enterprise was research for his latest novel, although Gideon was sure he had not meant to mislead him. It was more that the Irishman got wrapped up in his projects and seemed not to realize others might have more to gain—or lose—by their shared adventures.

And Gideon knew he would get no help in Sandsend. If he started raving about frog-mummies he'd be carted off to the loony bin.

Only one thing was certain. He wouldn't be taking the *Cold Drake* out, not tomorrow, not the day after. Not ever, if he didn't find out what had happened to his father and to Clive Clarke. Gideon couldn't put it all behind him and get on with life. Not when mysteries and the unknown seeped into Sandsend and his mind like the sea mist rolling in with the night. He just couldn't do it. He owed it to Arthur Smith—and with a sinking heart he realized he owed something to Clive Clarke as well.

Most of all, Gideon Smith owed it to himself to find answers. When the mystery had been solved, then perhaps he would live the life others wanted him to lead. But for now he had to do this, and he couldn't do it alone.

First thing in the morning, he would go and find Captain Lucian Trigger.

5

A Most Unusual Dinner

As Gideon packed a few provisions and the rest of the money he'd found in a stone jar under his father's bed, he felt a calm resolve come over him. He just had to convince Trigger to investigate. He, after all, was the hero, not Gideon.

He saw Peek's wagon negotiating the coast road. Gideon ran to the door and hailed him, and Peek squinted up at him and pulled on the reins until his old nag stopped.

"Are you going into Whitby?" asked Gideon. Mrs. Peek was hugging Tommy to her beside Peek; three more of their children were in the back of the cart.

Peek eyed him suspiciously. "Aye. Mrs. Peek wanted to take Tommy to the doctor. He's not been himself since last night."

Tommy smiled wanly at Gideon, who reached up to ruffle his hair, then handed an envelope to Peek. "There's a Mr. Stoker staying at lodgings on Royal Crescent; would you take this to him?"

Peek looked at the brown envelope. "I will. But why can't you take it yourself?"

"I'm going to London."

Peek gaped at him. "London?"

"Don't let anyone near Lythe Bank, especially the children," said Gideon.

Tommy looked wide-eyed. "Is that where the monster lives, Gideon?"

"Hush," said Mrs. Peek, glaring at Gideon. "There are no monsters, are there?"

Gideon bit his lip. You couldn't lie to children, not about such things. They instinctively knew. Instead he just winked at Tommy and said, "I'll be back soon. With help."

❧

Mr. Stoker, I am afraid I cannot join you in your research today. I wish I had time to speak to you in person, but that is one thing I just do not have. I now believe the search for your Count Dracula to be a blind alley. There is indeed an undead monster on the loose, but not the one you think. Perhaps the enclosed story-paper might prove illuminating. I have gone to London to engage the services of Captain Trigger. Yours, Gideon Smith.

Also in the envelope was an issue of *World Marvels & Wonders,* folded open to a Captain Lucian Trigger story. Stoker glanced at the periodical and put it unread to one side, pondering over his lunch of dressed crab. He had upset Mr. Smith. He had been careless with his words, given the young man the impression that he was merely on a jolly adventure, while for Gideon it could not have been more important.

A story, Gideon had said, with distaste. *Research. A novel.* He would have liked Mr. Smith's strong arm at his service, but he had let Gideon down, so it wasn't to be. He wouldn't make the same mistake again. Bram Stoker was stepping outside the comfortable confines of artifice and fancy, and tipping himself headlong into what he now knew to be a very real, very dangerous escapade. He would make amends. He would track down Vlad Dracula himself, and vanquish him. Stoker smiled as he finished his lunch. He had never felt more alive.

❧

The police had, of course, combed the moors in search of the dog, but they pronounced it gone. And relieved they seemed about it, too, thought Stoker. With murders and mysteries to be solved, a wild hound was low on the constabulary's list of worries. If it had run off toward the next police division, so be it. Stoker, of course, knew otherwise. The vampire had merely gone to ground and shed its transformed state.

He took a meandering route, making his painstaking way along the beach and scrambling up the rocks. He surveyed the moors rolling away from the coast, the farms and small holdings dotted around the patchwork landscape, any one of them potentially providing shelter—or a hearty meal—for Dracula. But why here? According to Le Fanu's account, Vlad Dracula was a Transylvanian nobleman of an ancient pedigree, and while the guise of a black hound might be suitable for effecting entry to England, surely rampaging like a rabid dog would not be the count's style.

Stoker's path took him back toward the abbey, and he knew from there he could descend the famous 199 steps down to the town. He resolved to sit in the ruins of the abbey and eat his provisions while he pondered his next move.

In the gathering dusk, just a hundred yards from the abbey, came a farmer, openly weeping and dragging a hessian sack. Stoker stopped him and said, "Good heavens, man, whatever is the matter?"

The man simply pulled open the neck of the sack and bade Stoker look inside. He did, then drew back in horror. There was the severed head of a sheepdog in there, the blind, milky eyes of the collie staring up at him.

"My old Shep," wailed the man. "He'd been missing all afternoon. He never goes missing. I found this yonder, near the abbey. What sort of monster would do that to a dog?"

What sort of monster indeed. His mouth set in a grim line, Stoker strode toward where the farmer had found the remains of his dog. The abbey. He fumbled in his satchel and took out a handful of stakes and his hammer, juggling them at his chest as he also delved in for the crucifix. In the gloom he slipped on a patch of dark wetness, which closer inspection revealed to be blood. His breath caught in his chest. The blood was before a dark opening, just off what must have once been the nave of the church, which led down half a dozen steps to an old cell or storage room. Stoker lit his small oil lamp with a painfully loud match strike. Was there a sudden movement from within? Holding the lamp high in one hand and clutching the stakes, hammer, and crucifix clumsily in the other, he descended, as boldly as he could, wishing he had Mr. Smith with him.

The cell was small and damp, but large enough for what it held: a long box beside one stone wall and a figure, clothed in a black cloak, hunkered down over what could only be the headless corpse of the old farmer's dog. His hands shaking, Stoker held up the crucifix and, summoning bravery as a bulwark against every other emotion screaming for him to flee the place, he said, "Count Dracula, I presume."

The shape paused in its repast, noticing for the first time the dim light illuminating the cell, as though it had been eating joyfully and with abandon, eyes closed. It straightened, and Stoker took an involuntary step back, then regained his composure and held the crucifix higher.

"You presume wrongly, Mr. Stoker," said the figure.

Stoker blinked and swayed with shock, both that the vampire knew his name and at the voice issuing from the creature. The vampire turned and smiled, its teeth the distended fangs of legend, its lower jaw slick with dark blood. But the face was that of a singularly beautiful woman, her complexion as pale as a white rose, her black hair falling about her shoulders in lustrous curls. She fixed him with her shining eyes and said in flawless English, "*Countess* Dracula, if you must. But why stand on ceremony?"

She advanced one step and Stoker moaned, the stakes falling from his weakening grip and clattering to the stone floor. She raised an exquisite eyebrow at his arsenal and said, "Call me Elizabeth." She smiled again, showing those dreadful, bloodstained fangs. "Elizabeth Bathory. And you are just in time for dinner."

❧

"Dinner?" asked Stoker, looking with horror at the corpse of the dog. "You mean you wish to share your foul meal with me . . . or I am to be your main course?"

Elizabeth Bathory laughed lightly, and it would have been a pleasing sound under other circumstances. She threw a sheet over the body of the sheepdog and took out a white handkerchief to wipe the gore from her chin. "I mean neither, Mr. Stoker. I have a basket with bread, cheese, and wine, if you would care to join me. And you can put down that crucifix; it is a rather pointless endeavor to keep brandishing it at me."

Stoker looked self-consciously at the cross and lowered it, touching his hand to his collar. "I apologize for my rudeness, Countess. But I must decline your kind offer. My appetite inexplicably deserts me."

Bathory cocked her head to one side to regard Stoker in a maneuver he found both wanton and ever so slightly alluring. "So," she said after a moment. "You are convinced a vampire is abroad on English soil and you are determined to rid the countryside of this foul beast. Am I correct?"

"Well," said Stoker, rather disarmed by Bathory's beauty and self-assured manner.

"And I should expect your satchel contains . . . let me see . . ." She placed an exquisitely painted nail to her full lips, as though lost in thought. "Garlic, wooden stakes, a Bible? An ax to chop off my head?"

When she put it like that, it did seem ridiculous. Then Stoker caught sight of the lumpy corpse of the dog, slowly coloring the sheet with dark blood, and his resolve stiffened.

"You surmise correctly, Countess," he said, raising the crucifix again. "Your reign of terror must end this night."

Bathory's cloak fell open, revealing a sumptuous ivory dress in an antique style plunging perilously at the neckline. She put her hand to the necklace hanging there and said, "It is hot in this cramped little hovel, Mr. Stoker. I intend to take some cheese and wine in the abbey grounds. Will you join me?"

Stoker risked a glance through the stone doorway, as the last of the bloodred rays of the setting sun faintly painted the ruined walls. Was there enough sunlight to cause the vampire ill if she stepped into it? Perhaps . . .

Bathory laughed again. "My dear Mr. Stoker," she said. "I can see I must tutor you in the ways of my kind. The sunlight will not harm me, nor will that crucifix. I intend to step out for some air whether you come or not; this hateful little place reminds me too much of the dungeon where I breathed my last as a living thing. This is the place where Walter Scott had that poor nun suffer a similar fate in *Marmion,* if I am not mistaken."

Stoker searched his memory of Le Fanu's document. Elizabeth Bathory, known as the Blood Countess for her habit of bathing in the blood of murdered young women to extend her youth. For her crimes she had been bricked up in her rooms in Csejte Castle in Hungary. Sometime in 1614, he thought he remembered. He blanched. Two hundred and seventy-six years ago. He stammered, "You are well read, Countess."

She smiled, showing those fearful fangs again. "I have had plenty of time to read, Mr. Stoker. And not just the classics. Why, I read in the newspaper you had been helping the local constabulary with their inquiries into the mystery of the ghost ship that fetched up on Whitby beach, did I not?"

"You did," said Stoker. Bathory grasped the handle of a wicker basket and moved toward him. He pressed himself against the cool stone wall, and she passed by him and into the grounds of the abbey.

Gathering his things, he followed, to find the countess laying out a gingham blanket on the unruly lawn, now painted silver by the fiercely glowing moon high above. Bathory sat down with her legs beneath her and closed her eyes, breathing deeply. "I always loved the smell of the sea."

Warily, Stoker circled around her. She began to lay out items from her basket: cheese, bread, and wine, just as she had said. "Please do sit down, Mr. Stoker. You are quite making me nervous with all this hopping around."

Stoker crouched on the corner of the blanket. He surveyed the food and raised an eyebrow as Bathory tore off a chunk of bread and began to nibble on it.

"I thought . . . blood . . ."

Bathory sighed and lay down her bread. "Mr. Stoker, you require water to survive?"

"Of course."

"So it is with vampires and blood. But just as you do not entirely subsist on water, so we do eat other food as well. Life would be rather dull if I had to only drink blood."

"Life?" said Stoker, pulling a face.

She shrugged. "Unlife. Undeath. Call it what you will. But mark this: I never felt more alive before I crossed over." She paused. "Lesson two. Sunlight does not cause vampires to shrivel and burn. It weakens me, yes, and it can hurt my eyes. But I am quite capable of walking in it. I enjoy the sunshine, Mr. Stoker. Number three, your crucifix means nothing to me, so please put it away. My kind may have been cast from the Kingdom of Heaven, but by men, not God. Men are not always right, you know. In fact, I find they rarely are at all. Are we not sitting on consecrated ground? With no ill effect to myself?"

"Garlic?" asked Stoker, rather hopelessly.

"I like it, in moderation," said Bathory. "This cheese is made with a small amount."

"A stake through the heart?"

Bathory smiled. "I dare say if I hammered a wooden stake through your heart, Mr. Stoker, it would sting a little."

His shoulders slumped, and he sat down properly on the blanket. Was all Le Fanu's lore useless? He could recall only one other fact. "Running water," he announced. "Vampires can't cross running water, can they?"

She gave him the look a schoolteacher might direct toward a particularly dull pupil. "I arrived by boat, Mr. Stoker."

He sighed. "That you did, Countess." He paused. "Do you mind if I have some cheese? I am dashed hungry, after all."

❧

It was quite the most unusual dinner he had ever had. He said, "I must say, you are rather not what I was expecting."

"What were you expecting?"

"A man, for one thing. Count Vlad Dracula of Transylvania, to be exact."

A cloud passed over Bathory's flawless face. "My husband," she said tightly.

Stoker felt suddenly fearful. "Your husband? Is he here?"

Bathory looked down at her glass of wine. "No, Mr. Stoker. My husband is not here. That is the reason I am." She looked up at him. "Dracula is dead, Mr. Stoker. Properly, finally dead. And I am on the trail of his murderers."

Stoker was burning with questions. Bathory smiled and said, "But enough for now. Have you tried this Wensleydale? There are cranberries in it. Most diverting."

Stoker munched thoughtfully and asked, "How did you . . . become as you are?"

"A vampire?" asked Bathory. "Dracula. He found me when I was near death and saved me."

"This was your death in the castle? Where you had been imprisoned?"

Bathory nodded. "I was not a good person, Mr. Stoker. I was a vain, arrogant woman who felt all the good things in life belonged to the young, and endeavored to extend my youth with the blood of virgins."

"And you bathed in it? And it restored your youth?"

"I did bathe in the blood of murdered women, yes. And no, it did not work. I was tried and jailed in my own castle to starve. And as I hovered between this life and the punishments of eternity, I was offered an opportunity to redeem myself."

"By Dracula?"

She nodded. "He had lived many lifetimes by then, and he had heard about me and my crimes. Where others could not venture, he breached the walls of my prison. At first I thought he was the angel of death, come to take me to my final judgment. Then he bestowed upon me his kiss, and drew his thumbnail across his forearm, and bade me drink of his own blood. Thus, I was transformed."

"Count Dracula and Elizabeth Bathory together," said Stoker wonderingly. "Your reign of terror must have been absolute."

A distant look entered her eye. "Men create their own monsters, Mr. Stoker. If you are not understood, you are to be feared and ultimately destroyed. Unless you strike first."

"But the stories . . . ," pressed Stoker. "Preying on innocent victims, drinking their blood . . . like that holidaymaker in Whitby." He paused. "And my dream the night before . . . the face at the window . . ."

She smiled. "I was curious, Mr. Stoker, about this man whom the newspapers said was *investigating*." Her face darkened. "As for that brute forcing himself upon the girl? He got everything he deserved."

Stoker frowned. "You were *protecting* her?"

Bathory looked Stoker in the eye. "My husband was demonized by those who said he took young girls and transformed them into monsters." She sat back and regarded him. "What do you know of women, Mr. Stoker?"

He frowned. "I am married, Countess."

She nodded. "Then you know when a girl's blood comes, it unlocks a new life for her. It is the transition between being a child and becoming an adult. You know what I mean by blood?"

Stoker reddened. He of course knew all about Florence's *monthlies*, but it was not a topic for polite conversation. As he had already established, however, this was a most unusual dinner. "Of course," he mumbled.

"The blood sets her free. It enables her to embrace the world of love and passion, and to create life herself. What Dracula understood, and I later came to understand, is that there can come a time when bloodletting can unlock yet another life, a third life beyond childhood and adulthood. Vampirism is yet another transition, Mr. Stoker. The giving and receiving of blood takes the woman on to the next level of existence. It is the ultimate emancipation for women who live their lives under the yoke of man's slavery."

"A rather . . . forward-thinking attitude," he murmured. "And you have . . . set many women free into this new and secret phase of life?"

"Dozens," said Bathory, her teeth gleaming in the moonlight. "At Castle Dracula, I have an army of them."

An army of vampiric women, all as passionate and abandoned and emancipated as Elizabeth Bathory. Stoker felt simultaneously sickened and excited.

That faraway look entered Bathory's eye again. "But that was not enough to save my husband. Castle Dracula, which has been my home for almost three centuries, is a beautiful place," said Bathory. "Its spires and towers reach for blue skies only recently sullied by the occasional passage of your empire's airships. It sits high in the Carpathian Mountains and can be reached only by the Gorgo Pass, on which no mortal will tread. The jagged peaks are covered with snow in the winter months, which thaws to form thunderous waterfalls and churning rivers in the spring. Raw, untamed forests spin out in every direction, haunted by things unknown to man, or forgotten by him. Wolves roam and sing in the moonlight, serenading Castle Dracula with the music of the children of the night. It is peaceful and happy. Or it was." She looked at him. "We were attacked, Mr. Stoker."

"An attack? But you said you had an army . . . the mountains were impassable."

"No plot of mere men could have unseated us. They came stealthily and in secret, traveling the watercourses, swimming upstream like black salmon against the melt-water torrents. They crawled like rats over the battlements of Castle Dracula while we slumbered as the summer sun burned in the sky."

"But what were they?" said Stoker.

Bathory shrugged. "If they had ever been human, it was a long time ago. They were dead things, wrapped in rags, with vicious claws and inhuman strength. Their faces were fearful to behold, Mr. Stoker: blank, round eyes and rows of pin-sharp teeth. As my husband beheld them I heard him shout, 'The Children of Heqet!' and he entered the fray."

She paused, then spat, startling Stoker. "Foolish, foolish man. Always had to play the protector and the hero." She cast her eyes down. "They tore him apart. They broke into our treasury and took one item, a jeweled scarab from ancient Egypt, picked up from somewhere or other by Vlad many centuries previously. For that they murdered my husband and turned my world upside down."

Stoker sat in silence for a long time after the story was finished. "And these Children of Heqet? What do you know of them?"

"Nothing. Vlad died before he could say anything further. They leaped into the rivers with their prize, and fled."

"So what brings you to Whitby?"

"I joined the battle at the side of my husband. The Children of Heqet did not escape without casualties. Come with me."

Without any of his earlier fear, Stoker followed Bathory back into the stone cell. She took a sturdy hatbox and opened it, bidding him to shine his lamp on it. He did so and drew back, horrified. Within was the severed head of one of the monsters Bathory had described, its withered skin stretched taut over a domelike head, its bulbous eyes staring sightlessly, its thin lips drawn back in a grinning rictus over daggerlike teeth.

"I have tasted their blood," said Bathory. "And as foul as it is, I continue to taste it, a drop or two a day. Because when it suffuses me I feel their presence, these hated Children of Heqet. They shine like a beacon in my mind. I have followed them here."

"To Whitby? But why?"

"I mean to find out. And they will know my wrath."

In the tiny cell, as Elizabeth Bathory drew herself up to her full height and bared her fangs, her eyes shining in the darkness, Stoker felt suddenly very afraid. No longer for himself . . . but for those who had wronged her.

"Mr. Stoker," said Bathory, holding out her hand. "Will you help me avenge my husband?"

Stoker had come seeking one monster, and he had found more to hunt. And he still felt as though he owed something of a debt to Gideon Smith. The young man had given freely of his time and energy to help Stoker, all—it had seemed—for nothing to help him in his quest for an explanation for his father's death. But now . . . it seemed likely the Children of Heqet could have done in the *Cold Drake*'s crew and Gideon's father. Perhaps, while Gideon was away seeking help in London, Stoker could go some way toward making amends.

He nodded and placed his hand in Elizabeth Bathory's, then said, "Madam, though I fear my contribution shall be wretchedly mortal and weak, I most assuredly will."

6

The House of Einstein

In Gideon's opinion, the mail coach wasn't worth half of what he'd paid. Pulled by a team of four horses, the battered old carriage was stuffed with sacks of letters. Gideon was invited to find a spot for the journey by the coachman, who didn't speak to him again other than to rouse him in darkness and tell him he was to get out. The driver just laughed when Gideon asked how close to London he was, and the coach rumbled away. Night had fallen and so, now, did a hard summer rain, drenching Gideon. He walked for what seemed like hours through bare countryside, no sign of civilization, nor an inn where he could beg for help.

Until he saw the house.

Gideon emerged from a thin copse on a gentle hillside and saw it nestling in a small valley, a large mansion of gray stone, almost invisible in the darkness against the black hills. A single lit window betrayed the presence of someone inhabiting the place. As he drew closer, the building emerged from the night as a rather singular work of architecture, a mashed-together riot of fairy-tale towers, rickety wooden lean-tos, a glass domed roof, and joists and pulleys swinging in the wind at the eaves. Before the terrace fronting the house there were small lawns, and Gideon saw a figure bent over a lawnmower, as though exhausted. Gideon hailed him, but a clap of thunder snatched his words away; the figure remained motionless. As he hurried closer, he saw the man was certainly some kind of domestic staff, given his tattered garb, but he could not understand why he was cutting the grass in such a storm.

"Ho," called Gideon as he neared. "Foul weather."

Gideon laid a hand on the man's arm. It was as hard and

unflinching as iron. Gideon frowned and bent closer. He *was* iron, or metal at least. A life-sized statue, leaning on a lawn mower, dressed in real clothes and boots. How odd. Gideon patted the metal man on his solid shoulder and said, "Think I'll ask for a bed for the night, before I end up a pile of rust like you."

The voice came little louder than a whisper. "The master is not in residence."

Gideon inspected the statue's face. Was there the faintest light behind those glass lens eyes, where before they had been dead and blank? He moved his hand in front of the glass and leaned in close to the rusted mouth.

"The master is not in residence."

"What are you?" whispered Gideon.

"The master is not in residence," said the figure, the last word a whine of clashing wheels and freezing gears. Then the dull light faded and the thing was silent once more.

❧

Gideon hammered hard on the flaking paint of the double doors for a full minute before he heard a shuffling sound from within the house. The wide stone steps were cracked and choked with weeds and dandelions and, up close, the house was in a dreadful state of disrepair.

"Who's there, at this time of night?" called a man's voice.

"My name is Gideon Smith. I am seeking refuge from the storm."

There was another agonizing moment of silence, then Gideon heard the jangling of keys and bolts being slid back. An oil lamp emerged first, followed by the screwed-up face of a man about the age of Gideon's father, snarling through rows of rotten teeth and with lank, wispy hair crowning his liver-spotted head. He looked Gideon up and down and asked, "What do you want?"

"Shelter," said Gideon. "A bed for the night, if there is one."

"The master of the house is not in residence," said the man, squinting beyond Gideon at the storm.

"I know. The lawnmower man told me."

The face creased unpleasantly, and the man laughed. "Old Bob? Nothing but a gimcrack novelty. Not a man at all. Just a toy." The man chewed his thin, dry lips. "Oh, you'd better come in."

❧

Gideon stood in the hall while the man slid the bolts back home in the door. There was a staircase sweeping up, and it would have made a grand entrance were it not piled from floor to ceiling with what Gideon could only term junk: tottering stacks of books, wooden boxes and crates in teetering columns, pieces of machinery, and piles of cogs and flywheels. The man looked down at the floor and tutted. "You're leaving a puddle."

"Sorry," said Gideon. "I've been walking for several hours." He held out his hand. "I'm Gideon Smith."

"Crowe," said the man, ignoring the hand. He was hunched over, a rough hessian blanket thrown over his shoulders. "I'm the caretaker here." He appraised Gideon and said, "I'll get you some clean clothes. The master's will probably fit you. I'm sure he won't miss some."

"Who is the master of the house?" asked Gideon. "I don't wish to impose unnecessarily."

"You're here now." Crowe shrugged. "And this is the house of Hermann Einstein, but he hasn't been here for six months. No one knows where he is, to tell the truth, so I wouldn't worry about being an imposition."

Crowe led Gideon up the dark stairs to a landing just as bizarrely stocked as the entrance hall, then opened a door into a bedroom. A snowstorm of dust puffed up and swirled at their passage. Crowe said, "There's a washroom and some towels. You can dry off and I'll put some clothes on the bed for you. Join me downstairs for a drink and a bite when you've finished, if you want."

❧

As good as his word, Crowe had laid out a fine meal of steaming meat pie, carrots, and turnips on a small card table in the center of the sitting room. He said, "Fill your boots, lad. You look famished."

Gideon was, and he set about the pie with gusto. Crowe watched him intently, still wrapped in his blanket, and said, "You come far?"

He said through a mouthful of food, "It's where I'm going that concerns me more. How far from London am I?"

Crowe cackled. "Depends on how you're planning to get there. Walking, I'd say you'll need a new pair of boots. Steam train, barely two hours. Omnibus goes from over the hill."

All of which, bar walking, would cost money. He looked around the sitting room. Some of the contraptions he could discern some kind of use for; others seemed foreign in the extreme. "This Mr. Einstein of yours . . . ," said Gideon. "What is his field of work?"

"It's *Professor* Einstein. And his field is anything and everything," said Crowe, taking a bottle and pouring amber liquid into two dirty tumblers. "The man's an inveterate tinkerer."

"Like the lawnmower man?"

Crowe laughed again. "Bob, we call him. Quite remarkable, in a way. You charge him up on the electrification and set him off, and he'll push that lawnmower right to the end of the turf, then stop before he falls off the edge, turn it around, and come straight back."

"It talked to me," said Gideon.

"Ner, not really," said Crowe. "Old Hermann put a cylinder in him, like you might get in a phonograph. He thought it was funny, for when guests came and the like, or peddlers."

Gideon took the whiskey Crowe handed him and sipped at it, grimacing at its bite. Crowe laughed again, and Gideon asked, "And where is Einstein now?"

Crowe scowled. "Quite rightly, I'm not meant to talk about it, given the nature of his work and all." He leaned in closer to Gideon. "Fact is, the old boy's gone missing. Properly missing. Quite put the wind up some folk in very high-up positions, let me tell you."

There was a crack of close-by thunder outside, and the rain pelted the sash windows with renewed vigor. Gideon dropped his own voice to a conspiratorial whisper. "High up? Nature of his work?"

Crowe looked from left to right, and, satisfied there were no eavesdroppers creeping around the piles of books, he said, "The British Government. Brought him over from Germany, had him holed up here. Working on an engine. For a special dirigible, so's I understand. A dirigible to the moon."

Gideon sighed. "That's no secret. They've had that in the newspapers. Everybody knows Queen Victoria wants to send a party to the moon."

Crowe waved him away. "Bluster and propaganda, lad. 'Course, everybody *wants* to go to the moon. But only Hermann Einstein can make it happen, and he's gone missing."

"Is there a telephone in the house?" asked Gideon. He thought to call the offices of *World Marvels & Wonders* again in the morning.

Crowe sighed. "We did have one, but it doesn't work. Old Hermann set this device up, called it a . . . a *dizzy rupture,* I think. Generates some sort of field, he said, though I'm not sure what he meant. He was always afeared someone would try to steal his work, spy on his ideas. He thought they had ear trumpets like telescopes and could listen in from miles away." Crowe shook his head. "Paranoid, that's what they call it. So he set up this dizzy rupture thing, which means the phones don't work now. A clever man, but a bloody odd one."

Gideon barely noticed Crowe refilling his glass, and the old man gave him a curious look. "I'll show you what I mean. I'll show you Maria."

Crowe made Gideon promise not to open his eyes as he manhandled something heavy and awkward into the sitting room. Roughly pushing books and packages out of the way, Crowe cleared a space near the hearth and told Gideon he could look. He saw an upright, slim creation, covered by a tarpaulin.

"This is Maria. First we'll need music," Crowe said.

Crowe located a phonograph and selected a wooden tube at random from a heap beside it. "Opus Forty by Camille Saint-Saëns," he read, then frowned. "Frenchie. *Danse Macabre*, it says. As good as anything."

The speaker of the phonograph issued a dusty, rhythmic hiss and then a harp sounded the same note, a dozen times like the tolling of a bell, with softly rising strings all around, as Crowe dragged the drop cloth off the marvel and took his place in his leather armchair.

Gideon stared, his mouth hanging open. Standing in front of them was a life-sized woman, with blond hair loosely tied on top of her head and a fine-featured if pale face. She was quite the most beguiling thing Gideon had ever seen. Her eyes were closed and her face downcast. She wore a leotard and tutu in faded, dusty pink, and fishnet stockings holed like the nets of the abandoned *Cold Drake*. Her feet, shod in ragged ballet pumps, were arranged with the heel of the right against the instep of the left, one thin arm languidly above her head, the other outstretched to the left.

"Maria," said Crowe, his eyes glowing.

"A woman?" said Gideon, not taking his eyes off her.

"Ah, what's the word?" asked Crowe, screwing up his face. He snapped his fingers. "*Automaton.* Now shush; it's about to start."

A violin cried out like an eerie beast, and xylophones rattled like dry old bones. Maria moved suddenly, jerkily, making Gideon jump. Crowe chuckled and placed a hand on his arm, and Gideon watched in amazement as the automaton's movements became more fluid. She danced in the small space Crowe had cleared near the hearth, moving faster and faster as the music became more frenzied and energetic. She whirled and whirled, kicking her leg repeatedly in the air with the perfect timing only finely tuned machinery could achieve, her hair falling free and swirling around her like a golden halo. She was a gale of limbs, a pink blur, and as the music reached a crescendo and died, she fell to the floorboards, one leg outstretched behind her, one leg in front, on which she rested her hands and chin, looking up at Gideon with black-rimmed eyes burning into his soul.

Gideon dared to breathe and glanced at Crowe, who had been getting more and more agitated throughout the performance, grimacing and twisting on his leather armchair.

"My God," said Gideon quietly.

"Maria," Crowe said in triumph. "The most wonderful creation in this entire lunatic menagerie. Clockwork. Gears. Flywheels and cogs. Come and look."

Crowe ran, hunched, to Maria and commanded, "Up! Up on your feet!"

Gideon stared at him. "She responds to your words?"

Crowe grinned as Maria stood and straightened, staring straight ahead. "A bloody wonder, it is." From on top of a pile of books he took a brass key, the width of two handspans. He roughly turned Maria around and tugged at her leotard, revealing a tiny, dark keyhole in the small of her exquisitely curved back. "You stick this in here, give it a couple of turns, and it's off. Clockwork." He saw Gideon staring at the automaton and said quietly. "Have a touch. It won't mind."

Gideon put out a tentative hand and laid his fingers on her bare shoulder, pulling them back as though burned. "She's warm!" he said. "As warm as you or I! And soft to the touch . . . like real flesh. What is she made of?"

Crowe shrugged. "Like I told you before, it's not my place to understand. Just to look after the inventions until such time as Professor Einstein decides to come home."

Crowe looked around conspiratorially again, then leaned in to Gideon. "I look after Maria, and it looks after me, too."

Gideon frowned. "What do you mean?"

"It does a *special* dance," said Crowe, running his tongue over his tooth stumps. "Just for me."

Gideon took a step back. "You don't mean . . . you make that thing . . ."

Crowe shrugged. "It's near as damnation a real woman."

He bared his teeth. " 'Cept it don't nag like one. Have a squeeze of its titties."

Gideon backed away farther. "I think I shall go to bed, Crowe. I plan to be away from here at first light. Thank you for your hospitality."

Crowe shrugged and turned back to the automaton. Gideon fled to the room where he had washed, and he lay in bed in the darkness as the sounds of the phonograph started again. Sick to his stomach, Gideon clamped his hands over his ears and begged for sleep to come.

Gideon was awake before dawn, staring out of his bedroom window at the blue sky and soaking lawns the passing storm had left in its wake. Crowe's whiskey, and his debased abuse of the automaton, had left a sour taste in Gideon's mouth. The way the automaton's eyes had met his at the close of that frenetic dance spoke to Gideon of some hidden, secret intelligence.

Gideon padded barefoot out of his room and along the corridor. He passed an open door from which emitted a groaning, sawing shriek, and he peered in to see Crowe, facedown and snoring loudly, the empty whiskey bottle on its side by his outstretched hand. Farther on he found a mismatched dark wooden door that, when he tried the round brass handle, swung open to reveal a tight spiral stone staircase. Gideon surmised he was in the fairy-tale tower that had been added to the west wing of the house, and curiosity drove him up the stairs to another door. As he looked around it, his breath caught in his throat; there was Maria, the automaton, sitting on a chair in a bare stone chamber, her head slumped on her chest. There was a table beside her on which rested the large brass key Crowe had spoken of. Gideon was surprised the old drunkard had summoned the wherewithal to return her to the tower at all. Along one side of the wall was a rail hung with frocks, blouses, and skirts of all kinds; Gideon felt slightly queasy at the thought of Crowe dressing the mannequin to suit his mood. She was still wearing the tattered ballerina outfit. Gideon walked across the stone floor and squatted before her.

He took a strand of her blond hair in his fingers and marveled at it; just like real hair. Hesitantly, he brushed her forearm with his fingers. Soft and yielding, just like real flesh. Gideon placed his hand on her chest, between her breasts, and felt the rhythmic pumping of some clockwork engine within. Gideon murmured, "Old Crowe was right about one thing: Professor Hermann Einstein is indeed a genius."

"Thank you," said the automaton with the slightest movement of her full, ruby-red lips.

Gideon yelled and rolled backward as the automaton's kohl-rimmed eyes flicked open and her head rose to regard him. Another of Einstein's surprises. Just like Bob, the lawnmower man, no doubt, talking with the help of a wax cylinder inside her.

"Not quite wound down, have you?" said Gideon with a smile. "My God, if I lived here for any length of time I would have a heart attack."

"Imagine what it's like for me," said Maria.

The color drained from Gideon's face. He peered at the automaton, and it blinked back and gave him a half smile.

"You're really speaking to me?" he whispered.

"I'm really speaking to you," said Maria.

Gideon was silent for a while, not quite knowing what to do next. He said eventually, "You thanked me. What for?"

Maria put her face down and looked at her hands, folded in her lap. "For not taking up Crowe on his offer."

Gideon bit his lip. "Does he do that often?"

She nodded sadly. Gideon put his hand to his mouth. "Good God," he said.

Maria smiled ruefully. "I have no God, sir, save Professor Einstein, who gave me life." She paused. "Do you have a name?"

"Gideon," he said. "Gideon Smith." He awkwardly put out his hand, and Maria placed hers in his palm. He felt the warmth from it, felt it pulsing with life.

"Are you *alive*?" asked Gideon. "Are you *real*?"

"Oil and fluid flow through my copper veins. Clockwork powers my limbs. A self-perpetuating hydraulic engine pumps inside my chest. My skin is the softest kid leather. Not alive, Mr. Smith. Not real."

"You look like a living, breathing woman," said Gideon. "Perhaps you have been hypnotized to believe you are a clockwork creation?"

"Are you easily shocked, Mr. Smith?" asked Maria.

Gideon shook his head. "Not anymore."

"Very well," she said. Maria deftly hooked her thumbs under the shoulder straps of her cotton leotard and pulled them down, revealing her bare torso. Gideon flushed, but she put a finger to her lips. "Hush. And watch."

Maria put one finger into her navel and Gideon heard a distinct clicking sound. Her stomach shuddered and a hairline crack appeared down the middle of her, from her breastbone to her hips. His eyes widened as the crack became a fissure, and Maria's torso opened up as though it were nothing more than a set of double doors. Instead of flesh and muscle, she had brass and glass; her veins were rendered as thin, metal pipes through which a dark, viscous liquid coursed. Her ribcage was a steel trap enclosing an intricate mesh of gears and flywheels, whirring and spinning as each muscle in her arms and face moved. There was indeed a box of valves and pistons pumping away, and cables of varying color and thickness that wound around the clockwork and up into the hidden areas behind her breasts and below her waist.

She pushed the doors closed and they fitted snugly together, the seam sinking into invisibility. Maria pulled up her leotard again to cover her modesty and spare Gideon's blushes.

"You are a wonder," he breathed. "A miracle. And Crowe

has debased you to sate his own perverse appetites. How long has this horror been visited upon you?"

"Since Professor Einstein left, six months ago," said Maria. "Crowe was cautious at first, merely looked at me for long weeks while . . . while he pleasured himself. Then he would undress me, and touch me. Then, when he became bolder, he would wind me up and have me dance for him. And . . ."

Maria put her face down again, and Gideon was shocked to see a single tear rolling down her cheek. "Did Crowe not know you could speak?"

She shook her head violently. "I would not waste words on that scoundrel. It was better to let him believe I was merely a mute object. He would have merely heaped more insults upon me and enjoyed my pain yet further if he thought I could . . . could *feel*."

"What is it like, when you wind down?" asked Gideon, after a while. "What do you feel then?"

"It is like sleep, I imagine," she said. "And sometimes, when I sleep, I dream."

"Nightmares, I shouldn't wonder," he said.

She shook her head. "No. Scattered, fractured dreams. Faces I cannot name and voices I cannot recognize. Dreams of London."

"London?" asked Gideon. "You have been to London?"

"I cannot have," said Maria. "But my dreams are of another life, without clockwork and pipes." She shook her head. "Cruel illusion."

"The clockwork and valves I can understand," said Gideon. "But your speech, your intelligence . . . how does one achieve that with gears and pistons?"

Maria looked at him. "There is another element, Mr. Smith, which I do not understand and cannot show you." She pointed to her forehead. "In my head there is a machine that powers my thought and gives life to my body. Something Professor Einstein invented, or found."

He stood and looked out the thin window, just as Bob whirred into life and began to noisily push his cutter across the lawn.

"I am going to London," said Gideon. He turned and knelt before her. "Come with me."

7

The Imitation Game

Maria looked startled. "Come with you?"

"What is there for you here? Abuse and degradation? Come with me. I shall keep you safe."

Maria blinked. "Keep me safe?"

"I have a mission in London," said Gideon. "I am to return home to Sandsend at the earliest opportunity, to deal with grave business there. But perhaps I can help you find your Professor Einstein."

She put her head to one side, the gears and wheels within her whirring. "Give me a moment to dress more appropriately. How shall we travel?"

Gideon punched the palm of his hand. "I have no resources, no money."

Maria said, "In the parlor there is a bicycle with a hydraulic engine. Take it to the front courtyard and I shall meet you downstairs."

After checking that Crowe still slept, Gideon quickly pulled on his socks and boots and stole downstairs. The bicycle was heavy and crowned with other junk and inventions, and something crashed with an alarming clatter as he pulled it free. He pushed it out into the warm morning sunshine before heading back inside. He stopped dead in the doorway as Maria descended the staircase with a fluid grace that would have been stunning from even the most well-bred lady. She wore a full skirt and a white blouse, a gray serge cape around her shoulders. Her feet stepped down the stairs in polished black laced boots, and her blond hair was arranged beneath a bonnet.

"Maria," he said. "You look beautiful."

She took his outstretched hand to step down from the final

stair. "The bicycle should get us to the next village. After that, we shall need money," she said.

She led him into a workroom and pulled open one of several drawers beneath a row of trestle tables piled high with cogs, devices, and test tubes, withdrawing a sheaf of pound notes.

"We can't," said Gideon. "It would be stealing."

"Professor Einstein kept it for emergencies," said Maria. "He was somewhat . . . disorganized. He secreted money for when tradesmen called or deliveries were made. I am sure he would be happy for you to take it, under the circumstances."

Gideon nodded uncertainly. "I shall pay back whatever I spend," he said. He took a book from the table and put the money inside it for safekeeping. He found a cloth bag and stuffed the book and money inside, along with Maria's brass key.

His heart sank to see Crowe standing in the hall, scratching his nether regions and yawning. He looked at Gideon and said, "Ah, up already? I was just going to put some breakfast on."

Then Crowe saw Maria and frowned. "What are you doing with the automaton? I could have sworn I put it back in the tower."

"You did," said Gideon. "And I have removed her. Your abuse of this poor girl is at an end, Crowe."

Crowe laughed. "Her? Poor girl? It's a *thing*, Smith. And a thing that doesn't belong to you. Now leave it be and get out. I'll not have you repaying my hospitality with theft, you blackguard."

"Oh, I'm leaving, all right," said Gideon, taking Maria by the hand. "And she is coming with me. This is not theft, Crowe. It's liberation."

Gideon barged past Crowe, dragging Maria with him toward the door. The old man shrieked and flew at him, and Gideon swatted him off easily. He strode out of the house and toward the motorized bicycle, muttering, "Could have done with a bit more time to figure out how this contraption works."

"There is a toggle on the box behind the seat," said Maria. "I observed Professor Einstein working on the vehicle."

Gideon hit the toggle and there was an alarming judder and a hiss of steam, which settled into a rhythmic vibration. He hopped on to the seat and Maria wrapped her hands around his chest, murmuring, "I suggest expedience, Mr. Smith. I think Crowe has a gun."

Gideon released the brake just as the first bullet whistled past his head. The bicycle surged forward, and Maria held on even tighter, which Gideon found most agreeable. The bicycle wavered perilously as it shot ahead at an alarming velocity.

"Come back with that clockwork tart!" shrieked Crowe. "It's mine! Bring it back!"

As he steadied the bicycle and piloted it along the drive toward the gates of the Einstein house, Gideon called over the noise of the motor, "Are you quite well, Maria?"

"Never better, Mr. Smith." She laughed delightedly as the drive curved upward and spilled them out onto a country lane. "Never better."

The bicycle sputtered and died as they came within sight of the village, a small, bustling hamlet called Hawerd. Gideon paid the postmaster from the wad of notes to take the bicycle back to the Einstein house. As he did, he noticed for the first time the book he had stuffed the money inside: *Investigations into the Atlantic Artifact and Experiments with the Aforementioned in Terms of the Animation of Automata.* He put it back in the bag and asked the postmaster if there was any transport headed toward London.

"You're in luck," said the man, glancing at his fob watch. "The express omnibus is due in half an hour. Have you in London by lunchtime."

He gripped Maria's hand and said, "Let us take some refreshment in the tearooms until the bus arrives." Then he paused. "Uh, forgive me, Maria, but do you actually eat or drink?"

She smiled demurely. "I don't have to, but I can. The food is processed within me and mulched down into liquid to lubricate my working parts."

Gideon grimaced. That somehow took the shine off the thought of a good strong cup of coffee. But his own stomach rumbled and reminded him he had not eaten since the night before.

As the coffee and pastries arrived, Maria said with a distant gaze, "London. Think of it. I can see in my mind's eye images of the Lady of Liberty flood barrier, the Threadneedle Ziggurat, the airships clustered around the Highgate Aerodrome."

"Perhaps you read of them in books," said Gideon. "Or newspaper articles. The Lady of Liberty statue is only five years old; perhaps your professor attended the dedication service when the French presented it to Britain to celebrate the defeat of the Yankee rebels in 1775."

"I have seen them," she insisted. "I have watched the airships circling the aerodrome in bright sunshine, seen the cascading foliage down the levels of the ziggurats." She looked at him. "I do not understand how I could have invented that. How could Professor Einstein have given me memories of things I have never seen?" She laid a hand on his bare arm and his hairs prickled. "Sometimes I wonder where they came from, whose they once were."

"Did he never speak of the memories and dreams he had given to you?" he asked gently.

She shook her head tightly. "Whatever reasons Professor Einstein had for keeping them a secret, he must have thought they were valid. However, he is gone and you have emancipated me from the yoke of dreadful Crowe. Now I can seek answers."

They stepped out into the sunshine just as the omnibus rattled through the village. Gideon paid the money and they were directed to a double seat halfway down the carriage.

"The outlook is fine for London today," the driver said with a smile. "Perfect weather for lovers."

Gideon flushed and tried to protest but Maria hushed him. She said, "Would you mind awfully if I took the window seat?"

As the bus steamed forward, Maria became lost in the countryside unfolding outside the window. Gideon reached into the cloth bag to count the remaining money, and his hand paused over the book. It was written in English, in diary form. Much of it was dense formulae and scientific jargon, but he reckoned he could get a sense of the book from the intermittent prose entries. He settled back in the seat and began to read.

> *January 11, 1888*—A most intriguing visit from a Mr. W, who represents the British Government and who I anticipated was here to, as the British say, "lean on me" to work faster toward our goal. I was all prepared to tell him going to the moon is not quite as simple as taking a train to Birmingham. But he came bearing gifts. A recent exploratory mission to the bed of the Atlantic Ocean by a Royal Navy submersible had uncovered the remains of a sunken Viking longship. Among the booty recovered from the wreck was a most unusual item that Mr. W. brought to me for my investigation, with the possibility that it might aid me in my endeavors.
>
> So: The item appears to be of some kind of opaque glass, frosted with a slight yellowish tinge, almost as though it had been forged from sand. It weighs three pounds and has a size of seventy-five cubic inches, and it is shaped like a rough, slightly distended half-sphere, the top being smooth and bisected by a slight indentation, the underside sporting exactly one hundred symmetrically arranged holes, each an eighth of an inch in diameter, and one larger hole. If it is indeed glass, it is extremely tough; I made the mistake of allowing Crowe to hold it, and the damn fool let

it slip from his fingers. It hit the floorboard of my workshop and did not crack, chip, or otherwise become damaged. Crowe's mishap did, though, reveal a hitherto unseen mechanism allowing the flat bottom of the artifact to open on tiny hinges, revealing a hollow interior.

Quite what the point of it is, I am at a loss to explain. Other items from the longship have been dated at the tenth century AD, so all I can say for certain is it is very, very old and manufactured by a very advanced civilization.

February 23, 1888—Investigations into the Atlantic Artifact have been sidelined of late, to allow me to concentrate on my work in other fields, but a strange occurrence today causes me to pick up my pen once more.

The artifact had been on my desk, gathering dust and proving no more use than a paperweight. But then Baxter, the venerable cat who patrols the grounds of the house, padded into my workroom bearing a present of a half-dead mouse, which he deposited proudly upon my desk, and the poor beast twitched as its life essence deserted it. It was then the development occurred. . . . Baxter had lain the mouse by the Atlantic Artifact, and almost immediately it was suffused from within by a red glow, faint but definite. I immediately placed both the dying mouse and the artifact in a glass fish tank, isolating them from external forces, and monitored the progress every ten minutes. Within half an hour the mouse had died. The red light continued to glow, and did so for a further seven hours, gradually dimming in the final sixty minutes. Curious.

March 14, 1888—My dear Albert's ninth birthday today. How I miss him and my darling Pauline. But the work the British Government has me doing here, while producing little of merit so far, is well paid, and they are both looked after in Munich, though I worry the constant infernal spats between the French and the Spanish will spill over into violence again, and Germany will be dragged into the hostilities.

The past three weeks have seen much progress with the Atlantic Artifact. I bade Baxter bring me more presents, and he obliged with a succession of dead and dying mice. The artifact seems to respond to living things as they are near death, and for a period of no more than seven hours after death has occurred. It is frightfully perplexing. Could I be on the brink of a major discovery? Is the artifact nothing less than an indicator or meter of the presence of the very soul?

March 21, 1888—A major breakthrough, and one of those accidental (or is it?) moments in which great discoveries are made. I was looking through a book of underwater creatures and marveling at a very distinct picture of *Chrysaora fuscescens*, the Pacific Sea Nettle jellyfish. I was idly pondering how its gelatinous dome and trailing fronds looked remarkably like a brain with the spinal cord attached when it struck me like a thunderbolt. The Atlantic Artifact was the rough shape, size, and weight of a human brain.

I have a small colony of frogs that I have been dissecting with the purpose of investigating the electrical impulses that power bodily functions. A small current applied to the nerve endings of a dead frog will cause the legs to twitch, and on an impulse of my own I rigged up a copper connector to one of the nerves of a recently deceased frog and inserted it into one of the many holes on the underside of the artifact, which glowed excitedly as I brought the animal to it.

The results were instantaneous. The frog's right leg moved immediately, proving the artifact is possessed of some internal electricity-generating component. Marvelous, given the age of the artifact.

But there is more.

With the ordinary electrical impulse, the frog's leg merely

jerked and twitched. When plugged into the artifact—which I have already begun to think of as a "brain"—the leg performed a fluid, natural movement, exactly in the same way the living frogs in my colony moved when swimming. The artifact was not merely running a current and exciting the animal's nerve endings; it was "remembering" how the frog would have moved in life, and replicating it.

I left the frog attached to the artifact overnight, and the next morning the artifact still glowed, much past the seven-hour limit when it is merely adjacent to a newly dead beast.

I must investigate further.

March 23, 1888—I have exhausted my colony of frogs. I tried different nerves and muscles attached to different housings in the base of the artifact. With one group, the forelegs moved. With another, the rear legs. I achieved a beating heart, an opening mouth and, with my final frog, I had the notion of placing its brain inside the artifact, which glowed brightly as though it somehow "approved" of this development. Within moments I gazed into the shining, unblinking, yet evidently seeing eyes of a frog dead for six hours.

I saw my own reflection in its black eyes. It was like seeing eternity.

Or perhaps God.

March 24, 1888—I had Crowe capture a magpie in the garden and after some rough surgery I have managed to connect its spinal cord to a large copper attachment, which fits snugly into the largest hole on the base and up into the hollow space within the artifact, where I reattached the cord to the unfortunate bird's brain. Immediately it began flapping around madly on the desk, its eyes swiveling, its ratcheting cries echoing around the room. I observed the thing for an hour before putting it out of its misery.

I need something bigger.

April 4, 1888, I have a heavy heart, but I knew what I must do. It is what Baxter would have wanted, being a very scientific cat, and his sad but natural death affords me an opportunity. As exciting as the impulses from the artifact are, do they necessarily indicate anything more than an advanced form of electrical charge allowing the nerves to "remember" their function in life? The real test is whether individual tastes and even memories of a specific living thing can be carried over and recharged by the artifact after death.

I wasted no time in attaching Baxter. Oh, the joy at seeing his eyes open and look at me! A test was called for. Baxter had always been a contrary cat, and, unlike his brethren, shunned fish. But he had a great love for chicken. I had Crowe bring me two bowls, one of tuna and one of chicken, which I placed before the reanimated cat.

He went straight for the chicken! It was not mere automatic electrical impulses driving Baxter. He had been restored to his former life and memories. Or at least partially . . . although he expressed his former interest in food, he seemed to regard me with blankness, as though he did not remember me at all. The poor thing was in pain and I swiftly administered a large dose of morphine, to keep him alive but unconscious.

I am somewhat at a loss what to do next. I know what I *wish* to do, what *needs* to be done, but dare I cross that threshold? And, if so, how?

June 9, 1888—More complications. Although the artifact gives life, it does not sustain it. I have had to allow poor Baxter to die a second death. His organs and flesh continued to deteriorate and putrefy, despite the reanimation, and he was in great pain even with the morphine. What use is returned life if the body continues to decompose? Conversely, Baxter's brain remained in a state of preservation within the hollow of the artifact. I have heard of such things . . .

experiments carried out with pyramidal shapes preserved foodstuffs longer than the same items kept within cubic boxes.

June 10, 1888—I am once again indebted to Crowe for his observations. We were having lunch and he wondered aloud whether a brain attached to an artifact would power a nonliving device, such as perhaps Bob or Maria. Bob, of course, is our lawnmower man, while Maria is perhaps my crowning achievement in the field of automata: a life-sized doll with such intricate clockwork workings she can perform astonishing feats of dexterity, and even dance. Hmm.

June 12, 1888—Success, but of an abominable sort. I managed to transfer the artifact, containing Baxter's brain, into the headspace of Maria. I connected her workings to the artifact and wound her up. She began to gambol about on all fours, sniffing at Baxter's bowls and rubbing her torso against my leg, as though indeed a cat in semi-human form. It was quite disconcerting, though Crowe seemed to find it all delightful. I disconnected her at once and ordered Crowe to bury Baxter's rotting corpse, brain and all. What is this strange device, and what can be its purpose? I dare not conceive of what I must do next. I dare not. But I must.

June 15, 1888—Another visit from Mr. W, who was "just passing." He wishes to know if my investigations into the Atlantic Artifact have borne much fruit. I did not reveal my full notes to him, but said progress was continuing apace. He asked pointedly if I required any further resources. I hesitated for but a moment. W. is a man of secrets and shadows, and while I do not feel he can be completely trusted, I imagine he is my best chance for what I require.

I told him I needed a fresh human brain.

He stroked his mustache and regarded me with a most ominous stare, but nodded. "Surprisingly, that is possible," he said. "I shall be most interested to see what results from your experimentation, Herr Professor."

What have I done?

June 29, 1888—W. has been in touch. He has a brain for me. He did not reveal its origin, and I did not ask. It will be delivered within three hours.

❧

There were no further journal entries. Gideon closed the book and let out a ragged sigh. He looked at Maria, who was still watching the countryside flash past. He asked gently, "What do you remember of when you first awoke in the Professor's house?"

She turned to him and said, "We played a parlor game."

"A parlor game?" Gideon frowned.

"Yes." Maria smiled. "They call it the Imitation Game. Do you know it?"

"We had little time for parlor games in Sandsend, I am afraid."

"One person plays the Interrogator, which was the Professor. Then two people go into separate rooms. One was myself and one was Crowe. We had a cook, then, and she was the go-between. The idea was both Crowe and I had to make the Professor think we were a woman by way of answering his questions, which were delivered to us by the cook, who also noted down our answers and returned them to him. Crowe had to deceive the Professor and I had to try to convince him. It was quite fun."

"What sort of questions? How was he to work out your answers?"

"Oh, logic, I think the Professor said. Things like, how long is your hair, do you wear skirts, how do you ride a horse?"

"And what was the result?"

Maria giggled. "What do you think? Crowe was hopeless at the game, while I managed to easily convince the Professor through my answers that I was the real woman."

She smiled at the memory and turned back to the window, watching the fields that stretched along both sides of Route 1. Gideon stared at Maria. Einstein had meddled in things he should never have touched. Maria was an automaton, a toy, but with a stolen brain. A pale imitation of a living woman. Had Professor Einstein created a monster? And had Gideon Smith unleashed it into the world?

She laid a hand excitedly on his arm, and if she noticed his involuntary flinch, she did not show it. "Look, Mr. Smith!" she said. "I can see London ahead!"

8

The Children of Heqet

When Stoker found Elizabeth Bathory at the foot of the 199 steps to the abbey, she was wearing a long, hooded cloak, and he could quite clearly see her reflection in the jet-shop window she was browsing; another vampiric myth untrue. The sight of her brought back his dreams of the previous night: haunting images of the severed, monstrous head, shot through with snatched glimpses of Bathory's alabaster flesh, her tongue running over pin-sharp fangs and ruby lips. Stoker had never been unfaithful to Florence, not even in thought, but it took half an hour in a cold bath to chase the night's visions away.

She looked up as he approached, her mirror image glancing at him over the rim of dark, round-rimmed glasses.

"Countess," he said. "How are you?"

"Rather hungry," she said, her voice as low as he remembered. He paled, and she laughed. "Perhaps for a currant teacake and a pot of Earl Grey."

"It is a devilishly hot day, Countess, and the sun burns terribly. Are you quite certain . . . ?"

"The sun will not kill me, but it will weaken me somewhat. However, I am acutely aware the accursed Children of Heqet could abscond at any moment, and I wish to locate them post-haste."

"So you know they are in Whitby and its environs, but not precisely where?"

"Exactly. And my resources are running low; the ichor of the monster coagulates and thickens in its veins. I fear I may only be able to sup from it one more time. That is why I cannot allow them to escape."

Stoker coughed and extended his elbow toward her. "Would you care to walk with me?"

Bathory inclined her head. "How gallant of you, sir." She placed her slim hand on his forearm and allowed him to lead her from the cell into the sunshine. "And you can tell me what you have learned about the Children of Heqet."

❧

Stoker had learned more than he expected to on his morning sojourn to the library, and he related it to Bathory as they wound through Whitby's streets. He caught people glancing at her, and more than one man took a second look at her astonishing beauty. He felt suddenly wretched; what if word got back to London that Bram Stoker was promenading through the town with such a creature on his arm? He pushed away the thought.

"I looked up various spellings before settling on the one I believe is pertinent: H-E-Q-E-T."

"Unusual," murmured Bathory. "It puts me in mind of Hecate, the Greek goddess of witchcraft."

Stoker nodded. "And also of childbirth, and nurturing the young. Hecate shares something with Heqet, who was one of the Nile goddesses, the goddess of birth and resurrection. She was often depicted with the face of a frog, which are prevalent along the Nile, and women would wear her image on talismans around their necks while they gave birth."

"The face of a frog," said Bathory, smiling at a woman with full skirts who passed by. " '*And the Lord spake unto Moses, Say unto Aaron, Stretch forth thine hand with thy rod over the streams, over the rivers, and over the ponds, and cause frogs to come up upon the land of Egypt.*' "

"Exodus," said Stoker thoughtfully. "The Old Testament plagues." He was silent for a moment, then glanced at Bathory. "Do you think it is possible the plague Moses brought forth was not merely frogs?"

Bathory smiled. "I find it entirely plausible. And do not

forget what the Children of Heqet stole from Castle Dracula: a jeweled scarab. Egyptian."

Stoker shook his head again. "But they would be impossible creatures, thousands of years old."

"Egypt is a strange land, with ancient ways lost to the rest of the world," said Bathory. "They did not consider death as you do. To the ancients the end of life was not a brick wall, nor a passage to some heaven of white light and sloping meadows. Death was a transformation, part of a cycle." She smiled. "We would have had much in common. Some would believe me an impossible creature, as well." She looked across the gambrel roofs of the town. "But where are they?"

"I asked my landlady, Mrs. Veasey, where the most unsalubrious district of the town is," said Stoker. "She warned me away from it. Perhaps a good place to start?"

The slums on the outskirts of Whitby were not pretty, but Stoker had seen far worse in London. The port's poor district was a haphazard warren of dirt tracks winding between tight terraces, home to those workers who earned such a low wage they could not afford accommodation in more prosperous parts of town, farmhands who toiled on the inland estates, the families of fishermen forced out of their traditional haunts by rising prices caused by an influx of richer folk, and the feckless, hopeless, and lawless.

The steam-cab deposited them on the outskirts of the district, where ragged children played with a battered leather ball on a dusty patch of land. Bathory pulled the hood of her cloak over her head and hid behind her dark spectacles; the sun was high and hot, and Stoker himself felt faint from its merciless rays.

They passed a knot of down-at-heel men who whistled and cat-called at Bathory. "We see what we can see," she said through gritted teeth, "and ask questions if need be."

They walked for an hour, losing themselves in the rammed-together, ramshackle houses, a patchwork of wood and brick spreading like a swamp. Most of the windows were smashed or without glass, and the sounds of violent arguments, wailing children, and cursing were almost more than Stoker could bear. They paused for a moment in the shadows and Stoker offered Bathory a drink from his water canteen. She took it and muttered, "Not enough."

"You require more water?" he asked, hoping for an excuse to call off their search. The dirt track was awash with raw sewage, and Stoker had held his kerchief to his nose and mouth for the last quarter of an hour.

She squinted at him, a look he couldn't read but which filled him with sudden dread. From behind him a chorus of shouts sounded, as a husband and wife roared at each other in the dark pit of their sorry home. He watched Bathory looking at the scene, and he saw her eyes widen at the distinct sound of the slap of flesh upon flesh. Stoker turned and looked in at the window; a corpulent man with a snarling face was standing over a shuddering woman on her knees, his fist raised. He paused in his unintelligible raving to meet Stoker's eye.

"An' what the fuck are you looking at?"

Stoker averted his gaze but heard Bathory's breath catch in her throat. Before he knew what she was doing, she elbowed past him and pushed open the rotten wooden door into the house.

"Countess!" he hissed, but she was already inside, and he saw the look of surprise and indignation on the man's face as she entered the tiny hovel.

"What do you want, bitch?" the man snarled, as though he were an actor playing his part in a dreadful little production laid out for Stoker's personal viewing.

"Get out," Bathory said to the cowering woman, who stumbled out of the door and, to Stoker's shock, into his arms.

Stoker watched what happened next, transfixed, wishing he could tear his eyes away. All he could do was hold the man's pathetic wife to him, so she wouldn't see Bathory picking him up by his shirt as if he were no heavier than a child's doll.

It was only when she bent to his neck in some obscene parody of a lover's embrace that Stoker at last found the strength to close his eyes.

When he opened them again, Bathory was returning to the street, seemingly taller and with a more dreadful bearing than before. Her mouth was slick with blood, and she took the kerchief Stoker still clutched to his face and wiped herself with it.

"He won't hit you again," she said curtly to the woman. "He won't hurt anyone, anymore." Then she turned to Stoker. "Even the Children of Heqet would shun this forsaken hole."

Stoker left the woman standing dumbly in the tight street and hurried after Bathory, who stalked along the track back toward the main road. When he caught up with her, she whirled round, her eyes flashing, and took his tie firmly in her hand.

"Don't be shocked. It is what I am. It is what I do. I try to limit myself to taking those who deserve it. To those who think it is acceptable to hurt women."

"Do you hate all men, then?" asked Stoker.

A smile curled the corners of her exquisite lips, and Stoker found it even more terrifying than her anger. "No," she said. "I was married, was I not?"

Bathory moved closer to him, and he felt the rustle of her skirts against his weakening knees. "Countess . . ."

"I miss Dracula so," she whispered, her mouth close to his ear. "I miss his ministrations. When the moon was full, we would transform into wolves and fuck all night in the forest."

Her lips brushed his ear, thrilling him; he was both terrified and aroused. "Would you like to run as a wolf, Bram? I could make it happen."

He closed his eyes and swallowed with some effort. "Countess. I am a married man. . . ."

She backed off, and when he opened his eyes she was smiling, patting down his tie. "That you are, Mr. Stoker," she said. "And I am a widow." She paused, looking toward the road. "Let us return to the abbey, to consider our next move. I shall meet you there."

Bathory took the hem of her cloak in her hand. She whirled it up and across her face, and Stoker blinked. In the space of that blink she was no more, but a raven was taking noisily to its wings, soaring into the blue sky above the stench of the stew, and heading toward the sea.

He watched it go, and the memory of Bathory sinking her teeth into that wretch's neck rose unbidden. He suddenly and uncontrollably vomited where he stood.

❧

Bathory was sitting on the grass, her cloak and skirts spread out around her. She looked quite the lady, protected from the sun in her hood and gazing at a small book of verse by Keats on her lap. Stoker cleared his throat as he approached and fixed a smile to his face. Bathory looked up over the rims of her spectacles. "Mr. Stoker. Watching me feed can be rather . . . unsettling. I would not have blamed you had you fled from me for good."

The specter of her bloodlust hung between them, and Stoker tried not to glance at the neckline of her frock hidden in the shadows of her cloak. She said, "I become a changed person, when the hunger is upon me. It can take some getting used to. You were horrified?"

He nodded. "I was horrified. But I understand. You weren't yourself."

Bathory shook her head violently. "No, Mr. Stoker. You miss the point. I *was* myself." She spread out her hands. "*This* is not me, Mr. Stoker. This is pretense and disguise. These are the trappings of civilization and respectability which vampires wear when we go abroad among mortals, but it is not us." She lowered her eyes, somewhat coquettishly, thought Stoker. "I spoke of wolves and forests. That is the true freedom vampirism bestows."

Stoker smiled wanly. "We mortals are artifice and show as

well, Countess. We are descended from the rude apes, as Darwin would have it. Underneath our clothes, we are all naked."

She smiled appreciatively. "I thank you for your understanding, Mr. Stoker." She looked into the distant blue sky. "But we are no closer to finding the Children of Heqet, are we?"

Stoker had walked by a pharmacy in town on the way to the abbey, and as he mounted the steps with his purchases something struck him, something so obvious he punched his own forehead. He said, "Countess, I believe I might have the answer. I should have thought of it immediately. Sometimes I stuff my mind so full of trivia I forget where I have put things. I was recently in the company of a young man from Sandsend. It is primarily a fishing village, though with a beautiful aspect. This young man was called Smith, and was rather desperately trying to get in touch with some hero from a penny dreadful he fancied could help him with a problem in Sandsend."

"What kind of problem?" asked Bathory as Stoker took her elbow and steered her toward the town.

"A fishing boat belonging to his father had turned up abandoned following a night of dense fog. The news was somewhat overshadowed by the arrival of your own ship, Countess. But the loss of his father and the ship's crew could perhaps be the work of the Children of Heqet, could it not? Mr. Smith and I parted company and he sent me a note. I remember it plainly now. He wrote: *There is indeed an undead monster on the loose, but not the one you think.* I fear I did Mr. Smith something of a disservice. Could he have seen one of the Children of Heqet?"

Bathory nodded. "In the absence of any other theory, Mr. Stoker, let us away to Sandsend immediately."

"It is already late in the afternoon," said Stoker. "Perhaps we could carry out a preliminary reconnaissance and return tomorrow? I should not like to be lost in those caves at nightfall."

Bathory said, "Mr. Stoker, I do my best work after nightfall."

⁂

They went to a hardware store for equipment and called in at Royal Crescent. Mrs. Veasey cast hooded glances at Elizabeth Bathory as Stoker ran down the stairs in excitement, brandishing the story-paper Gideon had sent to him.

"Look at this!" he called. "Oh, I was such a fool not to listen to Mr. Smith. Look!"

He held out the copy of *World Marvels & Wonders* to her and enjoyed watching her eyebrows rise as she saw the lurid illustrations to the story of the Faxmouth mummy. "Crude, but unmistakable," she said.

"Mr. Smith said he was going to London to seek out this Captain Lucian Trigger—I confess, I had always thought him a fictional character, but Mr. Smith was determined. Perhaps Mr. Smith has not yet departed. He spoke of strange happenings in his village, just outside Whitby. . . ."

Bathory nodded. "Then let us away there at once."

⁂

They took a carriage along the coast road to Sandsend, and Stoker led the way to the waterfront, where an aged, salty fisherman with leathery skin tamped down his pipe.

"Ho," said Stoker, and the man glanced at him, his gaze lingering longer on Bathory.

"Ho," he said, returning to his pipe.

"We're looking for a young chap, Smith," said Stoker.

The man nodded without looking up again. "Gideon Smith."

"That's the one." Stoker paused. "Do you know him, Mr. . . . ?"

"Peek," he said. "Aye, I know him."

"Might we find him somewhere?"

"You *should* be finding him fishing," grunted Peek. "But you won't. Apparently he's gone to London on some fool errand."

Stoker sighed. "I feared so. I say, Mr. Peek, you haven't heard of any . . . odd doings, have you?"

Peek shrugged. "My young lad had some fool tale about a frog as big as a man, terrorizing the village. Gideon was too ready to believe him. Reckoned it'd done for his dad." He shook his head. "Anyway, I've got work to do." He nodded at them. "Sir. Ma'am."

"Yes, yes," said Stoker absently as Peek strolled back to his crew. He looked at Bathory. "A frog as big as a man."

"I heard, Mr. Stoker," she said. "Shall we?"

❧

The sun had already dipped behind the imposing promontory on its westward descent; Stoker shivered in the cool shadows.

"I do not expect you to accompany me inside," said Bathory. "You may stand watch for innocent citizens. I would not want unnecessary bloodshed."

Stoker blanched. "It will really be that bad?"

She looked at him. "You were not in Castle Dracula. It was a massacre. They fight like animals." She paused. "No, animals know when to stop. They were relentless. Like engines."

"I have not come so far to skulk in the shadows, Countess."

Stoker had some experience of potholing, back in Ireland, but for sport and minor thrills, not on an errand to confront what he now feared was certain death. Florence had wept for a week when he had announced he was exploring the sinkholes and tunnels of Ireland; what would she say now? A large part of him wanted her to be there, forbidding him to go any further. *Think of Noel,* she would say. *Bram, think of me!*

Stoker pushed away their images, as painful as even this imaginary rejection was. Perhaps he should be thinking of them, not pleasing himself with strange adventures in the company of this beautiful, enigmatic woman.

Think of Noel.

Bram, think of me!

"I'm sorry," he whispered.

"You said something?" said Bathory.

He shook his head and, with his heart seemingly doubling in weight in his chest, led the way into the fissure, which opened into a seaweed-strewn chamber. His head-torch illuminated a sloping, low-ceilinged tunnel into which he could fit if he bent almost double. Bathory led the way and he followed until it opened out into a narrow but tall chamber in which they could stand upright. Stoker pointed his head-torch around and upward; he could make out a black opening some twenty feet above them. The rock wall was pitted with suitable hand- and footholds, and he began to scale the damp wall, Bathory close behind him.

The opening led to yet another tunnel, which shortly forked. Stoker allowed Bathory to join him in the narrow space, achingly conscious of the proximity of her body against his. He said, "What do you think? Should we split up?"

A little way into the left fork he made out a black domed object at odds with the glistening stones surrounding it. He inched forward and retrieved the policeman's helmet, shining the torch on the nametag stitched into the lining. "Constable Clive Clarke."

"We are on the right track," said Bathory. "Turn off your torch. I will lead now. I will see adequately. It is best if we do not speak further; tug on my skirts if you need my attention."

Stoker's heart leaped as they were plunged into blackness. He felt Bathory move past him, lithe and muscular like a cat, and caught a whiff of her earthy scent as she began to crawl down the tunnel, which gradually became wider and taller. Sometimes he could no longer hear her breathing and, panicked, put his hand out to feel the reassuring roughness of her black cloak.

He had no idea how long they had been stumbling along the tunnel when she whispered, "Ssshh!" and he was brought short, crashing into her back. "Look," she said.

He could make out the faintest of orange glows. Bathory whispered, "I will investigate."

He felt his way to the floor and sat among a pile of loose,

damp rocks: strangely shaped, smooth round ones and long ones slicked with what he presumed to be seaweed. Bathory seemed to have been gone a lifetime, and he feared she had been undone by the Children of Heqet. Oh, how he longed to see the sunshine again, longed to breathe fresh air. He tried to calm himself with thoughts of Florence and Noel. But even there in the blackness, Countess Bathory invaded his head, her full lips, her voluptuous figure.

"Bram."

Stoker almost leaped to his feet at the whisper in his ear. She had moved as silently as a phantom. She had addressed him with more urgency, more familiarity, which made his breath catch in his throat. He said, "Countess. Uh, Elizabeth. What did you see?"

"The Children of Heqet. The tunnel opens to a ledge above a chamber. They have a small wood-fire burning, illuminating an area where they appear to have been digging. They have unearthed a small wooden chest."

"How many?" asked Stoker, his blood chilling in his veins.

"A dozen, perhaps." She paused. "Too many. I . . . should not have brought you, Bram. You must go."

"Go?" he said.

There was silence. Stoker put out a hand but touched only cool rock. "Elizabeth?" he said more loudly.

Then there was the most horrendous racket, hisses and shrieks and the scrabbling of what sounded like claws upon stone. Horrified, Stoker fumbled for his head-torch and switched it on.

The first thing he saw was that the smooth rocks he had been sitting among were not rocks at all. They were the bones of men, picked clean of flesh. He pulled his hand away, but something was curled around it. A necklace of some description? He had no time to study it, though, as he looked up, his jaw dropping and his blood turning to ice water. He said wonderingly, "Elizabeth?"

Bathory was barely recognizable. She had transformed into

a beast, somewhere between human and bat, her cloak and dress in tatters around her horribly deformed limbs, which appeared to be dusted with fine gray hairs. Her face was stretched and mangled, her fangs bared beneath a dark nub of a nose and black, shining eyes, her ears hugely expanded. And from her arms hung curtained wings of black leather. She was locked in an obscene ballet with the thing that had haunted Stoker's nightmares. It snapped at Bathory—or the monster she had become—with cruel rows of slavering teeth, clawing at her with its elongated arms clothed in strips of dusty rags. Stoker, to his shame, felt a warm patch spreading across his trousers.

Bathory and the Child of Heqet were frozen in a grotesque tableau for a moment seeming to last an eternity, then she turned her transfigured, nightmarish face at him and hissed through her fangs, "Go, Stoker! Go!"

Behind her he saw movement as more of the bulbous-headed shapes swarmed into the tunnel. He sat, transfixed in terror, until Bathory roared, "*Go!*"

Then all Stoker could think of was escape. He began to crawl along the passage, ignoring the sharp stones cutting his hands and knees, and the low ridge into which he crashed his head, feeling blood trickling into his eyes. He could hear the sounds of pursuit behind him and he redoubled his efforts, whimpering and blinking back tears, the light from his torch spinning crazily around the confined, suddenly airless tunnel as he forced himself onward. He tumbled over a ledge, landing awkwardly with the wind knocked out of him, and abruptly felt he could go no farther. The game was up. Elizabeth was lost and he was now going to suffer the same fate as those fishermen: torn limb from limb by the Children of Heqet, eaten alive to sate their unholy appetites. At least he would look death in the face.

The beam from his head-torch picked out a sudden flurry of movement and he steeled himself, just as Bathory, still hideously transformed, burst out of the tunnel, held aloft on her leather wings. She was naked now, save for the gray fur covering her body, and her clawed feet plunged toward him, digging painfully into his chest as she hauled him upward. She soared through the fissure, strenuously flapping her wings, and into the dusk. The beach and sea wheeled alarmingly, then Stoker got an eyeful of tumbling, azure sky, before his mind, stretched to its breaking point, embraced black unconsciousness.

9

BENT OF THE *ARGUS*

Aloysius Bent writhed and moaned in the tangled pit of gray bedsheets, surfacing from the black void of unconsciousness with much farting and belching. A steam-hammer was banging like a two-shilling tart, the sound of a woodpecker ferreting for grubs, offering a fainter, yet no less annoying, counterpoint. He rearranged his morning erection in his sagging underwear and tried to separate the two sounds. The steam-hammer was the thudding hell of a hangover, evidenced by the stale gin sweat clinging to his tongue. The woodpecker was the ceaseless rapping on the door.

"Hold on a minute!" Bent yelled, his own voice driving into his head like a gravedigger's spade. He clutched his temples with both meaty fists and sank back into his pillow, murmuring, "Oh, sweet Jesus, fuck me sideways in a barrow of tripe."

Bent threw his bulk over the side of his bed, landing heavily on the bare floorboards with a thump, which prompted a volley of bangs with a broom handle from the spiteful old shrew below. Bent put his oily lips to a dusty knothole in the floor and shouted, "Fuck off!"

Bent prepared himself for the abject misery of standing upright. His room was a damp and airless box with peeling wallpaper on the third floor of the Fulwood Rents; he was surrounded on all sides by the villainous scum and victims of tragic hard-luck stories that were dried kindling to the misanthropic furnace that powered him. He felt an urge to piss, accompanied by a burning sensation that told him he'd probably picked up the clap again.

Finally upright, Bent stared at his reflection in the cracked, mottled mirror. A head as big as a rugby ball, pitted and pock-marked; a bulbous nose tipped with a spreading purple patch the shape of Australia. Teeth like fallen tombstones and a tongue as hairy as a Persian rug. His black hair—such as it was—was plastered to his scurvy pate. Some tart had once described his face as a stocking full of porridge. He frowned. One day he'd be rich, and everybody knew when you were rich it didn't matter how fat and ugly you were. But the blemish on his nose made him think of Big Henry, and the money Bent owed him. Big Henry was a crook, and they'd tried to transport him to Australia three times. He kept coming back—like a fucking boomerang, Bent thought, and chuckled to himself—and every time he did Bent got more and more in debt to him.

The knocking at the door continued. He hoped it wasn't one of Big Henry's thugs. Maybe *he* should bugger off to Australia; it might be full of crooks, snakes, and spiders, but at least the sun shone. Ah, who was he kidding? He was London through and through.

"All fucking right!" yelled Bent, the effort bringing up a dash of warm vomit into his mouth. He clamped his hand over his lips and forced it back down. Breakfast. Still in his grimy underthings, he wrenched open the door to a snot-nosed brat in rags and bare feet.

"God, mister, I thought you were dead."

"I feel it," mumbled Bent, staring at him through one yellow eye. He vaguely recognized the kid as one of the Fleet Street Irregulars, the army of urchins and strays who turned in decent tip-offs when they weren't hanging around with that bum-bandit private detective up near Marylebone. "What do you want?"

The boy held up a folded piece of paper, which Bent saw immediately had been torn from a policeman's notebook. "Rozzer told me to give you this. Said to tell you there'd been another one."

The hangover melted away as Bent opened up the note,

which simply said *Lomas Street.* He looked at the brat and said, "Don't suppose he sent a cab as well, did he?"

The boy snorted. "It's only four streets away, mister. Take you five minutes to walk." He cocked his head to one side, appraising the folds of fat spilling out of Bent's undershirt and over his shorts. "Fifteen, maybe."

Bent aimed a cuff at his dirty little head but missed. "Cheeky shite," he said. He gave the paper back to the boy. "You know Flash Harry, on Mount Street?"

"The snapper man?"

"That's the one. Take this to him, will you, and tell him Bent sent it. Hang on." Bent felt around in the trousers pooled by the sink and found a ha'penny, returned to the door and flipped it at the boy.

"The rozzer gave me a tanner," he protested.

"Lying shite-hawk," said Bent. "You'll be happy with that, or I'll put your dad on the front page of the *Argus.*"

"Ain't got a dad," snorted the boy again, turning to go.

"That figures, little bastard," muttered Bent. He said, "Flash Harry might be good for a couple of pennies. Tell him to come quick, as well. Tell him there's going to be money in this for him. Tell him Jack the fucking Ripper's struck again."

❧

Dressed in a gray suit fitting neither the fashion of the day nor Bent's sluggardly frame for the best part of ten years, he stood at the door to his house on the Rents and inhaled deeply. "Ah, London," he said. "You fucking stink."

The Fulwood Rents was located in the heart of the East End, close enough to the Royal London Hospital that Bent could hear the screams of the afflicted when the wind was blowing in the right direction. It was also a staggering distance from the Blind Beggar, where Bent liked to take his gin, and Raven Row, where he liked to play hide the sausage. He looked up. There was doubtless a blue July sky up there, somewhere, beyond the pall of low-lying smog punctured only by the occasional emergence of a dirigible, but he doubted he'd see it today. But who needed fresh air? Aloysius Bent had London, the only oxygen he required.

❧

The brat had lied; the walk was more like twenty minutes, although Bent had stopped to relieve himself against a dustbin on Whitechapel Road. He found the crime scene quickly enough, though, an alleyway snaking between a tripe shop and a florist on Lomas Street. Flash Harry was already there, setting up his tripod and filling his pan with flash powder. Bent patted the freelance photographer on the shoulder as he hunkered beneath the black cloak to fire off a shot of the scene, then went to find his contact.

"Albert." He nodded when he'd located the constable, and passed him an envelope, which the policeman secreted away in his tunic. "What we got?"

The constable looked around and said, "We'll have to be quick; Lestrade's on his way down."

"You're sure it's a Ripper?" said Bent.

Albert nodded and pulled back the sheet. The girl stared glassy-eyed, her white face streaked with blood. The top of her head, just below the hairline, had been perfectly sliced off and the cap of her skull lifted like a bottle top. It sat abandoned by her exposed, graying brain. Bent belched and tasted gin. He felt queasy again.

As Harry set up his camera, Bent turned to Albert. "What do we know?"

"Local girl, twenty-five."

"Whore?"

Albert nodded. "Party by the name of Frances Coles. Worked the streets in Whitechapel, Bow, and sometimes Shoreditch. Born to a respectable family by all accounts, before she fell into drink and prostitution. She was behind them bins. Four days, we reckon."

Bent held his nose. "That'll be why she stinks so much." He looked at the girl. "Quite pretty, if you scrubbed her up." He chuckled. "And put the top of her head back on, of course.

Oh, cover her up, Albert, she's quite giving me a fit of the vapors."

"Then I suggest you go and get some fresh air, Mr. Bent, preferably as far away from my crime scene as you can waddle."

Bent sighed and turned to face the short, ferret-faced man with a sallow complexion whose eyes shone like a rat's. "Hello, Lestrade," he said.

The detective scowled. "It's Inspector Lestrade to you, Bent. Now hop it. I've got a crime to solve."

"Already done it for you," said Bent as Harry's camera flashed with a white cloud of exploding powder. "Jack the Ripper, innit? Now all you've got to do is find the bugger."

Without warning, he felt his stomach convulse and he vomited a hot soup on the shoes of the stunned Inspector.

"Oh look," said Bent, wiping the back of his hand across his mouth and staring at the lumps of spicy sausage still visible in the steaming heap pooling around the policeman's shoes. "I forgot I'd had a bit of spicy sausage last night."

❧

The offices of the *Illustrated London Argus* were on the second floor of the enormous marble edifice of the London Newspaper and Magazine Publishing Company, squatting regally in the center of Fleet Street. Flags of all nations flew from its portico-heavy facade, and a doorman in green livery stood sentry as staff, customers, and clients streamed through the revolving doors.

"All right, Jug Ears," said Bent.

"Didn't you get the memorandum?" the doorman said, scowling.

Bent shrugged, feeling in the pockets of his jacket for the half a pasty he was sure he'd squirreled away there yesterday. The doorman went on, "You're not allowed to use the main entrance. You have to use the delivery door."

Bent snorted. "Union won't stand for that. *Argus* staff forced into the alley like barrow boys?"

"Not all staff." The doorman smirked. "Just you. Mr. Wright said you are not presenting the kind of frontline image expected of the London Newspaper and Magazine Publishing Company."

"Did he now?" said Bent, farting loudly and finally locating his pasty. "Well, I'll have to have a word with Mr. fucking Wright, won't I?"

He was pink faced and wheezing by the time he pushed open the double doors into the gloomy newsroom, passing the ranks of copy-takers and secretaries.

"Fear not," he boomed. "Aloysius Bent is here to save the day with another cracking front-page story."

The earnest, stiff-collared, and waxed-mustached gentlemen of the arts and culture section frowned at him as he lumbered past, heading toward the long desk of the City Editor, Gordon Bingley, who was squinting at a sheet of copy beneath the pool of light emitted by the gold and green banker's lamp perched behind his typewriter. He looked up and raised an eyebrow.

"Mr. Bent. So pleased to have you with us at last."

"Straight out on the job, Bingley old chap," said Bent, stuffing the last of his pasty into his mouth. "Clear the front of the afternoon edition. We've got another Ripper murder."

"Then you should get typing, Mr. Bent," said Bingley, allowing him a small smile.

Bent nodded and headed for his desk, which shone like a beacon of mess and chaos among the ordered ranks of his colleagues. Bingley turned his chair around and hollered, "Hold the front page!"

Bent grinned broadly. He loved it when Bingley did that.

❧

When he'd filed his story Bent felt he was due a treat, which was probably going to take the form of a drink in the Punch Tavern, provided he could take advantage of Bingley's agreeable mood and beg two shillings off him.

First, though, he had his board to update. The wall by

Bent's desk was dotted with photographs and scrawled notes, and to this array he added the print Flash Harry had dropped on his desk, the portrait of poor old Frances Coles.

Sixteen prostitutes with their heads sliced off. When it all first kicked off with Mary Ann Nichols in August 1888, Bent had wanted to dub the killer Jack the Slicer, on account of that's what he did—slice the tops of their heads off. But Wright had insisted on Ripper, and the name stuck. Sixteen, not counting Bent's ace in the hole—the woman no one else had ever drawn a Ripper link to. He'd tried to get his theories into print, but Wright wouldn't go for it without some firmer evidence. Annie Crook had died two summers ago, two months before Nichols. Witnesses said her body had been dumped by the Thames with the top of her head gone. Only trouble was, the body disappeared soon after: probably rats, possibly worse. The police refused to consider Annie Crook as a victim of Jack the Ripper, because they had no corpse, and therefore no proof. And, at the end of the day, she was just some lowly shopgirl about whom no one gave a flea's fart. There'd been talk of a commotion in her flat, of comings and goings in the dead of night. Every instinct Bent had told him there was a story there, a connection between Annie Crook and Jack the Ripper. Crook had sat for Walter Sickert, a painter on Cleveland Street. Bent had tried to get to him several times, and a year ago had managed to get a foot in his door. Sickert had the look of a haunted man about him, and he told Bent not to meddle in things that could turn very, very bad. Which, of course, was like a red rag to a bull.

Bent wandered over to the news desk and picked up a paper from some coastal town in Yorkshire. He glanced at the front page, then began to read with interest. He said to Belvoir, the deputy news editor, "Some Russian schooner found abandoned on a beach. And a bloke with his throat ripped out. And a fishing boat with no crew. All in one little shithole."

Belvoir shrugged. "We'll have stringers up north to deal with that."

Bent spied Bingley at the far end of the newsroom, through the Venetian blinds leading into Wright's office. Norman Wright, the editor of the *Argus*, had a broom handle so far up his arse he could brush his chair when he sat down. Bent hauled himself out of his chair and trundled down to the office, hoping to buttonhole Bingley when he came out. As he neared the office the door opened and a third man, led by a frowning Bingley, emerged. He was tall and thin, wearing an immaculate black frock-coat and carrying a topper and cane in his long hands. He had the eyes and nose of a hawk, and he regarded Bent with interest. From behind him, Wright bobbed his stern face over their shoulders.

"Ah, Mr. Bent," he said. "Most judicious you should be skulking around outside my office. I should like a word."

Bent gave Bingley a quizzical waggle of his eyebrows, but the City Editor looked away and escorted the visitor to the staircase. Bent shrugged. Wright probably wanted to grudgingly thank him for the Ripper story. He brightened. Maybe he could scrounge two shillings off him as well.

❧

"You're what?" said Bent, standing before the broad, tidy desk while Wright, ramrod-stiff, stood with his hands clasped behind his back, gazing out the wide window at the bustle of Fleet Street below.

"You are neither deaf nor, despite appearances to the contrary, stupid, Mr. Bent," said Wright. "You heard and understood. I am relieving you of your duties vis à vis any further Jack the Ripper stories."

"Have you seen the front page of the late edition?" asked Bent. "Where do you think that story came from, Wright? Did you think the fucking ink fairies left it under Bingley's pillow?"

"I shall not deny you have done good work, Bent," said Wright calmly. "But it is time for you to explore fresh ideas. New avenues. Different stories."

Bent waggled a finger at him. "I know what this is about. This is because I threw up on Inspector Lestrade's shoes this morning, isn't it? I wasn't drunk, you know. I think I had some dodgy jellied eels on Cleveland Street yesterday."

Wright frowned. "Why were you on Cleveland Street?"

"Ongoing inquiries," muttered Bent.

"Not ongoing inquiries into your spurious idea that the Crook girl is somehow wrapped up in the Jack the Ripper murders, by any chance? She was a shopgirl who died. A whole two years ago. Do you know how many people die in London each year, Mr. Bent? Do you know how desperate and uncaring life is among the lower classes?"

Bent shrugged. "Pretty much. I'm one of 'em."

Wright wrinkled his nose. "That you are, Mr. Bent. Smarten yourself up. And if you want a job to come to at all in this building in the future, your attitude will have to improve, also."

Bent glared at him. "You're threatening to give me the elbow?"

"If you do not desist with your wild theories, Mr. Bent, then yes. You are wasting your own time and that of this newspaper."

Bent screwed up his eyes and glanced back toward the door. "Who was that geezer? The one with the funny eyes and big nose?"

"Not your concern, Mr. Bent."

Bent tapped his lips thoughtfully, looking at the portrait of Queen Victoria hanging on the wall behind Wright's desk. "You've been got at, ain't you? Told to lay off the Annie Crook line. He stank of Secret Service. I'm right, ain't I? This goes right to the bloody top, doesn't it?"

Wright turned back to his window. "You are free to go, Mr. Bent. I look forward to seeing what new and exciting stories you dig up for the readers of the *Argus*."

Bent opened his mouth to let loose a stream of invective, then thought better of it. He paused at the door to Wright's office. "Uh, I don't suppose you could lend me two shillings until payday, could you?"

10

London

Gideon had never seen so many houses crushed together, never seen so many people living beside, on top of, and beneath each other. He tugged at his collar, suffocated just by the sight of the city. The sky had gradually disappeared behind a low-lying fog fed by chimneys as far as the eye could see, contributing plumes of black and gray smoke to the choking layer of smog that reduced the sun to a pale yellow orb struggling to pierce the murk.

The omnibus's speed on the M-Route had meant they made good time to the outskirts of London; now the vehicle crawled along Maida Vale, the roads clogged with bicycles, horse-drawn carriages, steam-cabs, and pedestrians. The omnibus beeped its air-horn repeatedly as children ran blithely in front of the lumbering leviathan, and velocipede riders wove in and out of the slow-moving traffic.

Gideon's disquiet at the revelations in Einstein's book was momentarily set aside; like so many new to London's sights and wonders, he was agog. He could see the soaring towers reaching into the smoggy clouds, smell the combined stench of a city home to six million souls wafting through the open windows of the omnibus. And the noise! He had never heard such a racket, such a relentless clamor. Machinery clanked, bells tolled, horses whinnied, people shouted, music tinkled, drunks roared, and babies cried. Gideon jumped as a face appeared at his window, a man in a creased suit and a battered brown derby, teetering on stilts as he kept pace with the omnibus, waving strings of picture postcards at them until the vehicle, entering the wider, more orderly thoroughfare of the Edgware Road, gained more momentum and pulled jerkily away.

The electric lights strung along Marylebone Road were fizzing into orange life in the artificial dusk brought on by the thickening smog, and the omnibus had to pause at the junction of Bayswater Road and Oxford Street as a marching band traversed the road in front of them.

"Look!" said Gideon, leaning across Maria to peer through the window. "Hyde Park! And the Taj Mahal!"

The Indian temple to true love glowed pinkly in the afternoon sun, and beyond it Gideon saw sweethearts punting on the Serpentine or walking in the shade of the trees. Everything he had ever dreamed of, everything he had thought he would only see in newspaper illustrations or grainy photographs, was laid out before him. Hungry for more, he peered far to the west and he saw the hazy shape of the Lady of Liberty flood barrier. She held her torch high in the sky, and though Gideon couldn't see it from where he sat, he knew she clutched with her left hand the book bearing the date of the failed revolution, April 18, 1775. He had always wanted to see America and dreamed that one day he would go there. He longed to see the vast plains peopled with the mysterious Red Indians, witness the ever-higher skyscrapers being built in New York, the city determined to be the grandest in the Empire. He even hoped he might visit New Spain, where the ancient lost cities of the Aztecs and Mayans had, for many years, inspired a long-lasting architectural fashion in London.

But yes: London. America could wait; he had never truly thought he would visit London, let alone New York or New Spain or Nyu Edo, and here he was. Dirigibles crisscrossed the sky—perhaps on their way to the Americas—and tethered blimps floating just above the rooftops advertised Cadbury's Cocoa, Beecham's Pills, Bovril, and, with a leering, painted devil, McIlhenny Tabasco Sauce.

Gideon yelped delightedly as there was a thunderous clattering from overhead, and he craned his neck back to Maria's window to watch the rapid-transit electric stilt-train rattling on its elevated rails across Hyde Park and toward Big Ben. Barely able to absorb any further wonders, he sat back in his seat, beaming broadly, as the omnibus crossed Piccadilly, heading between the tall townhouses toward the greenery-garlanded steps of the Victoria Ziggurat. The omnibus entered the artificial illumination of the cavernous transport ziggurat and was waved into a bay by a uniformed employee.

"We're here," said Gideon needlessly.

"Yes," said Maria, and if Gideon noticed the quiet dullness of her voice, he did not mention it. He led her off the omnibus and gasped. As he stepped onto the stone apron where the omnibus settled in a hiss of steam, he thought the Victoria Ziggurat might very well occupy him forever. Teeming masses crushed into its vast pyramid, which was styled after the ruins explorers had discovered in New Spain. London's high society was still delighted with the legends of human sacrifice and lost civilizations.

Travelers hurrying for their transport elbowed each other out of the way as match girls and flower sellers moved between them, forging serene paths through the chaos. A small boy with a dirt-lined face waved a rolled-up newspaper and hollered, "Jack the Ripper strikes again! Late afternoon edition! Jack the Ripper strikes again!"

A fat man in a top hat and bristling whiskers barged past them, dragging a train of children and a subservient, bonneted wife behind him, separating Gideon from Maria. As he was whirled away by the push and shove of the crowd he saw her face looking for him, and something inside him suddenly felt heavy and leaden. He had barely been able to look at her since reading Einstein's book. Yet, his heart insistently leaped each time he did meet her eyes, against everything his mind told him was right and proper. Gideon shook his head and forged through the masses until he was back at her side.

"We should get out of here," he said. "I can't think straight with so many people."

He cast around for an exit, took Maria's hand—not cold, not clammy, but still a thing possessed of strange, unholy life—and pulled her to where the crowds seemed thinner. They paused before a newsstand. Gideon momentarily delighted in a clanking ten-foot-tall brass man with oil lamps for eyes who danced in a heavy, marching gait. Steam hissed from his joints and onlookers threw coppers into the hat of his owner, who played a merry jig on a fiddle. A smiling man with a tidy goatee beard and an extravagantly ruffled shirt walked toward them, strumming what appeared to be a lute strung on a leather strap around his neck.

"Care for a song from the Guild of Scientific Troubadours?" he asked, grinning broadly and fixing a monocle to his right eye.

"You're American!" said Gideon with excitement. He had never met anyone from the New World before.

The man bowed low and doffed his cloth cap. "That I am, sir. Floridian, my family was, though we relocated north during the Clearances, when they built the Mason-Dixon Wall and the slavers began to strike in the far south. Now me and my fellow guildsmen sell songs, ha'penny a shout. What could I sing for you? 'Isopods In My Aquarium' perhaps? Or maybe 'Sixty-Four Actuators'? What about 'My Fingertips Are Weightless'?"

Maria pulled Gideon away, and she was about to murmur something in his ear when he spotted one of the periodicals hung up by a clothespin on the newsstand.

"*The Adventures of Captain Lucian Trigger Special Summer Issue*!" he gasped. Gideon took the magazine down from the newsstand and leafed through it. "All the Captain Trigger adventures of the last six numbers, in one edition. Plus a brand-new, exclusive story." He looked at Maria. "May I buy it?"

She shrugged. "You may do as you wish with that money, Mr. Smith. But there is something I must tell you. . . ."

Gideon paid for the penny magazine and stuffed it into his bag. "Maria? Did you want to say something?"

She looked at him with what he thought was sadness, and it stabbed him in his chest. Then she said, "Mr. Smith . . . I fear I am . . . winding down."

❧

Gideon took Maria into a quiet alley close to the transport hub and wound her back into clockwork life. She stood facing a red-brick wall with her hands braced against it while Gideon unlaced her corset and exposed her back and the small, brass-ringed aperture at the base of her spine. For one moment he considered leaving her, propped up against the wall, and fleeing. The thought shocked him.

He was Gideon Smith of Sandsend, seeker of adventure, avenger of deaths. Not Gideon Smith, abandoner of women. No matter how unreal they were. What did it mean, this collision of heart and mind, this thudding in his breast and sickness in his stomach? Maria was undoubtedly beautiful. But beautiful in the way that a well-turned piece of furniture was, or a work of art. She walked and talked and smiled—oh, how she smiled!—but no heart beat in her chest, no blood ran in her veins. The only part of Maria that could truly be said to be real was the brain that pulsed in her head . . . and that was not her own. Gideon had not had much time for girls, but he was still a man. Maria fascinated him, despite what she was. He pushed the thoughts away. What was the point? So he inserted the key, to a shallow gasp from Maria, and turned it until it held fast and she was once again herself. After winding Maria's workings and hiding the key back in the cotton bag, he stood awkwardly as Maria fixed her clothing, as though they had shared a most intimate act. His stomach rebelled, or fluttered. He didn't know which, or what it meant.

"What should be our next step, Mr. Smith?" she said.

"We should perhaps go to Fleet Street," he said. "They will be able to put me in touch with Captain Trigger."

"The man in the periodical?" said Maria. "Mr. Smith, could you tell me more of your errand in London? Perhaps we could take tea in one of the street cafés near the station."

They took a table on the street and ordered sandwiches and a pot of tea. Gideon goggled at the prices. "Is everything so expensive in London?" he hissed.

Maria sipped at her tea. "Now, Mr. Smith, your tale."

"And you think this Captain Trigger can aid you in your quest for justice?" she asked when he had finished.

Gideon nodded, taking the magazine from his bag. "He is the Hero of the Empire. He has faced the creature before. He will be able to help me defeat it and save Sandsend."

Maria contemplated her beverage. She said, "Mr. Smith? Would you awfully mind telling me about your father, and your childhood? What recollections I have are mere shadows, and I fear not even under my ownership, and would very much like to hear about where you grew up."

Gideon slowly closed out the sounds and bustle of London all around him, and transported himself back to Sandsend.

"I remember being happiest when I was ten years old. I had an older brother, Josiah, who was like all older brothers: joshing and harrying one moment, protective and loving the next. My mother was the most beautiful woman I had ever seen, and she was having another baby. Dad worked hard on the trawlers. We never had more money than we needed, but only rarely less. Sandsend was a wonderful place for a little boy, Maria. Tall cliffs and a beach, a river running down to the sea. We would walk along the sands to Whitby on market days, and on Sundays we would climb Lythe Bank to St. Oswald's Church. My dad didn't hold much with religion, but Mother insisted."

"It sounds idyllic," said Maria happily.

"It was," he agreed. "Then, that winter . . . Mother died in childbirth. I would have had a baby brother, but he was not strong enough to survive, either. Josiah had to look after me, and he gave up his schooling to help keep the house. But that didn't matter, because he was going into the business with Dad. He would have been a great fisherman."

"Would have been?"

"Six years ago he died from influenza. I took it very badly. He had been like . . . well, like a mother to me, or another dad. He looked after me. I had always been a bookish child, and sometimes the other boys poked fun at me." He smiled. "Not that I couldn't give as good as I got. I had always been strong. Just like Josiah." His smile turned to a frown. "That didn't save him from the influenza, though. It had him in the grave in a week."

"So it was just you and your father?"

Gideon nodded. "We were as happy as we could be, given what we had lost. Until that monster took him away from me, and left me with nothing."

Maria placed a hand on his. "So you are out for revenge. It will not bring your father back, I am sorry to say. No one returns from the dead, not even through vengeance."

Gideon shrugged. "Perhaps. But I cannot let his death lie. I must seek reparations. And who knows what evil the creature plots? It might have claimed more lives in Sandsend already."

"And you intend to return to Sandsend with Captain Trigger?"

He nodded, then realized he had also promised to help Maria find Professor Einstein, or at least some answers to her dreams. He knew the answer already, but he couldn't tell her out of . . . pity? Fear? He didn't know. Instead he spoke softly, forcing out each hateful word he knew he must utter. "Maria, I do not expect you to accompany me any further. You are free of Crowe and in London, as you wished. If you decide to go forth alone to find your . . . your creator, then I will not hold you to your pledge to aid me. We can part company now, if you desire it."

"If I desire it," she said leadenly. Gideon went to settle the exorbitant bill in the café. When he returned she was dabbing at her cheek with a paper napkin.

"Maria?" he asked, frowning.

She smiled, blinking at him. "It is quite all right, Mr. Smith. Merely a slight . . . leakage of fluid. It happens, on occasion."

They stood together in an awkward silence. Gideon said quickly, "I did not mean for us to part immediately, Maria. Come with me to the offices of *World Marvels & Wonders*, at least. Who knows, you might learn something about yourself on Fleet Street."

She smiled again. "I am already learning much about myself, Mr. Smith. But thank you, your offer is very kind, and I accept. Shall we take a steam-cab?"

❧

By the time the steam-cab—another new experience for Gideon—deposited them before the imposing facade of the offices of the London Newspaper and Magazine Publishing Company, Gideon was feeling wretched. Reverend Bastable would, he considered, be very proud of him. Despite the fact Gideon knew in his bones Maria was a good person, he had tried his very best to reject her, to push her away from him. He was a fool. And now, perhaps, it was too late. She was becoming increasingly distant from him, and when he had excitedly gripped her arm as they saw the famous Iron Guard patrolling outside Buckingham Palace, she had carefully extricated herself from his grip.

The money was dwindling alarmingly, he noted as he paid the cab driver and the vehicle steamed off. They stood in front of the portico, a sour-faced doorman glancing at them and then away. "Well," Gideon said. "I suppose we just go in and ask for Captain Trigger."

❧

Norman Wright could, in Aloysius Bent's considered opinion, go fuck himself. There were plenty of papers out there where Bent's experience and talent would be appreciated. Nurtured, even. Bent leaned back in his wooden chair and breathed out hard. He'd had a good couple of gins over at the Punch. Five, maybe. He could just have a little afternoon nap now. But he was too angry. Wright was willing to let himself be walked all over because Bent had gotten a little too close to the truth with his Annie Crook investigation. What kind of editor did that? What about freedom of speech? The inalienable right of the British press to shine a light on the dark doings of authority?

Still, no need to be hasty. He could bide his time. And time was one thing Aloysius Bent had plenty of. No point rocking the boat just yet, not when he had bills to pay and that tab at the Unicorn to settle. And Big Henry would want the money from that rummy game at Wapping back in June. He'd better just keep his head down, find something else to write about. He picked up the copy of the *Whitby Gazette*, the provincial rag he'd taken from the news desk. He shook his head as he read it. Son of a wool man found with his throat ripped out. And they said London was a violent place. This abandoned Russian schooner interested him as well. Witnesses said they'd seen a big black hound running from the hold. He turned back to the murder piece. Throat ripped out as though by a wild animal, it said. He shook his head again. Just how stupid were they out in the sticks? Black hound escapes from beached Russian ship, tourist has throat ripped out. And no one was making connections? He could work with this. The Wolf of Whitby. That had a nice ring to it. Feeling the familiar tickle at the back of his fat neck that signaled a germinating idea, Bent decided to reward himself with one last gin, perhaps over at Ye Olde Cheshire Cheese.

Bingley looked up as Bent stood and grabbed his coat. "Off again, Mr. Bent?"

Bent belched. "Going to find a new story, as per Mr. Wright's explicit instructions," he said, then paused thoughtfully. "Lend us two shillings, will you, Bingley old chap?"

❧

Bent was descending the staircase when he became aware of a minor commotion at the reception desk. There was a tall chap with curly dark hair, much too healthy looking to be a native Londoner, haranguing one of the harpies at the desk.

Behind him was a slim young woman, quite pretty from what Bent could see of her beneath her bonnet. He sauntered over.

"All right, Doris? Want me to call Jug Ears?"

The receptionist looked at Bent with exasperation. "Mr. Bent, I have been trying for the last ten minutes, with little success, to impress upon this young man that Captain Lucian Trigger does not receive visitors at the offices of *World Marvels & Wonders*. Can you assist me?"

Bent laughed, spraying spittle over the mahogany desk. "Trigger? You've come to see Trigger?"

The young man turned to him, fire in his eyes. "Sir, I have traveled a great distance to engage Captain Trigger's aid with an emergency situation."

Bent looked at him with interest. Not a London accent. Northern. "What's your name, lad? Where do you come from?"

"My name is Gideon Smith," said the boy. "And I have traveled from a small village near Whitby, sir."

"Whitby, you say," mused Bent. "I confess, the only time I'd heard that name before was in relation to the Prospect of Whitby, a public house with which I am acquainted." He paused. "Or was, until the landlord barred me at Christmas." He shook his head. "No matter. Fact is, Mr. Smith, I'm hearing the name *Whitby* quite a lot at the moment. You don't know about abandoned ships, do you? And wolves attacking innocent folk in the streets?"

"If it's wolves you want, or rather black dogs, you'd be better off speaking to a gentleman by the name of Bram Stoker," said Gideon. "But of abandoned ships . . . that is the very reason I am here." He lowered his voice and looked around. "There is evil abroad on the coast, sir. My father has been taken by . . . a thing beyond your understanding."

Bent couldn't resist rubbing his hands together. "Well, I think I might be able to help you there, son. My understanding has very distant borders indeed."

The young man shook his head. "I must see Captain Trigger at once. I simply must."

Bent smiled broadly. "Tell you what, Mr. Smith. I'll take you to see Captain Lucian Trigger, and you can tell me all about what's been going on in Whitby. What do you say?"

The boy glanced uncertainly at the young woman, then shrugged and turned back to Bent. "I suppose so, if that's the only way for me to get to Captain Trigger."

Bent placed his big hand on Gideon's shoulder. "Absolutely fucking top notch." He coughed into his fist. "Um, pardon my French."

11

Captain Trigger, at Last

Stoker thought he was inhabiting one of his dreams, which had become increasingly more bizarre and vivid of late, when he awoke with a pounding head beside the naked form of Elizabeth Bathory. They had made it back to the abbey, somehow, back to Bathory's cell. Around Stoker's palm was wrapped a leather thong with a piece of shining black stone hanging from it. He shoved it into his pocket, touched his head and felt the dried blood just below his scalp, and winced. Bathory was crumpled near her long box of earth, the lid shoved off. She was naked and bleeding, but at least she had shed that awful bat-form. He crawled toward her, fearing the worst, and laid a cautious hand on her pale shoulder.

"Elizabeth?" he whispered, then with more urgency, "Elizabeth?"

She moved and moaned, turning her head with great effort and opening her eyes. "Bram? We survived?"

"We did," he said. He cast around for the trunk containing her clothing and found a long, deep red cloak, which he wrapped around her nakedness. "But your wounds . . . you need a doctor."

She shook her head. "I need blood. You must help me. I must feed. Help me find someone."

Stoker shuffled backward, shocked. "Elizabeth, no, I cannot abet you in murder."

"I must feed, Bram," she said hollowly. "Or I may die."

Stoker scrabbled around for his bag, thanking his stars he had kept hold of it during their impossible flight from the caves. He said, "After watching you take that man in the stews, I vowed I would do all I could to stop you killing like that again."

Bathory, leaning on her box, smiled weakly. "So we are back to this, then. Is it to be a stake through my heart, Bram, then an ax to chop off my head? Now you have seen me for what I am, must I finally die?"

He returned to her with his bag, which still contained his garlic, crucifix, holy water, and stakes. But he left them and withdrew the bottle he had bought from the pharmacist earlier, now filled to the brim with dark, thick liquid. He rolled up his sleeve and showed her a bandage over the inside of his forearm.

"I took the liberty of drawing off a quantity of my own blood." He held it uncertainly to her. "Will it be enough?"

Stoker unstoppered the bottle and placed it to her lips. She enclosed his hands in her own and drank deeply, closing her eyes and shivering as the first gush of blood hit her tongue. They sat for a moment once she had drained it, hands clasped together around the bottle, and she smiled. Her hair had regained its former luster, and her skin shone with internal iridescence. Before Stoker's amazed eyes, the wounds on her exposed flesh began to close and knit, even the scars fading to nothingness within seconds. Bathory smiled at him.

"Bram. I thank you. You have saved my life."

"And I shall do it again, Countess," said Stoker. "If you can promise me you will not take innocent lives, then you can have all the blood I can spare."

Bathory frowned. "Innocence is a point of argument, Bram. But, yes, for now I agree to your pact. With one exception."

"One exception?"

"The Children of Heqet," said Bathory. "I can feel them in my mind, discern their intent. I can follow them."

"And I will follow you," said Stoker.

"Then take this," said Bathory, digging in her trunk and handing him a glistening bangle of gold and gems. "Get the best price you can for it in Whitby, and book us passage on a dirigible, as soon as possible."

"A dirigible, Countess?"

She looked into the middle distance, riding whatever secret currents flowed in the blood of the mummified demons. "London," she said at last. "We are going to London."

Gideon and Maria followed Bent back on to Fleet Street. "Now," the fat journalist said, running his grubby fingers through the snot dripping from his enormous nose. "Trigger lives over on Grosvenor Square. Very exclusive little address. Part of the Mayfair set. I'd suggest a steam-cab, but . . ." He patted his pockets. "Mr. Smith, are you, shall we say, *well resourced*?"

"We have a few pounds left," said Gideon, just as one of the overhead steam trains clattered by over a stone viaduct. "I'd quite like to try one of those things, though."

Bent frowned. "Ah, the old stilt-trains. Why, last year, there was a flower girl standing right under the tracks near Westminster when one of the boilers cracked on an engine passing overhead. Took the skin right off her, by all accounts. Steam-cab?"

Bent hailed a cab and they crushed into the back of it together. Bent laid his hands on his knees. "So. We should all get acquainted. My name is Aloysius Bent, and I am a journalist with the *Illustrated London Argus*."

"Not with *World Marvels & Wonders*?" Gideon frowned. "Then how do you know Captain Trigger?"

"We're all published by the same company," said Bent. He tapped a pudgy, tobacco-stained forefinger against his nose. "I know all sorts of things about Captain Lucian Trigger, young man. But tell me about yourself."

Gideon shrugged. "Gideon Smith, of Sandsend. There's not much to tell, other than that. Not until you've taken me to see Captain Trigger, at any rate."

Bent cackled. "Nearly had you there, didn't I? Never mind. And your young lady friend?"

"This is Maria."

"She's a Whitby girl, is she?"

Gideon shook his head. "She is on her own errand in London."

Bent pursed his lips. "And what errand might that be?"

Gideon thought he had better let Maria answer for herself. She glanced at him, then up at Bent. "I have strange dreams of London, though I do not believe I have ever been here before, at least not physically." She frowned and screwed up her face. "Dreams of . . . of Cleveland Street, I think. And a vast market, where I worked."

Bent tugged at his chin. "Tottenham Court Road." He looked thoughtfully at her. "Cleveland Street is just off it. Interesting."

As the steam-cab took them west, Gideon said, "You said you knew things about Captain Trigger. What kinds of things?"

Bent grinned. "That kind of depends on what you expect to find when we get to Grosvenor Square." He looked around, then whispered conspiratorially, "He's an invert, you know."

"Invert?" asked Gideon.

"You know," said Bent, grotesquely shoving his hips forward and back in a rhythmic movement. "A bum-jockey. An arse-bandit. He cruises, as they say, the Bourneville Boulevard."

Gideon looked blankly at Bent and Maria murmured, "I think Mr. Bent is trying to tell us Captain Trigger is a gentleman who enjoys the company of other men. In bed. A sodomite, Mr. Smith. A molly." She looked abruptly surprised, and put her hand to her mouth. "Oh. I wonder how I know that?"

Gideon flushed and looked angrily at Bent. "Sir, that is the Hero of the Empire you slur!"

Bent shrugged. "That's as may be, but that's what he is, Mr. Smith. What Oscar Wilde calls *earnest.* Trigger was drummed out of the Duke of Wellington's Regiment in 'eighty-one for buggering a molly, as Miss Maria would have it, from the junior ranks. Quite a scandal, it was." A cloud passed his face. "Or would have been. They hushed it up, on account of Trigger being, as you say, the Hero of the Empire and all."

The steam-cab lurched into a square of airy brick townhouses arranged around a pretty park enclosed by black railings. "We're here," said Bent. "Pay the driver, Mr. Smith, and let's go and find Trigger. And prepare yourself for a disappointment."

Gideon and Maria followed Bent to a black door at the top of a flight of stone steps and the journalist rapped sharply on the brass knocker. There was a pause and then the door was opened by a broad, ruddy woman in the black frock and white apron of a housekeeper.

Gideon said, "We are here to see Captain Lucian Trigger."

The woman frowned and made to shut the door. "I am sorry, but Captain Trigger is indisposed."

"Told you. He don't see anybody, doesn't old Trigger," Bent said.

"Then Dr. Reed!" said Gideon desperately. "Could I not speak to Dr. John Reed, in Captain Trigger's absence?"

Gideon became aware of a shadow behind the housekeeper, and then a voice as dry as autumn leaves said quietly, "Mrs. Cadwallader? Did someone mention John? Is there news?"

Mrs. Cadwallader turned to the figure who shuffled into the sunlight and said tenderly, "Captain Trigger, I told you that you were to rest this afternoon. Excitement does not do for you. I shall see to these people."

Gideon gaped at the figure whom the housekeeper had addressed as Captain Trigger. Surely there must be some mistake. There were some similarities between the small, thin man who stood in his housecoat and velvet slippers in the doorway and the illustration of the robust adventurer with his chest puffed out that proudly dominated the cover of the penny blood Gideon held out in his hand. Both had well-cut, silver-white hair, and both had gray mustaches with waxed tips. But there the likeness ended. The Captain Trigger who appeared in the flesh before Gideon Smith was thin to the point of emaciation, his face creased with lines of age and worry, his sad, milky eyes squinting in the strong afternoon sun. He looked like the shadow Gideon's Captain Trigger might cast, like a reflection in a tarnished mirror. Gideon felt his own shoulders slump, felt the breath knocked out of him. It had all been in vain. It had all been for nothing.

Captain Trigger smiled uncertainly and said, "What is your name?"

"Smith," said Gideon numbly. "Gideon Smith."

Gently, Trigger took the penny blood from Gideon's hands and felt in his housecoat pocket, withdrawing a fountain pen. With a shaking hand he wrote on the cover *To Gideon, from Captain Lucian Trigger, Hero of the Empire.* Then he handed the periodical back and said, "Good day to you, Mr. Smith. I hope you enjoy my adventures."

"Your adventures," said Gideon hollowly, looking down at the inscription.

Bent murmured, "Sorry you had to find out like this, lad. Old Trigger's nothing but a fraud. A romancer. You didn't . . . you didn't really think all that guff was actually *true,* did you?"

Gideon looked at the sad figure of Trigger and felt a sudden wave of loathing. He had placed his trust in Trigger, and it had been trodden into the dust. What of *This adventure, as always, is utterly true, and faithfully retold by my good friend, Doctor John Reed*? A lie. Nothing but a fiction. He shook his head in disgust. "So that's it, then? I cannot entreat Captain Lucian Trigger to help me in my hour of need?"

Trigger held his hands, palm upward, by his sides. "I am sorry. I am in no position to help anyone. I wish you luck in your endeavors, Mr. Smith."

The housekeeper put her face into the gap between

Trigger and the door and frowned at the three of them on the doorstep. As she began to close the door Gideon said, "So I am expected to just go back to Sandsend and deal with the mummy by myself?"

Bent nudged Maria. "There he goes again. Mummies. Have you got a clue what he's on about?"

Trigger held the door as it swung toward its frame. He waited a moment, then opened it again, despite Mrs. Cadwallader's protestations. He leaned out and looked quizzically at Gideon. Slowly he said, "Did you say mummies? As in Egyptian mummies?"

"You remember *The Shadow Over Faxmouth*? From the December issue last year?"

"Of course," said Trigger.

"The creature that threatens my home is the same," said Gideon. "*Exactly* the same."

Trigger's eyes widened, and as the housekeeper tried to take over the job of shutting the door he shooed her away with a wave of his thin hands. "Mr. Smith," he said, "I rather think you had better come in." He tapped his long forefinger against his chin. "Mrs. Cadwallader, I think we shall require some coffee in the trophy room."

❦

Trigger led them into the gloomy wood-paneled room hiding behind a net-curtained window in the shadowy rear of the townhouse. It was like walking straight into the pages of *World Marvels & Wonders*. Each wall was covered by a glass cabinet, and in each cabinet was a memento from every one of the adventures Gideon had devoured for as long as he could remember. He drifted, wide-eyed, past every display, his face reflecting dully in the glass. Here was hard evidence that, just as he had always believed, Captain Lucian Trigger's adventures were indisputably real.

"The Tongan Fetish," he said in wonder. "And the claw from the Exeter Werewolf. Lord Dexter's top hat! And is this . . . ?"

"The Book of the Expurgated Apostles," said Trigger, his own sallow reflection appearing beside Gideon's. "You are clearly an aficionado of the adventures, Mr. Smith."

Mrs. Cadwallader, glaring with hostility at the visitors, brought in a tray of coffee and fancies. "I'll thank you to not overly excite Captain Trigger," she said tartly. "He is very weak at present."

When the housekeeper had bustled out and closed the door behind her, Maria poured coffee for them all and Trigger sat lightly in his easy chair, resting his head on an antimacassar. He closed his eyes for so long Gideon feared he had fallen asleep, but just as he was about to clear his throat Trigger said, "Mrs. Cadwallader is quite correct, unfortunately. I am not the man I was."

"Like my old mum always said, you're only as old as the man you feel," cackled Bent.

Trigger opened his eyes and blinked at Bent, as though noticing the journalist for the first time. "It is not age wearies me, sir, but loss. However, I think it is about time introductions were effected. Mr. Smith has already stated his name and an intent causing my heart to beat like a drum. Who are you, sir?"

Bent extended a hand while he used the other to shovel fancies into his mouth. "Aloysius Bent, Captain Trigger, of the *Illustrated London Argus*. A lowly scribe, like your good self."

"A journalist," said Trigger primly.

Gideon said, "You've got it wrong, Mr. Bent. It isn't Captain Trigger who writes up the adventures, but Dr. John Reed." He looked around. "Is Dr. Reed not with you? I was given to understand you two spent much time together."

"In each other's pockets," guffawed Bent. "You might say, in each other's *trouser* pockets."

Trigger stared at Bent. "I am glad my life offers such amusement to you, Mr. Bent. Little more than I would expect from your publication, though."

Bent waved a protesting hand. "We've got the same paymasters at the end of the line, Trigger."

Trigger ignored him and addressed Maria. "And you, my dear? Mr. Smith's sweetheart, perhaps?"

Gideon saw a flush rise on Maria's pale cheeks. Einstein really had left nothing out of his automaton. She kept her eyes averted from him and gifted Trigger with a small smile, which caused Gideon's breath to catch in his throat. "We are merely traveling companions, Captain Trigger."

They sipped their coffee in silence for a moment, Gideon itching to stand and inspect further the trophies lining the cabinets. But then Trigger said, "I believe mummies were mentioned. Mr. Smith, I would be extremely grateful if you could tell me your story."

"Hang on a minute," said Bent. "He's giving me the tale, that's the deal. I bring him to you, he gives me the story of the Wolf of Whitby."

Gideon sighed. "For what seems like the hundredth time, there is no wolf in Whitby, Mr. Bent." He turned to Trigger. "Of course I shall tell you my story. That is why I am here. But you may have trouble believing it."

Trigger smiled, and for the first time since meeting him Gideon thought he detected a little of the elusive *something* that had made him the Hero of the Empire. "Oh, I doubt it, Mr. Smith," he said. "I am, after all, Captain Lucian Trigger."

❧

"That," said Bent, "is possibly the most ridiculous, fanciful, and far-fetched thing I have ever heard, and trust me, I've heard some fucking bullshit. Pardon my French." He paused. "Actually, no, don't pardon my fucking French. You've just wasted half my day on a wild goose chase. You should be in the bloody Bethlem Royal Hospital, chained to a wall, not running around loose in London."

Trigger continued to regard Gideon. "Is that right?" he asked. "Are you a lunatic? Is that a pack of lies?"

Gideon laid his hand on his chest. "Sir, it is the God's honest truth."

"Yes," said Trigger thoughtfully. "I do believe it is."

Bent stared at him. "Then you're as mad as he is. I'm in a house of madmen. True? Frog-faced mummies from Egypt attacking people in bloody Yorkshire? And let's say I could begin to stretch my credulity enough to accept such things exist. Do I need to point out the only person to see the thing is a *seven-year-old boy*?"

With some effort, Trigger got to his feet and strode to the trophy cabinet. "The stories in *World Marvels & Wonders* are, aside from a touch of literary license and the necessary alteration of details here and there to protect certain individuals, faithful reports of what happened. That particular case Mr. Smith alludes to, which appeared under the title *The Shadow Over Faxmouth*, occurred around two and a half years ago. A mummy liberated from the sands of Egypt was taken to Arkhamville, and was later revived by unknown means. It stole a ruby pendant and made for the sea. The mummy escaped but the pendant was recovered and brought back here, to this trophy room. It used to reside in this very cabinet."

"Used to?" asked Gideon, rising and joining Trigger at the glass case. There was indeed a velvet cushion, slightly indented but otherwise bare, and a small card inscribed with the words "Arkhamville necklace (originally Egyptian)."

"It has gone, with John. With Dr. Reed."

"He stole it?" asked Gideon, aghast. "He has abandoned you?"

Trigger shook his head. "Mr. Bent? What was it you said about me earlier? What did you call me?"

"A bum-jockey?" said Bent. "Oh, no, that was before we got here, in the cab. A fraud, that was it."

Trigger nodded. "A fraud. Quite. You see, Mr. Smith, Mr. Bent is correct. I am a fraud."

"But you said the stories were true!" protested Gideon.

"And so they are," said Trigger, smiling sadly. "But although they purport to be the adventures of Captain Lucian Trigger, that is not strictly correct. I said, did I not, that some things had been changed? The largest lie of all is that it is Captain Trigger who sallies forth into the world while his faithful companion Dr. Reed stays at home and transcribes his notes and journals. Quite the reverse is true. It is I, Lucian Trigger, who sits alone at the desk in the study and transforms into thrilling prose the rousing episodes of peril and triumph. And it is Dr. John Reed who is truly the Hero of the Empire."

"Then it is Dr. Reed I need to see," said Gideon.

Trigger sighed. "Would that were possible. He has been missing for more than a year. He embarked upon an adventure in Egypt. I am quite bereft without him."

"He's kicked the bucket?" said Bent.

Gideon glared at Bent. "Captain Trigger? Is he . . . ?"

Trigger shook his head sadly and touched his hand to his chest. "I do not know for sure. But if he were gone, I think I would feel it, here." He fixed his watery eyes on Gideon. "My heart aches every day, Mr. Smith, and I am convinced John is still alive."

Dusk had landed heavily on Grosvenor Square. Trigger sighed and lit the electric lamps in the room.

Eventually Gideon said, "Then it seems evident to me what must happen."

Trigger nodded sadly. "There is no help here, I am afraid. When you spoke on the doorstep of mummies, I dared to hope you might have some news of John. But it is not to be. You must face your peril in Sandsend without Captain Trigger, Mr. Smith."

Gideon stared at him. "That isn't what I mean at all, Captain Trigger."

"Then what, young man?"

Gideon looked at Trigger, then at Bent, then to Maria. "Isn't it obvious? If John Reed is really the man who tackled the Faxmouth mummy, then I've no choice. I have to go to Egypt and find him."

"Egypt?" said Bent. "Oh, this is getting priceless now. I'll give you this, Mr. Smith, you're awfully good value for money."

"But how do you anticipate traveling to Egypt?" asked Maria quietly.

Gideon began to stalk up and down the trophy room. "I do not know. How did Dr. Reed get there?"

"I believe on this occasion he secured the services of Rowena Fanshawe," said Trigger.

"The Belle of the Airways!" said Gideon. "From the adventures! Then she will be able to take me straight to where she saw him last."

"I have already spoken to her," said Trigger. "She merely transported him to Alexandria. Where he went from there, and how, I have no idea."

"I must see her, nonetheless," said Gideon. He paused, his face falling. "But . . . how much do you suppose passage to Alexandria would cost?"

"More than a steam-cab from Fleet Street to Grosvenor Square," Bent said, chuckling. "And you're broke, remember?"

Trigger was standing thoughtfully at the window, gazing out as the lamps flared into life in the square. "Mr. Smith," he said slowly, "if you truly mean to travel to Egypt in search of John . . ."

"I do," said Gideon. "I must have his help. That is, if the creature hasn't slaughtered the entire village by now."

". . . then I will finance your expedition," said Trigger. "John and I, we are not without resources. We are rather . . . affluent."

"Can we go to see Rowena Fanshawe now?" asked Gideon.

"I would suggest tomorrow," said Trigger. "This evening, I would like to extend to you an invitation to be my guests for dinner. I shall tell you . . . I shall tell you of John, and we can plan our next move in comfort. Do you and Miss Maria have somewhere to stay in London?"

"No," said Gideon. "I hadn't thought that far ahead."

"Then you must stay the night here," decided Trigger. "We have rooms, and you shall be quite comfortable."

"Sounds lovely!" Bent beamed.

Trigger looked at him. "You wish to stay, too, Mr. Bent? You may, of course. But I thought you considered Mr. Smith somewhat mad."

"He *is* mad," said Bent. "Mad as a hatter." He pointed at Trigger. "You're as much of a lunatic as he is, and you're a shirt-lifter to boot. She's a pretty little thing, but barely says a word and doesn't even know her own name. You're each as mad as the rest. But never let it be said that Aloysius Bent can't smell a good story when he steps in it." Bent put an arm around Gideon, who flinched at the smell of stale sweat wafting from his armpits. "I'm sticking to you like Lyle's Golden Syrup, my lad. Whitby, Egypt, or the fucking moon, you're going nowhere without me."

12

Dr. Reed's Casebook

I had (said Captain Lucian Trigger to his dinner guests) a long and largely illustrious career with the 1st Battalion of the Duke of Wellington's Regiment, traveling all over the world and rising to the rank of Captain. At the rear of this room, on the mannequin between those two cabinets, you will see my uniform. The brass buttons on the blue double-breasted tunic are polished every week, the red sash and trouser stripes are as bright and vital as they were in the merciless Indian sun, and the rapier is as keen as it was when I single-handedly faced a gang of bloodthirsty Thuggees in '76.

Alas, that career came to a rather abrupt end a little over a decade ago. The British Army takes a rather dim view of sodomy. You might have heard from your Mr. Bent that I was, variously, accused of visiting indignities upon youths in Calcutta, corrupting the junior ranks with the threat of disciplinary proceedings should they not succumb to my perverse demands, and even engaging in intercourse with a farmyard animal that differs in every version of the tale I have heard. The simple truth was, I fell in love. Unfortunately for the army, and for me, it was with a man.

Dr. John Reed was a medic attached to the regiment while we were stationed in Goa, formerly a Portuguese interest on the southwest coast of India. If paradise exists on Earth, then truly it is there. We would walk at sundown on Candolim Beach, where the sea fizzed with a most becoming phosphorescence as it broke on the golden sands. The fronds of palm trees swayed in the warm evening breeze and cows roamed freely while native women walked by in bright saris, holding fruit above their heads and murmuring in hypnotic, singsong voices *mango*, *banana*, *papaya*, over and over again.

Perhaps it was that sense of otherworldliness in Goa that caused us to drop our guard, but we consummated our love on the woodsmoke-wreathed dunes, and we became ever more careless about covering our tracks. Our indiscretions were duly discovered, and a court-martial took place.

My previous good character and exemplary military service ensured I received an honorable discharge with the minimum of fuss; I was already known to the readers of the more breathless periodicals for my adventures and achievements. But what I did not know until the court-martial was the past of my lover, Dr. Reed. No mere medical man was he: He was an explorer, archaeologist, adventurer, and more. He had signed up for a spell of military service to further his knowledge and experience, and the authorities decided his curriculum vitae was too good an opportunity to throw away for a mere punishment. So they offered us, behind closed courtroom doors, a deal.

Released from the shackles of military service, Dr. Reed would continue his adventures, free and without interference from the Crown. He would, however, be sometimes called upon to perform special tasks or undertake missions for Britain. Furthermore, as something of an inspiring fillip to the British public, his adventures would be recounted for publication on a regular basis. To ensure John could pass unhindered across the world's borders and boundaries, his identity would remain innocuous; as someone with a proud military service behind me, I would instead be the figurehead for these stories, which, having something of a poetic bent, I would also pen.

And so began a long and fruitful association. And, yes, a happy one. John and I were in love, and if his enforced absences were bitter, then our reunions were oh so sweet. I see you wincing, Mr. Bent. Perhaps you are also wondering why I did not accompany John on his missions and tours. The truth was, after a lifetime of military service, I had had enough of traversing the world and putting myself in peril. To sit at home in Grosvenor Square and await John's return while I crafted the tale of his latest adventure . . . that to me was bliss.

And so it continued. But in the last few years, John was called upon more and more by the Crown, much more often than they had ever indicated they would. His travels became an imposition; the danger mounted in each new mission. And sometimes, when he did have the satisfaction of earning the ancient artifacts and lost treasures he had fought so hard for, the Government would remove them from his possession. It troubled me to see John growing increasingly bitter and jaded.

Then, a year ago, he announced he was going to Egypt. During that very episode you mention, Mr. Smith, the *Shadow Over Faxmouth* event, John had learned from Professor Halifax about a lost tomb in the desert, the fabled Rhodopis Pyramid. It was said to hold great treasures and artifacts lost to humanity for two and a half thousand years. John was determined to find the lost pyramid and breach its walls. Last summer he departed upon his quest.

And I have not seen him since.

I contacted many of his traveling companions and regular acquaintances, of course, but aside from confirmation that he had indeed flown by dirigible to Alexandria, there was nothing. Why did I not go out there myself to find him? Alas, I have grown soft and weak since I left the regiment. When there was no word from John I sank into even deeper decline, and a melancholia has gripped me that I fear will never be shaken off. It is as though my heart has been rent in two, and half of it has whispered away. I very much expect I shall die before I ever seen John again, merely fading away in the shadows of this house.

From John Reed's "Unsolved Files"

Another summons from W. I confess I am getting heartily sick of the man's attitude. He seems to think I am but a dog to be ordered around, to roll over and play dead and perform tricks for him. This is not the deal we struck. W. is calling on my services more and more, so much that I spend more time in the employ of the Crown than I do on my own errands. This time there has been some kind of burglary at the British Museum. A burglary! Is this not work for Scotland Yard?

W. met me at the British Museum. It is quite rare for him to turn up on a job these days. The place was closed up, and the curator took us to the halls were the Egyptian relics were kept. One cabinet had been smashed crudely open, and the artifact snatched.

"What was it?" I asked the curator.

"A *shabti*," he said, and showed me a drawing of a small funerary figurine. It was well made and intact, but I had seen dozens of them in my time.

"Valuable?"

"Not particularly," said the curator.

"And not worth the effort put into stealing it," added W.

I inspected the smashed cabinet. "Not a very professional job," I noted. "There was no guard on duty?"

"There was," said W. "The past tense being appropriate." He lowered his voice. "Whoever was in here last night tore him to shreds. Literally."

Around the cabinet were signs of a scuffle. There was indeed blood, which W. confirmed was from the guard. And more . . . dried mud? I took a sample for testing.

How curious. Analysis of the mud samples from the British Museum reveals it to be a compound of a variety of different sources. The bulk of it is from the banks of the Thames, but there are traces of composted Egyptian lotus, which grows in abundance on the banks of the Lower Nile. Our burglar is evidently of an aquatic bent, and well traveled at that.

Notes on the Atlantic Submersible Mission

Lucian,

As promised, here are my notes on the submersible jolly with the Royal Navy. After that stunt W____ pulled as soon as we docked in Portsmouth, I'm not even sure it will make a suitable piece for World Marvels & Wonders *at all.*

Oh, don't get me wrong, there's plenty of excitement. That episode alone with the giant squid that tried to crack open the sub has enough drama to keep the story moving. Along with that Viking longship on the seabed, you've probably got the basis for a decent little tale. But my heart is not in the whole enterprise.

I was really quite excited about that artifact we found among the Viking hoard. It was a strange apparatus and no mistake, with a hard, glassy surface; it looks for all the world like a model of a human brain.

W____ took that off with him, of course. He did leave me some of the rest of the hoard, and I had it dated down at the British Museum. Among the treasures was a seal bearing the hieroglyph of the Pharaoh Amasis II, which was translated as being a label for clothing and chattels belonging to one Rhodopis. This is the second time I have heard this name, the first being from Professor Halifax in connection with that monstrosity I pursued to Faxmouth. You remember Reg, of course. Sad loss. I do wonder, though . . . is the fabled Rhodopis Pyramid he spoke of stuffed with such treasures?

One for a future jaunt, perhaps. Duty calls, at least this time only to Edinburgh. I will be back home before you know it.

All my love,
John

From John Reed's Journals

W. is up to something. W. is *always* up to something, but a theme seems to be emerging: Egypt. The strange brainlike artifact he took possession of following the Viking exploration on the bottom of the Atlantic was of Egyptian origin; then there was that murder and burglary at the British Museum, and he has since taken an inordinate interest in that business in Arkhamville. The latest piece in the puzzle comes from Walton Jones, whom I ran into in Bombay.

Oh, I do not flatter myself that W. employs only me for his missions across the world. He has many fingers in many pies. I learned that when we tackled Von Karloff on Everest and discovered that the Prussian had been sent to steal the Golden Apple of Shangri-La on W's explicit orders. That was when I first began to doubt W, to mistrust him.

I can quite understand W. employing the services of Von Karloff, but Walton Jones? The man is a base tomb robber, despite his claims of archaeological expertise and the fact that his young son Henry is, I understand, something of a brilliant medievalist even at his tender age, and bound for Oxford by all accounts. Jones Senior is nothing but a thief, and an indiscreet one at that. After a few gins in Bombay, his tongue was wagging like the tail of a mangy hound. He simply couldn't wait to tell me about his last mission, and the scroll he had procured for W.

It was a simple errand—his son could doubtless have pulled it off—that saw Jones in the Persian Gulf, where an alleged djinn was causing trouble to a garrison of British troops. Of course, it turned out to be nothing more than mischievous local tribes; I could have told W. that without even leaving Grosvenor Square. But while there Jones chanced upon an ancient papyrus scroll, Egyptian in origin, which he handed over to W. like a needy child desperate for a pat on the head.

"And what was of interest in the scroll?" I asked nonchalantly.

Jones tapped his nose with his forefinger, then proceeded to tell me anyway half an hour later. "Plans for some kind of ancient weapon, apparently. W. was most interested."

"Weapon? What kind of weapon?" I asked, interested myself.

Jones shrugged. "Don't know for sure. But it doesn't really matter, because the scroll put the thing in the pyramid of Rhodopis, which we all know nobody is going to find any time soon."

And there it was again. Rhodopis. W. is evidently assembling some kind of evidence for the existence of, as Jones would have it, a weapon of some description, buried in the lost tomb of Rhodopis. Unlike Walton Jones, I do not choose to underestimate W. His tendrils reach far and wide, and his resources are many and great. If W. is interested in the Rhodopis Pyramid, perhaps I should be interested as well. Whether he has designs on this so-called weapon for the good of the Empire or to feather his own nest, I would much rather find it first myself. Mr. W. must be made to understand that he cannot have everything his own way, and that the wonders of the world are not his alone to plunder.

NOTES FOR *THE CENTAUR OF THE CHAMPS ÉLYSÉES* (UNPUBLISHED)

Not a centaur, of course, but an insane and rather ghastly Spanish plot against the French. I'd stopped over in Paris after the wolf business in Cologne, and happened to see the thing firsthand. Crude automaton work, using the actual corpse of a headless horse, fitted with steam pistons, and a dummy human torso, head, and arms fitted to the neck. The horse's body was stuffed with gunpowder, and the Spanish spies let it loose down the Champs Élysées with the intention of it running smack into the Eiffel Tower and blowing it up. It might have worked, too, if the "centaur" hadn't gone awry, running around in circles before galloping off to the Seine, into which it plunged and rendered itself useless.

Not much of a tale for *World Marvels & Wonders,* with the best will in the world. But the episode is notable because of who I ran into while watching the blasted thing haring around Paris: Lord Arthur Somerset. He had just been involved in that terrible business on Cleveland Street, the molly house raided by the police. His name had been handed over to the constabulary as one of the clients, and he had been arrested. That was the last I had heard of him. How did he happen to be at liberty in Paris?

"It's not just who you know, old chap, it's what you know about them as well," said Somerset.

He claimed he wasn't going to say a word more, but the man has always been an inveterate gossip. It turned out that he had struck a deal; he would clear out of London in exchange for keeping his mouth shut.

"About what?" I asked.

"Can you keep a secret, old boy?" Somerset had asked. "It's about Eddy."

"Eddy? You mean Albert Victor, the Duke of Clarence?"

Somerset nodded. "Did you know he was to be married?"

"Some German, isn't it? Princess Mary of Teck?"

Somerset chuckled. "It is *now*, old bean. He'd set his cap for quite a different filly this time last year, mind. A shopgirl. Lived down the road from the molly house, in fact, on Cleveland Street. I saw her once or twice. She used to sit for Sickert."

"It's not unknown, though, Royalty mixing it up with the commoners on occasion. . . ."

Somerset shook his ruddy head, his ginger whiskers swaying. "That's not the secret, old boy. The secret is, they had her done away with. Quite brutally. Chopped the top of her head off and stole her brain, by all accounts."

"They?"

"The Government, old friend. Or at least, the shadows that work for it. I whispered a few words in the right ears, told 'em bits of what I knew, and intimated I'd make a bit of a fuss if they threw me in the clink." He spread his hands. "So here I am. Gay Paree. More wine?"

It was a gruesome enough tale, and something about it simply wouldn't leave me be. Somerset hadn't said the name, and I couldn't prove anything, but this had W's fingerprints all over it. I don't know how it fits into everything else, if it does at all, but I don't think there's much time to waste.

I'm about due for a little soirée to the land of the Sphinx.

Letter from Dr. Reed to Captain Lucian Trigger. Posted in Alexandria September 1889.

My darling Lucian,

I have arrived safely in Alex, thanks to the impeccable airmanship of Miss Rowena Fanshawe. And who should I meet as soon as we touch down on terra firma, but Louis Cockayne!

He has put me in touch with a local man who can take me up the Nile. I intend to spend a few days researching and gathering supplies, and then I will head out into the countryside to see what I can see.

The heat is infernal, the flies are persistent, and the blasted sand gets everywhere. I miss you, Lucian. I wish I could be with you.

Until I return,
John.

13

The Belle of the Airways

Each scribbled fragment, each journal entry, each note and letter forged Captain Trigger's loss even more keenly. But, to his surprise, the memories also awakened a delight Trigger had thought long dormant within him, if not even dead. They plotted and planned late into the night, studying maps of North Africa and reading through books piled high on the dinner table, as Mrs. Cadwallader huffed and puffed with her effort to remove the dinner plates and bring them wine and coffee. Not all of John's notes were relevant to their studies—indeed, there were personal notes he would never dream of sharing with the others—and while from his journals they knew John had been looking for the Rhodopis Pyramid, if he had made any detailed notes about its location he had taken them to Egypt with him.

"Rhodo-what?" asked Bent, flipping through a book on antiquities of ancient Egypt. "Piss?"

"This is hopeless," said Gideon, obviously deflated. "It could be anywhere. How big is Egypt, anyway?"

"It will look better in the morning," said Trigger. "Things often do."

Bent sat back and noisily quaffed a glass of wine. "You've perked up, Trigger. Almost got a bit of color in your cheeks."

Trigger shrugged. "For too long I have borne the burden of John's loss alone. It is gratifying to have someone share my trouble."

Bent yawned and stretched. "Well, I'm completely fucking exhausted now. Did you mention a bed?"

"Mrs. Cadwallader will show you to the room," said Trigger. "And Mr. Bent? If we are to spend much more time in each other's company, might I ask you to modify your profanity somewhat?"

"You might," agreed Bent. "And I might tell you to shove it up your arse. Good night, all."

Trigger watched him lumber out of the dining room in the wake of a horrified Mrs. Cadwallader. He sipped at his wine and watched Gideon following with his forefinger the course of the White Nile in an atlas, as Maria sat by his side. A most curious girl. There was a great sadness in her, thought Trigger, and he smiled ruefully. It took one to know one. There was an idea forming in his mind, and try as he might to push it away, it would not depart. It was a foolish, stupid idea, but he could not help but dwell on it. Perhaps the morning would bring with it a more sensible frame of mind.

"Why did you place your trust in the Captain Trigger of *World Marvels & Wonders*?" he asked eventually.

Gideon blinked up at him, as though not comprehending the question. "You . . . he . . . is the Hero of the Empire."

Trigger nodded thoughtfully. "And are you disappointed your hero has been found wanting?"

Gideon shook his head vehemently, waving his hand at the cabinets laden with souvenirs. "Wanting? I don't understand." He stood and walked to the nearest glass-fronted cupboard. "Every item here, every dagger and stone and gem . . . it's all like, like . . ." He paused, frustrated at his lack of language to describe how he felt. Then he said, "It's like when my father was fishing for cod, and sometimes, not often, but once or twice a year, they'd perhaps net a fish no one recognized. Not a cod, not a haddock. Some strange thing that had swum from some faraway place. That's what these things are, the Captain Trigger adventures. Strange things from faraway places. Disappointed, Captain Trigger? Oh, no."

Trigger joined him at the cabinet, his pale reflection at Gideon's shoulder. They stared at the strange things from faraway places, then Gideon placed a finger near the glass. "Another empty cushion . . ."

Trigger peered closer. "So there is."

Gideon read from the caption. "The Golden Apple of Shangri-La." He turned to Trigger. "But that's impossible."

Trigger raised an eyebrow. "How so?"

"You remember," insisted Gideon. "Captain Trigger and Jamyang the Tibetan mystic journeyed deep inside the Himalayas to the secret valley of Shangri-La, where time flows differently, an oasis amid the howling snow storms." His eyes shone as he quoted from memory, "*A verdant paradise of meadows ablaze with color, patchwork fields given over to swaying crops, blue pools, and white foaming rivers. Orchards of trees groaned with fruit and herds of deer grazed the lowlands near the bank of the river.*"

"I remember." Trigger smiled. "Remember writing it, anyway."

Gideon jabbed the glass again. "They confronted the rogue archaeologist Von Karloff who had stolen the Golden Apple, which was to be given by God to unite mankind in one tongue when their penance for the Tower of Babel was paid, and which was kept in Shangri-La for safekeeping until that day."

"Of course."

Gideon turned back to him. "At the end, Jamyang said '*Cui bono*.' We didn't do Latin at school. I had to look it up."

"To whose benefit?" said Trigger.

"To whose benefit?, yes. Jamyang was suggesting someone was pulling Von Karloff's strings; he was stealing the apple for a higher authority. The point is . . . in the story Captain Trigger returned the apple to the women of Shangri-La. If he hadn't, they would have aged and withered, and the lush valley would have fallen to the ravages of time and been destroyed."

Trigger was becoming somewhat impatient. "Yes, yes, I remember. So?"

"So . . . why is there a space for the apple in your cabinet, if it was supposed to have stayed in Shangri-La? And where is it now?"

Trigger shrugged. "I confess I am not familiar with every item in the house. I cannot really recall the apple, if it was ever there. Perhaps John prepared a space for it, but never brought it. Maybe a replica sat there, and has been lost. Now, Mr. Smith, I would humbly suggest we get some rest before tomorrow. . . ."

Gideon nodded and retired, and for a long moment Trigger stood alone, staring thoughtfully at the bare cushion, hidden behind a South Sea statue carved from volcanic rock.

"*Cui bono,*" he said softly.

Highgate Aerodrome commanded a prime spot on one of London's highest points, all the better for the dirigibles soaring in and out day and night to catch the winds bearing them aloft to all points of the Empire. Over the years most of Highgate Woods had been removed to accommodate the growing Aerodrome, and on the corner of Hampstead Heath were ranged the air traffic control towers coordinating the hundreds of airships spiraling around in the updrafts, waiting for their opportunity to land, and those tethered by steel cables to the large iron rings cemented into the macadam apron, poised to take off. Nearest the Heath were the ranks of vast intercontinental and trans-Atlantic passenger dirigibles, served by a small colony of hotels and departure lounges. Further back, away from the public gaze, the cargo dirigibles loaded and unloaded, a terminus of steam-lorries, locomotives, and stilt-trains waiting for the spoils of the world to be delivered and later disseminated among London's shops and markets.

"Miss Fanshawe runs a private dirigible business," said Trigger as the hansom cab deposited them at the main portico of the Aerodrome. "We'll find her at the far northeastern end, with the rest of the independent operators."

Trigger led them to a quarter of the Aerodrome that was far less luxurious and exciting than the Hampstead Heath side. They were in a much more perfunctory locale, a place of rundown wooden sheds and slightly shabby dirigibles in a variety of sizes, bobbing in the breeze. He took them to one of the more dilapidated structures, beside which there was a small dirigible, in relative terms; its balloon, long and slim like a cigar, was perhaps sixty feet from nose to tail, and betrayed signs of patching up and a make-do-and-mend program of repairs and maintenance. It floated a dozen feet off the ground, its gondola strung beneath it, small stanchions supporting idle propellers extended at either side. On the taut fabric of the balloon was the name of the ship, the *Skylady II*. Gideon looked at it rather doubtfully and Bent whispered, "Fucked if I'm going up in that wreck, Smith."

But Trigger was already hammering on the door of the shed, which had a printed notice nailed to it: FANSHAWE AERONAUTICAL ENDEAVORS.

The door was yanked open and a small man with a grease-blackened face appeared, dressed in oil-stained overalls and wearing a welding mask. Upon seeing Trigger, the man tore off his mask and smiled broadly, and then Gideon realized his mistake. It was not a man, but a woman . . . and not, on closer inspection, unattractive. She had shorter hair than Gideon had ever seen on a young woman, spiked and plum-colored, and a beaming smile of white teeth. Her overalls were unbuttoned scandalously low, and with the mask gone Gideon could see she was most shapely in the torso, and had slim legs and—when she turned to quiet the din of some kind of hammering machine behind her—a rather curvaceous backside. Bent whistled appreciatively and murmured, "Nice set of Cupid's kettle drums on that one."

"Lucian!" she squealed, and threw her arms around Trigger. "It's been such a long time. Have you news of John?"

He shook his head sadly. "No. But that is why I am here. Allow me to introduce my companions. This gentleman is Aloysius Bent, of the *London Illustrated Argus*. The lady is Miss Maria. And the young man is Gideon Smith, of Sandsend. This is my good friend Rowena Fanshawe—"

"The Belle of the Airways!" finished Gideon.

Fanshawe wiped her hands on an oily rag and presented it to Bent, who slobbered a kiss upon it; Maria, who shook it primly; and Gideon, who held on to it and gazed into her eyes. "The Belle of the Airways," he said again. "Miss Fanshawe, it is an honor to meet you."

She smiled broadly again. "A fan. Always nice to meet a good-looking one." She glanced around and whispered, "Some of the aficionados of Lucian's stories track me down sometimes, and want signed photographs. Mostly to fetch mettle to, I suspect."

Gideon looked blankly at her, and Bent leaned in toward him. "She means to wank over. Can't say I blame them. Have you seen those bubbies?"

They stood in silence for a moment, then Fanshawe said, "If you'll let me retrieve my hand, Mr. Smith, I'll take you inside and find you something to drink, and you can tell me why you're here."

❧

The offices of Fanshawe Aeronautical Endeavors were little more than a cluttered workshop with pieces of metal and machinery piled high on tables and a desk at one end, near a wall dominated by a map of the world, stuck with pins and scrawled notes. Fanshawe brewed a pot of tea on a gas burner and poured them all a tin cup, inviting them to grab stools, upturned crates, and rickety chairs.

"Tell me again when you last saw John," said Trigger.

Fanshawe shrugged. "Like I told you before, Lucian. He employed me a year ago to take him to Alexandria. We parted there and I never saw him again."

"No one ever saw him again," said Trigger sadly.

They sipped the strong tea in silence.

Fanshawe said, "I'm sorry if you were looking for more information, Lucian. I have none. And over the past year I have asked around, every time I've run into someone who might know John. There's nothing."

"That is why I think we must employ you again, Rowena,"

said Trigger. "Mr. Smith here has had recent adventures that could possibly provide some clue to John's disappearance. He has suggested he might travel to Alexandria on his own mission, which dovetails most agreeably with the search for John."

"Bloody fantasy, if you ask me," said Bent, laughing. "Mummies and nonsense."

Fanshawe tapped a finger thoughtfully on her chin. "It's a strange world out there, Mr. Bent. What most of London would see as rank nonsense is the stuff of life and death in the distant, shadowed corners of the globe." She looked at a ruled notebook on her desk. "I have a commission to take a cargo to Scandinavia, but not for another week or so. I suppose I could take you to Egypt."

Gideon stood. "When can we leave? Today? When would we arrive?"

Fanshawe laughed lightly. "Mr. Smith, it is two thousand and seventy one miles from London to Alexandria. Even with a following wind we would take the best part of two days. And such a journey needs preparation. It will take me a day, at least, to have the *Skylady II* ready."

"A day?" said Gideon, his face falling. "And two days' journey?"

"I'm guessing you've never flown in a 'stat before," said Fanshawe. "Perhaps you should come and see the *Skylady II*."

❧

"Most folks call 'em airships or dirigibles," said Fanshawe as she unlocked the door. "We in the trade refer to 'em as 'stats. Short for aerostat."

Fanshawe pointed at the balloon. "She's a rigid 'stat. See the skeleton, made of wood? It holds four different cells, and they're filled with helium. Helium's lighter than air, see, so it wants to rise up, even with the gondola and cargo or passengers. We crank her up and the engine powers the propellers, which drag her forward."

"Clockwork?" snorted Bent. "That's going to get to Egypt on clockwork?"

"Like the gearships," said Gideon quietly. "Our trawler back home was a gearship, same principle."

Fanshawe nodded. "The clockwork engines ain't as fast as the steam 'stats, and they take a hell of a lot of winding, but we save on space and coal. She'll get to Alexandria, no problem, provided Mr. Smith here is prepared to lend a hand with the winding." She put her own hand on Gideon's upper arm. "My. A bit of cranking shouldn't be a problem for you." She grinned at Trigger. "I'll have two of whatever he's had for breakfast."

Bent asked, "What happened to the *Skylady I*?"

Fanshawe smiled. "I believe there are bits of her still hanging off the north face of the Eiger." She paused. "That was a John Reed escapade, too. Why is it that when that man's name is mentioned, nothing is ever straightforward?"

Trigger coughed. "So you'll do it, Rowena?"

She looked at them all. "I'll do it. Who's coming? Just Mr. Smith?"

"Against my better nature, having seen that crate, I'm coming, too," sighed Bent.

"And I, also," said Trigger.

Everyone looked at him. Gideon said, "Captain Trigger? But I thought you to be indisposed . . . ?"

Trigger smiled. "Mr. Smith, I have been indisposed since John went missing. I have been in perpetual decline, some days not even rising from my bed. And so it would have continued, had you not come knocking at my door. You are vital and alive, Mr. Smith, and selfless. Could I let you go halfway around the world looking for John Reed, while I stay at home awaiting news? I could not. I am, after all, Captain Lucian Trigger, and I have my reputation as the Hero of the Empire to uphold."

Gideon clapped his hands delightedly and noticed that even Bent allowed himself a small smile. Fanshawe said, "And the girl?"

Gideon looked around. "Maria?" She was not there. He frowned. "Maria?"

"Perhaps she went back into the offices, out of the sun," suggested Trigger.

As Gideon went to look, Bent said, "An odd girl, that one. Something about her puts me in mind of something. Can't put my finger on it."

"She's a pretty little thing," conceded Fanshawe. "Beautiful, even. For an automaton."

"Automaton?" said Bent, frowning. "You mean like those mannequins that dance in Regent's Park with the German circus? You're effing joking."

Fanshawe shrugged. "Best I've ever seen. Most lifelike I've clapped eyes on, even better than the Bavarian ones, and they're mad for 'em over there."

Trigger stroked his mustache. "She certainly had me fooled. I thought she was a real girl."

Bent gaped at Fanshawe. "You can't actually mean she's not real? That she's like a toy, or something? That's impossible." He screwed his face up. "But how can a clockwork girl have dreams of London?"

Gideon appeared at the door of the office. "She's gone!" he said breathlessly. "I've looked all over. Maria's gone!"

14

MARIA ALONE

Maria didn't know where she was going, and didn't care. None of them would care. Since they had arrived in London, Gideon Smith had been terribly cold toward her, where he had shown such gentle kindness before. What had changed his mind? She was not angry at him, though, but at herself. She had made the mistake of allowing herself something like hope. He had shown her kindness and taken her away from the house of Einstein, and she had invested far too much in that. Stupid, she told herself. Stupid clockwork girl.

Maria walked away from the bustle of the Highgate Aerodrome. She had taken the bag with the brass key, and a few coppers. She thought she might find her way back to Einstein's house and throw herself on the mercy of Crowe. It was all she could expect. In an alleyway she tried to wind herself up. The awkwardness of the operation and the lack of leverage meant she only managed a couple of turns; it was enough, though, to give her the strength and energy to continue walking.

Maria didn't know where she was going, but her feet took her there all the same. With each moment she spent in London, she felt something infuse her, a sense of familiarity, a feeling that she was home. She walked through Regent's Park, watching with a faint prickle of jealousy the lovers who walked hand in hand, then she struck out east and found herself in the hubbub of the Tottenham Court Road. She smiled as a young hawker placed a rose into her hand, and a man with a dented brass instrument curled around his waist belted out a jolly tune while a monkey in a fez danced at his feet. More than once, a passerby glanced at her. Did they know her, perhaps? What if they merely sensed something about her, something out of place? Maria began to feel unnerved by the weight of humanity and took herself off down a side street. She gasped as whatever it was that lived in her head told her she knew this place, knew it well.

Maria looked up at the metal plate affixed to the sooty wall. Cleveland Street. She put a hand out to steady herself on the warm bricks. As she did so she saw a shape veering toward her on the pavement: a gentleman in a long black coat and a black topper, wearing a concerned frown.

"Ma'am?" he said. "I saw you stagger. Are you . . . ?"

"Mr. Sickert," she said. Her legs buckled and her eyes dimmed, and she fell into his arms.

❧

She awoke in a mild panic, in a shadowy room lit by gas lamps, the walls covered with framed portraits of women. Maria hadn't fainted before, didn't know she could. The man who had spoken to her was sitting opposite, staring at her.

"Oh!" said Maria, sitting up straight. "Where am I?"

"I do apologize," said the man. "You went into a deep swoon. I would not normally bring an unescorted lady back to my quarters, but under the circumstances . . ." He peered through the window, where the sun sank over the rooftops. "I did not consider it prudent to continue our discussions on the street."

"Prudent?" said Maria. "Who are you, sir?"

"My name is Walter Sickert," said the man, looking curiously at her. "You recognized me on the street. Do I know you?"

She shook her head tightly. "I . . . I do not know, Mr. Sickert. I do know you, but I cannot remember how or why. I am very much afraid I am afflicted with some strange malady."

Maria stood and walked over to the wall, steadying herself on the mantel. The painting above the fireplace depicted a lady resting in a sun-drenched park. "You are a painter, Mr. Sickert?"

"I was," he said, joining her. "After what happened . . . with Annie . . . well. I did not consider it judicious to continue taking young women into my studio."

"Annie . . . ," said Maria. "Do I know Annie?"

"Annie Crook," he said, then put a fist to his mouth. "I swore never to utter her name again." He regarded her with narrowed eyes. "Where do you know me from, really?"

She indicated the portrait. "Who is this?" she asked. "She looks familiar."

"That is she."

"Annie Crook? A shopgirl, yes?" Sickert nodded miserably. She asked, "Might you take me to her?"

He sat down, shaking his head. "No. Two years ago. She was found, horribly mutilated. She had . . ."

And there, in the shadows of the studio, Maria remembered. "She had no brain," she finished for Sickert. "They stole her brain."

He nodded miserably, then stood again, and clasped Maria's hands. "You must never speak of Annie Crook, hear me? Never utter her name. It would be bad for you, and bad for me if they knew I'd been talking to you. She was out of her depth. Mixed up in something big. She didn't even know who Eddy was . . . but no, I'll not have another visit by those men. I'll not say."

"Perhaps I should go," said Maria. "If you will not speak, then perhaps there are others who know me around here."

"But who are you?" he asked.

She shrugged delicately. "I am Maria. But I think I might also, once, have been Annie Crook. Or part of me might have." She tapped her head. "I think something of Annie Crook is up here."

Sickert giggled. If he had been high-strung before, his mind was becoming quite undone in Maria's presence. "Oh, there'll be others who remember Annie Crook," he said. "There'll be plenty who knew her. Perhaps not the sort you want to mix with."

She turned to him. "At the very least, Mr. Sickert, tell me this: Was she a lady of means? Was she highborn?"

Sickert laughed. "Highborn?" he said. "Dear Maria, Annie Crook was nothing but a lowly shopgirl, with a dash of common prostitute."

❧

Outside the *Argus* offices, Bent ran into one of the urchins from the Fleet Street Irregulars and gave him a full description of Maria. "You'll not miss her," he told the snot-faced boy. "Right pretty little baggage. And, apparently, an automaton."

"Like the dancing puppets in Regent's Park?" asked the boy, wide-eyed.

"Aye," said Bent, and gave him Trigger's address. "Just like that. You'll put the word out, yes?"

"Mr. Bent," said Bingley, leaning back on his chair as Bent stumbled into the office. "How nice to have you with us today."

Bent went straight to his desk and opened his drawer to retrieve his Jack the Ripper files. He stuffed them into a manila envelope and walked over to the news desk.

"On a big story, Bingley," he said, eyeing a half-eaten pastry on the City Editor's desk.

Bingley looked at him with narrowed eyes. "I don't trust you, Bent, that's the top and bottom of it. Now you sit down and tell me all about this big story of yours, or you make yourself available for whatever tasks I see fit. I have a paper to fill, you know."

"Can't do it, Bingley old chap," said Bent. "Utterly top secret right at the moment. But it's going to be the biggest story ever to grace the front page of this rag, I can tell you. Now, toodle-pip. I'll be in touch."

Bingley looked at him, aghast. "Where do you think you're going?"

"Mayfair," said Bent. "Then Egypt, perhaps."

"*Egypt*?"

"Big place in North Africa, full of sand."

"I know where Egypt is, Mr. Bent, and I can most assuredly say that you are not going there. Now sit down."

Bent held up his hands. "I'll be in touch as soon as I'm back."

"Bent!" roared Bingley, standing up. The journalist was already walking down the newsroom. "Bent! You get back here or you might not have a job to come back to when you return!"

But Bent had already gone.

❧

Gideon paced the study at Grosvenor Square, ignoring the tea Mrs. Cadwallader was trying to press upon him. "We should be out looking for Maria, not sitting here eating fancies," he said.

"London is a big place, with more than six million souls residing here," said Trigger gently. "This is the only place she knows; she will return here."

"If she's able," said Gideon. "She might be in trouble." He should have spoken to her at least, told her he would still help her to find Einstein. She must be feeling he'd abandoned her. She'd not be far wrong. He'd been so wrapped up in the thought of the trip to Egypt, so consumed by adventure. . . .

Bent was sitting at the table, flicking through the journals and notes Trigger had piled high the previous night. Bent's investigations in the newspaper archive had turned up a little on Rhodopis, but nothing very useful. He said, "Who's W? His name crops up a lot."

"John's contact in the Government," said Trigger. "A shadowy figure; I don't even know his real name."

Gideon paused. W? That sounded somewhat familiar. Bent said, "You met him?"

Trigger shrugged. "Tall. Thin. Always well turned out. Mustache. Rather hawkish nose. Piercing eyes."

Bent slapped his hand on the table. "That's the effer who had me taken off the Jack the Ripper story."

"How curious," said Trigger as Bent began to leaf through the journals again. Gideon snapped his fingers and went to find his bag. Maria had taken her key but left behind the book he had taken from Einstein's laboratory.

❦

When Gideon had finished reading Einstein's book, Bent shook his head. "This just gets more and more effing grotesque. Clockwork innards? But a human brain?" He coughed and murmured, "And she showed you her bubbies?"

Gideon ignored him. "The man who brought the Atlantic Artifact to Einstein is referred to merely as 'W.' Surely the same person? But what does it mean, if anything?"

Trigger took one of the journals from Bent and flicked through it. "Look here. These are John's notes on a mission he undertook with a Royal Navy submersible."

"I read that," said Bent. "W. took that . . . that brain-thing from him."

". . . and gave it to Einstein," said Gideon. "W. then provided him with a real brain—"

"Oh. My. Effing. God," breathed Bent. "I've just read this here about Lord Somerset."

Trigger frowned. "Mr. Bent, please limit yourself to the relevant entries. John's journals are not fuel for your salacious yellow journalism."

Bent shook his head violently. "No, no. Look. The Duke of Clarence was knobbing some shopgirl. W. had her seen to." He looked up, the ruddiness draining from his flabby cheeks. "W. provides Einstein with a brain at about the same time. That's when Annie Crook turned up dead by the banks of the Thames. With the top of her head sliced off, very definitely sans effing brain."

They considered this in silence for a moment. Trigger said, "I fear I am with Mr. Smith, Mr. Bent. You seem to be a little ahead of us. . . ."

"It could not be a stronger connection if it were pinned to the front of a steam omnibus crashing through your bay windows, Trigger. The artifact in Maria's head is Egyptian; she also has Annie Crook's brain. John Reed has gone off to Egypt. Could the artifact be from the Rhodopis Pyramid, like everything else seems to be?" He threw his hands into the air. "I'm going round in effing circles. I can't think straight. The mysterious Mr. W. seems to be casting a very long shadow over a lot of seemingly unconnected events."

Trigger steepled his long fingers beneath his chin. "Perhaps it would help if you could share with us your information on this Annie Crook, Mr. Bent."

Mrs. Cadwallader knocked and bustled inside, glaring at the journalist. "Captain Trigger, there's a half-starved waif on the doorstep, asking for him."

"Ah, the Fleet Street Irregulars," said Bent. He followed the housekeeper to the front door and returned in a moment, smiling. "The little buggers have done it. There's a sighting of a party matching Maria's description near Victoria Embankment."

"You can tell us of Annie Crook on the way," said Trigger. "Mrs. Cadwallader! Please organize us some transport, posthaste!"

Maria had prevailed upon Sickert to wind her, and although he had complied she feared the act had shattered what was left of his fragile mind. He sat in his chair, rocking and mumbling to himself, as she buttoned herself up and took her leave of his studio.

So. Her humiliation was complete. She was not only a clockwork toy, she was one with stolen memories, lifted from the mind of a common whore. Was it any wonder Gideon Smith had shunned her so? She must wear her degradation like a perfume. Now she knew why she so readily—and, yes, expertly—carried out Crowe's debased demands. Like a dog to its vomit, she had returned to her wicked ways, even after death.

Maria walked again. There was no one in London she

could count on. Who would want to see her, now that she knew she was an evil, unholy thing that had snatched rudely at a life she had no right to? Even though she now saw flashes of her former life, like half-recalled dreams, she could not remember anyone whom she might have called friend, then or now. She was truly alone.

Her steps took her to the river, and she stood on the Victoria Embankment, watching the sluggish flow of the Thames as the electrified lights strung along its length fizzed into pale life. A fog was rolling off the river, thick and sinewy around her ankles, and rising. Two sweethearts walked by, arm in arm, and whatever contraption Maria had for a heart ached.

Perhaps she should throw herself into the Thames. She didn't even know if that would do the job. But maybe, as she sunk to the bottom like a stone, dragged by her brass and iron workings, she would achieve some kind of peace.

There was a distant clamor of howling dogs, and beneath the caterwauling Maria heard another, closer sound. More passersby. She would wait until they had disappeared, to save any chance of anyone trying to save her. She turned to see who it was, then gasped. Out of the yellow fog shambled a shape, thin and elongated, buoyed along on the rhythmic scraping of its feet on the cobbles and a hissing exhalation of tomb-dry breath. As it emerged from the wreaths of mist Maria made out the glint of something sharp and cruel at the end of its clawlike hands. Was this the Jack the Ripper Gideon had spoken of, who murdered London's fallen women? A fitting end to her miserable existence. But as the figure stepped into the corona of light from the lamps she let loose a terrified scream that the smog all around her seemed to absorb into a leaden nothingness, of no interest to anyone.

15

Vampires of Shoreditch

The dirigible touched down at the Highgate Aerodrome, the tug-blimp guiding the vast leviathan of the sky into a berth where muscular stevedores grappled the trailing cables onto the huge iron rings set into the stone apron.

Bathory and Stoker disembarked and were directed to a waiting rank of steam-cabs, rickshaws, and horse-drawn carriages. They arranged for the box of earth and the countess's other baggage to be kept in storage at Highgate, then Stoker murmured, "Where should we begin?"

Bathory looked into the middle distance, her eyes narrowing. "They are here, in London. I can almost smell their briny stench."

As they settled into a steam-cab Stoker said, "Can you perhaps fix their location?"

Bathory concentrated, then shook her head. "South of here is the best I can suggest. The closer we get, the more brightly they will shine."

"A tour of London, please," said Stoker to the cabbie. "Head south, perhaps cross the river at Waterloo Bridge. I would show my companion the sights."

As the steam-cab trundled off, Stoker said quietly, "I took the liberty of drawing some more blood in the bathroom of the dirigible."

She nodded gratefully and took the glass bottle he surreptitiously passed over to her. "I cannot thank you enough for this, Bram," she said. "But it must be weakening you."

"Nonsense." He smiled. "I am a strong Irishman with blood to spare."

As Bathory sipped at the bottle, Stoker reflected he did, in fact, feel a little lightheaded, but as he looked at the back of their driver's head, his neck exposed, he wondered how many lives he had thus far saved, even if they may have been, in Elizabeth's opinion, not worth saving.

Bathory finished her meal, dabbed the corners of her mouth with her handkerchief, and looked out the window as they trundled into London.

"You have been here before?" Stoker asked.

She nodded. "On occasion."

He thrilled at the thought of Bathory and Dracula wandering among mortal folk, preying on them when their bloodlust overwhelmed them. "Are there many like you? Vampires?"

She looked at him. "Many," she said. "Especially on the Continent. England has, traditionally, not been a welcoming place for our kind. But we thrive in the mountains and forests of Europe. Germany, especially, has many resident vampires, as does Italy." She smiled at some memory of long ago. "Some Carnivale nights in Venice, there are more vampires than humans on the streets."

"And, wherever you go, do you . . . hunt?"

She nodded. "And we are hunted. Man and vampire find it difficult to live in harmony."

"Hardly surprising," sniffed Stoker, "when you steal our blood."

Bathory shrugged. "It is the way of things, the natural order. Just as man eats the animals on the farm, so we must feed on mortals."

Stoker looked at her for a long time. "Is that how you see me, Elizabeth? A . . . a sheep, or a cow, perhaps, to be milked for your sustenance?"

She laid a hand on his thigh and he closed his eyes, overcome. She whispered, "The blood pact was your idea, remember, Bram. And I am no more an animal than you. When you are hungry, do you tear apart a sheep in a field?"

"Of course not!"

"No. You control your appetites. You wait until an appropriate moment, and for appropriate food. So it is with me. I choose carefully." She smiled, showing her canines. "And I enjoy my food."

The steam-cab continued in silence for a while, then Stoker said, "I hope you do not mind me asking, Elizabeth, but the Children of Heqet have proved too strong for you and in overwhelming numbers twice before. How do you intend to fight them this time?"

She hesitated. "I said there were *few* vampires in London, Bram, but not *none*. I intend to procure some help. There is a . . . nest in Shoreditch."

Stoker felt unaccountably stung. He had somehow thought this adventure was for he and Bathory alone. "Vampires? A nest?"

She nodded tightly. "Common vampires," she said. "Not highborn like Dracula and me. A touch . . . difficult. But vampires, nonetheless. Can you ask the driver to take us there?"

Stoker tapped him on the shoulder. "Shoreditch," he said.

The driver deposited them on Shoreditch High Street, a wretched thoroughfare Stoker had never had the misfortune to visit in all his time in London. A warren of mazelike alleys and streets spread like a tumor, raw sewage roasted in the summer sun, and rats as big as dogs gamboled in plain view. They saw a man beating three small girls with a switch for some slight or other; Bathory murmured, "There would be good feeding here. I can see why Varney chose this foul place."

"Varney?" asked Stoker.

"One of the old school," said Bathory. "He was turned in the English Civil War. He was once a nobleman, Sir Francis Varney, but he lost his fortune and now scrabbles for a living with his family."

"His family? You mean . . . ?"

Bathory nodded. "Those he has turned, and those they in turn have turned. All vampires have an allegiance to their dark father or mother."

"Your army of wronged women in Castle Dracula." Stoker nodded.

She sighed longingly. "How I wish they were with me now. Then I would not have to beseech such a lowly hound as Varney for assistance."

A man reeling with gin crossed their path and smiled broadly at Bathory, his fetid breath emerging like a cloud. He was about to say something vile and inappropriate, but Bathory gave him a look that obviously reflected his own mortality, and he slunk away like a chastised mongrel.

A low arch led to a narrow courtyard rank with vermin and the stink of ordure. There was one barn-style door, uninvitingly closed, and Bathory nodded at it. "He's in there. Listen, Bram, I need you to do exactly as I say. Whatever you see, whatever I say, you must keep your own counsel and utter nothing. There are . . . protocols to follow when vampires deal with each other."

Stoker nodded and swallowed dryly. "I understand," he said. "Shall we get this over with?"

Bathory rapped smartly on the door. "Varney! Open up. You have a visitor from Castle Dracula."

There was silence for a moment, then a shuffling from within, and Stoker heard several bolts sliding back before the door opened a crack. It was pitch-black within, and he could just make out a pair of white eyes set in a dirty face, framed by brown hair.

"It's a terrified-looking gent and a woman with big knockers," said a voice.

There was a ripple of unpleasant laughter from within. Then the face disappeared, as though yanked away, and an eye of a most alarming yellow hue appeared at the crack, then widened with surprise. The door creaked further inward and a figure stood in the shadows. A dozen or more pairs of eager eyes were faintly reflected behind it in the darkness.

The owner of the yellow eyes was thin of body, wrapped in a dirty, dark cloak, with a bulbous, liver-spotted bald head. His face was long and taut, a thin, viperish tongue flicking over extended canine fangs, his nose barely two nostrils set in his snow-white flesh. He hunched over as though his huge head were too heavy for his wasted body to carry, but even so, he was almost as tall as Stoker. The yellow eyes trailed over Stoker greedily, then flicked back to Bathory.

"Countess Bathory," said the thing, its voice dripping with snakelike sibilance. "What an unexpected pleasure."

Bathory inclined her head slightly. "Varney. It's been a long time."

Varney shrugged his bony shoulders. "Fifty years? Seventy? I am trying to think . . . was Queen Victoria on the throne when we feasted upon children that full-moon night in Greenwich?"

Stoker glanced at Bathory, but she did not look back at him. "Your hospitality on that occasion was most welcome."

Varney put a long finger with a cruel, yellow nail to his bloodless lips. "Indeed. And yet . . . no reciprocation was forthcoming. No invitation to Castle Dracula landed on my doormat." He grinned horribly. "Unless it was lost in the post, of course."

Bathory nodded. "I apologize, Varney. It was most thoughtless of us. Events, unfortunately, have overtaken our desire to be good hosts at Castle Dracula."

"And now, here you are, on my doorstep once again," said Varney. He looked at Stoker. "But this time you bring a gift, yes? A little something for Varney's larder?"

Bathory took a step forward until her beautiful face was an inch from Varney's hideous visage. "My time is short, Varney, and my need great. Are you going to invite us inside, or would you prefer to conduct business in your doorway?"

Stoker had no desire to go into the dark space where flies buzzed ominously, but Varney acquiesced and stepped back, and Bathory strode forward, Stoker close behind.

There was a dry scraping of matches and an oil lamp was lit, casting a pale orange glow. As Stoker's eyes grew accustomed to the gloom, he put his handkerchief over his mouth to stop himself from gagging. The smell! It was only when the oil lamp began to burn properly that he saw the source of it; he was standing in a single space with a dirt-covered floor, perhaps thirty feet square, and in one corner were piled the putrefying corpses of half a dozen naked dead.

Varney grinned savagely at Stoker's falling face and spread his thin fingers toward the charnel scene. "Something to eat, Countess?"

She shook her head and smiled, showing her fangs. "I brought my own."

It took Stoker a moment to realize she was referring to him, and he looked at her in horror. Now that she was with her own kind, would she revert to type, forget their blood pact? Beyond Varney there were eleven or twelve other vampires, all young men. None were as grotesque as their—what had Bathory said? Their *dark father*?—but all had unnaturally white eyes and distended fangs. Varney said, "So you have. Are you planning to share?"

"Not at the moment," said Bathory. "He is a rare vintage."

Varney nodded. "Then this is evidently not a social visit, Countess. Perhaps we should get down to business. First, though, how is your husband? How is Count Dracula?"

Bathory cast down her eyes. "Varney, Count Dracula is dead."

The vampire put his hands together under his nose, his eyes widening. "Oh. Oh. How terrible." He paused, scrutinizing Bathory. "Then that is why you have come to me."

She nodded.

Varney clapped his hands together. "You have come to present yourself to me like the bitch in heat you are."

Stoker held his breath. What on earth was this fool doing?

But Bathory knelt down in the filth before the slavering creature and put her hands forward, palms down on his thin, bone-like thighs. Oh, how Stoker had wished for her to touch him like that! Now, all he could do was gaze on in horror as she said, "Yes, Varney. I wish you to be my master. I wish you to take me as your wife."

"Elizabeth, no! In the name of God!" cried Stoker.

Varney looked at him with interest. "He is rather outspoken, for lunch."

"Ignore him," said Bathory breathlessly. "What do you say, Varney? Have you not desired me for centuries? Have you not lusted after me, dreamed of the ministrations of these hands on your wracked body, imagined crawling over my flesh and debasing me in all the fashions you have learned over the years?"

He clapped his hands delightedly. "We shall wed this very day! Then we shall make our home in Castle Dracula!" He turned to the vampires assembled behind him. "Countess Bathory has populated the castle with beautiful females."

There was a cheer from Varney's foul family.

Bathory stood, and even though Stoker was crazed by fear he noticed a change in her, a shedding of the false subservience she had demonstrated in the face of Varney.

"Good," she said. "I accept your proposal of marriage, Varney, and in doing so I invoke my ancient right to a blood dowry."

The cheering tailed off and Varney looked at Bathory, his yellow eyes narrowed. "What? What did you say?"

She smiled. "Simply exercising my rights as a widowed vampire, Varney."

He bared his teeth. "I will still best you, Countess. Then you will feel my wrath yet further in our conjugal pit."

Stoker gasped as Varney, with barely the clenching of a single muscle, leaped straight upward and twisted so he clung to the bare brick ceiling, his cloak hanging down in tatters. Bathory hissed and stepped backward, adopting a fighting stance, her fingers curled like claws. There was a heartbeat, then another, then the battle was joined.

Varney flew at Bathory with a blood-chilling scream, but she adeptly cartwheeled to the left, landing with her booted feet on to the wall and crouching there for a moment before leaping back toward him and raking her nails along the back of his bald head. He yelped, and she stood and licked his ichor from her fingers.

"First blood to me," she said.

"And last to me," yelled Varney, tumbling forward in a somersault and slapping Bathory across the face. Her head whipped to one side, then back, and she launched herself at him.

Stoker backed into a corner and watched, horrified, as the unholy, impossible ballet unfolded before him. The combatants defied all laws of physics and gravity that Stoker knew to be absolute, bending time and space to perform feats of athletic battle. One moment saw them flying through the fetid air at such a crawl it appeared as though a kinetoscope film had been slowed and stretched; the next they were a flurry of limbs, a wind of claws. The other vampires cheered on Varney and cast hungry glances in Stoker's direction; he knew if Bathory fell, he was to be their victory feast.

But fall she did not. Varney gradually slowed and weakened under her onslaught, and after a misplaced strike he fell into Bathory's outstretched arms. Their eyes met momentarily, then she opened her mouth and sank her fangs into his thin neck.

There was a long silence as she fed hungrily, then let the withered corpse of the vampire drop heavily to the floor. Stoker felt his bile rise and his heart sink. How could he even think about civilizing such a creature? Bathory stood before Varney's family, her eyes shining.

"Your master is dead," she said. "Now you belong to me."

She turned to Stoker, and he felt terror, but then he saw her soften and smile. "Bram," she said. "I can feel them. The Children of Heqet. Varney's blood has empowered me. They are near the river, north of here." She turned to the vampires. "Run as dogs, cross the river." She stared into the gloom. "Embankment. Quickly."

The vampires fell to their knees and commenced such a howling and screeching Stoker had to close his eyes and clamp his hands over his ears. When he opened them again, there were a dozen hounds of varying size and breed tearing around the room, until Bathory flung open the doors. Dusk had fallen and the animals ran out into it, barking and yelping and disappearing into a fog that swirled and crept up the maze of narrow Shoreditch streets.

As Bathory and Stoker hurried after them, she said, "When old vampires like Varney and myself choose a mate, there are certain practices we must observe. They go back centuries, to when the world was wilder and more savage. A male can take a widowed female as his wife, but she may invoke the ancient trial of blood dowry to ensure his suitability, or if she is unhappy to willingly submit."

"It was a risk, though," said Stoker. "You might have lost."

She smiled. "I knew I wouldn't. Vampires like Varney . . . well, they're like most men, mortal or not. You always think you are right, and stronger, and better. Your arrogance is quite astonishing, really. I blame your mothers."

They left Shoreditch and hailed a cab. "Embankment, fast as you can," gasped Stoker. How could Bathory look so like a human being yet be so savagely *other*? Not for the first time since he'd met her, he felt within him the collision of fascination and revulsion, but now they were joined by another emotion: raw, primal fear.

The sound of howling rose through the fog ahead of them as they turned off Waterloo Bridge.

"Let us out here," said Bathory. She alighted from the cab and stood with the fog swirling around her, the flow of the Thames to her side, sniffing the air. The dogs, somewhere ahead of them, fell silent.

"Do you sense them?" whispered Stoker after paying off the cab driver. "The Children of Heqet?"

"Hush," she said, and closed her eyes. There was silence, then a piercing scream.

Bathory opened her eyes. "There. Now!"

She began to run and disappeared into the fog, Stoker hard on her heels.

16

The Attack on Embankment

"Come on, come on, come on!" said Gideon, slapping the leather of the seat's arm as the steam-cab ferried them agonizingly slowly from Mayfair to Embankment.

"Sorry, sir," said the driver, glancing over his shoulder. "The traffic's terrible, and this fog isn't helping any."

"Mr. Bent, wasn't it your theory that Annie Crook was the first victim of Jack the Ripper?" asked Trigger.

Bent leaned forward in the seat and rubbed his hands together. "You have to admit the old modus operandi is the same."

"Didn't Annie Crook die well before the current spate of killings?" pointed out Trigger, sitting opposite Bent and Gideon, his cane resting between his knees. "And am I right in recalling that while Jack the Ripper does indeed slice the heads off his victims, he does not go so far as to remove their brains?"

"What if Jack the Ripper's looking for something specific in his victims' heads?" said Gideon slowly. "What if he's after the Atlantic Artifact?"

"W," breathed Bent. "Christ, lad, you're effing right. Jack is W. He wants his artifact back."

Trigger frowned. "Mr. Bent, there are far too many holes in *that* argument."

"Real life ain't one of your stories, Trigger," said Bent. "Things aren't often neatly tied up in a dozen pages, with illustrations. But give me the benefit of your literary acumen, Trigger. Tell me the plot holes."

Trigger shrugged. "For starters, W. ostensibly has the artifact. He gave it to Einstein. He knows full well where it is."

"But does he?" said Bent. "Gideon said Einstein was missing."

"But Maria was not," countered Trigger. "She was in the house all along. Why couldn't W. just go back to the house and take her?"

"Maybe he didn't know," said Gideon. "There's nothing in Einstein's journals to say he actually told W. he'd transplanted the brain and the artifact into Maria. And there's something else. Einstein's manservant, Crowe, mentioned some device the professor had invented to stop people finding out things about the house. It's why the telephones didn't work. He called it a dizzy rupture."

"A disruptor," said Trigger. "Hmm. That could be the answer. If Einstein had told W. he no longer had the artifact . . . if W. had some kind of machine to aid his search for the artifact, then any disruptor devised by Einstein could conceivably block it, put him off the scent."

Bent's eyes were shining. "Say W. thinks Einstein's gone to ground with the brain and the artifact. Say he knows enough about the professor's work, but not everything. He knows Einstein would have done at least some research into the artifact, knows he'll have tried to use it with a brain. Stands to reason he'd make the leap to an automaton, given the professor's field of expertise. Maybe old W. saw Maria when she was a work in progress. Maybe that manservant, Crowe, told him about her. If Einstein's in London, W. would know about it. Unless he'd gone underground, living in the slums, with an automaton in the shape of a young girl. Which is why . . ."

"Why W's slicing heads off street-girls," said Gideon. "Looking for his artifact." He sat silently for a moment. "But would a representative of the Crown really stoop to that?"

Bent guffawed. "You'd be surprised how low the Crown would go, lad."

Trigger sighed. "But why, Mr. Bent? Why go to all that trouble?"

"Here's your motivation, Trigger," said Bent. "Here's your killer plot twist. W. wants the brain back because of what's in it. Because of what Annie Crook remembers." He looked up to the driver. "How long to Embankment?"

"Fifteen minutes, sir, if the traffic doesn't get any worse. Which I can't promise."

"Just enough time, I reckon," he said. "Gentlemen, let me take you back two years to June of 1888. London, Cleveland Street to be exact, and a young girl has just finished her shift at a tobacconist on the Tottenham Court Road. It's a balmy night when Annie Crook turns the key in the door of the house where she takes rooms, but she doesn't mind being cooped up inside, as small as her apartment is. Because Annie Crook is in love, and she's about to have a visit from her sweetheart. . . ."

❧

"It sounds preposterous, if I might say so," said Trigger.

"You might, but it'd be a bit effing rich coming from you, who spins them tall tales for *World Marvels & Wonders* every month," said Bent, sitting back with the satisfaction of a good tale well told.

"A fair point, I suppose," said Trigger. "But then, my tales are true."

"As is mine, sir," said Bent.

Trigger leaned forward in his seat as the steam-cab rumbled on. "So the Duke of Clarence, grandson of Queen Victoria and heir to the throne of the British Empire, falls in love and gets betrothed to a lowly tobacconist's assistant, and agents of the Crown . . . what? Murder her and steal her brain?"

"Your Mr. Reed said as much in his journals. I imagine the brain stealing was an afterthought. A mistake," said Bent. "W. dropped the ball on that, somewhat. He needed a brain for Einstein's experiments with the artifact, and W. needed to do away with someone. Happy coincidence." He paused. "Though not for Annie Crook, of course. And not for W, in the long run."

"So the Jack the Ripper killings can be ascribed to W, who wants the artifact back?" said Trigger. "Fascinating."

"And the brain," nodded Bent. "Because he couldn't have guessed at the time, but Einstein's experiments evidently preserved some of Annie's memories."

"Maria's dreams of London," said Gideon.

Bent nodded. "It's a bit of a jigsaw at the moment, and I'm not saying all the pieces fit properly. But I've survived thirty years in Fleet Street on hunches, and this one won't let go. As you say, Trigger, fascinating. But effing unprovable."

There was a sudden howling of dogs that caused them all to fall silent, and the driver pulled the steam-cab to a hissing halt. "We're here," he said. "Embankment."

"Will you wait for us?" Trigger asked the driver as he paid him. "We may need your services for the return journey."

Bent peered through the window. "We'll never see anything in that fog. Like trying to find an eel in a barrel of puke."

Then the night was rent by an ear-splitting scream.

❦

Enveloped in fog, Maria felt utterly alone, as though the rest of London had leaked away and there was only her, the thickening mist, and the terrible figure, inching toward her with painful deliberation. Its breathing came heavy and rhythmic, as though it was murmuring guttural but perversely comforting words in a language Maria had never heard.

"Why are you doing this?" she screamed. "Leave me alone!"

But still the figure walked on, closing the gap between them. The electric lights strung out along the river faded as the fog swallowed them, and Maria backed up as far as she could, coming up sharp against the balustrade separating the walkway from the river.

This had been what she wanted, wasn't it? Oblivion? To be thrown into the perpetual blackness? So why was the substance that passed for her blood hammering in her ears? Why did the collection of pistons, flywheels, and cogs in the place where her heart should be bang like a drum? Why did her cloth muscles clench and tighten as she readied to flee . . . or to fight? Could it be that Maria, the clockwork girl who was not alive, did not want to die?

She realized her revelation might have come too late. The dark shape was upon her, and with a fluid movement it tore off her bonnet. Finally, she saw its face.

But she had no time to recoil, as her instincts screamed at her to. Instead, Maria kicked her attacker in the shins and swung her arm, connecting with its head and knocking it off its feet. Now it was Maria's turn to stop in surprise. She looked at her hands as her assailant groaned at her feet. When had she become so strong? She had never had cause to use more strength than it took to pour a pot of tea, or undo the buttons on Crowe's breeches. But with all that clockwork and brass within her, those metal bones, the pistons and plumb-weights powering her limbs . . . well, was it any wonder? Professor Einstein had not merely given her life, he had created her. She was not inferior, by God. She was superior! It was not some evil soup flowing in her veins, but power. With a sneer, Maria aimed a kick at her attacker that snapped its head back; the creature fell upon the stone with a wet thud in a silent tangle of limbs. Maria had felled it. But what was it? She looked in horror at the figure on the cobbles.

"Maria!"

She turned, hoping against hope, as Gideon emerged, breathless, from the fog. Behind him were Captain Trigger and Mr. Bent, neither of them looking much the better for their exertions. But Gideon appeared as an avenging angel from the Old Testament, his dark, curly hair flying behind him as he ran, his white shirt plastered to his chest by the damp smog. He had come looking for her, her very own angel. He had come to her.

❧

"Maria!" cried Gideon again, and he ran up to embrace her. He felt as though his heart might burst. "Thank God we found you! But why did you—"

He paused, seeing the figure on the ground, and as Trigger and Bent puffed up he released his grip on Maria, feeling suddenly self-conscious. "Good God," he whispered.

"I was attacked," said Maria. "But it did not reckon on its victim fighting back."

Gideon turned to the motionless form on the ground. At last. The Faxmouth mummy, more horrible in the flesh than he could ever have imagined. Its limbs were thin and wiry, desiccated yet muscular. Its head was bulbous and gray, with huge orbs staring sightlessly at the fog-bound sky. Its mouth was indeed froglike and elongated, with rows of black, slavering teeth stretched in a perverse grin.

"But what is it doing in London?" said Gideon. He felt a sudden swell of something bigger than himself, something that threatened to swamp him. For the first time since leaving Sandsend he was aware that he was no longer driving his own destiny. He was being swept along. But toward what?

"Smith," Bent said to him. "Smith. Snap out of it. How many of these things did you say there were?"

Gideon blinked and looked at Bent. "What? One, of course."

He followed Bent's outstretched arms, and the journalist said, "Then what the eff are these buggers?"

All around them shapes were melting out of the fog, rangy, thin figures hissing and muttering in unison, their claws outstretched.

"That's twelve I make it, counting the one out cold on the floor," said Trigger. "Anyone got a plan?"

Bent let loose a long, wet fart. "Eff to a plan, does anybody have a *gun*?"

Gideon braced himself for their attack . . . just as a furry thunderbolt howled out of the fog and slammed into the ghoul.

❧

At an unspoken signal from Bathory, the dogs that had gathered in a frenzied, panting pack by the stone balustrade near the river surged forward with a great howling and barking.

Bathory stood with her cloak gathered about her and watched them go, Stoker wringing his hands by her side.

"I shall let Varney's curs soften them up first," she said. "But the last thing the final one standing will see before it falls will be my face."

She strode after the dogs, Stoker running to keep up with her. Ahead, through the mist, they heard the battle being joined . . . and human voices among the clamor.

"There are people there!" said Stoker.

They ran together through the curling fog to where the transmogrified vampire hounds wrestled with a dozen or more of the Children of Heqet as though, thought Stoker, in some obscene netherworld dinner dance. Stoker waved at the huddle of figures by the balustrade, a young couple and an older, white-haired man, as frail looking as the fourth—a portly, shabby gent—was fat. "Hi!" he called. "Over here!"

"Get them to safety," Bathory said. "Varney's dogs are not coming out of this too well."

"The odds are too great," said Stoker as the four people began to sidle along the balustrade away from the combat. "You cannot engage them."

Bathory looked at him, her eyes shining terribly. "I must." She laid a hand on his arm. "Bram, you must stop thinking of me as one of your polite London ladies. You have seen what I can do. But . . . if I fall in battle . . . I thank you for your assistance. You are a good man."

"Elizabeth . . . ," began Stoker, but he didn't know how to finish.

Madly, impossibly, he wanted to take her into his arms and kiss her. Instead he shook his head and did as she asked, stealing around the battle toward the group, his eyes widening with recognition.

"Gideon! Gideon Smith!" he called.

Gideon tore his eyes away from the slaughter at the sound of the lilting, Irish voice hollering through the mist. "Mr. Stoker!"

he cried. "But what are you doing here . . . and with the mummies?"

"A long and complicated tale," said Stoker, glancing back at Bathory, who still stood watching the carnage. "I suggest we get away from here."

"First effing words of sense anybody's spoken all day," said Bent, thrusting his hand at Stoker. "Aloysius Bent, of the *Illustrated London Argus*. You're Bram Stoker, ain't you? Do a bit of theater reviewing for us, from time to time?"

"I've got a long story of my own," said Gideon. Stoker's appearance had gladdened his heart; at the same time it reinforced his belief that he was being carried along by forces larger and more powerful than he could have guessed at.

"Can we please effing hear these long stories anywhere but effing here?" pleaded Bent.

"Bram!"

Gideon turned to the woman who stood watching the last of the dogs fall beneath the claws of the mummies. She was in full view, her black hair falling in curls around her long cloak. But the creatures were ignoring her and turning back toward Gideon's group.

"Run!" cried the woman. "I don't know what they are about . . ."

They ran. Gideon was first to the waiting steam-cab, rattling at the doors as the driver looked up from his newspaper. "Back to Grosvenor Square!" he gasped.

"Whoa!" said the driver. "Six? I'm only licensed to carry four passengers."

"Drive!" demanded Gideon through gritted teeth as he hauled the door closed. "Just drive!"

Bent and Trigger squeezed into the narrow forward-facing seat with Stoker's companion—who was so breathtakingly, exotically beautiful that she took Gideon's breath away—sandwiched between them. Stoker and Maria sat on the pull-down chairs facing the rear of the cab, leaving Gideon to squat in the foot-well as the steam-cab laboriously began to putter along Embankment.

Bent took the opportunity to give the woman a leisurely once-over. "Blimey," he said. "*Tout le monde sur le balcon*, as the Frenchies say. Whom do I have the pleasure of addressing?"

"This is Countess Elizabeth Bathory, my traveling companion," said Stoker.

"So you didn't find Dracula, then?" asked Gideon.

"No," said Stoker. "But we found your mummies, Mr. Smith. We have had quite an adventure. I got your message, and your magazine. Countess Bathory has faced the Children of Heqet before. They appear to be foul creatures that worship an ancient Egyptian deity. All rather fascinating. If deadly. We encountered them deep within the tunnels of that promontory near your home, Mr. Smith."

"Lythe Bank?" said Gideon. "You went into Lythe Bank?"

"And barely escaped with our lives," said Stoker. "Others weren't so lucky. We found a pile of freshly picked bones—" He paused and his hand flew to his mouth. "Oh, Mr. Smith. Oh, how insensitive of me. I am so sorry. . . ." He dug into his pocket and presented something to Gideon. "I found this. I'm not sure why I picked it up, nor if it means anything to you, but I thought it might belong to one of the dead men . . . do you recognize it, at all?"

Was it suddenly hot in the cab? Gideon felt a flush rise on his cheeks, needles pricking his eyes. Bones. Picked clean. And Stoker placed in his trembling hand the charm he had made for his daddy so long ago, the piece of Whitby jet he'd made into a good-luck charm. So the things had killed his father, after all. And his charm had brought Arthur Smith no luck.

"Stop the cab," he said quietly. "There needs to be a reckoning. We must go back and finish them off."

"Caution, Gideon," said Trigger. "A wise man knows when to fight, and when to retreat. We have no weapons, and you saw what they did to those dogs."

"I very much fear the battle might be coming back to us whether we like it or not," said Maria. "Look."

Gideon looked through the glass window and beyond the hissing steam engine mounted on the back of the cab. Something was following, catching them up at a terrific speed. It was tall and rangy, its limbs flailing as it pounded the road, gaining on them alarmingly.

"Christ, look at the effing speed of the thing," said Bent.

"Am I stopping, then?" called the driver.

"No!" said Gideon. "Faster!"

Bathory let loose a low, most uncountesslike growl as the mummy closed the final yards between them and leaped, landing on all fours on the engine. Bent recoiled from the window as it lunged forward, its mouth wide open, its milky eyes narrowed.

The driver glanced over his shoulder at the commotion and yelled, "What's that? What's on my cab?"

Gideon turned to him, peering through the front windscreen. "Drive!" he commanded. "What's that, up ahead?"

"Cleopatra's Needle," said the driver, as the back window smashed to a yell from Bent. "Who's breaking up my cab?"

"Head for that needle," said Gideon, and turned back to see the mummy's vicious claws raking the air of the cab. Its face was at the smashed window, uttering guttural sounds and hisses.

"What's it saying?" moaned Bent, bending forward from the waving claws.

"A language not heard for thousands of years," said Stoker.

"Perhaps it will understand this, then," said Gideon, grabbing Trigger's cane and forcing the metal tip into the forehead of the beast. It recoiled at the impact, then hissed loudly and lunged again.

Gideon continued to hit the thing as Maria screamed. Bathory muttered, "If I could turn around . . ."

"No," said Stoker. "Not here, Countess, I beg you. . . ."

Gideon ignored them and turned to Trigger. "Remember *The Bowie Steamcrawlers*?"

The mummy grasped hold of Bent's collar and the journalist screamed, "Gideon! This is not the time for reminiscing about the effing penny bloods!"

"I believe I know where Mr. Smith is going with this," said Trigger, pushing himself against the door to avoid the mummy's raking claws. "Of course I do, Gideon."

Gideon leaned forward and forced the cane hard into the mummy's mouth, wrestling with it as though it were the brake-shaft of a gearship until the creature fell back, clinging to the engine. "You—I mean, Dr. Reed—defeated Jim Bowie during a battle on an out-of-control steam engine on the Arkansas trail," he said through gritted teeth. "As I recall, Dr. Reed knocked the gasket off the engine, sending a cloud of steam—"

"Try that brass gasket-head directly beneath the thing's chest," suggested Trigger.

Gideon leaned forward just as the mummy forced itself through the smashed window and took hold of Gideon's hair. It appeared to smile wickedly, then opened its slavering mouth to deliver the fatal blow. Just as it had done to his father, no doubt. With renewed strength, Gideon flailed for the gasket with the cane as the thing pulled him toward it.

"Mr. Smith!" called Maria. "Oh, Mr. Smith!"

Gideon could feel the creature's fetid breath on his cheek. He closed his eyes and stabbed forward with the cane, and felt it connect with the brass gasket just as the steam-cab swerved to the left. "This is for my daddy," he whispered.

The explosion of steam thrust the mummy upward and outward, causing it to scrabble for purchase on the engine as it slipped toward the road. It grunted and grinned again, jabbering in its dead language as the steam hissed in its face. It was a good plan, but not good enough. Gideon pulled a face and stabbed at it again with the cane, which it deftly grabbed in its claws. The creature swung out over the road, tore the cane from Gideon's grasp, and then disintegrated in a mess of black ichor and gray flesh as it slammed into the side of Cleopatra's Needle.

The steam-cab, its engine dead, rolled to a halt. For a moment no one spoke, then Bent looked out of the window. "I can't see any more of the effers, but I shouldn't think we want to hang around here."

Gideon let himself out and went to inspect the remains of the mummy, dripping from the edge of the obelisk covered in Egyptian hieroglyphics, as the driver began to remonstrate with Trigger.

"I have given the driver a personal check," said Trigger, appearing at his elbow. "We should depart."

"Sorry," said Gideon, still staring at the remains of the mummy. "I'll pay you back. Somehow."

"Nonsense!" said Trigger. "Most excitement I've had in years. You saved our lives, Mr. Smith. Excellent work." He looked into the mist. "Still, we should get home. To Grosvenor Square. Let us head up Northumberland Street and find some transport, before word gets out and we're blacklisted by every cab driver in London."

Gideon stared into the mist. The Children of Heqet. Had they followed him to London? For what purpose? He turned to where the others waited. Enigmas, puzzles, and mysteries, the lot of them. He felt a sudden weight in his stomach, a longing and sickness for home. Maria was smiling, and he realized he didn't really know where home was, anymore.

Could he truly say it was back in the cottage in Sandsend, which would be cold and dark and dead with the absence of Arthur Smith? It was an emptiness that could never be filled, not even if Gideon went back there and filled it with a wife and children and grandchildren. His father had gone, and with it any notion Gideon had of home. Home was a transient thing now, ever shifting, walled in by the desire for justice, its hearth burning with the cold flames of revenge.

Gideon watched the black ichor drip from the monument. One down, thought Gideon. God knows how many to go. But he wouldn't rest until he'd hunted them all, and laid Arthur Smith properly to rest.

17

The Last Testament of Annie Crook

That night was what Gideon had dreamed of all his life. To be in such company, telling such tales. The moon was full and the fog was thick, and despite the season there was a chill in the air, so Mrs. Cadwallader built a small fire in the hearth. They drank ruby red wine and ate their chops and looked at each other, these strangers brought together by wild circumstance. One by one they told their stories, and Bent wore pencils to stubs as he furiously took down their words in shorthand in his rapidly filling notebook.

When they all had finished, Bent shook his head. "I wouldn't have believed it if I hadn't seen those things over on Embankment. If they hadn't nearly effing killed me." He paused and flicked through his notes. "This story's getting bigger and more complex by the hour. But a theme's running through everything. Egypt, of course. This bloody pyramid John Reed went off to find. The Children of Heqet. Our Mr. W. And . . ." He looked up. "Maria. Or should I say, Annie Crook?"

They all looked at Maria, who had been silent throughout the proceedings. Gideon said gently, "There are things we need to tell you, Maria."

She looked at her hands, knotted in her lap. "And things I must tell you, Mr. Smith. You are aware, of course, that I have dreams of London. When I left you at Highgate Aerodrome I followed the paths I had walked in my dreams. They took me to Cleveland Street."

Gideon felt Bent lean forward beside him. "And what did you see there, Miss Maria? What did you learn?"

She looked the journalist in the eye. "I met a man called

Sickert. I . . . remembered him." She tapped her forehead. "Or rather, what is in here did. He told me of Annie Crook, found without a brain. I know what I am now. Not human, not a machine. An unholy composite of both."

"Are . . . are you Annie Crook?" asked Gideon slowly.

She shook her head. "No, Mr. Smith, I am not Annie Crook."

"But you have her brain . . . ," said Bent. "And her memories."

"The memories are like half-forgotten dreams," said Maria softly. "Like stories I was told long ago and only barely remember. They do not feel as though they happened to me."

Trigger sat back thoughtfully in his chair. "Modern science tells us the brain is matter and electrical impulses. Can that truly be said to be what makes a person who they are?" He looked at Bent and placed his hand on his chest. "My heart aches because of the loss of John. But does it, really? My heart is a fleshy pump feeding blood to my organs. It is not truly where love resides, except in the language of poets. I cannot even begin to understand the miracle Hermann Einstein performed when he created his automaton and married the human brain of Annie Crook to the Atlantic Artifact within her. I should imagine Einstein himself does not fully understand it. I believe Maria is greater than the sum of her parts; she is Maria, and the life driving her is as much a mystery as that which animates our own earthly bodies."

Maria smiled at Trigger, and Gideon noticed her eyes were wet. He quietly dug into his satchel and took out Einstein's journal. "Maria," he said softly. "I took this from the laboratory. It . . . well, you should read it. It might help you understand a little more. I should not have kept it from you."

She took the book and looked at its dark leather cover. "Thank you, Mr. Smith." She looked up. "And thank you, Captain Trigger. Is there somewhere private I may go?"

"I shall have Mrs. Cadwallader show you to your room," said Trigger.

"One more thing," said Bent. "Miss Maria . . . do you recall anything about why you—rather, Annie Crook—might have been killed so terribly?"

Maria looked into the middle distance. "For love," she said eventually. "Forbidden love. With Eddy."

Bent slapped his hand on his thigh and chuckled. "At last. Gotcha. I effing knew it."

Maria, holding the journal to her breast, paused at the door. "Oh, and I remember one more thing. The last thing Annie Crook recalled before she died. You mentioned someone you refer to as W?"

Trigger looked up. "Yes?"

"I believe you may be referring to the man who murdered Annie Crook," said Maria. "His name is Walsingham."

As Maria left there was a knock at the door, and Mrs. Cadwallader hurried to answer it. She appeared at the study and said, "Captain Trigger, delivery men . . ."

"I took the liberty of telegraphing the Aerodrome and having Countess Bathory's things delivered here," said Stoker. "Captain Trigger had indicated there may be rooms for the night . . . ?"

"Of course," said Trigger, frowning as the deliverymen manhandled Bathory's long wooden box up the stairs. Gideon watched the arrivals with interest. There was more to Countess Bathory than either she or Stoker was telling, he thought. Their story of her arrival in Whitby and their subsequent encounters with the mummies had not been as thorough as Gideon might have expected from a writer of Stoker's stature.

The Countess smiled at Trigger. Was there something in that smile that spoke to Gideon of a strange darkness he could not identify? She said, "I do, unfortunately, travel with a great deal of baggage, Captain Trigger. I hope it does not inconvenience you overmuch."

"Not at all," said Trigger. He poured brandy for those who wanted it. "Now that we have told our stories, though, what now?"

"The writer in me demands some kind of concordance," said Stoker thoughtfully. "Where did it all begin? That's the ticket. To begin at the beginning."

"*The Shadow Over Faxmouth*," said Gideon. "Captain Trigger—well, John Reed, really—and the adventure in Arkhamville."

"Quite," agreed Trigger. "That was the first sighting of one of the Children of Heqet, though it was dormant and little more than a mummified grotesque. What revived it, I wonder?"

"It stole an item Professor Halifax had found on a previous trip to Egypt," said Gideon. "Could the proximity of the pendant have effected some kind of awakening in the thing?"

"When did all this supposedly happen?" asked Bent.

"Autumn of 1887," said Trigger.

Bent said, "What happened next? Old Hermann Einstein—wherever the hell *he* is now—was delivered of this Atlantic Artifact, which we now know to be inside the head of Maria, in January 1888."

"Evidently the Children of Heqet somehow knew of this," said Trigger, "and began their search for it. I wonder why they waited so long to strike?"

"Perhaps they had other items to plunder?" suggested Bathory.

Trigger held up a finger. "Or . . . what did Einstein's manservant say? There was some disruptor device. . . ."

"Quite," said Trigger. "If Einstein's paranoia about having the Atlantic Artifact stolen from him led him to create a suitable . . . I don't know, masking device, perhaps this clouded the Children of Heqet's talent for being able to locate the thing."

Stoker said, "So you suggest that once Maria left Einstein's house, and the influence of his disrupter, this made the Children of Heqet aware of its existence again, and they followed the trail to London?"

Bent pinched his nose between his thumb and forefinger.

"This is making my head hurt. Let's look at this from a different perspective. The mummies are after certain items. The scarab stolen from Countess Bathory; whatever they were digging for in Sandsend; the pendant John Reed acquired from Arkhamville University; and the artifact in Maria's head."

"Those notes from John Reed," said Gideon. "The break-in at the British Museum, where the guard was horribly murdered. A . . . figurine was stolen."

"The *shabti*." Captain Trigger nodded. "Of Egyptian origin."

"And now they have them all," said Stoker. He glanced at Trigger and coughed. "Presuming, of course, they managed to wrest the pendant from Dr. Reed in Egypt."

"I do not think there is any doubt," said Trigger. "John went in search of the Rhodopis Pyramid. He cannot have failed to encounter the Children of Heqet." His eyes fell. "And even he cannot have resisted those monsters."

There was an uncomfortable silence in the room. Bathory sat forward. "What were your plans?"

"We had arranged transport to Egypt," said Trigger. "We thought to look for John, so he could perhaps aid Mr. Smith with his troubles in Sandsend. Events seem to have overtaken us, though. The mummies are here in London . . . or at least were." He looked at Gideon. "It was your suggestion that we go to Egypt, Mr. Smith. Your home is no longer under threat. What do you wish to do now?"

Gideon opened his mouth, then paused. Trigger was right. The Children of Heqet no longer threatened Sandsend—they had gotten what they wanted, whatever had been buried within Lythe Bank in years or centuries past by smugglers or pirates. His quest was over. But he had promised Maria he would help her find Professor Einstein. He had a duty to Maria; he had made her a promise. And whether it was John Reed or Lucian Trigger who was truly the Hero of the Empire, Gideon knew one thing: Heroes kept their promises.

"I need to speak to Maria," he said. He would tell her he

was now free of his commitments and could devote his energies to searching for Professor Einstein. The thought of returning to Sandsend didn't occur to him until he stood on the carpeted landing at the top of the stairs. Return to Sandsend? Fish the shallows in the *Cold Drake*? Where running around London in the company of Captain Trigger had once seemed the highest, most improbable fantasy, now it was his old life that was beyond him. A warm breeze emerged from the billowing curtains at the end of the hallway, caressing his face, bringing with it the smells and faint clamor of London. He closed the gap between the top of the stairs and Maria's room, the middle one of three guest bedrooms, and placed his hand on the doorknob.

18

Clockwork Wishes

With each page Maria turned in the journal of her creator, she felt the memories of Annie Crook receding, becoming events that had happened to someone else. She wasn't angry that Gideon had kept the journal from her; she could see why he might have thought it would prove upsetting to her. That he considered her feelings—that he considered she could *have* feelings at all—caused whatever beat invisibly in her breast in place of a heart to hammer all the harder. In fact, reading the coldly scientific methods and results outlined by Einstein made her feel *better*. What man or woman truly knew where they came from, other than the collision of biology that brought sperm and egg together? It was the great question of the age, the desire to know what was the essential, mysterious spark giving self-awareness and humanity to mankind. Thanks to Einstein's journals, Maria had more idea than most people what animated her. And she was just as much a mystery as any flesh-and-blood woman. A brain, a clockwork body, a mysterious artifact. Who was to say her own life wasn't as God-given as anyone else's?

Since her adventures alone she had resolved to be less dependent on others. While living in Einstein's house she could always rely on the Professor or Crowe—loathsome, horrible Crowe! How she longed to pummel his face in with her newfound strength!—to wind her when required. Alone in the room she practiced winding herself, finally finding a position that allowed her, albeit awkwardly and slowly, to insert the key in the brass aperture and turn it until she felt strength and vitality in her clockwork muscles. She had asked Mrs. Cadwallader for a needle and thread and had sewn the small cotton bag that held her key tightly to her dress; she would not risk being without it, ever again.

However . . . with her liberty came something else. Her acceptance of what she was—and what she wasn't, because thanks to Captain Trigger she now knew she most definitely wasn't Annie Crook—had brought a thing she had never dared allow herself.

Hope.

Hope that she might live her own life. Hope that she might make her own way in the world. And . . . could she even think it? Hope that even she, Maria the clockwork girl, could find . . . love?

Mr. Gideon Smith. When he had appeared out of the fog on Embankment, she had almost swooned. Handsome, strong Gideon Smith. He had no family, very much like herself; no roots laid down, but instead a desire to see the world and all it offered; a thirst for adventure. The horizon never came any closer, no matter how far you traveled, considered Maria. Wouldn't it be a thing, to chase that horizon, for ever and ever? And wouldn't it be a thing to do it with Mr. Gideon Smith by her side?

She sighed again, recognizing the tiny differences in the emotions that seemed to emerge almost constantly now, since she had confronted what she thought she might be in Cleveland Street, and since she had learned what she actually was. This sigh was flecked with longing and fear. Mr. Smith had shown her kindness, but not love. She closed her eyes and wished very hard that he might come to her there and then.

One step at a time. Clockwork girls might be allowed life, of a sort. But were clockwork girls allowed wishes?

She started, and smiled, as she heard the soft padding of feet on the carpet outside her room, and very slowly the polished doorknob began to turn. Perhaps, just perhaps, they were.

Gideon paused with his hand on the doorknob, his fist raised to knock gently on the paneled wood. The breeze from the open window kissed his face once more, the curtains twisting and revealing the full, fat moon in the sky—framed within the jagged outline of shards of glass. Gideon frowned and let go of the door. The carpet beneath the small window was littered with smashed glass. Something had broken it.

Someone had entered the house.

Too late, he remembered the conversations downstairs. If the Children of Heqet had traced Maria to London all the way from Sandsend, what on earth had made Trigger and the others think she would be safe in Mayfair? With dread he flung open the door to Maria's room to find it empty. A tall-backed chair lay on its side, and Einstein's journal was cast haphazardly on the polished wooden floor. The bay window was open, the curtains blowing fiercely in the wind.

Maria, once again, was gone.

"Gone?" asked Bent. "She can't stay in one place for ten minutes, that one."

"She hasn't wandered off this time," said Gideon. "She's been taken."

He led them upstairs to the room and showed them the smashed window. Trigger said, "We can't be sure it was the Children of Heqet. . . ."

Stoker turned to Bathory. "You did not sense anything?"

Bent was on him, sharp as a tack. "Sense anything? What do you mean?"

Stoker coughed. "Countess Bathory has . . . she can sometimes know where the Children of Heqet are."

"No, Bram, I did not," said Bathory. To the others she said, "I do have certain . . . abilities. But they must be fueled. By . . ."

"By fuel we do not have," said Stoker quickly.

Gideon shook his head. "We must find Maria. Bent, can't you get those urchins on it again?"

"The Fleet Street Irregulars?" Bent scratched his head. "It's late. Even mudlarks like that have to sleep sometime. Besides, we got very lucky earlier."

"They won't be in London now," said Bathory. "Not with a prize like Maria in their grasp. They have the Atlantic Artifact. They'll be taking it back."

"Back?" said Gideon.

Bathory shrugged. "Have we not established that the Children of Heqet are connected in some way to the Rhodopis Pyramid? It makes sense they would head there with their bounty."

"And to whoever's waiting for them." Bent nodded. "Mr. effing Walsingham, my money's on."

"Gideon," said Trigger, "while you were up here we decided we would still travel to Egypt tomorrow. I need to know what happened to John. Countess Bathory wishes to take vengeance against the Children of Heqet—and whoever their master might be—for the murder of her husband. Mr. Stoker is accompanying the Countess, and Mr. Bent . . ."

"Mr. Bent's not letting go of the story of the decade," Bent said, cackling. "What about you, Smith?"

Gideon looked back at the broken window. Maria had trusted him, had thought she was safe. He had let her down. He said, "Then I'm going to Egypt as well."

"Just one thing," said Bent. "We're not exactly the Duke of Cornwall's Light effing Infantry, are we? In fact, the only weapon we seem to have is Trigger's cane, and that didn't come off too well against that thing back on Embankment—though Mr. Smith was exceedingly inventive with it."

Trigger allowed himself a small smile. "Mr. Bent, I think it's time I showed you the armory."

❧

"John did like to collect items from his various adventures," said Trigger as he opened the doors to the first-floor room. "And weaponry was no exception."

"Good Christ," said Bent as he wandered into the long,

narrow room. Rifles were ranked in cases all down one wall, and handguns were fixed to boards on the opposite side. Further down there were trays of grenades and larger, industrial-looking machines of war and killing that Trigger and Reed had collected over many years.

"We should perhaps take one or two items, as insurance," suggested Stoker.

Bent, his eyes shining, took down a four-barreled revolver from the wall. Trigger smiled. "The Lancaster. Fitted to take brass cartridges. Quite a kick."

"I'll take it," said Bent. He turned to the rifles. "Hang on, though . . . what's this?"

"Ah," said Trigger proudly. "The Lee-Enfield bolt-action repeater. One of John's favorites. Very new in design."

Bent put it down and selected a larger weapon. "This?"

"The Martini-Enfield. Rechambered to take .303 cartridges. You have to watch for inferior Khyber Pass copies; that's an original."

"I like it," said Bent, hefting it to his shoulder. Then his eyes widened. "Oh. Oh, good effing Christ."

He laid down the Martini-Enfield and walked reverently to a huge, gray barrel mounted on a tripod. "What is *this*?" he whispered.

Trigger smiled. "The QF three-pounder Hotchkiss. Designed as a coastal defense anti-dirigible gun."

"I'm having this," Bent said. "In fact, I'm taking them all."

"Mr. Bent, the Hotchkiss fires three-pound shells. I do not think Miss Fanshawe will be enamored of the extra weight."

"Miss Fanshawe can kiss my arse," said Bent. "She isn't going looking for blood-crazed mummies with teeth like a butcher's knife rack. Don't bother to wrap 'em, Trigger, I'll take them as they are."

Gideon took in his hand a straight-bladed, hilted sword. Trigger nodded. He liked the boy. He had a certain . . . simplicity of approach Trigger appreciated. "The Pattern Infantry Officer's Sword. Not yet in common use among the forces, but about to be rolled out, as I understand. John had very good contacts in the weapons industry."

"This will do for me," said Gideon, turning the sword so the blade caught the light from the electric lamps on the wall. "When I meet the Children of Heqet again, I want to be close enough to see the look in their eyes when they die."

Stoker awoke just after dawn, while the rest of the house was sleeping. Mrs. Cadwallader fixed him a breakfast of scrambled eggs, and he asked her to inform Captain Trigger and the rest he would be back before they departed for Highgate. Then he let himself out into the warm morning and went in search of a cab.

He liked London best in the morning, just before the bustle and squalor rose to the surface. On those rare quiet moments the city reminded him of Dublin, and if he closed his eyes he could imagine himself walking down Grafton Street or over the Ha'penny Bridge. Not for long, though; he was always brought short by a screeching cockney twang or the clank and hiss of some mechanical marvel or other. He hurried to hail a steam-cab and it conveyed him in no time at all to St. George's Square. He stood for a long time outside the door to number twenty-six, feeling as though he were some adulterer returning with his tail between his legs.

Despite the hour, Florence was in the kitchen, drinking tea while Adelaide prepared breakfast. She looked up at him, but her eyes betrayed no emotion; it was as though she had only seen him an hour before, not several weeks ago.

"Ah," she said. "You have returned."

"How is Noel?" asked Stoker, taking off his hat.

"Asleep," said Florence, sipping her tea.

"And in general?"

"Tolerable," she said. "He will be pleased to see you."

Stoker stared at his hands. "I cannot stay long."

Florence dismissed the maid, who hurried away, and looked at him. "So now we have it. You have come to tell me you have made a match with another, and you are leaving us. Or, rather, you want us out of here, so you can set up home with the other woman. Noel and myself are to put ourselves on the mercy of the parish, are we? Is it to be the poorhouse for us? The life of a street urchin for him?"

Stoker looked at his wife in horror. "Florence! What are you talking about?"

Tears flowed from her eyes freely. "You have hardly made a secret of it!" she said with controlled fury. "Hardly been discreet! Why, you are the talk of Whitby, Bram, and most of London, too. Gallivanting around in the company of some . . . some *strumpet*!"

The penny, finally, dropped. "Elizabeth?" he said. "You mean Elizabeth?"

"So she has a name!" said Florence, her lip trembling.

Stoker paused. How exactly was he going to explain this? "She is a noblewoman from Transylvania."

"How awfully exotic."

"Her name is Elizabeth Bathory. Countess Bathory. I have been assisting her with a problem."

"I daresay you have. While I have been here, nursing your sick son, you have been walking arm-in-arm with Countess Elizabeth Bathory, and holding secret assignations in the ruins of the abbey in Whitby. Oh, Bram, how could you? We took romantic walks there ourselves, have you forgotten?"

"No, of course not," he said, pinching his nose.

Her face crumpled. "Is she very beautiful, Bram? Is she younger than me?"

He laughed, this time without humor. "Younger? No. No, she is much older."

Florence looked at him with red-rimmed eyes. "Then why? Why have you abandoned us?"

He stepped forward and took her in his arms, despite her protestations. "You silly, silly old thing," he murmured. "I have not abandoned you. I do not feel that way about the Countess. It is merely . . ."

"Merely what, Bram?" she said, looking up at him, desperate to trust him.

He sighed. "I doubt you would believe me. But I must ask you to have faith."

"Father?"

He turned to see Noel standing at the door, rubbing sleep from his eyes. Stoker went to hug his son and held him at arm's length. "You are at least twice as strong as you were when I saw you last," he said.

"Are you home, father?" asked Noel, yawning.

Stoker turned to Florence. "I shall be, soon. I must first make a journey, but then I will come back and get you and we shall all repair to Whitby for the remainder of the summer."

"A journey?" said Florence. "To where?"

"Egypt."

"Egypt?" said Florence, aghast. "Bram, you are not serious."

He kissed her on the forehead. "I am, my darling. And I must go, now."

She shook her head. "I will not allow it. Egypt! Fancy!"

Stoker held her hands, and kissed them also. "I must, Florence. I will return. It should not take long."

"And is *she* going? Your Countess Elizabeth Bathory?"

He could not lie. "She is."

Florence's face hardened into a spiteful mask he had never seen before. She said, "Then go, if that is your will. But you should consider yourself very lucky if you have a family waiting for you when you choose to return."

"Please, Florence." He was not too proud to beg. "I must do this."

"You will do what you wish," she said, her words heavy with ice. "Do not worry yourself unduly about your son and your wife."

"Not in front of the boy," murmured Stoker, looking into Noel's wide eyes.

Florence snorted. "If only you were so discreet yourself."

With a heavy heart, Stoker kissed Noel on his head and let himself out into the sunshine. Despite his protestations, he still felt as though he had, in fact, betrayed Florence, that he was lying to her. Elizabeth was indeed very beautiful, and he could not deny her presence excited and thrilled him. He turned to see Florence at the window, staring sadly at him. She had been ever so good to him, allowing him his time to go off to Whitby and seek inspiration for his story. He had taken her goodwill for granted, and he had now stretched it to its limits.

He had gone to Whitby in search of art and ended up chasing monsters. Now, as he put his hat on his head and hurried to find a cab to take him back to Grosvenor Square, he briefly wondered if he had not, at least in the eyes of his beloved wife and son, become one.

To Egypt!

Rowena Fanshawe was waiting for them by the *Skylady II.* She wore black boots to her knees and a pair of tight jodhpurs. Gideon marveled at how little they left to the imagination regarding the lower regions of her female shape. Above the jodhpurs she had a crisp white shirt, the top three buttons open, and on her head was a brown leather helmet, upon which perched a pair of leather goggles with round glass lenses. Bent nudged Gideon as they unloaded their bags from the steam carriage. "She scrubs up well."

"The old girl's wound up and ready to fly," said Fanshawe. She looked at the assembly. "Passenger manifest changed somewhat since yesterday? No luck finding the girl?"

Trigger stepped forward and embraced Fanshawe. "We found Miss Maria, but she was cruelly snatched from us again. We believe she may well already be on her way to Egypt."

"White slavers?" frowned Fanshawe.

"Worse," said Trigger. "It is a long, fantastic story; its telling will give us something to do to while away the long journey."

Fanshawe cocked her head to one side and Gideon saw her regarding him as he piled cases up on the rough dirt. "I can think of one or two diversions to help pass the time," she said with a half smile. "But I'll listen to your story, Lucian. Who's the lady?"

Bathory stepped forward and held out her hand. "Countess Elizabeth Bathory," she said, inclining her head. "You are a brave woman, Miss Fanshawe, piloting this dirigible. It is an activity that I believe is commonly referred to as men's work."

Fanshawe shrugged. "I get by. You're awful beautiful, Countess."

Bathory smiled. "And you are as bold as you are brave, Miss Fanshawe."

"And this is Bram Stoker," said Trigger.

Stoker kissed Fanshawe's hand, and she said, "You're a writer, yes? Have I read some of your literary reviews in the *London Telegraph*?"

"How come she knows his stuff but has never read mine?" complained Bent.

Stoker looked impressed. "To Countess Bathory's list of adjectives I would add *intelligent* and, if I may dare, *beautiful* also."

Fanshawe waved him away with a small laugh, and Gideon felt Bent's elbow in his ribs. The journalist whispered in his ear, "She's got it all, that girl. And a pretty good rack with it. I tell you, son, you could be in there like a rat up a drainpipe." Gideon made a face and whispered for him to be quiet, but Bent ignored him and turned to glance at Bathory. "Maybe we could bunk up on a double date, you and the flygirl and me and the Countess."

As Bathory moved forward to admire the dirigible, she paused by Gideon and Bent and murmured, "I have exceptionally good hearing, Mr. Bent. Like a bat, you might say."

Gideon suppressed a smirk as Bent coughed and reddened. "Ah, well, Countess, no disrespect, and all that."

She gave him a smile. "It would be a *very* cold day in hell when I found myself in your arms, sir."

Bent shrugged cheerfully. "Worse things happen at sea, Countess. Never say never." He tapped the side of his nose and winked at Gideon.

Fanshawe went to survey the baggage that had been unloaded from the steam carriage. "What's in the big box?"

"That is mine," said Bathory. "I am afraid it is vital that it accompanies us. Will it be a problem?"

Fanshawe shook her head. "We aren't taking other cargo, and five passengers plus me isn't a problem for the *Skylady II*." She paused. "Anyone flown in a 'stat before?"

Gideon certainly hadn't and was keen to get on board. Stoker said, "We traveled to London on a passenger dirigible."

Fanshawe grinned. "I'm afraid you won't get the same level of luxury here, Mr. Stoker. Let me show you around the old girl."

Gideon followed Fanshawe up the steps into the cramped cabin of the gondola. The pilot waited until they were all in, Stoker having to crouch beneath the low roof, and said, "This is the communal area. Space is at a premium, so there are fold-down tables and seats fixed into the wall."

She indicated an oval doorway. "Back there's the general hold. Sometimes I leave it as one big space for cargo; as we don't have much I've divided it with drapes into sleeping quarters. Don't expect too much in the way of privacy."

"I'm happy to share with the Countess, if space is a problem," said Bent.

Bathory gave him a withering look. "You wouldn't want to, Mr. Bent. I shall need to be with my belongings, especially the long box."

Fanshawe nodded. "That can go at the back. We have a basic water closet and washroom, so there'll be no baths, I'm afraid."

"No problem for me," sniffed Bent.

Fanshawe turned the other way and squeezed past Gideon to open another oval door. He pressed himself against the inner hull of the 'stat but still felt the contours of her body traversing his chest. "In here's the cockpit. There's two seats, room for me and a copilot if necessary." She looked at them in turn. "I like to instruct someone in the basics once we're up, just in case."

"In case what?" asked Bent.

She shrugged. "In case I die. If that happens, you'll still want to have the best chance of landing in one piece. Mr. Smith, might I select you for the role?"

Gideon nodded. "If you like." He was going to be shown how to fly an airship, after all those times watching the dirigibles passing impossibly high and out of reach over Sandsend.

He'd never really thought he'd even get to ride in one as a passenger in his lifetime.

"Excellent," said Fanshawe. She looked at her watch, bound to her wrist on a brown leather strap. "Well, if you'd like to get your equipment loaded and make yourselves comfortable, we're nearing our slot for takeoff."

"How long shall we be in the air?" asked Stoker.

"If the wind is with us, I'd hope to be in Alexandria by nightfall tomorrow," said Fanshawe.

Stoker sighed and whispered to Trigger, "That's a long time to be cooped up. I rather wish we had persuaded Mr. Bent to bathe this morning."

"I heard that," said Bent. He grinned at Bathory. "Ears like a dog, me."

"If we're ready, you can pull the seats down and sit tight while I run the preliminary checks," said Fanshawe. "Then we can be off. Mr. Smith? Would you care to join me in the cockpit?"

The cockpit was tight, with two leather chairs close together and an instrument panel in front of them that Gideon found remarkably simple. Four glass windows looked out on the airfield. Fanshawe tapped the dials and levers in turn. "This is the altimeter, tells us how high we're flying. That one shows us the airspeed. This is the pressure gauge for the balloon, and if that drops past this red line here, we're in trouble. This is the winding meter—tells us when we need cranking up again. We use the steering wheel to angle the ailerons and take us to the left or right, pull it forward to lift and push to descend. That toggle puts the wipers on if we run into snow or rain. This down between us is the crank-brake; we let it go when we're airborne and it lets the clockwork engine power the propellers. And that's about it. Have a go with the wheel, get used to the feel of her."

Gideon turned the wheel to one side, and then the other, pushed it forward and pulled it back.

"Too hard," said Fanshawe. She placed her hand on his and directed him. "Do it too fast and you'll risk tipping her into the wind. Here, let me show you."

She squeezed behind his seat and leaned into him, placing her hands on his. He could feel her warm, sweet breath on his neck. "Push forward, like this. Not too hard, not too soft. Steady." She pushed his hands forward, then drew them back. "Steady. Keep a rhythm. Steady." Forward, and back. Her breath came faster as she pushed his hands. Forward, and back.

There was a high-pitched whistle from outside the 'stat, and Gideon coughed. Was it suddenly hot in the small cockpit? Fanshawe slipped back into her seat. Another button on her shirt had come undone, but Gideon thought it best not to mention it. Outside there was a uniformed Aerodrome worker, waving at them.

"Our slot," said Fanshawe. "You can sit back in the cabin, if you like."

Gideon let himself into the cabin where the others were strapped with leather belts to the fold-down seats. Gideon slid into the free one, between Bathory and Bent. Fanshawe leaned back to look into the cabin and said, "We're taking off. Just so you know, there's one rule and one rule only on the *Skylady II*: To wit, you do as I fucking say, each and every time, and no arguments."

Bent chuckled. "I like this girl," he said, then he gave a little yelp as the 'stat, freed from its moorings by the ground crew, lurched upward from the nose, and began to rise jerkily into the air.

"Oh good Christ," said Bent, peering through the small porthole in the cabin. "We're effing flying."

"That is somewhat the idea," said Trigger gently. The ground dropped away from them swiftly, and Bent turned away from the window, closing his eyes tight. "Jesus. I can't look."

"You should," said Gideon, gazing through the porthole

nearest to him. "London is spread out beneath us like a child's model. Look at the Lady of Liberty!"

He watched as the ground receded and the 'stat floated freely, buffeted by the winds that soared in the upper reaches of the atmosphere, then he heard the thrum of the clockwork engine as Fanshawe released the crank brake, and the propellers began to spin.

"Marvelous," said Trigger. "I do so enjoy flying." He paused and looked at Bent, who still had his face screwed up. "Mr. Bent? Are you quite well?"

"Where did she say the toilet was?" asked Bent weakly. "I really do hate to waste good food, but I think that fine breakfast your Mrs. Cadwallader served up for us this morning is shortly to make an unwelcome reappearance."

They had been flying an hour, the Kent hop-fields spread out like a summer patchwork quilt below them, when Fanshawe let herself into the cabin, a rolled-up map in her hand. She pulled down the table and sat in an empty chair, and Gideon saw her suppress a smile at the pale, sweating figure of Bent.

"Mr. Bent?" she said. "Does flying not agree with you?"

"If God had meant me to fly," said Bent, "he would not have made me so fat." He paused and looked at Fanshawe with one eye. "If I might ask, miss, as you are sitting here with us, who is actually piloting this effing thing?"

Fanshawe smiled. "I have her locked into a course for the moment. I should not need to adjust her for a while yet." She unfurled the map of the world and pointed to London. "We're going to head east, across Belgium and Germany, and then begin to bear south over Bohemia."

Gideon couldn't help smiling. He had read those names only in books and stories; he had never truly dared expect he might see them for himself, much less from the lofty vantage point of a dirigible.

"Would flying over France and Spain not be a more direct route?" asked Stoker.

"It would," agreed Fanshawe. "And also a more dangerous one. Both sides have been known to toss shells rather indiscriminately at passing 'stats."

Her finger continued southward. "Down the Croatian coast, and via Greece we head out over the Mediterranean. The next land we see will be Alex." She looked up. "Has anyone visited there before?"

They all shook their heads save Trigger. Fanshawe asked him, "Since the Bombardment of 'eighty-two?"

"No, it was prior to that. I remember it being a chaotic, lawless hole of a place."

She smiled. "It still is. But now it's a chaotic, lawless hole with the Union Flag flying above it."

Bent groaned again, and Fanshawe said, "I am going to check the instruments, then I shall break out some provisions. Mr. Bent, I often find the best cure for a spot of airsickness is to drink one's way out of it."

Bent opened one eye again. "You have drink?"

"I always carry a good stock of rum." She smiled.

Bent risked opening his other eye, and said to Gideon, "What did I tell you about that girl? She's almost perfect."

"Almost, Mr. Bent?" said Fanshawe, raising one eyebrow.

"Aye." Bent nodded. "And if you tell me you have some sausages in the back, I'll upgrade that to absolutely effing perfect, with no argument brooked."

20

Alive, Alive-o

Over rum and spiced sausage, Trigger apprised Fanshawe of as much of the situation as the travelers knew between them while Bent, his demeanor much improved by the fare, proclaimed undying love for the pilot and asked for her hand in marriage, which she deftly sidestepped with a good-natured cuff to the side of his head, winking at Gideon as she did so. He had never in all his life encountered a woman like Rowena Fanshawe, not even the trawlermen's daughters back in Sandsend, who were far from being highborn ladies. Fanshawe seemed more like a man than a woman, in attitude at least. In body . . . Gideon forced himself not to stare at her behind as she leaned into the cockpit to quickly check the instruments.

"So," said Stoker when she returned. "What do you make of our tale, Miss Fanshawe?"

"Rowena, please," she said. "And it sounds like one of the most fanciful of Lucian's stories for *World Marvels & Wonders*." She paused to take a draught of rum. "However, as I know all of Lucian's tales are indeed true, I have no choice but to believe you. As a 'stat pilot you see some strange things, Mr. Stoker, especially when you are acquainted with Dr. John Reed."

"I'm struggling to believe it, and I actually saw those creatures," said Bent, helping himself to another sausage.

Fanshawe drank her rum thoughtfully. "So why is this *your* problem? Why not alert the authorities, have the Fleet Air Arm or the infantry sent in to find this pyramid and destroy these mummies?"

"I fear even if we could persuade the government that our

story was not the rambling of madmen, it would take more time than we have to mobilize the necessary firepower to undertake the task," sighed Stoker.

"And the Government might not be so inclined to help," said Gideon. "In fact, they might be behind it somehow. Have you ever heard of Walsingham?"

Rowena paused with her drink at her lips. "Walsingham?"

"He was John's contact in the Crown," said Trigger.

"And mine, on occasion," said Fanshawe, placing her drink on the small table. "Lucian, I wish you'd mentioned this before."

He frowned. "It's a problem?"

She sighed. "It might be, if Walsingham's indeed involved." She tapped her chin with a finger. "Still, too late now. All I ask is when you get to Alex, and if you find your pyramid and Walsingham is indeed wrapped up in all this, you keep my name out of it."

They were flying into a clear night, above the wispy clouds, and Gideon looked through the porthole at an earthbound constellation of sharp lights. Fanshawe joined him, pressing close so she could see through the porthole as well, and said, "Berlin. I should go and adjust our course a tad."

Bathory stifled a yawn and one by one they went to their bunks, their small quarters separated by heavy velvet drapes. With Rowena checking their course in the cockpit, Trigger and Gideon cleared up the supper things.

"Mr. Smith, it must have been a dreadful disappointment for you when you came knocking on my door in Grosvenor Square. You came seeking a hero, and found a tired old man living in the reflected glories of others," Trigger said.

Gideon shrugged. "I found what I was looking for. Captain Lucian Trigger. We're here, aren't we? On an adventure?"

Trigger smiled. "It's more than that for you, though, isn't it, Mr. Smith? An errand of revenge. For your fallen father."

Gideon nodded soberly. "Yes. I swore I would find out who

had killed him. Now I know. Those hated creatures. I will not rest until they have been made to pay."

Trigger paused thoughtfully. "I had considered myself a mere purveyor of written confections of late, especially since John's disappearance. I had not realized, or had forgotten, that my words carry a responsibility. To people such as yourself, Gideon, who truly considered Captain Lucian Trigger a hero. You also feel responsibility for Maria, am I correct?"

"I promised to help her, and instead I put her in peril. Had I left her in the house of Einstein, she would have been safe . . . though she was suffering terrible indignities."

"That is the curse of heroism," said Trigger. "Fulfilling responsibilities, and making difficult decisions." He yawned. "Now I think I will go to bed. A long day awaits us tomorrow."

Gideon's bunk was in the section nearest the cabin, and he pulled his hinged bed down from the wall. As he was arranging the blankets he saw Fanshawe in the cabin.

"Will you sleep, also?" he called quietly.

"I will doze occasionally in the cockpit," she said. "I would appreciate it if you could perhaps steer the 'stat for a couple of hours come dawn, to give me the chance to get some proper sleep. It should only be a holding course by then."

He nodded his agreement and pulled the door closed, then stripped to his underthings and placed his folded breeches and shirt at the foot of the bed. It was a narrow, short bunk, and Gideon lay there in the dark, listening to the heavy snoring from Bent in the adjacent quarters. He stared at the low ceiling of the gondola, listening to the symphony of ticking and clicking from the clockwork engine at the rear of the 'stat. Sleep refused to come, and he tossed and turned, Bent's sawing snores driving into his skull.

A crack of starlight appeared at the door to the cabin, and the small form of Fanshawe slipped into the small space. Gideon said nothing and feigned sleep, and she padded over to him and stood by his bunk, breathing shallowly.

"Gideon," she whispered. "Are you awake?"

"Miss Fanshawe . . . Rowena. Yes. Is everything all right?"

Wordlessly, she took his hand and placed it upon her breast. Her white shirt was unbuttoned to the navel, and he touched her bare flesh, feeling the hard, hot nub of her nipple. He tried to withdraw his hand but she held it fast, her breathing coming quicker and quicker, and then she slid her own hand under the blanket and trailed her fingers across his inner thigh.

"Rowena . . . ," he whispered.

"It's all right," she said. "We can be quiet. Let me get out of these trousers."

She released his hand and he snatched it away as though he'd been burned. He could sense the raising of a quizzical eyebrow.

"Rowena . . . I cannot."

He gasped as she gripped him with a firm hand. "Your mouth says no, but your body says otherwise," she said. He felt her hot tongue on his. She brought his hands to her breasts again, and he moaned, then shook his head.

"I'm sorry."

With a sigh, she released her hold on him, and he heard her buttoning up her shirt. She said, "It is Maria, isn't it? You are in love with her."

"In love with her? No, Rowena, you've got it wrong. She's made of clockwork and . . . and . . ."

Fanshawe put a finger on his lips and kissed him lightly on the cheek. "Hush. It is all right. Don't tie yourself in knots over it. The workings of the heart are beyond all of us, Gideon. This never happened. See you at dawn."

With that she stole back into the cabin and quietly closed the door behind her.

Gideon lay silently for a long time, listening to the creaking and settling of the 'stat, until Bent said, "Good God, Gideon, you really are an effing lunatic, ain't you?"

True to her word, Fanshawe acted as though nothing had happened when Gideon woke, stiff and aching from his cramped night's sleep, and he might have been tempted to consider it all a dream but for Bent's volley of knowing winks and nudges over breakfast. Fanshawe had directed the *Skylady II* on a more southerly bearing, and they hugged a rocky coastline that plunged into azure seas, the bright sun above casting the perfect shadow of the 'stat on the millpond-calm waters far below.

While Fanshawe slept in the bunk Gideon had vacated, he sat in the cockpit, monitoring the gauges with an overeager eye. But she had set the 'stat on a course and he had instructions to meddle with the controls only if there was impending doom of some kind, and then only if he was unable to wake Fanshawe because she had mysteriously died in her sleep.

When she returned, Gideon went to help Trigger and Bathory put together a lunch, and in the afternoon they pored over their maps and books, trying to discern from John Reed's journals whether he had made any regular contacts on previous sojourns to Alexandria.

"We're hitting a bank of cloud," called Fanshawe from the cockpit. "If it gets dark, you might want to light the oil lamps."

"Is cloud bad?" asked Bent.

"It is if we hit another 'stat," said Fanshawe.

"Does that happen often?"

She shrugged. "Generally only once."

The cloud clung stubbornly to the *Skylady II* and after some hours brought with it a premature dusk, which Fanshawe suggested they alleviate with rum and cards.

"Are we making good time?" asked Trigger as she poured and Bent dealt.

"Not bad. This cloud is slowing us down. I've tried to rise above it but it's a pretty deep bank. I still think we'll get to Alexandria before midnight."

They passed the time with rum and cards, which, Gideon had to admit, did engender a convivial atmosphere. When Bent had lost too much and had to dole out IOUs to most of the assembly, he began to sing in a cracked, throaty voice: "Farewell and adieu to you, fair Spanish ladies, Farewell and adieu to you, ladies of Spain; For we've received orders for to sail for old England, But we hope in a short time to see you again."

Bent lapsed into a prolonged, heaving cackle, and his mood proved infectious. Even Countess Bathory smiled and glanced at Stoker, who held up his hands for quiet. As the rum had taken hold, his cultivated tones had begun to lapse back into his thick Irish brogue, and he stood unsteadily, laid his hand on his chest, and sang in a rumbling baritone, "In Dublin's fair city, where the girls are so pretty, I first set my eyes on sweet Molly Malone, As she wheeled her wheelbarrow, Through streets broad and narrow, Crying, 'Cockles and mussels, alive, alive-o!' "

They all joined in a chorus of *alive, alive-o!*s until Bent, obviously determined not to be outdone, downed his rum and stood also, patting Stoker on the shoulder and bidding him to sit. "I heard this one in the music hall in Clerkenwell just three nights ago. You won't know it, but you'll pick it up. A bouncy little ditty." He cleared his throat. "Show me the way to go home, I'm tired and I want to go to bed, I had a little drink about an hour ago and it's gone right to my head. Wherever I may roam, On land or sea or foam, You will always hear me singing this song, Show me the way to go home."

Bent banged his tin cup sharply three times on the table, then launched into the same verse again, beckoning Gideon to join in. Trigger laughed and did so as well, as did Stoker and Fanshawe. By the third repetition they were all singing and banging their cups on the table and repeating the verse faster and faster. Gideon laughed delightedly. Then Fanshawe frowned and held up her hand.

"What was that?"

They fell silent, and in a moment there was a distinct

thud, as though something had struck the gondola further down its length.

"Trouble with the engine?" asked Gideon. Fanshawe shook her head, stood, and made to pass through the oval door, Gideon behind her, when there was another smack, much closer, accompanied by the sound of splintering wood. Bent yelled as the hull of the 'stat bulged in near his head and a sharp metal point protruded an inch or so into the cabin.

Cursing, Fanshawe pushed Bent out of the way and peered through the porthole at the dark cloud. She squinted, then drew back and breathed, allowing Gideon to look out. He could just make out dark shapes in the cloud, balls or globes with something attached to the underside.

"Personal blimps," said Fanshawe. "One-man 'stats, balloons with frames suspended underneath."

"And what the eff is that?" asked Bent, pointing at the sharp point near his head.

"If I'm not mistaken, it's a harpoon," said Fanshawe.

Trigger frowned. "One-man 'stats? All the way out here?"

Fanshawe was squeezing past him to the cockpit, and Gideon followed her. "They don't have the range to get out here. Which means they're with a bigger . . . oh."

Ahead of them, emerging from the dark cloud like a vast, silent whale, was a huge dirigible, as big as a passenger 'stat, with a massive pale flower painted on the hull of its balloon.

"Shit," said Fanshawe.

"What is it?" said Gideon.

She bit her lip and looked at him. "Now we're really in trouble. That's the *Yellow Rose*."

As she scrabbled for her spyglass and put it to her eye, Gideon asked, "The *Yellow Rose*? Why is that bad? Mightn't they be rescuing us?"

"Double shit, and shit again," said Fanshawe. "Could this get any worse? Louis Cockayne's on the bridge."

"Louis Cockayne?" said Gideon. "From Captain Trigger's adventures? Then we're saved!"

21

The Sky Pirates of the *Yellow Rose*

"You really think so?" said Fanshawe.

Emerging from the black clouds, the *Yellow Rose* dwarfed the *Skylady II* as a shark might overshadow a minnow, thought Gideon. There were four of the drifting shapes loosing harpoons at the smaller 'stat, the shafts of the projectiles connected to thin steel cables that led back to the bigger dirigible. As the cables snapped taut, the *Skylady II* bucked and shuddered, sending Gideon crashing into Fanshawe.

Trigger staggered to the door of the cockpit, where Fanshawe was buckling herself into the leather seat and bidding Gideon do the same in the copilot chair. "Are we under attack?"

"Got it in one, Lucian," said Fanshawe, hauling the wheel to the right and causing the 'stat to dip and swing. "Texan pirates. Very bad news."

"I've never seen Texans in an airship before," said Trigger, steadying himself on the doorframe. "Between them, the British, Spanish, and Japanese have done their level best to keep stocks of helium away from the warlords. They have plenty of coal down there, and you're liable to see them on steamships or engines on their slaving missions, but not many airships."

"This is all very effing interesting," said Bent. "But they've obviously got one. Maybe they saved up their stamps and bought an effing airship."

"It's Louis Cockayne!" said Gideon. "Captain Trigger, he's one of your—one of John Reed's friends, yes?"

Trigger bit his lip. "Yes, but . . . perhaps his role in the stories was somewhat . . . whitewashed compared to reality."

"Break out the guns!" hollered Bent.

Fanshawe leaned back through the door and called, "No! No firearms! One stray shell, and we'll be on our way to the bottom of the Med."

The *Skylady II* lurched violently again. Fanshawe killed the clockwork motor. Gideon stared at her. "What are you doing? We need to get away from them."

"All we'll do is burn out the bearings," she muttered. "They're reeling us in."

Gideon felt the *Skylady II* buck and begin to move sideways. The travelers gathered in the cockpit and at the port-side portholes to observe the vaster vehicle, a black mass against the clouds. It was fully five hundred feet from its nose-cone to its arrangement of aft rudders, estimated Gideon, and the gondola slung beneath it was seven or eight times larger than the *Skylady II*'s, and it appeared to have at least two levels. On the port side to which they were being hauled, he could make out an open observation deck on which were situated the winding barrels that brought them in. The smaller blimps were alighting on the deck and, through his spyglass, Gideon could make out the tall figure of a man standing with his hands on his hips, dressed in a long black coat and wearing a dark sombrero-style scout hat with a narrow brim.

"Is that Louis Cockayne? The stories paint him as a hero . . . ," said Gideon.

Fanshawe raised an eyebrow as the *Skylady II* bumped against the rails of the observation deck, and looked out again at the smiling face of Louis Cockayne. "You've got a lot to learn."

❧

The door of the *Skylady II* was hauled open and a brisk wind whipped through the cabin, where Fanshawe had assembled them all. Through the open door Bent could make out seven figures. He said, "They've got guns. Why can't we have guns?"

"The *Yellow Rose* is covered with beaten aluminum panels," said Fanshawe. "They've got less to lose if a bullet hits them."

A young man with a weather-beaten face and a shock of dirty blond hair leaped across the three-foot gap between the observation platform and the cabin. In his hand he brandished a silver pistol with a six-bullet chamber. He turned and called through the door, "Two ladies, boss, purty ones as well. Four guys, one of 'em fat and two of 'em oldsters."

Bent raised an aggrieved eyebrow. "I'm not old."

From the platform, a more cultured voice called, "Bring them out, Bo. Tell 'em to mind the gap. It's a long way down."

Trigger said, "I shall go first and sort out this misunderstanding."

Bent followed him to the lip of the door, looking down at the dark sea far below, studded with green islands, as Trigger strode across the gap. There were five other young men, similarly dressed to Bo, and Louis Cockayne, smoking a cheroot. Studded belts hung loosely at the hips of his black trousers, holding holstered revolvers, and his black shirt was crisply pressed. He regarded Trigger with piercing blue eyes, and his full, black mustache twitched.

Bent looked down with horror. "Jesus effing Christ, I'm not going out there!"

A swift boot from Bo on Bent's backside assured he did, and the others followed until they were assembled before Louis Cockayne, who continued to smoke in silence, watching them all carefully. The crew entered the *Skylady II* and removed everything not nailed down, including the weapons and baggage, as well as Bathory's box of earth.

Fanshawe spoke up. "I'd like to remind you that this action is in direct contravention of British and international law, and we will be making complaints to Crown officials at our earliest opportunity. Louis, stop being an idiot."

Cockayne flicked his cigarette into the wind as fingers of cloud curled around them. "Rowena. I am merely inviting you aboard the *Yellow Rose* as a measure of our hospitality."

"Thank you," said Fanshawe in measured tones. "But we already have a 'stat of our own, and we are on an errand of some urgency."

"I must say, Mr. Cockayne, it is a pleasure to meet you," said Gideon, stepping forward and holding out his hand. "I have very much enjoyed your adventures."

Bent groaned. He worried about that boy sometimes. When was he going to learn life was not a penny dreadful?

Cockayne's mustache twitched, and he gave a wry smile. He looked at the smaller 'stat. "The *Skylady II.* Four-celled balloon, am I right?"

Fanshawe nodded. Cockayne turned to one of his crew. "Let her go."

Trigger smiled broadly. "I told you he would see sense, didn't I? Thank you, Mr. Cockayne. We shall get back on board and be on our way."

Cockayne grunted, and Bo pointed his revolver at Trigger. "Stay where you are, gramps."

Two of the *Yellow Rose* crew released the cables and the *Skylady II* bobbed for a moment, then began to float away from the bigger 'stat. Gideon frowned, and Fanshawe shook her head in dismay.

"Oh, eff," said Bent. "That's our ride."

Cockayne said, "Bo, get me a Winchester."

When the *Skylady II* was a full hundred feet away, turning at the mercy of the high winds in the blackening sky, Cockayne took the rifle his crewman handed to him and put its stock to his shoulder. He let off a shot with a deafening report, then re-aimed and fired off three more in quick succession. The balloon of the *Skylady II* crumpled in each of the places he had shot, and it began to deflate with an audible hiss of escaping helium, even from that distance. As the pressure dropped, the 'stat began to sink, aft-first, and fell into an increasingly rapid spiral toward the sea.

Cockayne smiled. "Oops."

"Mr. Cockayne, I must object!" said Stoker, aghast.

Cockayne raised an eyebrow. "Keep your hair on, Paddy. Bo, bring them to my quarters. I think we'll have a spot of dinner."

Cockayne's opulent private rooms were at the front of the gondola, with panoramic views of the darkened Mediterranean spread out before them through wide glass windows. There was soft music playing from a wind-up gramophone, and the rooms were decorated in flock wallpaper, very much like what Gideon imagined a gentlemen's club to be like. It was rather obvious now, though, that Louis Cockayne was no gentleman. Outside the cloud was dispersing, giving way to a black, starry sky, and the *Yellow Rose* was nosing north, back the way the *Skylady II* had come. Cockayne had a large mahogany table, lit by an electric chandelier set into the wooden ceiling, set for the dinner of fish and salad brought to them by a crewman with dark hair tied up in a rough ponytail. Gideon noticed he kept directing hooded glances at Bathory.

"I would rather you told us what is the meaning of this piracy, what your intentions are, and how you plan to recompense me for the destruction of my 'stat," said Fanshawe coolly.

Cockayne laid a broad hand on the breast of his shirt. "Piracy, Rowena? Really. And I will give you that information, in good time. Let us eat." He waggled a bottle at them. "More wine, anyone?"

There was a muted shaking of heads, save from Bent. Cockayne refilled his glass and said, "Let me see if I've got this right. I do have a generally shocking memory for names. Rowena's and my paths have crossed several times . . . remember that night in Budapest, Rowena?"

"I am still trying to forget it," she said sourly. "Absinthe is a terrible drink that quite robs a person of their senses, taste, and propriety."

Cockayne laughed richly. "And Captain Lucian Trigger. The first time we have met, though I have appeared in print alongside you, in your fictional confections, many times. How is dear John? Are you two still . . . ?"

"John is missing," said Trigger. "We are on a mission to locate him. Or rather, we were."

"You must tell me more," said Cockayne.

"I must say," said Trigger, "I have sorely misrepresented you in my stories. I had understood from John you were a valiant and noble Yankee, not a Texan pirate."

Cockayne nodded. "And so I am, Captain Trigger. I'm Connecticut born, not a Southerner."

"So why are you flying with the *Yellow Rose*?" asked Fanshawe.

He shrugged and took a mouthful of wine. "I go where the money is, Rowena. All us 'stat pilots are the same."

"Some of us are choosier than others, though," she said.

He made a face. "So I am not the flawless hero Captain Trigger's stories would suggest. Just goes to show, you should not believe everything you read in the periodicals."

"I object to that," said Bent, pushing a forkful of fried flatfish into his mouth. "But you do put on a damned good spread, Cockayne."

"Ah, Aloysius Bent," said Cockayne. "A member of Her Majesty's Press." He turned to Stoker. "And another scribe, Bram Stoker. My, I'm doing awfully well with these names." Cockayne put down his glass and sat back in his chair. "Countess Elizabeth Bathory. I must say, my dear, I have never met a more beauteous creature than yourself."

"Your flattery is wasted upon me, Mr. Cockayne," said Bathory. "You have the morals of a dog, sir, and are thus beneath my notice."

He laughed again and turned his gaze toward Gideon, who

met his stare unflinchingly. "And finally, Mr. Gideon Smith, of some one-horse town in the wilds of nowhere. What brings you together with these august personages, Mr. Smith? A hick like yourself, walking with greatness?"

Gideon bristled, but Trigger stepped in. "It is due to Mr. Smith that we are all assembled here today."

"Yes, thanks, Smith," muttered Bent. "Prisoners of sky pirates. Very good of you to go to the trouble."

"Mr. Bent does have a point," said Stoker. "What are your intentions, sir? Have you kidnapped us for nefarious purposes?"

"Finish your dinner," commanded Cockayne, "then we'll talk."

Gideon stared furiously at the untouched food on his plate. Yet another of his heroes had turned out to have feet of clay. The *World Marvels & Wonders* stories were fiction, after all. He looked at his knife, catching the light from the electric chandelier overhead, and glanced at the two tousle-haired cowboys with their guns. He sighed. If there truly were no heroes in the world, what chance did Gideon Smith have of saving the day?

Cockayne lit up another cheroot and said, "Bo, Luke, bring in the rest of the boys." He puffed on the cigarette and said to Trigger, "Why don't you tell me about your errand?"

"We were on our way to Egypt, where John was last seen a year ago," said Trigger. "We fear he may have come to harm. There is some plot afoot, Cockayne, a most fantastic one."

"I'll park my disbelief," said Cockayne. "Do tell."

Trigger leaned forward. "Long dead, inhuman mummies terrorizing London. We believe they have taken John and caused much death. We are on a rescue mission and a voyage of revenge."

"You were," corrected Cockayne.

Trigger frowned. "Are you ready to tell us where this dirigible is going, Cockayne, and what your plans are?"

"I am." Cockayne nodded. "We have been to the west

coast of Africa, where we have been rounding up Negroes for sale in the Texan slave markets."

Stoker stared at him. "Abominable, sir."

"Lucrative, Mr. Stoker. The southern states are blessed with ideal conditions for the growing of cotton. It's tough work, and the Africans are well suited to toiling in the sun." He chewed thoughtfully. "Of course, the slave markets don't just deal in Negroes. Texas is littered with coal that needs mining and farms that need working as well as cotton that needs picking."

Gideon shook his head. "Slavery is still rife in America? But surely—"

"Down in Texas they do what they want, as far as I understand it," said Bent. "Which is sort of why they built the wall to keep 'em out."

"I can't believe Britain allows it," said Gideon.

"New York is a long way from London," said Cockayne. "The British would like to stamp out the Texan warlords, but they just don't have the resources."

"Like we didn't have the resources back in 'thirty-four when the southern states seceded from British rule to form the Confederacy," said Bent. "Come on, Gideon, you did find a bit of time for schooling among all that fishing, surely?"

Cockayne smirked. "The Confederacy is a veritable utopia compared with Texas, Mr. Bent. They're decent folks down there, just like you and me."

"But with slaves," said Bent.

Cockayne shrugged. "Just like the rest of the Empire, before it passed the Abolition Act in 1833. Texas, though, that's a different kettle of fish. The British took advantage of New Spain's gradual withdrawal from the territory there to make war with France and took over some of the old New Spanish outposts, such as San Antonio. It didn't last. After they built the Mason-Dixon Wall on Queen Victoria's command in—when was it, 'thirty-eight, they started?—the British Governors in Texas got increasingly pissed. Can't say I blame 'em.

The Confederacy and French Louisiana to the east, New Spain to the southwest, the Japs coming in from the Pacific coast . . . well, who could blame 'em for seceding themselves forty years ago? And if Boston and New York couldn't do more'n build a wall to thumb their noses at the Confederacy, they sure as shit weren't going to do much when the likes of Artemis Pinch in San Antonio decided to go it alone with their own rather . . . loose brand of justice and morality."

Rowena pointed a fork at him. "And yet you're running slaves for the likes of this Artemis Pinch?"

"Artemis is long gone; it's his son, Thaddeus, who rules San Antonio now, or Steamtown as they like to call it."

There was movement in the corridor outside, and Cockayne's eyes flicked toward Fanshawe's. He whispered, just loud enough for Gideon to hear, "Rowena, I'm in the shit. I need your help."

Bo and Luke bustled in with the other crewmen, all armed and in an excitable mood. They nudged each other and pointed at Bathory and Fanshawe in a way that made Gideon very uneasy indeed.

Trigger stood, and there was a volley of clicks as the crew pointed their revolvers at him. He sat slowly, his eyes narrowed. "Whatever you're planning, we cannot allow this, Cockayne."

"You cannot stop it, sir. You're all coming back to Texas with me, to be sold in the slave markets."

"I don't think I'd last long, picking cotton," said Bent. "Manual labor doesn't agree with me."

"Put them in the hold," said Cockayne.

Cockayne's boys began to manhandle Stoker and Bent out of their seats. Gideon stood before they got to him and aimed a punch across the table at Cockayne, who easily avoided his swing and slapped his hand down on the table, deftly flipping up his steak knife, bringing it down hard, and pinning Gideon's sleeve to the table.

"Naughty, naughty, boy from nowhere." Cockayne smiled.

Gideon saw Bathory quietly put her cutlery on her plate. "Bram?" she said, turning to Stoker as two men grabbed his shoulders.

"Yes, Countess?"

"I think it would be a most judicious time for you to release me from our blood pact, don't you?"

Stoker looked down at the untouched food on his plate as the men began to pull him from the table. "Yes, Elizabeth," Stoker said softly. "I very much think it would be."

22

Countess Bathory Unleashed

What followed could only be described, even by one with the literary pretensions of Stoker, as a massacre. Bathory tore the six crewmen apart before they had the time to fire off another revolver shot, the needle of the gramophone squalling off the cylinder with a shriek as she sent the furniture of the stateroom into disarray. Three of the crewmen tried to fight; the remainder saw the futility of such an action and tried to scramble toward the closed double doors of the quarters. But none were spared. With tooth and claw she ripped and shredded them, painting Cockayne's quarters scarlet and reveling in the rising charnel mist as one might carelessly abandon oneself to a light summer rain. With strength that good men attest only the devil can confer, she tore one man's arm from his shoulder and dropped it to the wooden floor, still clutching the useless gun with which the man had thought to defend himself. The cacophony of shrieks and screams seemed to spur Bathory on, as though it were an inspirational symphony rousing her to yet more carnage. The crewman Bo, who had directed particularly lascivious glances at her earlier, she saved for her special kiss. She held his head with firm, strong claws as she lowered her slavering, beastlike maw to his neck and drank deeply, even as his scream tailed off and bubbled up through the wound she rent in his flesh. Stoker heard Bent mumble something like a prayer as Bathory, the dead and dying spread around her like an obscene work of art, laid her shining eyes on Cockayne and walked toward him with purpose.

He had backed up against the windows and drawn his twin pistols, pearl handled and black barreled. She swiped them away from his shaking hands and took him by the lapels in one grotesquely clawed hand, her blood-soaked fangs widening for the kill.

"Wait," he said, with admirable calm. "I can take you to John Reed."

Bathory was past caring, but Stoker, still sitting at the table, caught Trigger's glance from across the room. He said, "Elizabeth. Hold, if you can."

She turned to Stoker and hissed at him, but she seemed to recognize him, and she paused in temporary, if grudging, assent. Trigger stood uncertainly and whispered at Stoker, "Is she safe? Will she attack us?"

"I am not her keeper." Stoker frowned. "And I have never seen her so filled with the bloodlust. But . . . yes. I think she is safe. To us."

Trigger said to Cockayne, "Is this some trick to spare your life?"

Cockayne said, not taking his eyes off Bathory's jaws, "No. I saw him in Alexandria a year ago. He was searching for a pyramid. The Rhodopis Pyramid, or some such?"

"Please," said Fanshawe. She put her hand on Bathory's arm, and the Countess hissed. "Louis, you said . . . you said you needed our help."

"I do," said Cockayne. "Rather, I did. I think you just gave it to me."

Bathory's grip loosened, and her face began to distort and shrink back to her human form, as though made of elastic. Within seconds the light had dulled in her eyes and she was back to the woman they recognized, albeit dressed in tattered rags and with a face smeared in gore.

One by one the travelers emerged from their hiding places, Gideon ashen faced and Bent feeling his way with his eyes tightly closed. Fanshawe glanced at Gideon and they shrugged at each other. Trigger relieved Cockayne of his guns as Bathory stepped back, taking a handful of napkins and wiping her mouth.

Bent started to applaud, though no one followed him. "Well, I for one am glad you're on our side, Countess," he said with forced jollity. "And, um, sorry about what I said before, at the Aerodrome. About your titties. Breasts. No hard feelings, eh?"

Cockayne coolly surveyed the bloodied remnants of his crew. "I guess this rather puts a different perspective on things, doesn't it?" he said.

"It certainly does," said Trigger, training both pistols on him. "You have an explanation for us. No more tricks, now."

Cockayne sighed. "Got myself in a heap of shit. Rowena will testify. I may not be the lily-white hero of Trigger's prose, but I'm not—" he gestured at the remains dripping with gore "—one of these guys."

"How'd you end up doing slaver runs, then?" asked Fanshawe.

"You ever been down San Antonio way? Place they call Steamtown? No? Keep it that way. Of all the warlords south of the Mason-Dixon Wall, Thaddeus Pinch must be the craziest bastard among 'em."

"Don't tell me, Louis. Poker."

Cockayne grinned. "You got it, Rowena. I won the *Yellow Rose* fair and square in Houston. Unfortunately, Pinch found out about it and called in some old gambling debts—the kind that I *didn't* win. I was to fill a hold with Negroes for the Steamtown mines to pay them off. Or it would have been my ass on the chopping block."

"Your friends?" asked Gideon sourly.

"Hand picked by Thaddeus Pinch," said Cockayne. "Crew and minders, all in one. I was trying to find some way of getting the hell out of this shit when we sighted your 'stat."

"Lucky you," said Fanshawe with a light smile. "Though I suppose this means, as you say, your ass is back on the block."

"I concur," said Trigger. "You aren't taking your cargo to Texas. Mr. Cockayne, I think now would be a good opportunity to turn this dirigible around. We are going to Alexandria after all, and you are taking us."

"In case anyone was wondering, or is too polite to ask, I am a vampire," said Elizabeth Bathory. "You take Mr. Cockayne, and I shall clean up in here. I apologize if I caused any of you distress or fright, but I hope you will agree that, as drastic a course of action as it was, it was necessary."

"Did you really have to kill them all?" asked Cockayne. "Good men are hard to find."

Bathory walked toward him and put her face close to his. "*Good* men, Mr. Cockayne?"

"Good men who can fly a 'stat like they could," said Cockayne with a small shrug. "As it goes, I didn't like them that much personally. A little uncouth."

Trigger waved the pistols, and Cockayne led them out of his stateroom and to a ladder leading to the bridge, directly above his quarters. There was a much bigger instrument panel laid out before the windows than the one Gideon had seen on the *Skylady II*, and a wheel very much like the one on his father's trawler. Cockayne released a lever on the wheel and began to spin it, and almost immediately the *Yellow Rose* began to nose its way around into a wide turning arc.

"She has good handling," said Fanshawe appreciatively. "Quick. Is she packing a hybrid?"

Cockayne smiled. "A tripler. Electric, steam, and clockwork. I can flick this lever and toggle between the three, depending on need, fuel stocks, and prevailing conditions. Self-winding mechanism, as well. She can practically be flown single-handed."

"So why the crew?" asked Gideon. He didn't fully understand half of what Cockayne had said, but he got the gist. This was a state-of-the-art vehicle.

"Rounding up Negroes takes a bit of manpower, Smith."

Gideon pulled a face. "Yes. We'll be freeing them as soon as we get to Alexandria."

Cockayne turned and raised an eyebrow. "If I don't take those slaves back to Texas, I can never show my face below the Mason-Dixon Wall again."

"Perhaps you'd like to discuss that with Countess Bathory?" said Gideon.

Cockayne grunted and turned his attention to the instrument panel. "We're on a course for Alex," he said. "We should make landfall in two hours."

"Two hours?" said Fanshawe, impressed. "This bird can really fly." She tapped a finger on her chin. "I never had you down as a 'stat pilot, Cockayne. And I thought the *Yellow Rose* was under the command of Trey McFarlane."

"I won her off McFarlane in Houston, eighteen months ago," said Cockayne. "It's good to broaden one's horizons. You can never have too many brands in the fire."

"So that makes you Brethren, then," said Fanshawe thoughtfully.

"I guess it does." Cockayne nodded. "The Esteemed Brethren of International Airshipmen. Noble pathfinders of the global skyways."

"Why don't you tell us about when you last saw Dr. Reed?" suggested Gideon. He felt unaccountably stung every time Fanshawe and Cockayne spoke together.

Cockayne locked the wheel and turned to them. "It was about a year ago," he said. "I met up with Reed in Alexandria. Come to think about it, I think he did say Rowena had dropped him off."

She nodded. Trigger said, "Did he leave Alexandria while you were there? What were his plans?"

"You know John, he never gave too much away when he was adventuring. He was going to procure some local knowledge. I put him in touch with Mr. Okoth. A Ugandan. Strange character, but he knows the Nile like the back of his hand. He'd worked with some professor from up Massachusetts way—"

"Professor Halifax from Arkhamville University," said Gideon. "From *The Shadow Over Faxmouth*."

"That'd be the guy. Okoth had taken him up the river to where old Sais used to be. I took Reed to Okoth and left 'em to it. I left Alex after that. Haven't seen or heard from Reed since."

"Then you will take us to this Mr. Okoth," said Gideon. "What time will we land in Alexandria?"

Cockayne consulted his pocket watch. "Ten o'clock, local time, by my reckoning. I'd imagine we'd be better off starting in the morning. We can sleep on the *Yellow Rose* tonight."

Bent frowned. "And have you kill us all in our effing beds, Cockayne?"

"Oh, he won't do that," said Fanshawe.

"How can you be so sure?" said Gideon.

She smiled. "Because he's going to take the Pledge, aren't you Louis?"

Cockayne remained impassive. She continued, "As a member of the Esteemed Brethren of International Airshipmen, Mr. Cockayne has an implicit duty to support and assist any other member in trouble or need. All he has to do is take the Pledge in my presence, and he won't be killing any of us, in our beds or otherwise."

Cockayne sighed and held up his left hand, then recited, "As one who makes his way across the fair world by its high and windblown paths, I hereby pledge my allegiance to Rowena Fanshawe and her companions until such time as she releases me from my pledge, yadda yadda yadda."

"And that's it?" said Bent, aghast. "You think one promise from this effing blackguard is going to help me sleep like a baby tonight?"

"Oh, he'll keep his word," said Fanshawe. "Men like Cockayne have seen too much to risk bad juju. He lives on his wits and his luck; if he broke the Pledge he'd never know when that luck was going to run out. And with the life he leads, he just can't risk it."

Gideon turned as Stoker climbed the ladder to the bridge. Cockayne asked, "Where's the vamp?"

"Countess Bathory has gone to find fresh clothes from the baggage your men brought on board," said Stoker, glaring at him.

Bent chuckled. "Shame. I thought them rags showed off her knockers to great effect." He paused and looked around. "She can't hear me from here, can she?"

"I must say, Cockayne," said Fanshawe, "you didn't look too perturbed by the Countess's transformation."

He shrugged again. "Like you said, Rowena. Folks like me and you, we've seen a lot. Stuff that'd make normal folks' toes curl."

Gideon felt himself flush. Was he just *normal folks* to these great adventurers? Trigger, as much a fraud as he was, had at least seen the world and moved in its stranger circles, albeit in John Reed's shadow. Even Bent, Londoner through and through, seemed to have a greater understanding of life. Gideon Smith was just a hick, true enough. A boy from nowhere.

"I ran into a vampire couple of years ago," said Cockayne. He nodded at Trigger. "With John Reed, actually. Over in Gothenburg, Sweden. I think you might have written it up."

"*The Endless Night of the North,*" said Gideon. "*World Marvels & Wonders,* February 1889. I read it."

Cockayne smirked. "You read it, boy? I lived it."

"And did you heroically dispatch the vampire, Mr. Cockayne?"

Bathory had emerged onto the bridge, clean and clothed in a fresh dress, her leather bodice restrung, new boots on her feet.

"That we did, Countess. It had been preying on young girls in the long winter nights. John Reed held it down while I drove a stake into its heart."

She applauded. "How brave. And was it a terrible, ancient vampire possessed of unnatural strength and fearsome supernatural capabilities?"

"It was, as far as I recall." Gideon nodded.

Cockayne glanced at Trigger, who said, "It was in the final

draft. In John's notes . . . I believe it was little more than a child."

"Hey, it was still killing girls," protested Cockayne. "Besides, what kind of monster turns a kid into a vampire, anyhow?"

"Mr. Cockayne, please desist from baiting the Countess," said Stoker angrily. "We have cleaned up your stateroom. The . . . remains of your crew we have consigned to the waves far below, from the observation deck. I recited a small prayer."

"I'm sure their immortal souls'll be very grateful," said Cockayne.

"Well, I would just like to say, you are looking beautiful, Countess, and I know I speak for the rest of us when I say I thank you for saving us from those miscreants," said Bent, rubbing his hands together and bowing slightly.

"Mr. Bent, you do not have to be so obsequious. I am no different a person than I was before I revealed my true nature. Please treat me as you did before." She paused. "Well, perhaps without so many references to my breasts."

"What if she gets hungry again?" said Cockayne.

Bent frowned. "He does have a point, Countess."

She walked to Bent and patted him on the shoulder. He flinched only slightly. "Rest assured, Mr. Bent, should the bloodlust take me, I think you personally will be quite safe. I might as well drink a bottle of rum as feast on your blood." She turned to the rest of them. "If that is a general worry, then please do not fret. I can quite control myself. And Mr. Stoker, bless his heart, has been providing sustenance for me in times of need."

Bent murmured, "You're a dark horse, Stoker. Does the missus know?"

"Well, that's us locked on a course for Alex," said Cockayne. He put his back to the dark vista before the 'stat and surveyed them all. "What a ragtag bunch you are, eh? You really mean to do this? Take on these mummies?"

"If we have to," said Gideon.

Cockayne chewed his lip for a moment. "You won't last five minutes, even with that little armory we took off your 'stat. Even with your pet vampire."

Bathory hissed at him and he shrugged. "Sun's fierce in Egypt, Countess."

"Don't worry about us," said Gideon.

"But I do, Smith," said Cockayne. "I do. Come with me."

❦

Unwilling to be ordered about by Cockayne, but still intrigued by him, Gideon followed the Yankee off the bridge, up a ladder, and into what appeared to be a gymnasium, complete with iron weights, a vaulting horse, and climbing ropes. Trigger followed and positioned himself by the door as Cockayne took off his hat and coat and rolled up his shirt sleeves.

"You hit like a girl, Smith," said Cockayne.

Gideon glanced at Trigger, who gave a shrug. He said, "The table was in the way. . . ."

"Table schmable, Smith. Have another swing. This one's free. Go ahead."

Gideon frowned, but Cockayne held open his hands. "So long as Rowena's holding me to the Pledge, I might as well give you the benefit of my experience. Look, you have done me a favor, getting my Texan minders out of the way. Even if it was a bit gory . . . anyhow, that's a long way of saying I guess I owe you one. Hit me."

Without saying a word, Gideon threw a punch. Cockayne deftly dodged it, took hold of Gideon's wrist, and flicked him on to his back.

"Terrible," said Cockayne. "Stand up."

Gideon rubbed his rump and glared at the Yankee. Cockayne put his left fist high and banged his right into his sternum. "Keep this up here and this one down here. Go on."

Gideon reluctantly adopted the pose, and Cockayne jabbed at him with his left fist. Gideon ducked, and Cockayne brought his right hand up, hard, into Gideon's chin.

"Ow," said Gideon, staring with narrow eyes at Cockayne.

He flung another punch, and Cockayne smacked him sharply on the cheek.

"Awful. Try again."

They sparred for an hour, Gideon following Cockayne's instructions and getting hit less, and coming closer to landing a shot on the American's chin. Eventually, Cockayne held up his hand. "OK, here endeth the lesson. I need to check our course. You don't hit like a girl anymore, Smith. You hit like a lady. But it's an improvement, I suppose."

Cockayne turned to go, and Gideon said, "Mr. Cockayne?"

The American turned. "No need to thank—"

Gideon's punch landed square on Cockayne's jaw, knocking him off his feet and onto his backside. He stared at Gideon for a moment, then laughed and climbed to his feet.

"Good, Smith," he said, nodding. "Good. You might last ten minutes now, not five."

Laughing to himself, Cockayne headed out of the gymnasium. Gideon looked at Trigger. "What was all that about?"

Trigger smiled tightly. "I might be very much mistaken, Gideon, but it strikes me our Mr. Cockayne actually rather likes you."

Gideon snorted. "I can do without the likes of him—"

Trigger held up his hand. "Do not be too quick to judge, Mr. Smith. Cockayne might not have covered himself with glory in our first meeting, but he was perhaps acting for other reasons than we first thought."

Gideon shrugged. "Self-preservation. No more honorable than slaving for profit."

Trigger stroked his chin and looked at Gideon mildly. "Perhaps, Mr. Smith, perhaps. But until our own lives are forfeit, who knows how we will behave?"

Gideon and Trigger joined the others on the bridge, where Cockayne was pointing out a pinprick of light in the blackness ahead of them.

"The Pharos lighthouse," he said. "We're almost there."

23

Red Hot in Alex

As they began to descend, Trigger asked Gideon, "What do you know of Alexandria?"

"What they taught me at school." Gideon shrugged.

Trigger said, "After the Bombardment, our architects set to work on creating a new lighthouse, bigger and better than before."

"One of the Wonders of the World." Gideon nodded.

Trigger stroked his mustache. "There are so many wonders, these days."

Cockayne piloted the 'stat to the airfield—little more than a vast expanse of orange dirt—to the east, between the sprawling city and the verdant fields on the banks of the Nile.

"I'll go to the Customs House, clear our arrival," said Cockayne. He threw a ring of jangling keys at Gideon. "The Negroes are in the hold, Mr. Savior. Be careful, though. They're savages. They might not consider you any better than me, Smith. Big Bad White Man, and all that."

"I hate that man," said Gideon when Cockayne and Fanshawe had gone. "Can't we just leave him now?"

"I concur, but I think we need to keep him with us," said Trigger. "At least until we verify his story about this Ugandan. And, of course, we have no transport; if this Pledge of Rowena's does indeed hold water, perhaps we can prevail upon him to take us to the site of the pyramid, and even back to London afterward."

Gideon scowled. He did not like Fanshawe being in Cockayne's company for longer than necessary. What had he meant, about that night in Budapest? He brushed the thought aside and said, "Let us go and see these Negroes."

It was dark, hot, and airless in the hold, and Gideon held up his lamp to see the backs of a hundred men, seated in fours on wooden benches that ran the length of the tight space. They were all stripped to the waist, and as he drew closer he saw they were chained to each other at the ankles and wrists.

Bathory appeared at his shoulder and hissed. "And men think vampires to be inhuman," she said.

Gideon held up the keys and shook them. "We, uh, we are going to set you free." The eyes regarded him coolly. "Does anyone speak English?"

There was a silence, and then, with a rattle of chains, one man halfway down the rows held up his arms. "Here. My name is Souleymane. Are we in Texas?"

Gideon shook his head. "No. We are in Alexandria. Where are you from?"

"You call it the Ivory Coast," said Souleymane. "Alexandria? al-Iskandariyya? Egypt?"

Gideon nodded enthusiastically. "Yes. Egypt. We have . . . the men who took you are dead. You are free."

Souleymane muttered to his neighbor in his own tongue and a ripple of whispers spread through the men. Gideon stood by the nearest man and inspected the lock on his chains. It took him a minute to find the right key, then the shackles fell from the man's wrists. Gideon turned to the next man, and the next, then handed the key over and allowed the men to free themselves with a rising tumult of conversation.

Stoker located a hatch at the bottom of the hold and unlocked a staircase that descended down to the ground below. Gideon saw him draw back as a wave of heat hit him from beneath. Within minutes the men were free, and Souleymane presented himself to Gideon with another, older man.

"This is the chief of my village," he said. "He thanks you for what you have done."

Gideon smiled and shook the man's hand. "Are you far from the Ivory Coast? From your home?"

"We are," said Souleymane. "But not as far as we would be in Texas. We will make it. We will see our families again. I will see my wife and my children, and my father."

A sudden sadness hit Gideon at the thought that he would never see his own dad again. Tears pricked his eyes. Without warning, Souleymane embraced him, and asked, "What is your name?"

"Gideon Smith."

"They say London is the home of heroes," said Souleymane. "Are you a hero?"

Gideon shook his head. "Hero? No, not me. I have friends . . . they are the heroes. I didn't do anything, really."

Souleymane and the chief led the other men down the steps. They fell to their knees and kissed the dry earth, then set out, a long, dark column, toward Alexandria, and the south.

"He is right, Gideon," said Trigger, whom he had not noticed at his side. "You *are* a hero. You are the truest among us. You do not lie, or cheat, or pretend to be something you are not. You have made this happen."

Gideon shook his head and looked to the distant lights of Alexandria, then beyond the city to what he could not see, the vast, shifting sands of Egypt. "No," he said. "Like Cockayne said, I'm just nobody."

Trigger pursed his lips. "Gideon, people say a lot of silly things about heroism. But there are two things I've heard that ring very true. The first was said by a countryman of Mr. Cockayne, one Ralph Waldo Emerson. He said a hero is no braver than an ordinary man, but he is braver five minutes longer."

Gideon smiled. "And the other?"

"Heroes are not born. They are made. Actions speak louder than words, Gideon. And, lest I descend completely into cliché, let me leave you with one more thought. Despite the stories I wrote and am eternally gratified you devoured so voraciously, appearances can often be deceiving. John . . . he did not see himself as a hero. An adventurer, perhaps, but not a hero. In truth, he was little different from our American friend. He would be the first to admit he was no angel, and sometimes he did what he did for less than noble reasons. But, all this aside, I love him. Because that's what we do, isn't it, Gideon? Overlook . . . imperfections. For love. That, I believe, is true heroism. The rest of it? Stories for children, really."

"Jesus effing Christ," said Bent, squinting into the sun. He nudged Stoker. "How hot is it? It's only eight o'clock in the effing morning."

They stood on the dirt beside the *Yellow Rose* while Cockayne handed out leather canteens of water. "Take small sips often, don't glug it all away at once. You need to keep hydrated in this heat."

"I can't effing cope with this," muttered Bent. "Is it going to get any hotter?"

"Measurably, I would imagine," said Stoker, stowing the canteen in his satchel. He looked at Bathory. "Will you be all right?"

She nodded, though with a grim set to her face. "If we can keep in the shadows as much as possible. Did you . . . ?"

He nodded and patted his bag. "I drew a bottle earlier. I must confess it is weakening me somewhat now."

"Then no more," she decided. "I know your intentions are honorable, Bram, but this will kill you."

"But if I don't, you will kill someone else," he murmured. He looked at Cockayne, who pulled the brim of his scout hat over his eyes. The Yankee was his favorite should Elizabeth get the bloodlust upon her, he thought. Cockayne caught his eye and frowned at him, then said, "Trigger, are you going to give me my pistols back?"

They had recovered their weapons from the *Yellow Rose*, and Gideon had the sword hanging from his belt. Trigger looked doubtful, as well he might, thought Stoker, but Fanshawe said, "Give them to him, Lucian. He will honor the Pledge. I promise."

Cockayne holstered the pistols with satisfaction, glancing at Stoker and Bathory. Evidently he, too, believed he might feel the ire of the Countess before long. "Come on, then. Let's get into the city."

❧

"Is this place really as rough as everyone keeps saying?" asked Bent. He'd survived a lifetime in London, and he couldn't see how this hole would possibly be any worse.

"Just keep close to me and ignore everyone," Cockayne told him as he led them through the tumultuous chaos of the Customs House, where the officials were swamped by people of all colors and languages, waving pieces of paper and assaulting Bent's senses with shouts and cries. It was little better outside, he considered; a wide dirt track led down toward the whitewashed buildings of Alexandria that spread along the coast on either side of the Nile delta. The road was lined with tents and stalls, and those who were obviously new arrivals were approached from all sides by beggars with horrendous disabilities, smiling holy men silently asking for alms, and traders showing swatches of silk, battered cups and lamps, dried fruit, and livestock. Bent tripped over a goat and fell in a tangle of his own limbs and sweat-stained clothing, raising a smile even from Cockayne.

"Effing hell," moaned Bent. "I can't stand this. All these bloody people. And it's so hot! Look, this blighter's selling hats. What money do they take here?"

Trigger gave him a handful of shillings. "I imagine good old British sterling shall do as well as anything. Would you like some help at the stall?"

The smiling Egyptian wearing a fez held his hands out to invite Bent into the shop. He grinned. "I think I can handle this geezer." He said loudly, "I require hat. Hat for head. Hat to stop, um, el sol making me, ah, loco. Capeesh?"

The man nodded, his smile fixed to his face. "Try this. Very good hat for English gentleman."

He handed Bent a pith helmet, gray from many years in

the desert. "Oh, yes. I think this will do a treat. How much do you want for it?" He looked at Trigger. "Ten shillings?"

Trigger shook his head violently, but the man grabbed Bent's arm. "Ten English shillings, did you say?"

Seeing Trigger's anguished look, Bent said, "Erm, no, I meant . . . a shilling. That do you?"

The man's bottom lip curled. "Ten of your shillings."

"Ten shillings?" scoffed Bent, getting into the swing of it. "Two shillings, and that's my final offer."

"Eight shillings."

"Three-and-six, and you're not having another ha'penny off me," said Bent, and forced the money into his hand. The man bowed, and Bent walked back to the others.

Cockayne nodded at the helmet. "Good value, if you don't mind a dead man's hat."

Bent began to laugh, then furrowed his brow. He took off the pith helmet and Cockayne pointed to a neat round hole, just above the peak. "Bullet," he said.

Bent stuck his little finger through the hole and looked at Trigger. "Is that bad luck, then?"

"It certainly was for the previous owner." Trigger chuckled. "But look at it this way, Mr. Bent . . . lightning rarely strikes the same place twice."

❦

The souk delighted Gideon. It was a warren of streets and alleys, covered with brightly colored tent awnings, every imaginable stall selling every imaginable thing. Gideon had never seen so many different faces: Greeks and Turks, Arabs and Africans, English and Europeans, all mixed and mingled together, jabbering at each other in their own languages, yet somehow still making themselves understood. He counted off the different peoples he knew only from *World Marvels & Wonders*'s breathless features on distant cities and exotic lands. Women in white muslin dresses and headscarves that showed only their eyes drifted past like ghosts; turbaned Hindoos with bare chests argued with corpulent Egyptians in tasseled fezzes; naked Fellaheen children ran between everyone's legs; Coptic priests debated with each other and tugged their beards; Jewish traders ordered Nubian workers to pile this thing high, take that stock elsewhere. A brace of drunken English sailors, hanging on each other's shoulders and dragging jugs of rum with them, sang unintelligibly as they wove through the bazaar. The scent of woodsmoke drifted lazily through the souk, and the smell of roasting meats caused Gideon's mouth to water. Bladders of water hung like limbless pigs on a rope strung between two high walls, and a line of ancient men with rheumy eyes watched the group's passage, sitting cross-legged on elaborate rugs and smoking water pipes.

"This is amazing," said Gideon. He reveled in the noise and the smells, the foreign, exotic heat, and the hooded glances of veiled women. This was what he was born to do, adventure in far-flung corners of the world.

"I am dying for a piss," announced Bent.

Trigger frowned at him. "Did you drink all your water?"

Bent waved his empty canteen. "It's hotter than Hades here, and twice as effing busy. I'll never complain about the Tottenham Court Road again."

"We're here, anyway," announced Cockayne. Between two stalls was a striped curtain covering a stone staircase. "Okoth's."

"Let me go first," said Bent, elbowing past Gideon. "He's got to have a toilet."

Gideon followed him to the top of the stairs, where Bent pushed open a wooden door and popped his head around. "Okoth? Mr. Okoth?"

He gasped, and looking over his shoulder Gideon saw a mountain of a man, with skin so black it looked purple. He was clothed in a tentlike robe of shimmering blues and greens, and he bared white teeth in a grimace, his eyes wide. In the man's giant hand was a huge hatchet glinting in the light.

"Die, you astonishingly ugly bastard!" yelled the man, letting loose the hatchet. "Die!"

As the weapon hit home with a solid *thunk,* Bent made a liquid, strangled sound and slid down the doorframe to the floor at Gideon's feet.

24

The Astonishing Mr. Okoth

As Gideon manhandled Bent into a chair, Okoth said, "Did I get him? Did he die?"

Trigger and Stoker had fumbled for their pistols, but Cockayne had bid them to belay the idea. The Yankee intercepted the cup of water Okoth offered to Gideon and threw it in Bent's face.

Okoth strode across the room, which was spartanly furnished with a single chair, a desk, and a chart of the course of the Nile, to retrieve his hatchet. He broke into a wide smile. "I did! I did get him! Oh, come and look!"

Gideon followed the gigantic black man to the wall where the weapon was embedded; there was a fly, neatly bisected by the sharp blade, still twitching on the white plaster wall.

Okoth clapped his hands together. "Astonishing! I hate flies. Hate 'em! What do you think of that, an African who hates flies? Is it not astonishing?"

Gideon held out his hand. "Mr. Okoth. I am Gideon Smith, from England. We have come on an errand with which we hope you might help us."

"Hang on," shouted Bent, straightening his pith helmet. "Did he try to effing kill me or not?"

Okoth bounded over to Bent, his colorful robe flapping. "Kill you, honored guest? Oh, no. Not esteemed visitors from England, in the company of my good friend Mr. Louis Cockayne."

Gideon had never seen a man of Okoth's size move so swiftly, crossing the room and clapping the Yankee on both shoulders. "Mr. Cockayne! It is a very long time since I saw you last. How goes the slave trade? Brisk?" before turning to

Gideon and, in a stage whisper behind his hand, hissing, "These Americans are astonishingly stupid. You must speak to them with simple words they can understand. They are like babies, or camels."

Cockayne frowned and lit a cigarillo. He introduced them all one by one, and Okoth called into a back room for coffee. "My son, Mori, is in the other room." He nudged Bent. "His name means *one who is born before the loan on the wife's dowry is paid off,*" and doubled over with great, resounding laughter, smacking his knees. "My name means *born during rains,* which is astonishing given my sunny disposition, yes?" He straightened and considered the journalist with a cocked head. "Bent. Means crooked. Or . . . the man who likes other men. If that is your preference, Mr. Bent, I can have Mori make some inquiries in the souk. . . ."

Evidently flustered, Bent waved him away. "That's Trigger's bag, not mine. I'm a committed tit man."

Okoth mimed hefting a pair of imaginary breasts and guffawed, winking at Gideon as a thin boy with a smattering of hair on his jawline, wearing a plain cotton shirt and trousers, emerged from the other room.

"Coffee!" announced Okoth. "Thank you, Mori."

The boy nodded and smiled, stealing glances at Bathory and Fanshawe. Okoth shooed him away by flapping the hem of his robes at him. "Go! Stop leering! You think you are committed English tit man, like the esteemed Mr. Bent? Astonishing cheek, that boy."

Cockayne sighed. "Okoth. We need information."

Okoth sipped at his dark, sweet coffee. "Where are your boys, Mr. Cockayne? Out raping and plundering, putting babies in local girls, hmm?" He turned to Gideon. "Very raucous, Mr. Cockayne's boys."

"My crew's dead," said Cockayne, nodding at Bathory. "Thanks to her."

Okoth inspected Bathory. "Ah. You are *obayifo,* am I correct, Countess?"

She inclined her head and smiled. Okoth said, "Vampire."

Trigger raised an eyebrow. Okoth shrugged. "Many strange and astonishing things in Africa, Captain Trigger. And Okoth has seen them all! Now, information is required, yes?"

"Yes," said Trigger. "Cockayne said you had seen John Reed when he traveled to Alexandria a year ago."

Okoth sat down on one of the rickety chairs near his table. "Ah, John Reed. The great adventurer." He shook his head. "Very sad."

Gideon felt Trigger slump beside him, and he put out a supporting arm. Trigger said, "He's . . . dead, then?"

Okoth gave a massive shrug of his shoulders. "Dead? Who can tell? And what is death, anyway? You know, the Egyptians believe in—"

"Stow the theology," said Cockayne testily. "Is Reed dead, or not?"

Okoth placed his hands on his knees. "Well, all I can say is he went into the pyramid, and he never came out."

"The pyramid?" said Gideon. "The lost Rhodopis Pyramid? He found it?"

Okoth laughed richly. "You English are astonishingly funny, Mr. Gideon Smith. You always think something is lost unless you find it yourselves."

Gideon helped Trigger to a chair. He had grown suddenly old and feeble, much as he had first looked when he stood on his doorstep on Grosvenor Square. Trigger put his hand to his head. "I always thought . . . John always survived. No matter what happened, he always won out, at the end."

"Did you actually see him die?" asked Gideon quietly.

"I did not," said Okoth. "He went into the pyramid and did not come out. I waited for a day and a night, and returned every few days for a month, but there was no sign."

"He could have survived," said Gideon, though he sounded doubtful even to himself. "Perhaps he is still inside, or effected an escape while Mr. Okoth was not there."

Trigger shook his head sadly. "If John had left the pyramid, why would he have not come home to me? He has fallen victim to the Children of Heqet, undoubtedly. And even if he did manage to survive those fiends . . . he would not have lasted long in the pyramid."

"There might have been food," said Gideon desperately.

Trigger's voice dropped to a whisper. "John had . . . other hungers. He was no stranger to Limehouse, if you get my meaning."

Gideon did not, and he looked up. Bent laid a hand on his shoulder. "I think Trigger means he was an opium addict."

Trigger nodded sadly. "He would have died in a mindless frenzy without the drug, even before the hunger got him."

Okoth leaned forward and said seriously, "I knew about Doctor Reed's . . . requirements. I had to get Mori to procure something for him in the souk." He rubbed his finger and thumb together. "Kef, from Morocco. Hashish."

They stood silently in the hot, airless room for a moment, then Gideon said, "We cannot give up hope. Mr. Okoth, can you take us to the Rhodopis Pyramid?"

He broke out into a wide grin. "Astonishingly, I can do just that." He frowned. "But wait. You said Heqet, did you not? The astonishingly ugly frog-faced goddess of these heathen Egyptians?"

Gideon glanced at Trigger. "We did, yes. You know of them? The Children of Heqet?"

"Astonishing commotion in the souk today," said Okoth. "An Egyptian fisherman came running through, all of a fluster, claiming to have seen monsters in the river."

"Monsters?" said Gideon.

"Monsters," agreed Okoth. "Frog-faced monsters, he said, with cruel teeth. And more! Astonishing! They had a woman with them, an English woman, blond of hair and pale of skin! Under the water, but *her eyes were open*!"

Gideon gasped. "Maria!"

"When was this, Okoth?" said Cockayne.

Okoth shrugged. "Dawn, he said."

"We've got to go after them!" said Gideon. "Mr. Cockayne . . . ?"

Cockayne shrugged. "OK. I'm interested. We can take the *Yellow Rose* upriver for a bit, if you like. But I ain't putting myself in harm's way for anyone, Pledge or no Pledge."

"All pyramids are built to the west of the Nile," Okoth said, when Alexandria was far behind them and lost to sight. He had directed Cockayne to follow the vast river until it was time to bank off into the desert. "For that is where the sun sets, and thus that way lies the land of the dead."

"Are all pyramids tombs?" asked Gideon. He could not believe a people who lived in such rich sunlight and among such suffocating heat could be so obsessed with the cold darkness of death.

"Indeed," nodded Okoth. "They were built to resemble Ben-ben, the mound that rose from the primordial waters of Nu, and on which the first rays of the sun fell." He laughed. "Those Egyptians were astonishingly crazy. Everybody knows the world was created by Katonda, the big eye in the sky, the father of all the gods and the father of all living men."

For a while Gideon watched the passage of the Nile below them, the land around it remarkably green and fertile. Gideon had thought Egypt a place of sand and little else. Vast tracts of land near the river were swollen and flooded, and he could make out lumpish gray shapes gathered in the shallows of the floodwaters. "What are those?"

"That is the hippopotamus!" Okoth grinned. "The big fat river horse." He cocked his head and regarded Bent. "There is not an insignificant likeness to yourself, good sir."

"Cheeky ass," sniffed Bent as Gideon hid a smirk behind his hand. "What else have you got down there?"

"Birds with long curved bills, the ibises, very important in Egypt. The mongoose. Tortoises. The Nile monitor, very nasty lizard, very strong jaws." Okoth snapped his hands together in a sharp clap.

"Don't like the sound of that much," said Bent.

Okoth said, "Very temperamental creatures. But not as bad as the crocodiles."

Bent stared at him. "Crocodiles? Running wild?"

"Oh yes," said Okoth. "Wild and fast. Snap, snap, snap!" He collapsed into peals of laughter again.

Okoth tapped Gideon on the shoulder and pointed toward the river. "Now, isn't that a most astonishingly curious sight?"

❧

At first, Gideon couldn't see anything beyond the wading birds and half-hidden hippos, but as he stared beyond Okoth's outstretched finger he eventually made out a disturbance in the center of the wide river, a series of swirling eddies and the occasional small black shape breaking the surface.

"Is that them?" he said quietly. "Maria?"

"I'll bring us down a little," said Cockayne, and the *Yellow Rose* dipped, casting a widening shadow over the brown waters. As the 'stat drew level with the activity in the river below, Cockayne killed the engines.

"Great Scott," said Trigger. "It is truly them. The Children of Heqet."

"And Maria!" said Gideon. "Encircled within them!"

"Are you telling me they've effing swum from London to Egypt?" asked Bent.

"She isn't moving," said Gideon, peering down from the window.

"I suppose if they are after what is in her head they would not care if she lived or died," observed Bathory.

Stoker raised an eyebrow and murmured, "Elizabeth . . ."

She glanced at him, then at Gideon. "Apologies. I did not mean . . ."

"We don't know if Maria can truly die," put in Trigger quickly.

"What with her not being alive to begin with," said Cockayne. He turned to Gideon, resting on the instrument panel. "So, what's your plan?"

"Might I make a suggestion?" asked Trigger.

"No," said Cockayne, continuing to stare coolly at Gideon. "I want to know what Mr. Smith is going to do."

Gideon swallowed dryly and looked from face to face. Fanshawe gave him an encouraging smile. "Er," said Gideon, then closed his eyes and breathed deeply. "Remember *Vanuatu, West of Fiji*?"

Trigger nodded. "Go on."

"John Reed rescued Mr. Cockayne from the caldera of the volcano after accompanying a rescue mission with the Fleet Air Arm dirigible *John Carter*."

Cockayne smiled crookedly. "Not how I remember it. Must be your artistic license, Trigger. But let's say he did. How?"

"A cable," said Gideon. "We could . . . we could use those cables you used to harpoon Rowena's 'stat. Lower someone down to get Maria."

Cockayne mused. "Might work. But how would you get her from those creatures?"

Gideon thought for a moment. "A diversion. Something to scatter them. Perhaps some gunfire, or . . ."

"Or that effing big gun!" said Bent excitedly. "You said you had one, didn't you, Cockayne?"

Cockayne smiled tightly. "Good plan, Smith. I'd propose lowering Rowena down."

Gideon looked up. "What? No. No, I'll go."

"I'm lighter," said Fanshawe. "I'll need someone strong to haul me up, especially when I get Maria. You should do that."

"Mr. Okoth can take the wheel of the *Yellow Rose*." Cockayne nodded. "We'll get out onto the observation deck. Come, Mr. Bent, let us bring out the Hotchkiss. Mr. Stoker? We could probably do with your help. It's rather a fearsome beast."

"Wait," said Bathory. They turned to her. "I have traveled halfway across the world for my revenge. I will not be denied now. I must engage the Children of Heqet."

"They appear to be in their natural element," said Stoker. "Is it wise, at this stage?"

"Why don't we see how Mr. Smith's plan works out," said Cockayne. "Okoth, the *Yellow Rose* is yours."

Okoth grinned broadly and took the wheel as Cockayne led them to the observation deck, sheltered from the sun beneath the huge balloon of the 'stat. Fanshawe began to clip the thick cable from the winding mechanism that had snared the *Skylady II* to her belt, and Cockayne had Stoker and Gideon help him manhandle the huge gun and its tripod out to the deck.

"How interesting, they can survive in the seas and fresh water," said Stoker.

"Perhaps they are more amphibian than aquatic," suggested Trigger. "Or perhaps they can breathe both, as I believe manatees do."

"She moved!" said Gideon excitedly as he peered over the railing. "I saw Maria move!"

"Then we need to be careful where we aim," said Cockayne. "Though, from what you've said, the automaton's pretty hardy. Mr. Bent!"

Bent nodded, positioned behind the Hotchkiss. Cockayne said, "The recoil's going to blow you on your fat ass if you're not careful, so be ready. Take into account the fact the Children of Heqet are moving forward, and we're drifting slightly to the left of them. Got them in your sights? Good, then swing it forward . . . a little smoother . . . not so far . . . wait . . . now!"

The Hotchkiss boomed and, as Cockayne had warned, threw Bent backward. Gideon peered over the side as the shell impacted into the water, throwing up a huge gout of brown water.

"Reload!" said Cockayne. "And another one! Behind them this time!"

Bent let loose a second shell, the observation deck shuddering, and began to reload again. His third shot was placed to the right of the Children of Heqet, and it seemed to do the job.

The creatures scattered in the river, leaving Maria floating alone, her arms bound tightly to her sides with a coil of rope.

"I'm going over," announced Fanshawe. Gideon took up the winding handle and braced himself as she stood with her boot heels on the lip of the deck, leaning backward out into thin air. She gave him a salute and a wink. "Don't worry, Gideon, I'll get your girl back."

"She's not my—" Gideon started to say, but Fanshawe had kicked out and begun to descend. He grabbed the handle and arrested her fall, then began to reel out more cable, already sweating in the fierce sun.

Cockayne, who was looking over the side, shouted, "Enough, Smith, she's down."

"What's happening?" asked Gideon.

"Oh, bravo, Rowena!" announced Trigger. "She's got Maria!"

"The frogs are closing in." Cockayne frowned. "They sure move fast."

"Oh!" gasped Trigger. "One of the Children of Heqet has grasped Maria's ankle!"

Cockayne picked up the rifle he'd leaned against the railings, then paused. "Stoker, take the crank. Gideon, come here."

Gideon did as he was bid, and Cockayne thrust the gun into his hands. "Stoker, keep winding. Gideon, hit that thing."

"Me?" said Gideon. "For God's sake, Cockayne, do it!"

"I concur," said Trigger. "This isn't a training exercise, Mr. Cockayne."

Cockayne continued to stare at Gideon, until he sighed and hefted the stock of the rifle to his shoulder. "I've never fired one of these things," he muttered.

"Line up the crosshairs in the sight," said Cockayne. "Get the thing's face right in the middle."

Below, Fanshawe was grimly holding onto the ropes around Maria as the mummy clutched the clockwork girl's ankle. He could see Maria's panic-stricken face, and more Children of Heqet closing in. Sweat beaded on his forehead as his finger tightened on the trigger. He had one chance, then the rest of the creatures would be upon Maria. Why the hell couldn't Cockayne have done it? He brought the mummy's face into sharp relief in the sight, its wide mouth dribbling and its teeth gnashing as it reached another clawed hand toward Maria, then squeezed.

The report deafened him and the recoil punched him away from the railing. There was silence for a moment as he regained his balance, then Cockayne let loose a whoop. "You did it, Gideon! Smack in the forehead! Wind that crank, Mr. Stoker!"

Gideon threw the rifle at Cockayne and elbowed Stoker away from the winding mechanism. "I'll do it," he said, turning the handle until he saw Fanshawe's hand wave at him from the edge of the deck. Trigger and Cockayne rushed to help her up, and together they hauled Maria over the side.

She was drenched, her clothes in rags, her hair matted and tangled with weeds. She was utterly beautiful. She gasped and looked at them, from face to face, until she finally settled on Gideon.

"You came for me. Across the world. You came and rescued me," she murmured.

Cockayne patted Gideon on the shoulder. "You did good, Smith. You did good."

He was about to say something to Maria that was only half-formed in his head, buoyed upon feelings he didn't really know how to explain, when Bathory hissed. They turned to see her leaning over the railing.

"The Children of Heqet have sunk below the surface," she said. "The reckoning is still to come."

They helped Maria onto the bridge, and Okoth clapped his hands as Cockayne took the wheel. Trigger said, "Mr. Okoth, back in Alexandria you said you might be able to take us to the site of the Rhodopis Pyramid. . . ."

Okoth beamed. "Astonishingly," he said, "I can do just that. We must go west. West to the land of the dead."

25

The Lost Pyramid of Rhodopis

"Is that it?" asked Bent. "Somebody tell me we didn't come halfway across the effing world for that."

Bent had temporarily removed himself from the cool shadow in the lee of the *Yellow Rose.* True to the big Ugandan's word, there were slabs of ancient, cracked pale stone scattered on the sand to which the Yankee could moor the 'stat. There was also a structure that Okoth had proudly introduced as the Pyramid of Rhodopis. After seeing it, Bent had to chuckle. He liked this Okoth; he was a man with a sense of humor, which this venture had been sorely lacking to date. The pyramid was made from the same stone as the blocks and broken columns half-buried in the white, hot sand, its four sides rising to a sharp point. It stood all of fifteen feet tall.

"I suppose this effing Rhodopis was some kind of effing circus dwarf?" complained Bent. He was all for a giggle, but not one that took so much effing effort, and in such heat.

Gideon said, "I don't understand. I was given to believe the pyramids were huge."

Okoth nodded enthusiastically. "Astonishing. Monstrous." Then he laughed deeply, holding on to Gideon's shoulder. "Oh, Mr. Smith. I see your confusion. You thought this was the Rhodopis Pyramid, in its majestic entirety? Oh, dear me. How astonishing. No, no. Mr. Smith . . . all of you . . . you must understand Egypt is a capricious, secretive place. What one sees one day might be gone forever the next. The landscape moves and shifts like an ocean, or a living thing. That is why there are no real maps of Egypt! Might as well just have a piece of yellow paper." He laughed again. "This is merely the tip of the pyramid. The rest is far below, under the desert, lost to the moving sands of time. And so it has been for many generations."

"But you said John Reed had entered the pyramid," said Gideon. "You said you would take us to where—"

"I said I would take you to the pyramid, which I have done." Okoth smiled. "Do you wish also to see the place where Dr. Reed gained access?"

Trigger looked up. Gideon breathed out and said, "Yes, Mr. Okoth, yes we would."

"Then back aboard Mr. Cockayne's astonishing airship!" commanded Okoth. "Back east, Mr. Cockayne, to the river."

❧

"Pretty little thing, for a machine," Cockayne said, seemingly half to himself, as he piloted the 'stat back toward the Nile.

Bent dropped his voice to a whisper. "Gideon said he saw her bubbies."

Cockayne smirked. "Careful what you say about that. The boy's in love with her."

Bent stared at him.

Cockayne shrugged. "Seen stranger things in the world, Mr. Bent."

Fanshawe had taken Maria off to wash away the detritus of her journey and get her some new clothes, and Bent saw Gideon waiting expectantly on the bridge for their return. Could he really be in love with Maria? The more Bent thought about it, the more he wondered if it was such an outrageous thing. She was pretty, she was intelligent, she was . . . well, for all intents and purposes, she wasn't much different than a real woman. He grinned to himself. And if she got to nagging, you could always let her wind down.

❧

Gideon gasped. Maria, her hair tied in a loose bun, stepped onto the bridge, wearing brown leather boots, beige jodhpurs, and a crisp white shirt.

"We're almost the same size." Fanshawe smiled. "It's been

a long time since I had a female friend to gossip with. What do you think?"

Gideon didn't know what to say. He felt a shiver on his thighs and an itch on his scalp, a dryness in his mouth and a flight of butterflies in his gut. So this was what they meant when they said someone looked *breathtaking.* His mouth worked but nothing came out, and Trigger stepped in. "You look enchanting, Maria. How are you feeling after your travails?"

"Better," she said. "Miss Fanshawe kindly wound me."

And there it was. The eternally present reminder that Maria was not like other women. But as her eyes met Gideon's, he couldn't help but wonder . . . did she, too, feel the dryness of mouth, the dancing of her stomach? She held his gaze and looked down demurely. "I'd like to thank you all for saving me. It's becoming something of a habit."

"Hey, what's a hero without a damsel in distress?" Cockayne smiled. He winked at Gideon, who realized the American was talking about *him* when he said hero. He flushed.

As the others gathered around Cockayne, looking toward the Nile, Gideon self-consciously sidled over to Maria. He said, "I, uh, I'm glad you're well."

She looked at him coolly. "Glad? Well . . . thank you, Mr. Smith."

More than glad! He wanted to shout, to holler. *More than glad! So much more that I don't know what words to use!*

"Maria . . . ," he said. He stopped, and started again. "Maria . . . in one of the Lucian Trigger adventures, John Reed meets a woman."

"A woman?"

"In the valley of Shangri-La. Her name is Kella. She loves him. But he cannot love her back."

"Of course." Maria nodded. "Because he is . . . well, he loves Captain Trigger."

Gideon pinched his nose. "No . . . well, yes. I know that's

what it means now. But when I read it . . . he meant they were too different. They were from different worlds."

Maria said nothing. Gideon went on, "But that didn't stop her loving him. I suppose."

"But he could not love her back," said Maria.

"No," said Gideon. "Because he loved Captain Trigger." He paused. This wasn't quite going as he intended it to. He tried to start again, but Maria held up her hand.

"I think I understand you, Mr. Smith. People who are so very different cannot find common ground for love to flourish. I thank you for taking the time to explain that to me."

To Gideon's dismay, Maria smiled tightly and walked over to the others. That wasn't what he had meant at all. What he had meant was . . . he sighed. Perhaps not everything in life could be adequately explained using *World Marvels & Wonders.*

The riverside, at least, was cooler, and Bent reveled in the breeze blowing off the Nile. Cockayne had tethered the 'stat to a thick-trunked palm tree. There was more shade, and the verdant landscape made the heat more tolerable. Almost like Hyde Park by the Serpentine. Though, Bent considered, there were no crocodiles in the Serpentine. Okoth's son, Mori, was standing on the bank with a rather unusual vessel moored in the river behind him.

"What is that?" asked Gideon. It had the shape of a turtle's shell, with curved glass windows at the front, and its smooth, black surface was warm and dry to the touch.

"My boat!" said Okoth proudly. "She is—"

"Astonishing, we know," said Bent. "Funny-looking boat, if you ask me."

"I do not think we understand," said Bathory. "Mr. Okoth, we were given to believe Dr. Reed was in the pyramid . . . why do you now bring us to the river?"

"All will be revealed," said Okoth. "Everyone, board my ship."

A hatch was set into the side of the strange hull, almost invisible until Mori pulled it open. Bent had his doubts, of course, but he allowed Mori to help him inside, the boy pushing against Bent's rump when he became wedged in the narrow opening.

"She is hulled with rubber," said Okoth proudly. "From Malaya, of all places. Not a single drop of water can get in."

"As one born in the rains, I thought you'd be all right with a bit of river water," said Bent.

"Hate the stuff. Bah." Okoth frowned. Bent double, he scuttled to a wheel and a series of levers and toggles. "All will be revealed," he said. "Steam engine, you know. Very powerful."

He fired up the engine and manipulated the levers, and the boat pulled away from the bank, holding steady against the flowing Nile. Then it lurched and began to sink, the green river water lapping at the glass windows. Bent felt his bile rising, pushed up by panic. "Eff!" he shouted.

Okoth slapped his forehead. "Oh no! Mr. Bent! You are too fat! We are sinking!"

Bent moaned and scrambled for the hatch, but Okoth burst out laughing. "Only joking, Mr. Bent! We are supposed to be sinking! That is why Dr. Reed employed me to help him in his search. Mr. Okoth's boat, she is an *underwater* boat!"

Bent scowled at the Ugandan. "Very effing funny, Okoth."

"A submersible," said Stoker wonderingly, as the water closed over the top of the windows. True to Okoth's word, not a drop managed to work its way into the cabin through the rubber seals around the glass and the hatch.

"She is, I am sure you will agree, astonishing."

❧

"Crocodile," said Okoth, nudging Gideon and pointing into the green, silty water beyond the windows.

Maria cried out and grabbed Gideon's other arm as the beast, its jaws yawning, swam past them, its cruel eyes peering in the windows, then moving on. She coughed, released him, and took a step away, though inside he cried out for her not to. The bed of the Nile was fronded with reeds and waving plants. Fish swam in bright, smartly moving shoals, and eels moved between the weeds. Okoth's submersible had a pair of strong, oil-burning headlights on the front, and they illuminated the dank, silted depths of the river as sand and debris floated and turned in the strong beams.

"You brought John Reed down here?" asked Gideon. He had to confess he had been as panicked as Bent when the submersible began to descend. After a lifetime around fishermen, he had lost too many friends and acquaintances to the cruel waves.

"Certainly I did, Mr. Smith. He had learned of another way into the pyramid. Those ancient Egyptians were rather clever."

"I thought you said they were stupid, before," sniffed Bent.

Okoth shrugged. "In some things, stupid. In others, clever." He paused. "Like anyone. Like yourselves."

Stoker took the opportunity to quietly inquire after Bathory's health.

"The sun robs me of my strength so," she whispered. "I have never felt its intensity so strongly and for such a long time."

"Do you need . . . blood?" Stoker blanched at the thought. He felt weak himself, and he did not know if he could siphon more from his arm, which ached considerably.

She shook her head. "You are not strong enough, Bram. You have helped me a great deal. I will be all right."

Fanshawe edged toward Gideon. "I'm worried about Lucian," she murmured.

Trigger sat, cross-legged, staring at his hands. His shoulders were hunched and his face slack and pale. Gideon said,

"The further we get into this, the less I think we are going to find anything positive about the fate of John Reed."

"This is the place," said Okoth. He killed the engine and the boat drifted in the currents. He turned it around so it was facing the sandy wall of the west bank. There, set into the rock, was an almost perfectly circular hole, a dozen feet across.

"A secret tunnel," said Cockayne. "And it goes straight to the pyramid?"

"That is what Dr. Reed believed," said Okoth.

Gideon turned to him. "But how did he get in there? We're so far underwater . . . it would be madness to try to swim. You would have no idea how far to go before there was air."

Okoth laughed. "Then it is an astonishingly good job Okoth comes well prepared. Mori, break out the tanks."

❧

"No," said Bent. "No, no, and no."

"I'm tempted to agree with our Mr. Bent on this one," said Bathory.

"And I," said Stoker.

"Nonsense!" said Okoth. "They are perfectly safe. These tanks are filled with air from my bellows . . . enough for a full half hour. Trust me, I have tried it myself." He paused. "Well, I got Mori to try it. And he is the fruit of my loins. It is as if I had done it myself."

Gideon took hold of a heavy metal sphere with a glass window in the front. It felt heavy, and his palms were starting to sweat. A tunnel. A tunnel. He tried to force the thought away. "And you put this on your head?"

"Yes, yes, and feed the air pipe in here, thusly. It cannot fail. The air tank is on your back. All you do is swim until you find a tunnel or cave with air."

Trigger stood forward and inspected the tank. "If John trusted Mr. Okoth, then so do I. I shall go. I do not expect you all to join me." He looked at Gideon. "Mr. Smith, you have been brave beyond all expectations thus far, but perhaps your mission is completed. You have killed at least two of the creatures now, and you have rescued Maria." He looked around. "But if anyone does wish to come with me . . ."

Gideon said nothing. No one looked at him. They all expected him to go. No one even thought he might not. . . .

Cockayne shrugged. "It's not my bag. But I'll wait with the *Yellow Rose*. You're going to need a ride out of here." He grimaced. "Hopefully."

"I'd quite like to not go," said Bent. "But I know I'm going to." He grinned. "Never did do what makes most sense when it comes to a story."

"My revenge is so close I can almost taste it," said Bathory.

"And I will go where the Countess goes," said Stoker.

Trigger looked at Fanshawe. "Rowena. I think you should stay with Cockayne. Ensure he is true to his word. If things go wrong . . . go and get help from Alexandria. And Miss Maria should stay as well."

Maria raised an eyebrow. "Because I am a woman, Captain Trigger? Or because I am *not*?"

Trigger opened his mouth, then closed it again. He smiled. "Touché, Miss Maria. I confess I acted out of valor toward a member of the fairer sex rather than prejudice against your origins. But you, of course, must decide yourself."

She nodded. "I will go where Mr. Smith goes."

Okoth held up a long rubber hold-all. "Anything you like, guns and whatnot, will fit in here. Dry as you like." He frowned. "But first . . . there is one other thing."

"Crocodiles?" asked Bent.

"Worse!" whispered Okoth loudly. "The curse! Awfully superstitious, those Egyptians. Look."

Gideon followed his finger, peering into the gloom to see the line of pictures etched into the stone lintel around the dark opening.

"Hieroglyphics," said Stoker. "Do you know what it says, Okoth?"

He nodded soberly. "*Whoso dares to lead enemies to desecrate this tomb shall die in the arms of their beloved*."

They pondered for a moment, then Trigger said, "That settles it. I no longer believe I have anything to lose, save the opportunity for revenge. I'm going first. Mr. Smith, do you concur?"

Gideon looked through the window at the tunnel, and he could already feel the cold, dead space pressing down on him, crushing the breath from him. Shapes swam in front of his eyes and coalesced into the grinning, awful faces of Oliver Thwaite and all those who had died in Lythe Bank, beckoning him into the dark opening. He licked his lips, but no moisture would come. He felt his legs buckle and put a hand out to steady himself on the wall of the submersible.

"I can't," he said in a small voice. "I'm terribly sorry, Captain Trigger, I just can't."

26

Beneath the River, Beneath the Sand

Mr. Okoth showed them how to breathe through the tubes, and how the helmets fitted snugly on their shoulders, the rubber seals tight across their chests to stop water getting in and precious air escaping. Bent staggered slightly under the weight of the helmet, and the last thing Stoker heard before the brass-and-glass globe muffled the journalist's complaining voice was, "If God had meant me to swim underwater, he wouldn't have made me a smoker."

Through the slightly warped glass window set into the brass dome, Stoker regarded the others suiting up, and Gideon, standing alone to one side, his eyes downcast. Curious. Whereas everything—even the chase by that mummy on Embankment, which had been rather thrilling—had seemed part of a wonderful adventure before, suddenly Stoker felt anxious and, if he was honest with himself, a little foolish. What on earth was he doing, getting suited up in this nonsense and preparing to enter an underwater tunnel, two thousand miles from home? It was as though a spell had been broken, as though Gideon Smith had been the glue holding the entire enterprise together. His sudden refusal at the fence had allowed things to fall apart.

But there was no opportunity to back out now. Mr. Okoth was indicating it was his turn. He waited in the airlock until he heard the distant rap of three knocks, their prearranged signal, then he opened the hatch, gasping in the helmet as the Nile rushed in, soaking him with cold water as it rose rapidly around him and filled the airlock. He felt a moment of panic as the water surrounded him, then relaxed as he continued to breathe in the helmet. The circular opening was ten feet ahead of him. All he had to do was leap forward and let the current take him toward it. There were oil lamps in the bag, but they would have to push through the tunnel in darkness until—*if,* he thought dourly—they found a dry section of the tunnel. Trigger was waiting in the dark circle of the opening, leaning back on the stone aperture, his clothing flowing with the rushing waters of the Nile. If, as Stoker was sure they would, they found the bones of John Reed in there, what would that do to Trigger? Stoker redoubled his grip on the bag, then leaped forward, letting the spring-hinged hatch close behind him. The water would drain out, and Mori would send Elizabeth and Bent through. He kicked off against the boat as Trigger stretched out his hand, and Stoker labored against the currents, the weight of the bag and the brass helmet dragging him downward. His outstretched fingers caught Trigger's, and the old adventurer pulled him into the tunnel. It was already so dark Stoker couldn't see the other man's face, so he patted him on the shoulder, and they turned to wait for Bent to come flailing through the silt-fogged water.

Above them, the faded hieroglyphics spelled out their ancient curse. If such a thing existed, then Trigger had already invoked it. To die in the arms of one's beloved . . . Stoker felt a pang of longing for Florence, and a wave of guilt at his adventures with—and unchivalrous thoughts toward—Elizabeth. He idly wondered whether he would die in Elizabeth's arms within this labyrinth, and shocked himself out of his reverie with the thought.

Stoker and Trigger pulled Bent into the tunnel. Bathory came next, her hands outstretched and finding Stoker's. He held her for a moment, in a different world, the Nile flowing over and between them, their eyes meeting through the glass. But where his eyes held a confused, tightly laced longing, there was something feral in Elizabeth's gaze, something animal. It made him shudder. The farther they had gotten from London, the less and less likely it seemed that Stoker could ever civilize Elizabeth Bathory. He sighed. What had he been thinking? That she was some toy, some pet project he could show off around London? Or had he harbored thoughts of . . . He pushed away the image that rose, of him attending functions and theater openings with Elizabeth on his arm despite the shocked, scandalized stares of those who had known him and Florence.

So that was it. Four of them against the Children of Heqet. As Trigger forged forward into the black tunnel, Stoker fell in behind him. Stoker wished Gideon was here, but he had recognized the look in his eye, the abject fear. The boy had a phobia of enclosed spaces. Stoker shook his head. They all had their weaknesses, it seemed.

They kept close together as they waded slowly into the interminable blackness. Half an hour of air, Okoth had said. He had promised to keep the submersible underwater for an hour, but they all knew by that time they would either be inside or dead. Stoker tried to mark time in his head, deciding to ask Trigger to turn back if they passed the quarter-hour mark beneath the river. Was the tunnel sloping gently upward, or was it his imagination? It was so hard to tell in the pitch black.

He felt Trigger move and jerk in front of him, and his breath came shallow and fast in the helmet. Were they under attack? Then he felt hands upon his helmet, and at the same time his shoulders breached the surface of the water. The tunnel had, indeed, sloped upward, and now they were thankfully in the air. With each step they drew above the waterline, and when it was at his waist Stoker tore at the rubber fastenings and pulled off the helmet.

His first, deep lungful of air was dry but fresh. Evidently the pyramid, despite being largely under the sands, had access to a source of air, presumably through some lost or hidden tunnel. Holding the bag above the water, Stoker felt inside for an oil lamp and matches, and he felt a palpable sense of relief from those behind him as the light illuminated the tunnel ahead. The water ended at stone steps, and he helped Elizabeth and Bent up them before lighting four more oil lamps.

"Thank eff for that," gasped Bent as he tore off his helmet. "I couldn't have gone much longer with that thing on."

They stood, dripping wet, and piled up the air tanks and helmets. "I rather hope we find another way out of here," said Trigger. "I'm not sure if we have enough air left to go back."

"Wonderful," said Bent, patting his pockets. "Oh, shit. I left my tobacco in my coat. Should have put it in that hold-all with my new hat."

The lamps showed the tunnel ahead leveled off, a square, stone passageway continuing beyond the reach of the dim light. Bathory, her hair plastered to her head, her long skirts sticking to her legs, asked, "What now? We just continue and hope this brings us to the pyramid?"

"I fear we have no other choice," said Stoker.

Stoker tried not to stare at the sopping Countess Bathory, though Bent obviously had no such compunction. He and the journalist were in silent agreement on one thing, then; the Countess looked most comely in her drenched clothes.

"We could make a bit of a fire," said Bent, looking around. "Dry off a bit."

Stoker frowned. "Fire eats oxygen, and we do not know how plentiful it is. Besides, what would we use as kindling?"

"There's a pile of sticks here," said Bent, bending down a little way up the tunnel. "Almost as though someone's left them here for that purpose."

"They aren't sticks," murmured Bathory. "They're bones."

Bent leaped back as though burned. Stoker glanced at Trigger, knowing what he was thinking. "John's bones?" asked Trigger in a whisper.

Stoker picked one up, and it crumbled to dust in his fingers. "They are immeasurably ancient. Tomb robbers from long ago, perhaps." He looked at them. "I have heard tell that the pyramids of the ancients are replete with devices and traps to deter robbers."

"Maybe they thought the curse was deterrent enough," said Bathory.

Trigger crouched and ran his fingers through the dusty

bones. "I pray the curse is real," he said quietly. "I would give everything to die in John's arms."

As Stoker sorted through the bag and checked the weapons, Bent took him to one side and said, "The Countess is here to avenge her fallen husband. Trigger's after his bum-chum. But what the eff are you and me doing here, Stoker?"

Stoker shrugged. "I promised to help Countess Bathory."

"Get off it. You wouldn't be putting your life at risk for a vampire you hardly know. Not a respectable married geezer like you."

Bent's words hit home hard, making the gulf between Stoker and Florence seem more painfully acute. "So what is *your* reason, Mr. Bent?"

Bent shrugged. "Same as yours, at the end of the day. You're expecting to get a book out of this, whether you admit it or not. I want the big story."

Stoker made a thoughtful face. "That is how this enterprise began," he admitted. "I was holidaying in Whitby, seeking inspiration."

Bent laughed. "You've certainly got that. Bet you weren't expecting to end up in some bloody tunnel in Egypt."

"Art takes us where it will, Mr. Bent." He looked briefly at Bathory, then at Trigger. "Just like love."

"Art my arse," sniffed Bent. "Deep down you're the same as me. You want to spin a good yarn. Tell a good story. It's in our blood. We'll go to the ends of the effing earth if we have to—well, we've proved that. And we'll put our lives on the line." He paused, staring into the oil lamp's flame. "Crackers, ain't it?"

Stoker had to smile despite himself, despite their situation. "Yes, Mr. Bent," he said, looking at Bathory once more. "Thank you for putting it all into context for me. It is, as you say, crackers."

And suddenly, very suddenly, he felt a stinging, aching sense of absence. Florence. He had put her to one side for a spell, forgotten she was as integral to him as his hand or, yes, his heart. Now, as the adventure unraveled without Mr.

Gideon Smith, regret flooded him. How could he have set her aside? How could he have done that?

"You all right, Stoker?" asked Bent.

"Yes." He nodded. "Just some dust in my eye."

He handed out the rifles and pistols they had brought from Trigger's home, along with others that Gideon had persuaded Cockayne to liberate from the armory of the *Yellow Rose*. He said, "Elizabeth, you are the only one of us who has really engaged these monstrosities hand to hand. Do you have any advice?"

She looked Stoker in the eye. "They are relentless. Keep firing, even when you are sure you have downed one. And if they keep coming . . ." She shrugged and turned away. "Perhaps you should think about turning those weapons on yourselves."

"Never," said Trigger. "Their reign of terror is at an end. It is up to us to stop them, for who knows what further carnage and misery they are plotting right at this moment?"

"The thing with a good story," said Stoker thoughtfully as he holstered a handgun in the waistband of his trousers, "is that even the most foul villain needs some kind of motivation. What, I wonder, are the Children of Heqet about? Why have they been amassing these strange artifacts?"

"I'll tell you what," said Bathory. "We'll ask the last one standing that question just before it dies. Now come on."

They walked for two hours along the seemingly unending stone corridor. "We must be nearly effing there," muttered Bent. "My fallen arches are effing killing me."

Trigger, in the lead, held up his hand, and they stopped. Stoker said, "What is it?"

Trigger pointed, and they saw the corpse hanging from a cruel metal spike, protruding from the stone wall, that had penetrated its skull. He said, "John?"

Stoker rifled through the wallet in the dried body's leather jacket. "Walton Jones. Wasn't he one of Walsingham's men, according to Reed's notes?"

Trigger nodded vaguely. "He's losing it," whispered Bent to Stoker. "He'll be about as much use as a chocolate fireguard when push comes to shove."

Bathory crouched and inspected the floor. "There's something different here. See how the tunnel has become squares of stone for as far as we can see?"

Stoker leaned forward with his lamp outstretched. "There are holes ranged on both sides of the wall, all along the passage." He squinted in the gloom. "There appears to be a lever of some kind, perhaps fifty yards hence. There is evidently some fiendish mechanism behind these walls."

Stoker emptied the rations from the hold-all and tossed it ahead of him, past the skeleton. As it hit the ground another metal spike extended from one of the holes in the wall at a frightening velocity, quivering as it reached its limit. Stoker turned to look at them. "Had that been one of us, we would have been skewered."

He fell to his hands and knees and inspected the square stones. "There is evidently some kind of pattern to follow, to prevent the trap springing. The question is, what is it, and how do we decode it?"

Bathory sighed. "We do not have time. Gentlemen, avert your eyes."

❦

Stoker closed his eyes and tried to remember the words to a music hall song he'd heard awhile back, begging himself not to weaken. From behind him he heard a strange, alien sound, as though something was being stretched and distorted. Bathory made a soft, animal growl, and he bit his lip. He heard Bent moaning, "I can't do it. I have to look."

The journalist evidently wished he hadn't done so. "There's an effing dog in here!"

Bent staggered back to the wall of the corridor as the beast, its jaws slavering, leaped. Stoker smiled. "Not a dog. A wolf."

"That's the Countess?" asked Trigger mildly.

Stoker nodded. Bent said, "I've heard of one or two women

in Whitechapel who apparently have the reputations of dogs, but this is something effing else entirely."

The wolf paused at the start of the booby-trapped corridor, sniffing the dry air, then bounded forward. As soon as the vast paws hit the ground, it leaped again, as a spike struck into the space it had just vacated. With two more bounds, and two more spikes, the wolf was at the other side. Bent picked up the lamp and squinted; he rubbed his eyes and shielded the back of the lamp so to better direct the beam. He swore softly. In the wolf's place was the naked form of Bathory, crouched on all fours.

"I have died and gone to heaven," he said. "Let those effing mummies take me now. I have seen a little slice of the great hereafter."

"You shall die and go somewhere, for sure," said Stoker, "if we cannot find a way to get the rest of us across."

In the thin beam of light, Stoker saw Bathory haul on the lever set into the stone wall, and the spikes receded, the one nearest to him spilling the desiccated corpse to the floor with a dry smack. The dried head separated from the shoulders and rolled across the corridor. No spikes issued forth.

"Do you think it's safe?" said Bent.

"Someone needs to test it," said Stoker.

"Mr. Bent?" called Bathory from the other side. "Could you be a darling and bring me my clothes?"

Bent had picked up the fallen skirts and was halfway down the corridor toward Bathory before he realized what he had done.

Trigger gave a lopsided smile. "It's safe. She has disarmed the mechanism."

Stoker applauded. "Excellent work, Countess! And bravo, Mr. Bent! Your courage knows no bounds."

They gave Bathory a few moments to dress, then gingerly crossed the tiled floor, as Bent stood with his back to the Countess, his hands over his eyes, slowly counting to a thousand. "It's all right, Mr. Bent," said Stoker. "The Countess is decent."

Bent grabbed his arm. "You won't tell anyone, will you, Stoker?"

"Tell them what?"

Bent cocked his head toward Bathory. "That I finally found my dream woman." He dropped his voice to a whisper. "But she effing terrifies me."

❧

After seeing Countess Bathory's bloodlust on the *Yellow Rose,* and now her supernatural ability to transform into a powerful-looking wolf, Stoker began to feel they might just have a fighting chance against the Children of Heqet. Looking forward, he almost tripped over something at his feet.

Stoker crouched and peered in the light of his lamp at one of Okoth's helmets and air tanks. Trigger bent down and covered his mouth.

"John's," he said at last.

Stoker tried to smile. "Then at least we know he made it safely this far."

"Perhaps this ancient sepulcher is John's tomb also," said Trigger hollowly.

They walked on in silence, and a sudden draft caused the flames in their oil lamps to flicker. Stoker peered ahead. "Fresh air. And I can see light, though it's very faint."

They hurried forward, and Stoker murmured to Bathory, "Are you well, Countess? You look paler than usual."

She smiled, but thinly. "The transformation took more out of me than I expected. It is the harsh sun I have endured, and the lack of sustenance."

Stoker stroked his beard. "If you really need to feed . . ."

She shook her head and pointed forward. "Some kind of open doorway ahead, Bram."

"Careful!" called Bent. "Might be another effing booby trap!"

Stoker and Bathory paused by the stone opening through which the tunnel widened to a room, with a similar, darkened doorway some thirty feet opposite.

Stoker poked his head around the opening. "It is lit with torches," he observed. "Set into sconces on the walls. Evidently, we are entering inhabited territory."

"The Children of Heqet," said Bathory grimly.

"Curious room, innit?" said Bent.

The floor, ceiling, and walls were composed of black and white tiles, though not symmetrically laid, and of quite a different nature than the stones in the booby-trapped tunnel. Some of the black tiles had smaller white squares set into opposing corners, giving an appearance that straight lines were in fact wavy, while tiles of diminishing sizes and rounded edges tricked the eye into seeing extended vanishing points where there were none, and swirls of tiles, though static, appeared to be rotating slowly, first one way, then the other.

Bent shouldered past Stoker for a look, then pulled back and pushed the pith helmet back on his head. "Giving me a fit of the vapors."

"We know how fiendish these ancients were," said Stoker. "It would be best to tread carefully."

"Check your ammunition," ordered Trigger, spinning the chamber of his revolver. "We're close to them. I can feel it."

Stoker looked around on the ground and found a few fallen stones, which he cast in a handful across the checkerboard floor. Nothing moved. Holding the pistol aloft, he took a step onto the tiles, then another. He turned and shrugged, and Trigger followed him, rifle in hands. The two men padded to the center of the room, then beckoned for the others to follow. The other doorway was ahead of them, doused in darkness. Trigger said quietly, "Whatever we want is through there. Keep your wits about you now."

As Bathory and Bent joined them in the center of the room, Stoker cocked his head. "What was that?"

Beneath their feet, hidden cogs and gears began to turn, and the ground began to thrum with their regulated movement. Bent frowned and said, "It could be my imagination, but . . . is this room moving?"

Your Fear Is a Lie

"Tea!" called Okoth, clapping his hands and waving them at Mori.

Cockayne stared at Gideon until he met the American's eyes and said irritably, "What?"

Cockayne shrugged. "Wasn't expecting that from you, Smith."

Gideon looked at his hands. They were trembling. "I couldn't," he said in a small voice. "I just couldn't."

"What scares you?" said Cockayne.

"Leave him, Louis," said Fanshawe quietly.

Gideon shook his head. "It's the tunnels. When I was a small boy . . . I got lost. Underground."

Gideon Smith first truly knew fear when he was nine years old. Oliver Thwaite had been reported missing a scant hour before, and the men were getting organized to comb the moors. Gideon knew where he was, though; Oliver Thwaite spoke of nothing else other than the pirate gold that lay within the catacombs of Lythe Bank. He'd tried to tell his dad but had been unable to penetrate the carefully controlled panic infecting the grown-ups. So he decided to rescue Oliver himself.

Thanks to his already vast knowledge of Trigger's stories, Gideon knew exactly what was required for a descent into the underworld. He would need light, of course, and had borrowed an oil lamp from his daddy's shed. Chasms or sheer stone faces would need to be traversed or scaled; he hadn't dared take a rope from the *Cold Drake,* but his mother's spare washing line would do. A ball of string, tied to the entrance of the caves and unwound behind him, would ensure he wouldn't get lost. Gideon wasn't sure why, but he did know brandy was something of a cure-all, so he decanted a couple of inches from his daddy's bottle into a stone jug.

Gideon had never ventured inside Lythe Bank before, of course. As he stood before the black fissure, he felt something inside his throat catch, felt his chest constrict. The crack in the high walls seemed to beckon him into a world not his, a world where thousands of tons of rock waited to press down upon him, a world without sunlight or fresh air.

Unfurling the string behind him and holding the oil lamp high, Gideon sidled with ungainly crab-movements along the narrow passage, his back against the rough wall. He shouted Oliver's name and the caves mockingly echoed his words. His adventure was not quite as thrilling as he would have hoped. The weight of his situation pressed down on him, all those tons and tons of rock gathered around his thin nine-year-old self. Gideon began to breathe quickly and shallowly, panic rising. One stumble, and the oil lamp crashed to the sharp rocks. Plunged into blackness, Gideon began to wail, then sob, and hurriedly retraced his steps along the string . . . which hung limply in his hands, sheared off by the angular rocks. He began to run blindly onward, falling and scuffing the palms of his hands. He was as lost as Oliver Thwaite. But more than that . . . he couldn't breathe. The caves had lured him from the wide-open spaces. Gideon's eyes bulged and he clawed at his throat, but it was no use.

He was dying.

He didn't know how long he lay there, dying in the impenetrable black, before a faint glow appeared and grew into an oil lamp carried by a frowning Arthur Smith, who picked him up and carried him back toward the light. With each step, Gideon's imminent death seemed to recede, and his breath came in ragged rasps. Shame mingling with relief, he realized he had walked barely thirty steps into the tunnels, and in seconds Arthur had him out.

"You went to look for him? You're a brave lad. Foolish, but brave. Promise me you'll never go in there again," Arthur said into Gideon's hair. "I couldn't bear it if I lost you."

Then he frowned and put Gideon down, and looked back at Lythe Bank. Gideon knew what he was thinking. "I'd better get the men, though. If Oliver Thwaite's in there . . ."

Arthur Smith knew, and Gideon could sense, there wouldn't be a second small boy brought out of those tunnels that day.

❧

Cockayne nodded. "And this fear has lived with you ever since." He ruminated for a moment, then said, "Your fear is a lie, Smith."

Gideon frowned. "I'm not lying. You weren't there. You didn't see me. I couldn't breathe. I couldn't move."

"I didn't say you were lying. I said your *fear* is a lie," said Cockayne. "What, you think the walls are going to close in on you? The roof will collapse? You'll be lost in the darkness forever?"

Gideon nodded. "All those things."

Cockayne waved his hand. "We're, what, thirty feet below the surface here? The submersible could crack. Water could pour in and drown us. Crocodiles could eat us. Those goddamn mummies could come back. Why the hell aren't you curled up in a ball, whimpering for your mother?"

Gideon took a breath. "I don't know."

Cockayne smirked. "You flew from London to Alexandria strung under a balloon. That didn't scare you?"

Gideon shrugged. Cockayne went on, "Your fear is a lie, Gideon. It only hurts you because you believe it. Stop believing it. Tell it to go jump in the lake."

"What would you know about it?" asked Gideon, not intending to sneer but doing so anyway.

Cockayne stroked his mustache. After a long moment he said, "What do you think I'm scared of, Gideon?"

"I don't know."

"I'm scared of being more than twenty feet off the ground." Cockayne smiled.

Fanshawe laughed. "Louis, you're a 'stat pilot."

He turned to her and nodded. "Yes. And how do I do it? Because I stopped believing the lie." He paused and looked back to Gideon. "When I was nine years old I lived on a farm in Connecticut. I had two brothers. We had a grain tower, and my brothers liked to climb it, play pirates. I was always too little. One day I followed them up the ladder and out around the rim. I looked down. I couldn't move. I was frozen to the spot."

Cockayne accepted a cup of tea from Mori and sipped at it, pulling a face. He handed it back. "Needs sugar, kid." He looked into the middle distance. "Robert, who was my eldest brother, came up to help me. He climbed across the domed roof of the grain tower and tried to get me to scramble back to the ladder. I couldn't move. He tried to grab me, told me he'd kick my ass if I didn't move."

Gideon looked on, listening despite himself.

Cockayne said, "Robert fell. Lost his grip. His eyes met mine as he fell. He held my gaze all the way down."

"What happened?" said Gideon.

Cockayne shook his head. "I don't really remember. I was in shock, I guess. They got me down somehow."

"Robert? Your brother?"

Cockayne looked down. "He died. I could barely climb the stairs after that. I knew everybody blamed me, even if they didn't say so. I'd look out of my bedroom window, I'd get dizzy. But I knew it would ruin my life, if I let it. So I looked my fear dead in the eye, and told it to go jump in the lake." He stood silently for a moment. "Don't think it doesn't creep up on me. Don't think I never stand on the observation deck of the *Yellow Rose* and feel that tingle in my feet, my stomach turning somersaults. Don't think I never look over the edge and suddenly don't know which is up and which is down. But my fear's a lie, Gideon, and I'll be fucked seven ways to Sunday before I let a lie bring me down."

Gideon turned away and stared through the window, at the black hole of the tunnel. He said softly, "That's what it means to be a hero."

"If you like," said Cockayne. "Maybe that's just what it means to be a human being. You kick a dog often enough, it knows if it comes near you, it'll get kicked. So it keeps away. That's the difference between a man and a dog. Kick a man, a real man, and he'll bide his time until he can kick you back, only harder. That's what you've got to do, Gideon. Kick back. Don't let a lie bring you down. Tell your fear—"

"To go jump in the lake," said Gideon. He turned around and smiled. "Mr. Okoth? Do you have any of those air tanks left?"

"I'm coming with you," said Maria.

They all looked at her. Gideon said, "No. It'll be dangerous."

Fanshawe sighed. "Didn't Maria deck one of those mummies with one punch?" She shook her head. "You men really are full of your own hot air, aren't you?"

Cockayne raised his eyebrow. "Really? One punch?"

"I'm stronger than I look, Mr. Cockayne," said Maria. "And I don't need an air tank. Not after the Children of Heqet brought me halfway across the world under the water."

Gideon shook his head again. "Maria, no. I insist."

She smiled tightly. "Mr. Smith, you are being what I believe Mr. Cockayne would call an asshole." She looked at the American. "Is that right?"

Cockayne grinned. "Perfectly, Miss Maria."

As she helped put the air tank on Gideon's back, Fanshawe gave him a hot, deep kiss. "For luck," she said.

She tightened the rubber seals on the helmet and stepped back. Gideon, the sword hanging at his side, gave her a little wave, then tugged at Maria's arm. The pair of them entered the airlock and Okoth shut them in it.

"Nice story," said Fanshawe to Cockayne. "I assume all of that was complete balderdash?"

He shrugged. "Actually, no. It was the truth."

She looked at him and blinked. "Louis Cockayne. Could it be you're human after all?"

He grinned. "Maybe. But keep it to yourself, hey? I've got a reputation to uphold."

They watched as Gideon flailed about in the water, Maria, eerily floating without helmet or air tank, guiding him toward the tunnel. Fanshawe said, "He must be petrified."

"If he does this, he'll be a hell of a lot stronger," said Cockayne.

"And if he doesn't?"

Cockayne shrugged. Fanshawe looked at her watch. "Let's give them half an hour and get up to the top. I need some sun and fresh air."

As they paused on the lip of the tunnel, Maria and Gideon looked back to the submersible. Cockayne pressed close to the window and winked, and raised his right hand, the thumb and forefinger curled together in an 'O', the other fingers extended. He said, almost to himself, "Kick some ass, kid."

As he staggered up the sloping passage, the water sloshing around his thighs, then his calves, then his ankles, Gideon unclipped the helmet and let it fall with a gasp. All he could feel was the darkness, heavy and oppressive, and beyond it the rough rock, pressing down on him, squeezing the breath from him. He tried to fill his lungs, but they wouldn't expand, and pinpricks of light danced in front of his eyes.

He felt Maria's wet hand take his, smelled her river-sodden hair as she came in close. There was no breath on his cheek, but he felt her lips brush his ear. "Are you all right?"

"I can't . . . breathe . . . ," he whispered. "I can't do this."

"Your fear is a lie," she murmured, and he felt her hands on his waist, her body aligning itself against his. "When Rowena kissed you—"

"For luck."

"When she kissed you for luck . . . did you like that?"

He nodded, finally gulping down the cool, dry air of the darkness.

Then Maria kissed him.

Your fear is a lie.

His hands found her body, sopping wet.

Your fear is a lie.

And, indeed, his anxiety receded. His fear evaporated. Not just the fear of the darkness, of the rock surrounding him.

His fear of the differences between them.

Finally, Gideon abandoned himself to Maria, met her tongue with his own, without question, felt his body stir against hers, felt himself dissolving into her.

She pulled away, planting a lighter kiss on his lips, as though signing off a letter. Gideon felt his heart hammering, though not from fear. When it calmed to a manageable cadence, he retrieved the oil lamps and matches.

As the flame flared, Maria smiled at him out of the darkness. She was beautiful. The lamps revealed a tight, roughly hewn passageway extending into the blackness. He held up his oil lamp. Whatever there was to fear, it was not the ages-old rock, nor the clockwork girl. Whatever there was to fear, it lay ahead of them.

Your fear is a lie. All *fear is a lie.*

He felt something dig into him, in his pocket, and pulled it out. The jet charm he had, a lifetime ago, given to his father. He tied the cord around Maria's neck. "Perhaps it will serve you better," he whispered.

From somewhere deep within the dark earth, something ground against something else, something turned, something shuddered. Gideon looked quizzically at Maria.

"Did the earth move?" he asked. He put his hand on the

reassuring hilt of the sword, and in his other he took Maria's. "Come on."

It was not Bent's imagination. The room was turning in a clockwise direction, gathering speed. Then they all yelled as the floor tipped them forward, and the wall with the doorway in it rushed toward them. With another turn, they were on what had been the ceiling, the torches clattering from their sconces and rolling free.

"I can't get my bearings," shouted Stoker. "This infernal chessboard . . ."

He no longer knew what was up or down. He heard Bent being violently sick as the room rotated one way, then the other. The door was now in front of them again, and he tried to strike out for it, but he felt his feet slipping from underneath him, his sense of balance utterly destroyed. Even when he closed his eyes he saw the shifting black and white shapes, and his head pounded.

Then, as abruptly as it had started, the movement stopped. Stoker picked himself up from the floor and looked around. Everyone else seemed to be in one piece, though ragged from the ordeal. He found his pistol on the floor and drew his sword. Something was going to happen.

"Stoker . . . ," said Bent weakly.

He looked up. Ahead of them, framed in the black doorway—he no longer knew if it was the door by which they had entered or the one facing it—was a shambling figure stepping into the light from the scattered torches and rolling lamps.

"The Children of Heqet, at last," said Trigger.

There were eight of the things, and they came at the adventurers in a relentless wave. Stoker emptied five shots from his chamber into the first creature, and though the impact sent it spinning backward, it picked itself up and came at him again. He heard the sound of gunfire and the clatter of spent cartridges all around, smelled the rising stench of gunpowder.

"Elizabeth!" cried Stoker. "Elizabeth, if your nature can serve us at all, then now is the time . . . !"

Bathory needed no further imperative. She snarled and crouched like a cat, her eyes shining and her jaw displaying her extended canines. Then she leaped at the nearest mummy and tore into it.

Bent swung at the creature with the stock of his rifle as Trigger emptied his gun into it. Stoker saw Bathory tear through another mummy. She was by far having the best time of it; their bullets were slowing the things down, but not stopping them. He noticed Trigger, backed into a corner and pumping shots into the stomach of a mummy that refused to go down. Bathory had been cornered by two, and she was bleeding profusely from a row of claw marks across her face. Stoker cried out and began to fire into one of the mummies, blasting holes into its torso until it glanced down, almost comically, at the gaping wound in its chest, and collapsed into two.

Stoker ran to Bathory. There were three Children of Heqet down. Bent and Trigger were firing at the others, but then there was the terribly final click of their empty weapons.

"Elizabeth is sorely wounded," shouted Stoker.

The Children of Heqet advanced, spreading out to come at them, hissing and muttering in their dry, dead language. Stoker bit his lip. They were not going to escape from this, he knew with sudden certainty. The nearest creature grinned widely and launched itself at him.

And paused, blinking its milky eyes in surprise. Black ichor began to trickle, then flowed more freely, from a perfect line across its thin, ragged neck.

Its head toppled from its body, and the creature collapsed.

Behind it, brandishing a dripping sword, was Gideon Smith.

❧

"Mr. Smith!" cried Trigger. Gideon grinned, but there was no time for self-congratulations. There were four Children of Heqet left, and they turned and opened their wide mouths at Gideon, clicking and whistling in their strange tongue.

Bathory looked in a bad way; Bent was sitting on the floor, breathing hard. They had felled three mummies between them already, but they looked the worse for it. And the battle was not won yet.

Maria stepped forward to Gideon's side. He felt a tingle in his sword arm, a blood-rush to his head. Vengeance was in his grasp. Vengeance for his father, vengeance for the crew of the *Cold Drake* and the countless others slain by the Children of Heqet. With a roar that built up deep within him and issued forth like a battle cry, Gideon swung the sword at the nearest monster, connecting with the parched skin of its shoulder. There was a momentary resistance as the blade met bone, then he was through and swinging freely. The creature looked at him for a second with its pale eyes, then its right arm and part of its desiccated, rag-bound torso separated, and it collapsed in a dry heap at Gideon's feet.

The three remaining mummies backed off, allowing Gideon and Maria to run to the others. She aimed the guns they had brought, firing into the nearest creature until the chambers were empty.

"Guns have little effect on them," gasped Stoker. "Mr. Smith, it is damned good to see you, if you'll excuse my uncouth language."

"It's *effing* good to see you, Smith," corrected Bent. "But there's three of 'em left. And they're closing in."

Bent was right. Could Gideon stave them off? Not, he feared, without someone falling under their claws. He brandished his sword and commanded the others to get back. If he was going to die here, deep underground, at the claws and teeth of these monsters, he wouldn't go down without a fight. And, he realized with surprise, he wasn't scared anymore. He looked at Maria, and she looked at him and smiled. Gideon gripped the hilt of the sword more firmly.

"Let's have your best shot," he murmured.

Hissing and creeping, the Children of Heqet walked slowly

toward them, their thin muscles tensing as they readied to pounce.

"Hold!"

Gideon tore his gaze away from the mummies, to another figure standing in the open doorway. It was a man, broad-chested and pale, dressed in a dirty, ragged shirt open to his waist, ripped trousers, and battered brown boots, a worn satchel slung over his shoulder. He was middle-aged and undeniably handsome, his hair gone to gray and a little long and shaggy, his features fine and pronounced beneath the rough gray beard. About his neck was a gold chain with a red gem set into a golden clasp. He regarded them with piercing blue eyes and held up his hand, palm outward. Incredibly, the Children of Heqet paused and stood still, though they continued to hiss softly and bare their teeth.

Trigger, crouching on the floor beside Bathory, blinked and frowned at the man. He rose slowly and said, very softly, "John?"

What Happened to Dr. John Reed

"John." Tears flowed down Trigger's dusty face. "John. My God, I truly thought you were dead."

Trigger took a step forward, but the Children of Heqet hissed and raised their claws. Gideon glanced at Stoker, then back at the man who, incredibly, Trigger had addressed as John Reed. Was it really him, or some infernal trick? The way the mummies gathered behind Reed made Gideon redouble his grip on the hilt of the sword; something felt terribly, terribly not right about this.

Reed looked curiously from face to face, lingering on Maria's beautiful face. One of the mummies muttered something to him in its alien language of whistles, clicks, and singsong syllables; Reed nodded thoughtfully and eventually said, "Lucian. You shouldn't have come here."

"We came to rescue you!" said Trigger. "Do these creatures have you prisoner? Do they work for Walsingham? Has he taken the weapon?"

Reed cocked an eyebrow and frowned, as though trying to keep up with Trigger's rapid-fire questions. "Walsingham? No, Lucian, they don't work for Walsingham. They work for me." He took a step forward, ignoring Trigger's outstretched arms and instead standing in front of Maria. Gideon tried to muscle between them, but Reed ignored him. "As to the weapon . . . well, you have done your research, Lucian. Very good. And thank you, also."

"Thank you? For coming to rescue you?" said Trigger.

Reed turned to him. "No. Thank you for bringing me the final piece of the puzzle." He glanced almost casually over his shoulder and said to the mummies. "Bring the girl into the tomb. If anyone tries to stop you, kill them."

"John!" said Trigger in horror.

"Trigger," said Bent gently. "Ain't it obvious what's going on here? It's not the mummies, not your Mr. Walsingham. There's nobody behind all this but John Reed. He's only the effing villain of the piece."

"Don't be ridiculous," said Trigger shortly. "John, tell him. For God's sake, tell him."

At last, as though finally fully recognizing Trigger, Reed gifted him a smile. "Come with me. Bring your friends."

Gideon tried to intervene as two of the Children of Heqet gripped Maria's arms, but she shook her head. "Wait," she murmured. "Let's see what's going on first. You'll just get yourself killed."

Reed instructed one of the other mummies to relieve Gideon of his sword and the rest of them of their guns, which were spent of ammunition anyway. Then they were shepherded through the doorway and along a short, dark corridor into a large square room lit by flaming torches ranged along inward-sloping walls that merged into a dark point far above them. They were finally inside the pyramid, Gideon realized. Before them were twin thrones, ornately carved from flaking yellow stone, set upon a raised dais. On the wall behind the thrones was a series of ancient paintings, surrounded by hieroglyphics. Two huge statues reared up behind the thrones, sporting the same horrific frog faces as the Children of Heqet. There was a pool, or a bath, fed by a constant flow of clear water, and a table groaning with fruits and vegetables. On an open fire with a metal grill mounted on bricks, an animal Gideon couldn't identify roasted in its own juices. He could almost hear Bent salivating beside him. And it was a tomb, as Reed had said; before the thrones were laid two sarcophagi carved with impassive faces, one female, one male. He had a sense there were doorways and arches that led off into other rooms, but his eyes were drawn to the right and a curious sight: what looked for all the world like the prow of a small boat, perhaps fifteen feet from the nose to the flat back. There was a wooden throne within it, and some kind of hood or canopy was open above it, giving it the look of a yawning mouth—just like that crocodile they had seen from the submersible, thought Gideon.

Reed nodded to this strange boat-shape, and the two Children of Heqet dragged Maria toward it and stepped over the rim. The outside of the structure shone dully in the torchlight—some kind of metal, realized Gideon. Brass. They sat Maria heavily in the wooden seat and stood sentry at either side. Gideon caught her eye and she gave him a tight smile that seemed to say *Wait. Bide your time.*

"What's the meaning of this, Reed?" demanded Gideon. "What are you doing with Maria?"

"John?" asked Trigger. "Is he right? Are you really the villain?"

Reed made a face. "What's a villain, Lucian? What's a hero, come to that?" He paused, as though lost in some reverie, then shook his head a little and looked up. "Who are your friends, Lucian?"

Trigger introduced them all one by one. Reed's gaze lingered on Gideon, and he said, "Gideon Smith. That name . . . a madman once told me a Gideon Smith would destroy the world."

"Takes one to know one," muttered Bent, then said more loudly, "Ah, Dr. Reed, you mentioned food . . . ?"

Reed gestured toward the table and Bent stepped forward, shrinking back as the nearest mummy bared its teeth.

"It's all right, let him get food. Let them all get food, if they want it," instructed Reed, and the creature fell back.

"They obey you," said Gideon. "They understand you?"

Reed nodded. "And I them."

"Impossible," said Stoker, helping the weakened Countess Bathory, who hung on to his shoulder. "Their language has not been heard for two thousand years or more. You could not have learned it, no matter how long you have been in here."

"I didn't need to." Reed smiled. He delved into his satchel and withdrew a small ball shining brightly in the reflected torchlight.

"The Golden Apple of Shangri-La," breathed Gideon.

God gifted mankind the golden apple, which removes the barriers of language. It was kept here in Shangri-La, to which it also gives the bounty of lush protection from the Himalayan winter. When mankind is ready, the golden apple will once again unite the nations of the world in one tongue.

Reed nodded. "You are familiar with my adventures, Mr. Smith."

"And I recall you climbed to the peak of Everest to recover the apple from Von Karloff," said Gideon. "You didn't return it to Shangri-La. The valley must have died."

Reed looked into the shining apple. "Poor Shangri-La. It was the nearest I will ever come to paradise, I think. And now . . . a snowy wasteland. Once I realized Walsingham had dispatched Von Karloff there, I couldn't leave the apple in Shangri-La."

"Even though removing it would mean the valley would die, and all the people in it?" asked Gideon.

"Even though they would all die," agreed Reed, focusing on Gideon and the others. "That was when I knew. When I realized."

"Realized what, John?" asked Trigger.

"*Cui bono*," said Gideon quietly.

Reed smiled at him. "Very good, Mr. Smith. *Cui bono*. To whose benefit? It was then I realized John Reed was being taken for a fool. And it was not going to continue. Lucian, I expect you have many questions. I owe you answers, at least."

"You can tell me on the way home," said Trigger briskly. "Louis Cockayne and Rowena Fanshawe are waiting up above us with a dirigible. Let's get you back to London." He shook his head. "You've really been down here all this time? For a year?"

"A year? Has it been that long?" Reed pinched his nose. "Time seems to pass differently here."

"John," said Trigger softly. "You are . . . you do not seem well. Let us return to London at once."

"London, yes," said Reed. "London, of course." He smiled. "But I think I shall make my own way. By dragon."

Bent shook his head, tearing into a hunk of roasted flesh. "I thought this lot was effing bonkers, but you take the biscuit, Reed." He chewed thoughtfully. "What is this, anyway?"

Reed shrugged. "Some kind of lizard, I imagine. The Children of Heqet bring my food." He paused. "Where to start . . . ?"

"At the beginning," suggested Stoker. "I always find that best."

"The cycle of life has many beginnings," said Reed. "But, to choose one . . . I set off from London in search of the fabled Rhodopis Pyramid, and riches beyond my wildest dreams. I could not have guessed what I would find here. I found freedom. The shackles that had been forged for me dropped away, the scales fell from my eyes. I found *enlightenment*."

Reed stood up from the chair and strode toward Maria, still seated in the high-backed wooden chair on the strange boat. He said, "It started off as many adventures do. A journey across the skies with the Belle of the Airways. A chance meeting with a friend, Louis Cockayne, in the mélange of the Alexandria souk. Whispered rumors, introductions. Okoth, and his vows to bring me to the pyramid." Reed smiled crookedly. "I imagine your reaction to seeing the small peak of the pyramid, poking through the sand." He looked up, where the sloping walls of the chamber converged in the darkness. "Foiled, I returned to Alexandria, knowing there must be another way inside."

"Did you know what you'd find?" asked Gideon. "These creatures? These murderous things?"

Reed frowned. "They do not act out of malice, Mr. Smith.

They merely do what they were created for, what they waited for over long millennia."

"Tell that to my father," said Gideon. "And his crew. Those creatures killed them and picked his bones clean."

"I am genuinely sorry if that is the case, Mr. Smith," said Reed. "The Children of Heqet are very . . . single-minded when it comes to fulfilling their purpose."

"Which is?" asked Gideon.

Reed held up his hand. "My research in Alexandria revealed another possible entrance beneath the surface of the Nile, and I employed Mr. Okoth and his submersible. I found the secret tunnel and avoided the traps." He smiled. "I see you were resourceful enough to do the same, Lucian."

"Others weren't so lucky," said Trigger. "We found the body of Walton Jones."

Reed raised an eyebrow. "Jones? He always was an idiot. And Walsingham is twice the idiot if he employed him. But even Jones's failure means Walsingham is getting closer to the pyramid . . . it is fortuitous you arrived when you did."

Gideon felt suddenly sick. He had delivered Maria straight to Reed. His stupid thirst for adventure and heroism had ruined everything. But what was Reed planning?

"You found the Children of Heqet here?" he asked. "Are they the weapon you made mention of in your notes?"

"You are shrewd and intelligent, Mr. Smith," said Reed. "No, they are not the weapon. And I did not find them—they found me. In the turning room."

Reed's face darkened. "I have no idea how long I was there. Days, surely. I had no food, and my body ached for that which enslaved me."

"The opium," whispered Trigger.

Reed nodded. "I had only a ball of kef, procured by Okoth. In desperation, curled on the floor, little more than an animal, I ate it. And achieved my enlightenment. My ascension."

"You ate a whole ball of hashish?" said Trigger. "You must have been out of your mind."

"I was," agreed Reed. "I stepped out of my mind, out of the prison I had built for myself. The kef liberated my mind and opened it up to the truth."

"Which was?" asked Gideon.

"That Walsingham, and the Crown, had taken me for a fool. That they had set me to work as if I were little more than a dog."

"But you were the Hero of the Empire!"

Reed grinned without humor. "That's what I said. Unfortunately, truth and fiction diverged somewhat radically around the time of the Shangri-La incident. For all Lucian's talent with the quill, he could not write a happy ending for me. Once I realized Von Karloff was in the pay of Walsingham, up there on the frozen peak of Everest, my world came crashing down. If Walsingham could play us all off against each other so easily, sending Von Karloff on one little errand and Walton Jones on another, myself on a third . . . well, what was the point? We thought ourselves free spirits, roaming the globe at will. We were merely puppets. And once I realized that, I saw I was being betrayed at every turn. I gave my life to the British Empire, and traveled the world on Walsingham's command. And how did they treat me? As though I were a mere errand boy, a foot-soldier in their endless quest to know everything and rule all."

Reed paused thoughtfully. "Lucian, before I set off for Egypt, Walsingham called me in to Whitehall. He wanted to retire me."

"Would that have been such a bad thing?" whispered Trigger. "To sit at home, with me, in Mayfair?"

"*Retire* me," said Reed. "As though I were merely some employee. Thank you for all your years of service, Dr. Reed. Have a meager pension and the thanks of a nation. Not only that, Lucian, but they sought to impose *conditions.* I was not, in my retirement, to adventure any further. Not to, in their words, feather my own nest." He barked a laugh. "They all but called me a buccaneer. Said I no longer fit the sort of image England wanted to project." He shook his head.

"So you came here," said Gideon. "One last hurrah. Fill

your coffers with the treasure of the Rhodopis Pyramid for your retirement."

"At first, yes." Reed nodded. "But a . . . bigger picture emerged. Thanks to the Children of Heqet."

"Why did they not kill you?" asked Stoker. "Forgive me, but you were a mere tomb robber to them."

"Because of this," said Reed, touching the pendant hanging at his pale chest. "Because they recognized it."

So did Gideon. "The amulet from Arkhamville University," he said.

Reed smiled at Trigger. "He really is good, isn't he? Yes, Mr. Smith. The amulet. They recognized it for what it was, and thanks to the Golden Apple of Shangri-La, I was able to converse with them." He paused. "Can you imagine, talking to things that remembered ancient Egypt?"

"So why not leave?" asked Gideon. "Why sit in here for a year?"

"In truth, I don't think they would have let me, even if I had wanted to," said Reed. "They are simple creatures, with one sole purpose. My possession of the amulet—" He smiled. "Do you know of the *ka*, which the ancients believed is the life force inside every man, and continues on his eternal journey once his body is turned to dust? I think the Children of Heqet feel me to be some kind of reincarnation of their master, the Pharaoh Amasis II."

"I still do not understand," said Bathory, her voice ragged. Gideon turned to look at her, leaning on Stoker's shoulder. She looked pale and weak, her eyes fluttering. "Your creatures . . . they attacked Castle Dracula. Slew my husband. For what?"

Reed took the amulet from his neck and placed it on a low stone table. He reached into his bag and withdrew a golden scarab. "For this, Countess."

He placed it alongside the amulet and took out a small stone idol, fashioned roughly into the shape of a man. Gideon said, "The *shabti* stolen from the British Museum. By the Children of Heqet, we presume?"

Reed nodded. "The same one I confronted in Faxmouth. It is dead now, battered against Cleopatra's Needle." He paused. "A fitting death, I suppose." His eyes narrowed. "That was you, wasn't it?"

"It attacked us," said Trigger.

"As I said, driven by a sole purpose," said Reed. He took a small box made of some precious metal, engraved and inlaid with jewels, from his bag. "Hidden beneath the rocks on the Yorkshire coast," he said.

"And for that my father died," said Gideon.

Finally, Reed removed a ring inset with a huge ruby. He held it up to the light, turning it as it caught the flickering flames. "Taken from the finger of a mutilated body on the banks of the Thames."

Maria gasped and Bent said, "Annie Crook!"

Reed shrugged. Gideon said, "But what are all these things? What do they mean?"

"Together with what is in the clockwork girl's head, they mean everything," said Reed. "They mean I can finally leave this place."

Reed laid the ring down and surveyed them all. The ring, the *shabti*, the amulet, the scarab, the box. He sighed and said, "You will have to indulge me. Allow me to tell you a story." Reed stroked his beard. "Mr. Smith, you echoed the words of my erstwhile colleague Jamyang earlier. *Cui bono*. To whose benefit?"

"Walsingham," said Gideon. "Walsingham's benefit. That's what you discovered in Shangri-La. That's why you're here now. Why we're all here."

Reed nodded. "That *was* the answer. Things have changed."

"What do you mean?" asked Gideon.

"To whose benefit?" asked John Reed. "*Mine*, Mr. Smith. It is all to my benefit now."

29

The Tale of Rhodopis

Toward the end of the Twenty-sixth Dynasty of Egypt (said John Reed), five hundred years before the birth of Jesus Christ, when Egypt was about to fall to the Persian hordes, a slave girl from Greece worked in the house of an old man. During the precious time she got to herself, Rhodopis would steal away among the olive trees and sway to music she heard in her head, perhaps the tunes of her long-lost home in Greece. One day, the elderly master, walking in the olive trees, saw Rhodopis dancing. He was entranced, and when she had finished he applauded her most enthusiastically. The very next day he presented her with a gift: a pair of ruby-red slippers in which she could dance to her heart's content.

One day, scrubbing laundry on the rocks on the banks of the Nile, her beloved slippers got wet, and she placed them on a rock to dry. A huge falcon swooped down from the sky and snatched up one of her slippers. Unknown to Rhodopis, the falcon was actually Horus, most ancient and noble of all the Nile gods. He flew with the slipper to Sais, and the court of the Pharaoh, Amasis II, and dropped the slipper from a great height into his lap.

Amasis had yet to take a wife, and he recognized this as a message from the gods. Whoever the slipper fitted he would marry. All the maidens of the region were invited to the celebrations at Sais, and each one eagerly tried the slipper throughout the course of the festivities. Rhodopis, of course, had not gone to the festivities, because the other girls, jealous of their master's attention to her, had locked her in a cupboard. Failing to find anyone whom the slipper fit, Amasis decreed he would travel the land and find every maiden, and she would try on the slipper. Eventually his search led him to the house of the old man, and Rhodopis was revealed as the maiden whose foot fitted the slipper, and Amasis joyfully took her to his palace in Sais to be his bride.

"Cinderella," said Gideon. Reed had been seduced by a tale for children.

Reed nodded. "But this was no fairy story; there was no happily ever after. It is the story behind the story that counts." He paused, as though gathering his thoughts, then said, "These were dark times, and the Persian hordes were massing under the conquering Xerxes, who swept all before him. Amasis knew it was only a matter of time before the Persians overran Egypt, so he set his scientists and theologians the task of creating a weapon so powerful and destructive that it would save Egypt from the invading armies.

"They worked on this, and at the same time Amasis ordered a pyramid built to honor Rhodopis, and to provide both a sepulcher for the couple when they died and a place for this terrible new weapon to be developed in secret, away from the eyes of the Persian spies.

"Amasis called upon Heqet, the goddess of the Nile, to provide an honor guard for what was to be kept within. Heqet is the goddess of fertility and childbirth. She selected fifteen women to give birth to her children, which were nurtured and raised to adulthood in Heqet's temple in Sais. When the pyramid was completed they were put to the sword and embalmed, given eternal undeath by the frog-mother, and placed here to help Amasis's plans come to fruition.

"And there they lay for nigh on two and a half thousand years. The rising waters of the Nile during particularly heavy rains caused the sepulcher to flood; one of the mummified bodies of the Children of Heqet was carried out into the river, and thence it was found by Professor Reginald Halifax, who took it to the New World.

"Halifax had found, during prior excavations, this jewel.

The proximity of the amulet to the mummified Child of Heqet revived it, and the guardian of the sepulcher knew its time had come to live again. It attempted to return the jewel to the pyramid, but I intervened, and it left empty handed. It returned to the pyramid and woke the others, to begin their work in preparation for the return of Amasis."

Gideon pointed to the items on the stone table. "Then these . . . and the artifact in Maria's head . . ."

Reed nodded. "They had been scattered across the world; they were being transported from Sais when bandits attacked and made off with them, and from there they were traded and stolen and transported across the globe. The Children of Heqet, once awakened, set out on their task to locate them all."

"It seems a lot of trouble to go to for some trinkets," said Bent, looking around. "This pyramid's stuffed with treasures. Haven't you got enough here?"

"Do you not understand, Mr. Bent? They are merely disguised as jewels and treasures. They are, in fact, ancient Egyptian technology, indistinguishable from magic to our modern minds. They are the *weapon*, or at least what powers it."

"What manner of weapon is this thing?" asked Gideon. He truly feared Reed's sanity had ebbed away, with only the company of those foul mummies. It would drive anyone insane.

"Like nothing the ancients had conceived of before," said Reed. If he was insane, thought Gideon, he was like no raving lunatic Gideon had ever imagined. There was a coldness to him that seemed to make even the torch flames shiver. "It required the best minds and philosophers of the ancient world to create it. But time was running out. Once the Persians attacked the caravan, the weapon was rendered useless. The pieces had been forged in science and magic in temples and laboratories. A single day more, and they would have arrived here, and the weapon would have been completed. The Persians swarmed over Sais, and both Amasis and Rhodopis died in the conflict. They were taken into the pyramid and embalmed, and the sands of time conspired to hide them. The treasures were scattered across the world over the subsequent centuries."

"Until now," said Gideon.

Reed stood from his throne. "Finally the pieces are assembled, and the weapon is ready to be activated."

Reed gathered up the artifacts and walked to where Maria sat patiently, listening. Gideon moved forward, but the Children of Heqet closed the gap between him and Reed.

"Not long now," said Reed soothingly to the mummies. "Not long, then eternal sleep can be yours."

"I won't help you," said Maria. "Whatever is in my head isn't yours, Dr. Reed."

"You're lucky you have a head at all," said Reed. "I wanted the artifact, not you. You can thank the Children of Heqet you aren't headless at the bottom of the ocean. They knew, more than I, that the artifact had to be aligned to a living brain. Two thousand years ago it would have been a slave; today it would have had to be some innocent stolen from the hinterland of Alexandria, I suppose. You have saved me from what I imagine would have been some rather amateur and painful surgery upon a stranger, Maria."

Between the Children of Heqet who blocked his path, Gideon could see there was a flat wooden panel in front of Maria's chair, with five differently shaped recesses set into it. Into the first Reed placed the amulet. "As to helping me, Maria," he said, "if I understand everything correctly, then the choice simply isn't yours."

The amulet slid home with a dry sigh. Did Maria stiffen as it did so? Gideon peered at her. Was it in fear of what was to come, or something more? Reed pried the ruby—or whatever it was—from Annie Crook's ring and placed it in the second aperture. There! Maria definitely shuddered, gazing hard into the middle distance. Gideon tried to get a better look, but one of the mummies pushed him back with a hiss and a shove to his chest.

"Trigger," murmured Gideon. "He's up to something."

Trigger was pale, his eyes hollow, very much like he'd looked on his doorstep in Mayfair. Then he'd thought he'd lost John Reed. Now he *knew* he had.

As Reed placed the scarab in the fourth carved hole Maria gasped, looking straight up into the darkness. Was there a redness about her eyes, a pale, diffuse glow? Into a rectangular hole went the box, and Maria cried out in pain and surprise. Gideon shook his head and elbowed past the Children of Heqet, or tried to; this time one punched him hard in the gut, sending him sprawling.

Reed looked at the *shabti* for a moment, turning it in his fingers. "This is the last one," he said. "When I place this into its housing, the weapon is activated." He looked at Gideon, climbing to his feet, winded. "Any last words for the girl?"

Gideon looked at her, then back at Reed. He knew what he should say. He *knew*. But what good would it do? Instead he said, "Let her go, you fiend."

Reed smirked. "The poet could not have done better." He slid the *shabti* into the aperture and stepped backward, until he stood behind Maria's tall chair. She began to shake and gasp, her arms extending stiffly in front of her, fingers splayed as though she were about to play the treasures like some kind of ancient, alien piano.

Then she spoke. Gideon frowned and looked at Trigger. It was her voice, but she was speaking no words Gideon could understand. She hissed and clicked and jabbered in a guttural tongue: the language of the Children of Heqet.

"Excellent!" said Reed. "It works! It actually works!"

"Reed! Stop now, while you can!" called Gideon.

Behind him, Stoker shook Trigger roughly. "For God's sake, say something to him, man! You're the only one he'll possibly listen to now!"

"Look," said Bent. "Eff me, look."

The long brass hood hanging over Maria began to jerkily close, as a crocodile's mouth might. "Stop!" screamed Gideon. "In God's name, Reed. What have you done to Maria?"

"There is no Maria!" Reed laughed. "Whatever fiction she had built for herself, now there is only Apep."

"Apep?" said Bent. "What's he on about now?"

Reed's eyes met Gideon's as the hood—which he could now see had two large glass portholes very much like eyes—closed slowly, swallowing Maria and Reed. The look that passed between them was dripping with malice. What was it they said? About revenge being a dish best served cold? John Reed had let his vengeance chill in the sunless shadows of that pyramid, forged it in the frozen crucible of that dead, ancient air, until he had finally been delivered of the means to test the keenness of its edge.

"He's effing insane!" shouted Bent. "Properly effing insane."

"No, he's not," said Gideon. "He's possibly the sanest man in the world. That's why he's so bloody dangerous."

Maria was still uttering her unknown words—chanting, really—as the hood finally closed. Gideon could see Maria through one eye-porthole, Reed through the other.

"It is too late!" cried Reed, his voice distant within what Gideon realized with cold clarity *was*, in fact, a cruel-looking crocodile head, with rows of brass teeth beneath the—cockpit? *Cockpit*?—that Reed and Maria occupied. "Apep lives! Even the darkness bends toward my will! Just as Apep shunned order and lived to snuff out the light of Ma'at, so he shall draw a veil over the modern Babylon of London!"

Apep. The ground cracked before the crocodile vessel, a zigzagging, widening black line parting the interior of the pyramid, separating Gideon from the rest of the adventurers. The Children of Heqet fell back. The sloping walls shuddered and sent trickles of dust down. The crack widened further, and Gideon heard Bent groan as the table of food buckled and fell into it, as though the parched sand itself was hungry.

Apep. The cockpit—yes, the cockpit, because Gideon knew now what Apep was—began to rise with a hiss of ancient hydraulics and the exhalation of hidden exhausts. A neck wider than an oak tree, scaled with brass, rose up from out of the cracked earth.

Apep. One vast claw, then another, gripping the parting ground, climbing up from the bowels of the pyramid. With a terrible groaning the floor rose in the middle, sending Gideon rolling down toward the back of the pyramid. Something was forcing itself up, drawn up on those fierce claws, an obscene birth from the darkness below.

Apep. A muscular brass rear leg, then another. Then the head, the cockpit, disappeared into the shadows above, and there was a rending sound, a flood of bricks and stone and the sudden, unfamiliar sight of daylight, a clear blue lightning strike above.

"Gideon!" shouted Stoker. "Gideon! Are you alive?"

Gideon shrugged off the sand and mortar and crawled up the buckled floor, watching as the brass hind legs disappeared into the sky, dragging what looked like a many-jointed *tail* that petered down to a point.

"Bent is down, hit by a rock," called Stoker. "Elizabeth is most weak. Trigger . . ."

Gideon knew. Trigger was a husk, as though Reed had sucked the life out of him. "The whole place is about to come down," said Gideon. "We need to get out of here."

"I concur," shouted Stoker across the rapidly dividing room. "What's your plan, Gideon?"

Plan? Gideon peered through the sand and dust. He couldn't even see the others. They expected him to have a plan? A chunk of falling masonry narrowly missed him and he pressed against a column, which shook alarmingly. He looked up. A grotesque, froglike face leered down at him. No, not a column. A statue. Heqet, evidently. He coughed and spat a glob of dusty spit onto the stone floor. A statue.

"Trigger! Captain Trigger!" he called. "Stoker, can he speak?"

He heard Stoker shouting sharply, then a weak voice: "Mr. Smith?"

"Captain Trigger!" called Gideon. More stone was falling; the sky kept tantalizingly appearing far above then disappearing again, as though the sands were the tides of the sea. "Do you remember *The Temple of Death*?"

"The Temple of . . . Death, did you say?"

"Yes!" shouted Gideon. "*The Temple of Death*, from the . . . the March issue two years ago, or the April one. . . ."

"I think so," said Trigger, distant and uncertain.

"The Thuggee temple in India!" said Gideon. "It collapsed, remember? Dr. Reed pushed over a statue of Kali and it stopped the roof from coming in. Do you think that would work with these statues of Heqet?"

There was silence. "Captain Trigger?"

"Yes," said Trigger doubtfully. "I remember that episode."

"*Would it work?*" shouted Gideon. "Should I push the statue over? Or will that make it worse?"

"That episode . . . ," called Trigger.

"Yes?"

"That episode . . . I'm afraid I rather embellished John's notes, Mr. Smith."

"Embellished?"

"I made it up, Mr. Smith. I'm very sorry. I'm afraid I made quite a lot of it up. The derring-do and suchlike."

Gideon snarled and punched the statue. He heard Stoker's voice: "Gideon, we're trapped here. If you have any kind of plan . . ."

He made it up. Despite the mounting evidence, Gideon had still held firm in his belief in Captain Lucian Trigger. From Sandsend to London, from London to Egypt, one constant had remained absolute: *This adventure, as always, is utterly true, and faithfully retold by my good friend, Doctor John Reed.* He had lived his life by that, by what he'd read in the pages of *World Marvels & Wonders.* And now . . . *Trigger had fucking made it up.*

There was a fearsome crack from above, and stone and sand began to rain down on Gideon. He heard Stoker yell something formless and terrified. Gideon took a deep breath, got behind the statue of Heqet, and began to push with all his might.

Gideon clambered up the statue, which had fallen diagonally across the chamber, its head poking through to the sun-drenched desert, precariously holding the collapsing pyramid together. Gideon scrambled along its length. It would not hold for long. He breached the surface, and he took a welcome lungful of burning air before turning to help Bent up through the gap, his arm twisted horribly, his head bleeding, but alive and staggering. Ashen-faced Trigger came next, and Gideon peered down for Stoker and Bathory.

"Mr. Stoker?" he called. "Countess?"

"We are here," called Stoker, though Gideon couldn't see him. "Elizabeth is losing consciousness. Mr. Smith, do you think you might lend a—"

Gideon leaped backward as the sand suddenly shifted beneath him like water, and there was a thunderous crack as the shattered wall of the pyramid toppled inward, sending an avalanche of stone blocks down below.

"Stoker!" called Gideon. "Stoker! Can you hear me?"

There was no answer, but Gideon became aware of someone tugging on his shirt. It was Bent.

"Erm, Gideon," he said slowly. "I really think you need to see this. . . ."

30

A Dragon to Eat the Sun

"Now that is somewhat astonishing," said Okoth. Fanshawe and Cockayne were sitting on the grass in the shadow of the *Yellow Rose*, enjoying the breeze drifting off the Nile. As she turned to follow Okoth's outstretched finger and saw the column of dust rising from far out into the desert, she began to get a bad feeling in her gut that told her she should perhaps have kept her wishes to herself.

"Roundabout where that pyramid is, ain't it?" said Cockayne. He checked his pockets and withdrew a collapsible telescope. He watched for a moment, then took it away from his eye, as if he couldn't quite believe what he saw.

"What's that?" asked Fanshawe. "Something coming out of the ground?" Cockayne handed her the telescope.

Something bright and shining in the sunlight, like a tall mirrored column, had pushed up through the broken granite stones. She frowned and adjusted the focus. It looked for all the world like the head of a crocodile with glinting glass eyes. She swore softly as the rest of it emerged, a fat, sleek body made of overlapping scales forged and hammered from what appeared to be brass, two powerful hind legs with glinting clawed feet, and a pair of smaller forearms. Then it unfurled a pair of vast leathery bat wings and rose into the air, its hinged tail swinging beneath it.

"It's a dragon," she said wonderingly. "A brass dragon."

"I think we'd better get over there," said Cockayne.

For once, she agreed with him.

Stoker coughed as a cloud of dust billowed up and began to slowly settle. The rocks had fallen and taken him and Bathory with them, sliding back down to the sepulcher below. He could still see the bright sunlight lancing through the dust, though it was terribly distant, and bordered by a shuddering blackness. He could not, however, feel his legs. It was only when he put his hands down to his waist and brought them back slick with his own blood that he realized his lower half was crushed under a huge stone slab.

"Elizabeth?" he coughed. "Elizabeth? Are you alive?"

As the dust settled he saw her, lying in a pool of sunlight shining through the wreckage of the pyramid above them.

"Elizabeth," he said weakly. "You must rise. Get to the surface. Get help."

"I . . . cannot . . . Bram," she said, her voice barely a whisper. "The battle with the Children of Heqet . . . I was already weak . . . the harsh Egyptian sun drains me. . . ."

"What are they doing up there?" moaned Stoker. "Why aren't they coming to help?"

"Perhaps . . . battle is joined . . . ," she said. "Feel so very tired, Bram . . . must sleep. . . ."

"No!" he said sharply. "Elizabeth, no! You must save yourself. . . . Oh!"

He felt his legs, then, felt the pain of his crushed nerve endings sending sluggish telegrams of emergency to his brain. He coughed into his sleeve, and it was wet with blood as well as spit when he took his arm away.

"I have been such a fool," he whispered. "Elizabeth . . ."

"Hush," said Bathory. "You need not say anything."

He tried to turn his head to look at her, but the blackness that edged his vision was spreading. She said, "What would you do, Bram, if you were not here? What would be your wish?"

"I would so like to walk the corridors of Trinity College in Dublin again," he said hoarsely. "Gaze upon the Book of Kells once more. But before that . . . Hyde Park, on a warm day . . . I would be hand in hand with Florence, and Noel would be running ahead, spinning a top. And I would tell her . . . tell her I was sorry for everything, and I wished I had been a better husband, and a better father. . . ."

He slipped into a reverie, and when he came to, sharply, he did not know if he had in fact slept. He whispered, "Elizabeth?"

There was no answer. "Elizabeth?"

She made a small sound, almost an agreeable one, as though she merely dozed. He put out a hand to her and felt her bare arm. She was cold.

"Thank you . . . ," she said, "for all that blood you drew for me. . . ."

He blinked. "Of course," he said softly. "Elizabeth, listen to me. There is no need for both of us to die. I cannot recover. But take my blood. . . ."

"I . . . cannot . . . ," she said, almost dreamily. "It would kill you, Bram."

"I am dead anyway. Take it." He thrust his arm toward her. "Take it from my wrist. Drain me. It shall be easier for me, that way. I am in such pain. . . ."

For a moment she did nothing, then he felt her cool lips upon the inside of his forearm. A kiss, and nothing more.

"Take it!" he urged. "Help them stop Reed. Florence and Noel are in London. . . ."

He felt twin pinpricks on his wrist, and he was glad he could not see Elizabeth in her vampire state. He pictured her, beautiful and serene, in his head, as she drained his blood and he slowly slipped into the darkness for the final time.

❧

Apep was above them, framed against the blue sky, the sun bouncing off every brass scale on its magnificent body. It hung in the sky, the huge metal wings flapping down and up, down and up, and seemed to regard them with its baleful porthole eyes.

"What the eff's keeping it up in the sky?" asked Bent wonderingly. "Helium, do you think, like a dirigible?"

"Science," said Gideon. "Witchcraft. I don't know. Look at the thing. It defies all rational explanation."

One of the eyes glinted in the sun, and Gideon saw it was opening. Reed's head emerged. He roared at them from the dragon, "They always say the sun will never set on Britannia. Apep is the sun-eater, and he shall rain fiery death upon that foul and debased place. It is good you live, because when I am done those who are left will need to know who did this. One final story for you to pen, Lucian."

And then, Gideon remembered his dream of so long ago. The night it all started. The day that was the last of the life he once knew.

He had dreamed a dragon ate the sun.

"No!" he shouted. "You will not do this, John Reed! You will not!"

Reed laughed from his perch atop the brass dragon. "And who are you to tell me, the Hero of the Empire, what I will and will not do?"

"I am Gideon Smith!" he cried. "And I will stop you, John Reed, if it takes my final breath."

Reed closed the porthole, and the dragon executed a tight turn in the sky and began to fly north. Gideon watched it go, powered by arcane means, piloted by the enslaved Maria. The rescue mission had now turned into something far more urgent. "We need to get to London," he said. "To warn them."

There was a scrabbling behind them, and Gideon turned to see Bathory climbing through the fissure in the rock-strewn sand. Bent said, "Stoker?" and she looked away, giving the smallest shake of her head.

"We should get his body out," said Bent. "Christ, my arm. My effing head."

"We'll send someone later," said Gideon. "We must go now, or there will be many more corpses to disinter from what is left of London."

"But how?" asked Trigger hollowly.

A shadow fell across them, the vast balloon of the *Yellow Rose,* banking and descending so the observation platform turned to them. Fanshawe stood there, leaning on the rails.

"What the hell was that?" she called. "We saw it from the river and reckoned you might need our help."

Gideon looked at Apep, now a dot in the clear sky. "That was death, Rowena. And it is bound for London. We must follow it."

She unfurled a rope ladder as Cockayne, on the bridge, brought the *Yellow Rose* down as low as he could. Gideon said, "Let's get moving. I'd hate John Reed to think I wasn't a man of my word."

"You know, I'm not being what you might call unpatriotic or nothing," said Bent, wincing as Fanshawe strapped a splint to his broken arm, "but some might say Reed's got something of a point."

Gideon stared at him. "You are joking, of course?"

"I don't agree with his methods or anything, all this raining death on London with a brass dragon and all, but . . . well. Let's just say the British Government doesn't always act with the most honorable intentions, shall we?

"Take your Maria, for example, and that brain. All Annie Crook did was fall in love with a geezer who just happened to be a member of the royal family. And what does the Crown do? Whisks him away and kills the Crook girl. All because it wouldn't look good, and it might give the great unwashed ideas above their station. Is that any way to behave? And Reed himself . . . he goes to all that trouble to find these lost treasures scattered about the world, just to have scoundrels like Walsingham come and pick and choose what he wants."

"For the greater good, though," said Gideon, but doubtfully.

Bent laughed. "You really think so? You think the Government's more shadowy side really does anything to benefit the likes of me and you?"

"Einstein was working on an airship to the moon," said Gideon. "I read it in his notes. That is why he was given the Atlantic Artifact."

Bent shrugged. "That's as may be. But why go to the moon? So you and me can stand in Trafalgar Square and wave our flags? You can bet your last farthing if they want to go to the moon there'll be something in it other than a couple of verses of 'Land of Hope and Glory'."

Gideon sighed. "You are awfully cynical, Bent. So that excuses Reed destroying London?"

"Of course it doesn't," said Bent. "But it makes you think, don't it?"

Gideon walked over to Bathory. "How are you, Countess?"

She looked up. "Why do men ruin everything?"

Gideon had no answer, and he withdrew quietly. He turned to where Trigger sat, hunched over on a bench at one side of the bridge, staring listlessly at his hands. Bent had a broken arm and a fierce-looking injury to his head. Stoker was dead, Trigger a pale shadow of a man. He had found Maria and lost her again, to God knew what. Was this what heroes did—cause everything they touched to crumble to dust?

"I should never have brought us all here," Trigger said without looking up. "Now he will destroy London with that infernal device." He buried his face in his pale, shaking hands. "What have I done? What is John doing?"

"We must stop him," said Gideon softly. He wanted to be angry with Trigger, wanted to shout at him and hit him for his lies, for his fiction. But looking at the broken old man, he felt only pity. He said, "But I cannot do it alone. I need you, Lucian."

"What use am I?" spat Trigger. "An effete old man, a spinner of tales, nothing more. Abandoned by my lover." He looked up at Gideon. "Do you think him mad? Or can he really be evil, and I have been blinded by love all these years?"

Gideon could easily believe either. He asked, "What do you think, Lucian?"

"*Something* has caused him to stop loving me," said Trigger, and tears rolled down his dusty cheeks. "I think that even if he were driven mad by his ordeal in the pyramid, something of our love would remain."

"One way or the other, we will bring him to his senses, Lucian. Save London. But we must do it together, yes?"

Trigger looked at him, then down at his feet again. "I am of no use to you, Gideon. The fate of London is in your hands."

⁂

They left Alexandria far behind them and bore north by northwest, the glittering Aegean Sea below. Gideon peered through the windows at the black dot in the distance. "Is that it? Apep?"

Cockayne nodded. "It's moving quickly, but so are we. The *Yellow Rose* is a little speedier than the ship you came in on." He ruminated for a moment. "Was it bad down there? In the pyramid?"

Gideon nodded. "I had thought I was going on a grand adventure. I didn't realize people would die."

Cockayne shrugged. "It ain't like the stories, that's for sure. Trigger presents what you might call a sanitized version of events for public consumption. The reality . . . well. You saw what it was like firsthand." He paused. "It gets easier, though. Easier to deal with. Next time, you'll have learned lessons. You'll handle things differently. You'll still screw up, but less so. And the time after that . . . It gets better, is all."

Gideon stared at him. "You think there'll be a next time?"

Cockayne kept his eyes on the horizon. "From what I heard, Gideon, you did pretty good. Have faith in yourself. It's the only way you'll survive, if you're going to be an adventurer."

Unless Gideon was very mistaken, Louis Cockayne had just as near as damnation paid him a compliment. "I think I'll go to the galley, see if I can find some food for us all," he said.

Cockayne nodded. "You do that, Gideon." He winked at him and returned to his contemplation of the sky.

Over lunch in the stateroom, Cockayne asked, "So, what's the plan of engagement?"

Gideon had to confess he didn't have one. "Rule number one, kid," said Cockayne. "Be prepared. Rule number two, if you can't be prepared, be lucky."

Fanshawe cocked an eyebrow. "What's this, are you two now in some kind of adventurers' club or something?"

Cockayne held up his hands. "I'm merely the pilot for this endeavor. Please, don't anyone labor under the misapprehension that I will be risking my life to save London. I just wondered what the hell you plan to do when we catch up with that goddamn dragon."

Gideon looked around. "Does anyone have any ideas?"

Cockayne pushed his hat back on his head. "Can't say I've ever fought a dragon before, so I can't offer you much in the way of advice. But think about it. Whatever that thing is, however it's actually flying, whether it's ancient science we know nothing about or some freaky hoodoo, it operates on basic principles. It needs its power source to keep moving. And, if I've got this right, that power source is based around your little friend Maria. Take her out, and the game's up for John Reed."

Gideon shook his head vehemently. "No. We're not going to hurt Maria."

"She ain't even alive. You're balancing her against . . . how many people in London? Six million? Rule number three. Weigh up the odds, and don't bet on a pair if the other guy's got a royal flush. Now, what kind of weaponry is that dragon packing?"

"I don't know. Reed talked of raining fire on London. I don't know if he was being literal or metaphorical."

"I'm a dab hand with the three-pounder Hotchkiss, as we've already effing seen," said Bent.

"Not with that arm," said Cockayne. "Look, I'm going to the bridge, check our bearing. You guys . . . you've been through the mill. You look beat. Why don't you take a couple of hours of sleep? I'll wake you up when we see the white cliffs of Dover."

Gideon headed for the cabin and lay on the bunk, staring at the ceiling and listening to the steady thrum of the engines. He had no idea what he was going to do if they eventually caught up with the Apep dragon. Harpoons and guns . . . were they going to be enough? And what kind of damage could John Reed inflict before they managed to stop him?

The responsibility weighed suffocatingly on Gideon, but he knew there was no one else to shoulder it. Bent was well meaning but injured. Cockayne had refused to engage. Bathory was still weakened, and she had no loyalties to Britain. Her mission of revenge was fulfilled, the last of the Children of Heqet buried under the collapsed pyramid of Rhodopis. Rowena would do what she could, he knew, but by the same token her loyalties were really to herself. And Trigger . . . the lifeless look in his eyes told Gideon that Trigger considered himself dead already.

It was up to him. He closed his eyes and willed sleep to come, knowing that when it did he would inevitably dream of dragons again.

31

Apep

Maria could not remember a time when she was not Apep, and Apep was not her. She felt every beat of the—of *her*—wings, knew instinctively how to steer with her tail and how to lean into the wind by flexing the pistons and gears in her powerful hind legs. Memories of ancient sand and heat mingled with her more recent recollections and ultimately subsumed them.

Every nerve and thought entangled with what she had become. She had a purpose. She had instructions, a map, in her head. Testing out her new body, her new being, she swooped low over the sand and then high into the blue sky, twisting the brass beast in a balletic turn, then straightening and flying on.

"I am Apep," she said in a tongue at once utterly foreign to her and completely natural. "I am the destroyer." She paused. "I am at the command of one man alone." She looked away from the blue sky that met the yellow sand ahead of them. "Are you Amasis?"

"Yes," said John Reed. "I am your Amasis. You were created to wage war on an empire that threatened to swamp the world."

She paused again, considering, allowing the ancient programming to settle and calm within her. She nodded. "What are your orders, Amasis?"

He shrugged and smiled. "As they always were. To wage war on the Empire. To London."

On John Reed's instructions to Maria, who was changed in ways he could only guess at, Apep flew high and fast, keeping to the clouds where possible and following the line of Italy's western coastline. In Rome, Reed knew, the people would be pausing at their coffees and looking up as the shadow of the gigantic beast fell over the Immortal City, and in Livorno he saw how they fled for cover in the churches. Reed had commanded Maria to set a course for London, and she had instinctively and unerringly done so, her eyes wide as she sat ramrod stiff in the reclining leather seat, the artifact in her head feeding to each cog, flywheel, and pinion that powered and moved Apep, each piston and hydraulic pump, each tiny combustion chamber and grinding gearwheel.

Reed, the Golden Apple of Shangri-La in his hand, had her soar over the glistening blue sea. In Marseille, French cannons fired hopelessly at Apep, and horses stampeded in fright on the Camargue. Partisans took pot shots, and Reed knew by now word would have gotten to British Gibraltar. They'd be telegraphing the headquarters of the Fleet Air Arm. Yeovilton wouldn't quite know what to make of it all, he thought, but when panicked reports began to come in from France and Spain that *something* strange was in the air and headed for Britain, they would think it prudent to do something, at least. He was right. He peered through his spyglass at the three RS-3s, the lightest and most maneuverable of the Crown's military dirigibles, taking up a holding pattern just over the cliffs of Dover.

Apep flew out of the sun on its huge pumping wings. Reed felt bold and ordered Maria to push Apep forward into a steep dive, then pull out of it at the last minute, just to make sure everyone got a damned good look at them. The two flanking RS-3s moved into a defensive position and trained their two-pound guns on Apep, presumably waiting for the order to be flashed up to them via heliograph from below. As Apep bore down on them, the message came, and Reed, with his long years of military service, decoded the series of sunbursts in his head almost without trying:

Fire at will.

Both RS-3s let loose their shells, which bounced harmlessly off Apep's hide. The central 'stat was loading up its guns when Apep responded.

"Maria," Reed said. "Attack."

She stiffened again, and her hands played over the glowing instrument panel in front of her. Reed felt a grinding of gears from below, and the sensation that something was opening.

There was a moment's silence, in which the pride of the Empire's mastery of the air faced off against the ancient technology long buried beneath the shifting sands of Egypt.

Apep roared.

A burning ball of gas issued from Apep's now gaping maw, a blue and orange and yellow comet that slammed into the central RS-3 and engulfed it in a conflagration that quickly overwhelmed the fragile balloon and incinerated the small wooden gondola, leaving only a rain of ashes to fall on the stunned soldiers below.

Reed, his blood surging, saw the heliograph message from the ground ordering the remaining two RS-3s to engage, but before they could load their shells, they, too, felt the fierce heat of Apep's roar, and were disintegrated.

In the *Yellow Rose* they watched in silence from the bridge.

"Well," said Bent. "First blood to John Reed."

Bathory looked sharply at him. "He has already claimed first blood. Bram."

Bent frowned at her. "Are you well, Countess? You look awfully pale."

She waved him away, though her brow furrowed with evident pain.

Cockayne chewed his cigarillo. "So the dragon really does breathe fire. Well, at least we know what we're dealing with now." He looked at Gideon. "Rule number four. Know your enemy."

"Can we outrun it?" asked Gideon. "Beat them to London?"

Cockayne shook his head. "I don't know what juice that

thing is running on, but it beats the hell out of what we're packing."

Cockayne boosted the propellers as Apep cast its shadow across the patchwork countryside of England. Without looking at Gideon he asked, "You got a plan yet?"

"I'm working on it," said Gideon through gritted teeth. "You just concentrate on keeping up with them."

Cockayne gave him an amused look and winked at Fanshawe. "Aye aye, captain."

⁂

Near Biggin Hill a fleet of five beefy Albert-class 'stats, bristling with firepower and the best maneuverability the Fleet Air Arm could boast, blockaded the sky in their famous "five of clubs" formation, while a crowd of cheering civilians gathered below, waving Union flags.

"No one knows what we are," said Reed. "All they know is that we are a threat. But this empire has grown so corpulent, so arrogant, that it does not fear threats anymore. It merely expects they shall fail."

The Fleet Air Arm enjoyed moderate success that surprised Reed. The first volley of bullets managed to shatter one of the glass "eye" windows of Apep, to a suddenly audible rousing cheer from the crowd below. But Apep's retaliation was swift and terrible. With five well-aimed fireballs, Apep sent each of the Albert-class 'stats hurtling in flames to the fields, the last plunging into the crowd of fleeing onlookers. A pall of smoke and a terrible silence hung over Biggin Hill, and a satisfied Reed had Apep move on.

⁂

"At last," said Reed, looking out over Bexleyheath at the line of carts and people flowing northwest along the Watling Street Road, to what they must have believed was the relative safety of London Town. "Word of our presence precedes us."

As Apep scooted low along the wide avenue, Reed experimented with a series of short bursts of fireballs, laying a sustained carpet of flame that took hold of the ancient wooden houses to either side and roasted the fleeing refugees where they stood. Reed had Maria turn a victory roll and swiftly ascend high into the sky, as the charnel stench of blackened flesh rose in a hellish cloud from burning Bexleyheath below.

In the *Yellow Rose,* Gideon hung his head as they passed the slaughter in the blazing streets. Cockayne had given the 'stat all the power he could muster, and with a following wind they had finally made up the time in pursuit of the dragon. Gideon almost wished they hadn't. Too late to halt the destruction, but in time to witness the aftermath of the carnage. The wreckage of the Albert-class 'stats had been bad enough, especially the one that had hurtled into the hill and claimed the lives of the cheering crowd. But the deliberate murders of the unfortunates fleeing Apep's arrival . . . that was almost too much to bear witness to.

"I could have stopped this," said Gideon, quiet and fierce. "I should never have taken Maria into the pyramid."

Seething, he grabbed a horrified Trigger by the front of his shirt. "How many are dead down there, Trigger? Reed can't be allowed to get away with this. You've got to *do* something."

"No," mumbled Trigger, refusing to meet Gideon's stare. "No. You are right. John is gone from me. He might as well be dead already." Finally, Trigger looked up at Gideon. There were tears in the old man's eyes. "As might I."

Disgusted, Gideon pushed him away. To Cockayne he said, "Give her all you've got. We need to catch Apep, before there is more slaughter."

"You got a plan at last?"

Gideon grimly said again, "I'm working on it."

The wind whistled in through the window, caressing Reed's face. "Ah, London," he said. "How I have missed you. How you will beg for mercy."

Maria watched impassively from the pilot seat. She said,

"Is this the empire that threatens the world? I see no ranks of soldiers. No armies. I see only . . . innocents."

"There are no innocents in London, Maria. Every man, woman, and child is complicit in the crimes of the British Empire; they are all cogs that move forward the inexorable machine that crushes the human spirit, subsumes it into the single entity that is Britannia. Victoria will not rest until she has remade the entire world in her image, until there are no corners of any foreign fields that are not forever England."

He leaned forward to peer through the windows. "Ah. Greenwich approaches. Look, Maria, the Lady of Liberty flood barrier! Shall we show them what we think of their liberty, their freedom to do whatever they like, so long as the Crown approves? Take off its head, Maria."

Her hands hovered above the instrument panel, but she hesitated. Reed laughed. "You cannot deny me, Maria. You are merely a passenger in your own body. Apep is the dominant force. Obey me!"

She banked Apep sharply, and it circled the tall verdigris-covered statue flanking the Thames, its feet mired in the mud of the river, ready to hold hard against sudden rushes of water from upstream. When Reed was sure he had enough of an audience below, he ordered her to let loose Apep's dragon roar. The impassive face of Lady Liberty blackened and began to melt, then the head toppled from the shoulders of the huge metal statue and crashed into the river.

"Now for the climax!" cried Reed. "Let us strike the Empire at its very heart. Maria, to Buckingham Palace!"

❦

"The Empire does not appear to be beaten yet," observed Maria, reporting a flotilla of dirigibles converging on the city, gunships of all sizes from the Fleet Air Arm's bases, every 'stat the Crown could muster. It was as though she saw across the city with Apep's vast glass eyes, as though she were plugged into not just the dragon's workings but a greater network of chattering telephone calls and telegraphic communications.

He watched those on London's packed streets seek out the parks for sanctuary, and space to move should more conflagration fall from the sky. Apep banked and wheeled above Hyde Park, performing yet smoother and more daring feats of aerobatics as Maria settled into her control of the great brass dragon.

"You are enjoying this, are you not?" asked Reed.

Maria said nothing, but a small smile played around her lips. *Yes,* thought Reed, *you're enjoying this almost as much as I am.*

He looked down at the chanting, jeering mass of humanity gathered below. He told Maria to launch a series of fireballs at the Serpentine, and the lake hissed and steamed. Reed nodded appreciatively. "A sense of theater is called for on occasions such as this," he said. "People must remember where they were when the Empire died." He held up a finger. "But first! There is business to take care of. Maria, have Apep hover at a fair altitude, so we can see Buckingham Palace. Before we can lay waste to Victoria's nest, we must first deal with those who have harried us since Egypt."

"Gideon Smith," she said, a little uncertainly.

"You sense them following us?" asked Reed. "You hope your paramour comes to rescue us?" Reed cocked his head. "You are mine now, Maria. You belong to Amasis."

❧

Apep hovered on its beating wings, stately and otherwise motionless, facing Buckingham Palace. On the streets Gideon could see panic and the massing of the Iron Guard outside the palace gates. There were other 'stats in the sky, but they were far away and moving slowly. It was up to them.

"Well?" said Cockayne.

Gideon ignored him and looked at Trigger. "Come on," Gideon said. "Think. What can I do?"

Trigger shook his head wretchedly. Gideon swore. There must be *something,* something in all the *World Marvels & Wonders* adventures he'd read. Gideon closed his eyes, breathing deeply. There was nothing he could count on, no episode he could re-create. There was no blueprint for this. It was not a Lucian Trigger adventure. And if Trigger, and Cockayne, and Fanshawe and all the others, if they couldn't come up with a plan, with all their experience and greatness, what chance did he have? He had blundered from one happening to another, trying to do the right thing but barely surviving. He wasn't an adventurer, he wasn't a hero. He was just a fisherman.

Gideon opened his eyes. He was just a fisherman.

This wasn't a Lucian Trigger adventure.

He was just a fisherman.

It was a Gideon Smith adventure.

He looked at Cockayne. "I've got a plan," he said. "We're going fishing."

32

The Battle of London

"You intend to do *what*?" asked Bent.

"Harpoon the dragon," said Gideon again. "It worked when Cockayne reeled in the *Skylady II*."

"But the *Skylady II* was a lot smaller, lighter, and slower than the *Yellow Rose*," said Fanshawe. "Apep is powerful and fast and nippy in the air. Oh, and there's the small matter of those fireballs. . . ."

"And that thing's brass," said Bent. "You'll never get a harpoon through that hide."

"Not necessarily," said Cockayne thoughtfully. "What's the dragon doing now?"

"Hovering above Hyde Park," said Fanshawe. "About six hundred feet up." She looked at Gideon. "And facing Buckingham Palace."

"I need to get above Apep," said Gideon. "Can we do that?"

"Sure," said Cockayne. "Let's get out on the observation deck, via the armory. Rowena, you think you can fly the *Yellow Rose*?"

She smiled. "I've handled bigger." Then she frowned. "But . . . Gideon? What are you planning to do?"

"Board the dragon," he said.

She shook her head. "It's impossible. Reed will murder you."

Gideon shrugged. "Who else is there? Bent's got a broken arm, Trigger . . ." He pointed to where the old man stood by the windows of the bridge, staring listlessly out. "The Countess is too weak. You need to fly the *Yellow Rose*."

They both looked at Cockayne. "And Louis is just along for the ride. But I'll do this for you, Smith. I'll harpoon your damned dragon. Come on."

⁂

Cockayne and Gideon dragged a harpoon gun mounted on a thick iron pillar out onto the windswept observation deck and planted it near the railings.

Breathing hard, Cockayne held up a long harpoon shaft, but with a flat round head instead of a sharp point. "Magnetic harpoon," he said with a grin.

Bent frowned. "Is brass magnetic?"

"It is if there's iron or nickel in the alloy," said Cockayne, loading the harpoon into the gun and fastening the end of a coiled steel cable to it. "So here's hoping."

They waited while Fanshawe banked the *Yellow Rose* up and around until the observation deck was looking down on the dragon, a hundred feet away. Gideon said, "God bless the Fleet Air Arm for breaking that window. That should make getting inside easier."

"Yeah, if you live that long," said Cockayne. He got behind the harpoon gun and sighted the dragon in the cross-hairs. "You ready, Gideon?"

"As I'll ever be. Let her go."

Cockayne squeezed the trigger and the harpoon ripped out with a violent crack, the thin steel cable unspooling with a zipping whisper. It hit the head of Apep with a clanking sound, and Cockayne slapped a brake on the coil, holding it fast.

"Release the cable as soon as I'm down," said Gideon. "And give me your gun belts."

Cockayne unbuckled the studded belt and handed it over. "Finest cowhide."

"That's what I was banking on," said Gideon. He wrapped the belt around one hand, passed it over the taut cable, and gripped the other end tightly. "Wish me luck."

"You don't need luck, you need this," said Cockayne, taking a pearl-handled six-gun from inside his long black coat. He stuffed it into the waistband of Gideon's trousers. "And remember rule number five: Heroism is for chumps. Valor?

Britain and America can't even agree on how to spell it. Just get in there and finish the job." He paused. "But good luck anyway."

"Hear effing hear!" called out Bent. "Best of British to you, Gideon."

"Mr. Smith?" said Trigger softly. "I was wondering . . . when you confront John . . ."

Gideon, the wind whipping his hair about his face, looked at him. "Don't ask, Captain Trigger. Please. Don't ask."

Trigger nodded and averted his eyes. Gideon looked down, at the people crawling over the green grass of Hyde Park like insects, at the steaming pond of the Serpentine. Trigger was going to ask him to spare Reed. No botched jobs, no half measures, not anymore. He took one more look at the panic below, then threw himself over the railings.

❧

"How interesting," said Reed. "It appears the young man is coming to rescue you, by quite ingenious means. Maria, burn their ship to cinders."

Maria considered this. The greater part of her that was Apep moved to follow the orders, but the tiny core of her that was still Maria hesitated.

Reed said, "You do as you are bid, Maria. Apep is absolute."

There was a dull thud on the roof of the dragon's head. Reed cocked his head and said, "Wait. Hold your fire." He cracked his knuckles. "Perhaps I should settle this in the manner of a true hero after all."

❧

Gideon's downward slide along the cable almost wrenched his arms from his sockets, and though smoke and great flakes of leather flew in clouds, the belt held, tattered as it was when his boots finally struck Apep's head. He tossed it aside and waved at Cockayne, a hundred feet distant, who released the cable immediately. It swung down from the harpoon gun and dangled from Apep's head as the *Yellow Rose* wheeled away to put distance between itself and the dragon. Gideon crouched on the head of Apep, the wind whistling past his ears. He could feel a sick, tickling sensation in the soles of his feet. One swift maneuver from the dragon, and he would be thrown to his death. He needed to get inside, and quick.

But Reed evidently had other ideas. As Gideon inched forward he saw the bearded face of the other man appear at the porthole.

"Mr. Smith," said Reed as he crawled out of the window and onto the snout of Apep. "A shame you have followed Maria halfway across the world, and back again, only to die."

Gideon fumbled for Cockayne's pistol. "It's not too late," he said. "You can give this up now, take your punishment. There doesn't have to be any more death."

Reed laughed. "You think I can just stop? Do you not understand anything you have seen or heard? I am compelled, Smith. I will have my pound of flesh."

"And what if you do burn Buckingham Palace, kill Queen Victoria? What then?"

"Then I dance in the ruins, Smith. Liberate Victoria's coffers of those ill-gotten gains. And I turn Apep on Whitehall, and Walsingham and his cronies die. Then I fly into the sunset on my dragon, and be at peace. And woe betide any fool who follows me."

Gideon shook his head. "You think it is that easy? You kill the Queen and the world quietly forgets about it? London is not like that, Dr. Reed. Britain is not like that." He waved toward the crowds gathered below. "You hear them? You think they are calling for you, begging for you to commit your atrocities to satisfy your own tiny sense of injustice, calling for you to have your pound of flesh from the bones of their children? No, Reed, they are not shouting for you, other than for your head."

And then it hit him, with such force his breath was snatched away by the wind. They were not shouting for Reed, of course not. They didn't know Gideon's name, or who he was, but they could see, as they huddled below, certain death hovering above them, that there was someone who fought for them. Someone on their side. A hero.

"They're shouting for me," said Gideon slowly.

And John Reed leaped.

"What are you *doing*?" muttered Cockayne. "Rule number six. Noble speechifyin' is for the penny dreadfuls, not real life. If you have a gun, use it. Don't talk about it."

Bent put his hand to his mouth. "Oh, no. Reed has tackled Smith. Effing hell. There goes the gun."

Gideon was thrown backward, landing on the smooth curve of Apep's head. The pistol skittered out of his hand and over the side, into the wind-swept abyss. Reed pummeled him in the face with his fists, landing heavily astride Gideon.

"You will die a hero's death," he said "That's what you want, isn't it, boy? To be a hero?"

Gideon swung his fist, just like Cockayne had taught him, and connected with Reed's head. Reed recovered quickly and kicked out, sweeping Gideon's legs out from under him. He hauled Gideon up by his lapels and threw him around in a wide circle, so Gideon skittered along the dimpled nose of Apep, toward the shattered porthole. Was this his chance? He dragged himself forward and peered in, upside down, and saw Maria.

Oh, Maria. Clockwork Maria. He was flooded with—say it! Say it!—flooded with *love* for her. She saw him and her eyes widened, then teared up in anguish.

"Mr. Smith . . . ," she said with great effort. "I am undone. I cannot fight the machinery."

Reed grabbed Gideon by the shoulders and dug his knee into his back. "Maria!" he called. "You may fire at will. Raze Buckingham Palace to the ground."

"No, Maria!" cried Gideon, but Reed dragged him away and punched him in the face.

❧

The flotilla of dirigibles was drawing closer, led by a huge 'stat in the black-and-white livery of the London Constabulary. On the police 'stat's observation deck, an officer with a bullhorn called: "Desist at once, and land that . . . that dragon. Or we'll open fire."

"Eff!" said Bent. "Cockayne, you've got to do something. If Reed doesn't kill Gideon, those trigger-happy coppers will. You're a dead-eye dick with the guns. Can't you take Reed out?"

"Not at this range," said Cockayne. "And not with Rowena swinging the *Yellow Rose* around like it's a soap cart."

"We must do something," said Bent. "The boy's getting the worst of it."

Trigger joined them at the railings. "Oh dear. John is rather giving him a beating, isn't he?"

"Oh, Gideon got a good one in then!" shouted Bent, punching the air with his good arm. "Go on, Gideon lad. Give him another!" He paused. "Hang on. What's happening now?"

"The dragon opens its mouth," said Cockayne.

"Good gravy, it's going to firebomb Buck House," gaped Bent.

"I should do something," said Trigger, his head in his hands. "This is all my fault. John is my responsibility." He looked at his hands, pale and thin and shaking. "What can I do? I can't do what John does. What you all do. I'm not a hero."

"Don't worry, Trigger," said Cockayne mildly. "The only thing Britain loves more than a hero is a failure."

Trigger stared at him, then back at the battle being played out on the hovering Apep.

"Mr. Cockayne," said Trigger. "I would very much like your assistance with something."

❧

Gideon could quite have been convinced that John Reed, as his mummy servants believed, hosted in his soul some supernatural entity lending strength to his muscles, so relentless and ferocious was his attack. He had Gideon in an iron grip around his throat, choking the life out of him even as he pushed him backward, toward the edge. And just below him, beneath the layers of hammered brass, was Maria, entrapped, tantalizingly close. The thought gave him renewed vigor, and he gripped Reed's wrist with both his hands and tried to force the choke hold away.

Reed's grip slackened, and Gideon put the sole of his boot to the other man's chest and kicked him backward. He rose and launched a punch at Reed, landing on his shoulder.

"That is for Bram Stoker!"

Another hit: "For Sandsend!"

Another. "For Maria!"

And with the hardest punch of all, which sent Reed spinning, Gideon roared: "For my father!"

Reed staggered but did not fall. Gideon was spent, ragged. One more. One more blow would do it. One more for London. But he didn't have one more. Reed looked down at him, then up, over his shoulder.

❧

Inside the cockpit, Maria helplessly watched her own hands moving in arcane patterns over the glowing controls. Apep had hijacked her clockwork body, and at the commands from Reed she could do nothing but watch as the artifact in her head detached itself from her conscious efforts and moved her limbs. But the cloud in her head was lifting somewhat, the mist thinning. Had she heard? Had she really heard . . . ?

Outside, there was a voice on the breeze, tantalizingly close, then snatched away.

It was Gideon. It sounded like . . .

She felt a sudden weight around her neck. The simple charm of jet that Gideon had tied around her neck in the bowels of the earth. The stone seemed heavy, and hot, and it burned the mist from her mind.

Reed punched Gideon in the face, but he shouted it again. "Maria! I love you! You must fight it."

There it was again. Could it be? Could it really be true? Mr. Smith . . . *loved* her?

"I love you, Maria, but you must fight it!"

Joy coursed through her brass workings and piston-powered heart, and gave strength to her to bring her hands to a shaking standstill above the instrument panel. But Apep was not going to relinquish control so easily. She felt with dismay her hands moving against her will, completing the deadly sequence.

⁂

Gideon chanced a look behind him at the same time the wind turned and brought with it a tumultuous cheering from both below and the *Yellow Rose,* sweeping in toward Apep. There, looming up out of the blind side of the dragon, was Captain Lucian Trigger, strapped into a personal blimp from the *Yellow Rose.* The clockwork-powered propellers on the metal framework pushed him forward. In his hands he held a rifle, cocked and aimed at Reed. It was the chance Gideon needed. Recalling everything Cockayne had taught him, he clenched his fist hard, drew it back, and hit John Reed on the jaw.

Reed looked at him with surprise, his head snapping back and his legs kicking out from beneath him. He twisted in mid air and landed heavily on the back of the dragon, the breath knocked out of him. And something else was gone, as well. It was as though Gideon's final punch had broken his will to fight. He looked dully at Gideon, then over his shoulder at Trigger.

"John!" called Trigger. "You have had your last warning. This ends here."

Trigger alighted on the top of Apep, swiftly releasing the leather straps of his harness so the blimp floated away from him.

"Captain Trigger." Gideon nodded, grinning. "Thank you for coming to my aid."

"I believe I am officially the Hero of the Empire, after all, at least in print." Trigger smiled, then turned back to Reed. "On your feet, John."

Reed stood slowly, glowering at Trigger, who walked forward, let the rifle fall to his side, and delivered a solid punch to Reed's jaw, which sent him whirling back on to his rump.

"You deserved that," said Trigger.

Reed touched his mouth, his fingers red with blood. He blinked. "Lucian? You hit me?"

Reed scrambled to his feet, and Trigger narrowed his eyes. "John. This is not you. You are not yourself. Fight it. Look at me. Remember our love."

Reed shook his head, more from confusion than anger. "No . . . it's gone too far . . . I can't back down now. . . ."

"John. You are John Reed. A good man."

"I must have vengeance! I am—"

"John Reed," insisted Trigger. "The man I love."

Then he cast the rifle away from him, stepped forward, and took Reed's face in his hands. Reed whispered, "Lucian? I . . . I haven't been very well. Can you make it better?"

Trigger nodded kindly, then kissed him.

❦

Gideon Smith could only imagine what those on the ground made of what happened next. The wind fell, the crowd far below went silent, and even the engines of the dirigibles dimmed and softened. Some might think Trigger had lured Reed into a trap, others assume Reed fought his lover off, while yet more would blame it on a mere accident. Gideon thought it happened as a consequence of the two men's world receding and becoming less solid as their stolen second of true love was made flesh. Trigger and Reed, entwined, slipped from the dragon, in neither panic nor violence, and Gideon watched them fall toward Hyde Park, far below.

There would be those—and Gideon counted himself among them—who would swear blind that Trigger and Reed continued to embrace, and kiss, all the way to their deaths.

❦

Gideon sat heavily on the roof of Apep. So the curse had gotten Trigger after all. *Whoso dares to lead enemies to desecrate this tomb shall die in the arms of their beloved.* Captain Lucian Trigger, Hero of the Empire, had been granted his heart's desire. Exhausted, Gideon saluted the space into which Trigger and Reed had plunged. With Reed gone, so was his control over Maria. The vast, deadly maw of Apep began to close. The danger was past. Gideon looked up as the *Yellow Rose* banked in close, the observation deck looming against the tail of the dragon. Cockayne leaped onto Apep and held out a hand for Gideon.

Gideon climbed up the rope ladder Bent had lowered toward the dirigible. "Wait. Maria."

"I'll take care of her," shouted Cockayne, holding his hat. "We need to figure out how to get this thing down without blowing up half of London."

"No," said Gideon, trying to step down from the ladder, but the *Yellow Rose* bucked and turned, swinging him away from the dragon. Bent hauled him up to the observation deck with his good arm.

"Go get Rowena!" shouted Cockayne. "I need her on the observation deck. Get her to lock the wheel for a minute!"

Bent nodded and disappeared into the gondola, while Gideon stood at the railings, anxiously frowning at Cockayne. He was so close to being reunited with Maria . . . but Cockayne was right. They had to get the dragon down safely. The police 'stat was trying to come alongside the *Yellow Rose.*

"Clear Hyde Park!" shouted Gideon. "We're taking the dragon down."

The constable nodded, and the dirigible began to bank away as Fanshawe came on to the deck. "I saw Lucian fall . . . ," she said, biting her lip.

Gideon nodded and took her hands. "He saved us. Saved London. He really was the Hero of the Empire after all."

"Hey, Rowena!" shouted Cockayne. They had drifted away from the dragon now. "How did you like handling the *Yellow Rose*?"

She cupped her hands around her mouth. "Piece of cake, Cockayne."

"Then she's yours. Reimbursement for the *Skylady II*."

She frowned and glanced at Gideon, then shouted back, "But what are you going to do?"

Cockayne grinned and shuffled along the head of Apep, pausing at the shattered porthole. "I figure I've got my reward at last, Rowena." He raised his hat. "Don't try to follow me, Gideon, because I swear to God I'll blow you out of the sky."

Gideon stared as Cockayne slid into the cockpit, not quite believing what was happening.

❧

Inside Apep, Cockayne touched the brim of his hat. "Miss Maria, good to make your acquaintance at last."

She sat stiffly, still locked into Apep's ancient technology. What she said was unintelligible.

"Shit," said Cockayne. What the hell language was she speaking? Cockayne looked around the cramped cockpit. This was going to go very badly, very quickly. He had taught Gideon Smith to hit hard and fast. He glanced down as something rolled against his boot. A golden apple? He bent to pick it up.

"Who are you?" asked Maria. She spoke in the same strange language, but suddenly Cockayne understood every word.

"Louis Cockayne," he said with a grin.

"I am . . ." She shook her head, pinching her nose. "I am Maria. No, Apep. No, Maria." She stiffened and looked at him. "I am Apep. Only Amasis may command me. Are you Amasis?"

Cockayne shrugged. "If you like."

She nodded. "Then what are your orders, Amasis?"

Cockayne gave a little whoop. "We're going west, Miss Maria, and we don't stop until we hit America. They're going to love you down in Texas, mark my words. Louis Cockayne is going to be a very rich man."

"Gideon . . . ," said Maria, suddenly ascendant again, but her body was not her own, and was already doing Cockayne's bidding.

"Don't you fret about Gideon Smith," said Cockayne, sliding into the seat behind Maria and lighting up a cigarillo. "He's going to be all right. All you concentrate on is going west, my dear, and don't spare those goddamn horses!"

Gideon punched the railing, then said fiercely, "Get me one of those personal blimps. I can catch him."

Fanshawe laid a hand on his shoulder. "Gideon. You can't. Look at that thing go."

"Then get after it!" he yelled. "Turn this 'stat around and get after it!"

She shook her head. "We'll never catch him, Gideon. The people here need help. Bent and the Countess . . . and there's everything to sort out . . . Lucian and John . . ."

Gideon felt tears pricking his eyes. As he watched Apep flying into the late afternoon sun, he put his head in his hands and wept, not feeling very heroic at all.

The Hero of the Empire

There was a special issue of *World Marvels & Wonders* rushed out within three days of what the newspapers were proudly proclaiming to be The Battle of London, and Gideon Smith was gratified and embarrassed and proud, all at once, to hold it in his hands with himself on the cover. What lay within was a highly sanitized version of events, of course. There was no mention of mummies or vampires, nor of John Reed's treachery against the Crown. The dragon was presented as a somewhat foggy anarchist plot, foiled by the combined efforts of Lucian Trigger, the Hero of the Empire, and his cohort of companions. There was a pen-and-ink illustration that made Gideon laugh out loud; Bent was portrayed as handsome and strong, his chest puffed out, wielding his pencil and notepad as though they were the sword and shield of a valiant knight. Of Louis Cockayne there was no mention; the disappearance of the dragon was ascribed to a chaotic, uncontrolled flight path that took it out of harm's way and into the sea, where it would be recovered.

It was not all rousing triumph, though. There was tragedy, too. Captain Trigger and Dr. Reed had lost their lives battling the anarchists, and it was only the efforts of Gideon Smith that saved the day. Gideon flushed slightly as he read; the triumph in the skies was ascribed wholly to him, with Trigger and Reed demoted to tragic bit parts in the final battle. Not how it was at all, of course. Nevertheless, a statue to Captain Trigger had already been commissioned and was to be positioned in Hyde Park, at the spot where Trigger and Reed fell to their deaths. The theatrical manager and writer Bram Stoker was also missing in action in foreign climes; a party was to be sent to see if they could rescue him, and failing that, recover his body. There was also the sobering matter of the innocent victims of Apep, the dozens on Biggin Hill and the hundreds in Bexleyheath. The French had quickly offered to repair the Lady of Liberty flood barrier, but Queen Victoria had said no; let its melted visage remain, a stark reminder that the people of the Empire had to be forever watchful against fanatics and terrorists.

❧

Gideon handed the penny blood back to little Tommy, whom Peek was holding in his arms. "Did your pappy read the story to you?" asked Gideon.

Tommy thrust out his lip. "I read it myself!" His face darkened. "Are there monsters out there? Really?"

Gideon glanced at Peek. He'd said Tommy had been troubled by nightmares ever since the confrontation with the Child of Heqet in the mist. He crouched down and looked him in the eye. "Tommy," he said. "Sometimes, monsters just turn out to be people. And sometimes, people can be monsters. Do you understand?"

Tommy nodded uncertainly. "And who will fight the monsters, now that Captain Trigger is dead?"

To that, Gideon didn't have an answer. "Someone, I'm sure," he said. "But don't you be afraid. Someone said to me that fear is a lie. Do you know what I mean?"

"I *think* so," said Tommy.

"You're a clever lad," said Gideon, ruffling his hair. He stood and nodded to Peek. "Thanks for coming."

"How could I not?" said Peek. They were both dressed in black suits, standing on Lythe Bank, St. Oswald's Church behind them. As soon as he was able, Gideon had returned to Sandsend and ventured into the tunnels where Stoker and Bathory had fought the Children of Heqet. There he found the bones of the *Cold Drake*'s crew, and those of Clive Clarke, the police officer. The Reverend Bastable had just led a funeral service for Sandsend's fallen.

"I suppose what happened to them will always be a mystery," said Peek, looking shrewdly at Gideon.

Gideon looked out to sea, where the Newcastle & Gateshead factory farms still steamed on the far horizon. "Aye, I suppose it will." A number of serious-faced men in sober suits and top hats had told them at Scotland Yard exactly what they could and could not say about the adventure. Those men had also, presumably, been responsible for the rather pedestrian write-up in *World Marvels & Wonders*; Bent would be furious at the dour prose. No connection had been made publicly between the deaths of Arthur Smith and his crew and the events in London. In truth, there were few connections to make. The *Cold Drake* had merely been in the wrong place at the wrong time, in the path of the Children of Heqet when they needed to feed. But at least the monsters were gone, some at Gideon's own hand, the last handful beneath the crushing stones of the fallen Pyramid of Rhodopis.

"But what happened next, Mr. Smith?" asked little Tommy.

Gideon grinned. "Mr. Smith? It's Gideon to you, lad."

Tommy screwed up his face. "I did know a Gideon, but he was just like everybody else. He went away. You're a hero, Mr. Smith. But the story ends with those anarchists throwing Captain Trigger off that big brass dragon. It doesn't say what happens next."

What happened next was that Fanshawe had taken the *Yellow Rose* down to land in Hyde Park, the crowd cheering and clapping most riotously as the adventurers emerged. After the debriefing at Scotland Yard, Bent, who had begun raving and laughing like a lunatic, was deemed to have a head injury and taken to St. Thomas's Hospital in Southwark for treatment for that and his broken arm. Elizabeth Bathory was returning, with the help of Rowena Fanshawe, to Castle Dracula in Transylvania. Gideon had held out his hand to Bathory, but she had embraced him. "You were valiant, Gideon Smith, and it is you I have to thank for allowing me to avenge my husband."

"Perhaps I will see you again?"

"Perhaps," she agreed. "But know this, Mr. Smith: I bear no love for your country or your Empire. It encroaches on every corner of the world, and there will come a day when your people venture too close to Castle Dracula. Pity them if they do. Your men in authority did that cruel and base thing to Annie Crook, and who knows how many others. Tell them Countess Bathory and Britain are at peace, but only for now, and it is a fragile peace."

As Fanshawe prepared to return Bathory to the Carpathian Mountains, Gideon hugged her and whispered, "Be careful."

She kissed him on the mouth. "We'll find Maria. We'll get her back. I promise."

Peek brought him out of his reverie. "You left this place as little more than a boy with fancy ideas, Gideon. You've come back a man." He pointed to the harbor. "The *Cold Drake*'s still there, waiting for you."

Gideon had entertained the idea of trying to take the gearship out across the Atlantic, searching for Cockayne and Maria. But it would never make the journey, and the Americas were a huge territory. He could not undertake such an enterprise alone. And if the thought of settling down in his old life had occurred to him, it had done so only briefly, and he had pushed it away.

"I can't stay in Sandsend, Peek. I've seen too much. The world's too big. I have to know more of it. The *Cold Drake*'s yours, if you'll have her. But I shall not be going out in her. My life has to take a different path now."

Peek shrugged. " 'Course, it's not for the likes of me to know, but I'd reckon you've done what you set out to, Gideon Smith. I reckon your daddy will rest at peace, now."

Gideon smiled. "Perhaps."

"But what happens next?" asked Tommy insistently.

What was it Trigger had said about heroism? Stories for children. And was that such a bad thing? If stories of heroism could inspire one child, allow one boy to dream of doing good himself? Gideon mussed Tommy's hair again, then winked at him. "That," he said, "is a story for another day."

Gideon, in a fine suit with tails and a collar that made his neck itch, was shown by a footman into a lavish room, the carpets thick and luxurious. Bent and Fanshawe were already there, Bent looking as dapper as Gideon had ever seen him in a topper and holding a cane, Fanshawe looking beautiful and womanly in a silk gown.

"Gideon!" she squealed, hitching her skirts up and running toward him.

"How was Castle Dracula? Not tempted to stay?"

She pulled a face. "Too many women. Too many vampires." She cast a thumb over her shoulder. "He'd have liked it, though. They breed 'em sturdy over there."

Bent, his arm in a sling, grinned and waved. "You're looking every inch a hero, Smith."

Gideon extricated himself from Fanshawe's embrace and shook Bent's good hand. "As are you, Mr. Bent. New suit?"

"Not half," said Bent, giving a little twirl. "I must say, the matter of that small reward for our efforts was most welcome. I even got Big Henry off my back."

"And how is your arm?"

"Mending." Bent nodded. "But that's not the real problem. Took a knock to the head in that pyramid. Would've been dead, but for my hat. The pith helmet everybody laughed at. God bless that little feller in the souk who sold it to me. As it was, it gave me a bit of concussion, said the quacks. And something else." He lowered his voice. "Listen. Effing. Eff. Eff off. Eff me."

Gideon made a face and shook his head. "What?"

"Well, you know old Trigger told me to watch my lingo. That stone on the head did something to me. I can't say it any more. Eff."

"Can't say what?"

"*Eff*," said Bent. "Eff you sea kay. Try as I might, it just comes out like this. Eff. It's an effing liberty, if you ask me. Words are my livelihood, Smith. They can't just take one off me like that."

Gideon laughed as the footman, in a powdered wig with his nose in the air, appeared. "Gentlemen. Miss Fanshawe. It is time. Queen Victoria will see you now."

Bent whispered, "Nervous?"

"Yes," said Gideon. "I've seen mummies, vampires, and a dragon. But this terrifies me. I mean, it's the *queen*."

"Just imagine her on the toilet when you see her." Bent chuckled. "It's a great leveler, is shitting."

The footman coughed and open the doors, then said loudly, "Her Royal Majesty Queen Victoria."

Victoria, in a long, blue velvet dress, sat on an elaborate throne inlaid with gold leaf. She was much older than she looked in her pictures, thought Gideon. Her face was dry and powdered, creviced with deep wrinkles, her gray hair gathered in a lace-covered bun. But her eyes were bright and intelligent, and as the group reached the appointed spot ten yards from her, stopped, and bowed, she regarded each of them in turn. The footman withdrew, leaving them alone in the royal presence.

After a moment, Victoria said, "Mr. Smith. Miss Fanshawe. Mr. Bent. Britain thanks you for your bravery and heroism in dealing with the threat against our shores and, indeed, our self. In the normal run of things, such an investiture as this would be attended by the great and the good, and accompanied by much pomp and circumstance." She smiled, which was something Gideon had been given to think she did rarely. "But as we know, this has not been what anyone might describe as a normal endeavor." Victoria paused, as though lost in thought, and said, "I am seventy-one years old. I have reigned for fifty-three years. In that time Britain has extended its reach across the globe. In ten years we shall be in a new century. The twentieth century. Can you imagine it?"

They took a moment to do just that. "How very strange it sounds. But although we move inexorably to the future, the world stubbornly remains a very strange place. No matter how bright a light we shine into its dark corners, it still throws us constant surprises. The events you have all participated in show us that. We are conquering science by degrees every single day, but there is so very much still beyond our understanding."

Victoria had on her lap a velvet cushion, on which lay three medals. She touched them for a moment, then said, "Miss Fanshawe. Please step forward."

Fanshawe crossed the distance to the foot of Victoria's throne and curtseyed, remaining crouched down with her eyes on the carpet, as she had been told.

"Oh, look at us, dear," Victoria said, sighing. "We do not need to stand on ceremony too much. There is no one looking."

Fanshawe smiled and looked up at the queen. Victoria ruminated. "There are those who think a woman's place is in the home. Had we subscribed to that notion we would not have spent the last half a century ruling much of the known world. Your adventures in your dirigible are well known, Miss Fanshawe, and you are an inspiration to young girls everywhere. We fully expect there are small girls now who will take to heart your exploits and be inspired to great things themselves. For your part in defeating the machinations of poor, deluded John Reed, we award you the Conspicuous Gallantry Medal. And well deserved it is, too."

Fanshawe leaned forward to allow Victoria to place the blue ribbon around her neck and rest the medal against her breastbone. "May you fly high for many more years to come."

As Fanshawe retreated back to the line, Victoria said, "Ah, Mr. Aloysius Bent. Please come forward."

As Bent kneeled awkwardly before the Queen, she said, "Mr. Bent. It is one of our great points of pride that we have such freedom of speech in Great Britain, and it is never more sharply brought into focus than by the gentlemen of the press, of which we believe you to be one of the foremost exemplars."

Bent grinned broadly, and Gideon willed him not to cuss in delight. Victoria continued, "You, Mr. Bent, have transcended your appointed role as recorder of facts to take an active part in protecting London from its direst threat. For that, we award you, too, the Conspicuous Gallantry Medal."

When Bent had returned, admiring his medal, Victoria allowed herself another of her rare smiles. "And, finally, Mr. Gideon Smith of Sandsend."

Gideon took up his position, and Victoria looked at him for a long time. "The others who were involved in this enterprise were no strangers to such endeavors. Even Mr. Bent, as a journalist, is more worldly-wise than an ordinary citizen. But you, Mr. Smith . . . we find it quite astonishing that one such as yourself would embark upon such a dangerous mission and give such a soaring account of yourself in the bargain. You galvanized those around you, Mr. Smith, and acted with the greatest heroism any ruler could wish to see from her subjects. In recognition of your efforts, we would like to present you with the highest honor available to us. The Victoria Cross."

Burning with pride, Gideon lowered his head to receive the medal. He waited for Victoria to dismiss him, but she tapped her dry lips thoughtfully with a long fingernail for a moment, then said, "Mr. Smith, we have been giving a certain matter much thought since your valiant battle in the skies over London, and its rather sad consequences for certain individuals in your party.

"Britain has thrilled to the adventures of Captain Lucian Trigger for some time now. We assembled here know the truth of those adventures, and how they came about. But that is information for ourselves. It would not do for the people of Britain to find out their heroes had feet of clay."

She mused again, then said, "It does, however, leave us

something of a problem. There is suddenly a Captain Trigger–shaped hole within the fabric of Britain. It needs filling."

Gideon raised an eyebrow. Victoria said, "Mr. Smith. Britain needs a hero, one whose adventures can inspire, delight, and soothe. We would very much like it if you would become that hero."

Gideon gaped at her and said, "Me?"

"You, Mr. Smith." Victoria smiled. "Our new Hero of the Empire. One to take us into the future. We would very much appreciate it if you would become an agent of the Crown, and look after the more *outlandish*, shall we say, threats that are leveled against Britain from time to time." She leaned forward. "To begin with, there is the problem of a purloined dragon that has the potential to cause much embarrassment for our interests in the New World."

"I don't know what to say," said Gideon.

"Yes would be a good start," said Victoria. "And a thank-you would not go amiss."

He broke into a beaming smile. "Yes, of course, Your Majesty. And thank you. Thank you so very much."

❦

Outside, in a sunlit courtyard, Bent lit a cigarette and the adventurers admired each other's medals. "Looks like you're going to search for Maria after all," he said.

Fanshawe embraced him. "Oh, Gideon, I'm so pleased. If you need any help in America . . ."

"I will," he said. "Can I count on you?"

She kissed him. "Of course. The *Yellow Rose* is called the *Skylady III* now, by the way. Consider her at your service."

"You sure you want to work for this gang? You've seen what they can do," Bent said.

Gideon shrugged. "I can only be the best I can, Mr. Bent. If I can make the world a better place, save perhaps one life . . . Like Mr. Cockayne said, it's about balance."

Bent shook Gideon's hand. "Give me a shout when you get back. You'll need someone to tell your story to the world."

Bent watched them leave. In his opinion, Gideon should forget that clockwork girl and make a go of it with Fanshawe. She was a right saucy little number. He wasn't particularly looking forward to his pit of a bed in the Fulwood Rents, if he was honest with himself. Perhaps he should think of bettering his position. As he finished his cigarette, he became aware of a figure walking toward him, a pale, thin man in a black overcoat despite the sunshine, with a drooping white mustache. Bent narrowed his eyes. Where had he seen him before? That was it. In the newsroom.

"Mr. Bent," said the man.

"Mr. Walsingham." Bent nodded. "I was wondering when you'd show your hand. Is this where you confess to being Jack the Ripper?"

"Jack the Ripper? Mr. Bent, I have done many things in the service of this country, but killing prostitutes is not one of them."

"Someone's doing it," said Bent. "Someone who thinks there's a treasure in the head of some whore. You gave Annie Crook's brain to Einstein. Bit of a schoolboy error, eh? Considering what memories she had?"

Walsingham looked piercingly at Bent. "We could not have known what Einstein was going to do with Annie Crook's brain. But if we had wanted it back, we would have taken it from Einstein, not skulked around in the shadows. Yes, Mr. Bent, someone is slicing prostitutes' heads. It is not us. We know full well where the automaton is, and it is not on the streets of London. But we shall find out who is doing it." He paused thoughtfully. "Perhaps it will be a job for our new Hero of the Empire."

Bent shrugged and picked his nose. Walsingham said, "What are your immediate plans?"

Bent scratched his bandaged head. "Not been into the *Argus* since we got back. Only got out of hospital two days ago." He sniffed. "Thought the effers would have come to visit me, bring me some grapes."

Walsingham smiled thinly. "No one came to visit because you are no longer part of the staff."

Bent gaped at him. "They sacked me? For going off to Egypt? But I'm a bloody hero! And I've got the biggest story in history to tell!"

"They sacked you because I told your editor to," said Walsingham. "And you are not telling your story to anyone." He looked out across the lawns of Buckingham Palace, at the spires and ziggurats of London beyond. "The public does not need to know in such detail the measures we have to take to protect it."

Bent pointed his cigarette at him. "Forget it. I've been on the Annie Crook story for two years. You're not taking it off me now I've had firsthand experience. No effing way."

"Mr. Bent, need I remind you we can be quite persuasive?"

Bent opened his mouth and then paused. "You'll have me seen to?"

"As I say," said Walsingham. "The measures we must take to protect the public." He shook his head sadly.

Bent's shoulders slumped. "So that's it, is it? You swap me a medal for a job, and my silence? What do I do now?"

Walsingham smiled. "We have procured another position for you."

"Oh aye?" said Bent suspiciously.

"A role in the same stable of periodicals as the *Argus*. *World Marvels & Wonders*, to be precise."

"The penny blood? What are you talking about?"

"Mr. Bent," said Walsingham. "Did you not hear Her Majesty say Mr. Smith is to be the new Hero of the Empire? His endeavors will only be useful to the Crown if they are properly presented, to inspire the citizenry. That is where you come in. I can see it now: *This adventure is utterly true, and faithfully retold by Gideon Smith's constant companion, Mr. Aloysius Bent.*"

Bent sighed. "Can I refuse?"

"No. It's a great opportunity, Mr. Bent. You will travel the world."

Bent stared at him. "You mean I actually have to go with him on these crackpot exploits? Won't it be dangerous?"

Walsingham nodded. "Very. But time is wasting. You may recuperate for a short while as Mr. Smith undergoes a period of military training, and then you will receive a message to present yourself at Highgate Aerodrome. There will be a dirigible leaving for New York, and you will be on it." He smiled. "Don't forget your notebook, and in the meantime, please remember: Careless talk costs lives."

Walsingham turned and left without another word. Bent watched his receding back for a while, then lit another cigarette. "Eff," he said, with feeling.

Two Weeks Later

August was hot and sunny, but it was cool inside twenty-six St. George's Square. Thick drapes kept back the light, though Florence Stoker thought them not conducive to Noel's recuperation. One more week, and they would ease back their mourning. Life must go on.

She sat listlessly in the study, rereading the same page of her book. The sound of the doorbell intruded into the silence, and Florence groaned. She called, "Tell them I am not receiving visitors, Adelaide. And if it is another journalist, tell them we have told our story to Mr. Aloysius Bent and he has quite admirably handled Mr. Stoker's obituary."

There had been a stream of visitors since Bram's death. Henry Irving, Ellen Terry, a slew of famous actors and actresses. Theatrical types, literary types, all kinds of people. Dour men in black who had told her she must not discuss too much of anything Bram had told her before he died, and made her sign papers to that effect. As if he had told her anything! All she could think was that their last meeting had been so strained and painful. She wished she had told him how much she loved him.

There were other visitors, too. Mr. Gideon Smith, who told her such a tale she could scarcely believe it. In fact, she didn't believe it. But they said Mr. Smith was a hero, and he told her Bram was a hero, too, and he had died trying to stop that terrible brass dragon attacking London.

Adelaide shrieked, and Florence looked up. What now? With a sigh, she crossed the study, opening the door to see Adelaide crumpled on the floor. In the doorway was a tall figure, the sun behind him.

"I'm afraid she's fainted."

Florence feared she would, too. That voice . . . a cruel joke. She said weakly, "Bram?"

He stepped over the threshold. Bram indeed. Tall, strong, smiling through his beard. He wore tight breeches and a loose white shirt. She looked at him, bewildered. "They said you'd died."

"They thought I had. Oh, Florence, I have such stories to tell."

"Why didn't you telegraph? How did you get home?"

"I flew." He flapped his arms. "Most exhausting."

She cried then, tears of joy, and Bram took her in his arms. "It's really you," she said.

"Where is Noel?"

"I shall get him directly. Let me hold you for a moment. I'm worried you will disappear like a phantom. They said you were crushed under the pyramid's stones."

"I was," he said, smelling her hair. "Somehow, I found the strength to escape. I crossed France. When I reached Calais I was bereft of the accoutrements a gentleman requires, having lost my wallet and most of my clothing in Egypt. I procured a peasant's outfit from . . . well, a criminal."

"I shall swoon, Bram, I swear. You had dealings with the underworld? *French* criminals to boot?"

"Briefly." Bram smiled. "We . . . had lunch together. After a fashion."

She shook her head and they held each other until Adelaide stirred. Florence stepped back, smoothed her dress. "When she is recovered, we shall have brunch. You must be starving."

Stoker wiped an almost imperceptible red spot from the corner of his mouth, and smiled. He ran his tongue over his keen canines. He, too, had thought he'd died, especially when Elizabeth took his blood. But before she left, as he hovered in darkness, she'd gifted him a few drops of her own blood into his parched mouth. An acquired taste, but one he'd come to relish.

"It is quite all right," he said, his eyes shining, where before they had only twinkled. "I have already eaten."